"A rich, complex book . . . We need more novels like this, which critically examine the larger world and our role in it, both as Americans and individuals."
— *Cleveland Plain Dealer*

"*Forgetfulness* is a novel of deep nuance offered through suspense, but it also makes a profound statement about revenge and the capacity to forgive . . . This may be the best novel in Just's illustrious career."
— *Deseret Morning News*

"Addresses the randomness of terrorism with shuddering realism."
— *Columbus Dispatch*

"Like Hemingway's best prose, Just's writing is understated and beautifully precise . . . *Forgetfulness* is quite possibly the best, most intelligent work of fiction among the growing number of novels that explore the post–Sept. 11 world."
— *Richmond Times-Dispatch*

"Searing and accomplished . . . as readable as it is profound."
— *Baltimore Sun*

"The prose is so sinuous, probing, and serpentine, filled with details, moods, facts, and strange episodes, that I was hooked in an instant . . . This is a splendid, lyrically seductive novel."
— *Providence Journal*

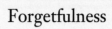

Forgetfulness

Books by Ward Just

NOVELS

A Soldier of the Revolution 1970

Stringer 1974

Nicholson at Large 1975

A Family Trust 1978

In the City of Fear 1982

The American Blues 1984

The American Ambassador 1987

Jack Gance 1989

The Translator 1991

Ambition & Love 1994

Echo House 1997

A Dangerous Friend 1999

The Weather in Berlin 2002

An Unfinished Season 2004

Forgetfulness 2006

SHORT STORIES

The Congressman Who Loved Flaubert 1973

Honor, Power, Riches, Fame, and the Love of Women 1979

Twenty-one: Selected Stories 1990
   (reissued in 1998 as *The Congressman Who Loved Flaubert:
   21 Stories and Novellas*)

NONFICTION

To What End 1968

Military Men 1970

PLAYS

Lowell Limpett 2001

FORGETFULNESS

Ward Just

A MARINER BOOK
Houghton Mifflin Company
BOSTON   NEW YORK

FIRST MARINER BOOKS EDITION 2007

Copyright © 2006 by Ward Just

www.houghtonmifflinbooks.com

Library of Congress Cataloging-in-Publication Data

Just, Ward S.
    Forgetfulness / Ward Just.
        p. cm.
    ISBN-13: 978-0-618-63463-7
    ISBN-10: 0-618-63463-0
1. Painters—Fiction.   2. Americans—France—Fiction.
3. Terrorists—Fiction.   4. Pyrenees—Fiction.   I. Title.
PS3560.U75F67   2006
813'.54—dc22   2006013906
    ISBN-13: 978-0-618-91849-2 (pbk.)
    ISBN-10: 0-618-91849-3 (pbk.)

Book design by Anne Chalmers
Typefaces: Janson Text, Trixie, Europa Arabesque

Printed in the United States of America

QUM 10 9 8 7 6 5 4 3 2

A portion of this novel appeared, in slightly
different form, in *Narrative* magazine.

To Sarah

and to Kib and Tess Bramhall

and to the memory of Fred Busch

PART ONE

Florette

THE WAY DOWN was hard, the trail winding and slick underfoot, insecure. Late autumn, the air cold, no breeze, the setting sun casting long shadows, deceptive in the gathering darkness. The four men carrying the stretcher—two in front, two behind—had begun to curse. In the beginning they were silent, concentrating on their footing, but the way down was so very hard that they could not now restrain themselves, their boots slipping on the damp earth, the stretcher hard to handle. Each time the stretcher tipped the injured woman groaned, and when a part of her body grazed a rock or a tree branch she gasped, a kind of lumbar whistle, most annoying. They passed through wide-bellied fir trees and slender white birches, the smell of the forest in her nostrils, an odor so thick she found breathing difficult, a weight in her lungs that pressed painfully against her. She was bothered that the pain in her leg was migrating, an unwelcome undocumented alien. She was trying to put her mind in another place altogether but was so far unsuccessful. She was unable to free herself of the forest. It seemed to her the very end of the known world so she conjured images of unwelcome aliens. For now she was in the hands of strangers, dubious men who did not belong here. So she spoke aloud, telling them to be careful, to take their time, not to be so rough. She was no longer young, as they could see. And she was injured and not herself. She thought to add, "Please."

The bearers grew impatient, and as dusk turned to nightfall and their vision failed the stretcher became as heavy as a coffin despite the injured woman's average height and weight. The bearers in the rear could not avoid looking at her lower leg, loose as a rag doll's,

3

leaking blood. Her trousers were torn and one of her shoes was missing. Of course the situation was difficult for her, injuries were never pleasant, and she was not dressed properly. Her espadrilles were made for a picnic or a stroll in the park. Her sweater was woven of fine wool, soft as babies' hair. But the situation was difficult for everyone and she could have the courtesy and fortitude to shut up about her own inconvenience. Still, it was well known that Americans were complainers when fate went against them. Americans believed they occupied a unique place in the world, a place under God's special benevolence. And if God was absent, anyone would do. The women were no better than the men. Wherever they went in the world they expected cooperation, and if they did not get it they complained.

This American in fine clothes was a flatlander, too old for mountain work, anyone could see that. She was lucky they had agreed to help her. She was not their responsibility and they had business of their own. But there she was, sprawled immodestly on the ground near the shelter, semiconscious, demanding to be taken care of. No telling how long she had been there but probably not longer than an hour or two, a harmless old woman who had lost her way, unsuitably dressed for the mountains, quarrelsome in the manner of Americans. Her good luck that the shelter contained an army-issue stretcher, placed there years ago for just such an emergency. She knew it was there, too. So she was twice lucky and should give thanks instead of complaining because by rights they should have left her where she was. Their business did not include rescue work. But they were mindful also of the tradition of hospitality, so after an argument they agreed to take her at least partway down the trail and they knew now they had made a mistake. The autumn light continued to fail and they knew they would not be free of the mountain before nightfall and they suspected, by the heaviness of the air, that a storm was coming. None of this—the weather, their slow progress—was to their advantage. The rescue of the American woman was an error and they would pay for it.

She heard them talking, the words indistinct except for the oldest one, the one with the lisp, the one who seemed to be the leader. All four were filthy, as if they hadn't bathed in a week, but he was the filthiest. Also, he smelled. When he bent close to her, his balaclava glowed silvery in the dying sunlight. He had the face of a conquistador, his lean nose, tiny pig's eyes that burned with contempt. He was thick around the middle. She had known men like him her entire life, reckless, savage, concerned for themselves alone. They stormed into your life and took what they wanted. These four carried small Adidas packs on their shoulders and looked as if they had been in the mountains for some time. She wondered if they had come over the high country from Catalonia. Or perhaps they were returning. She had no idea the direction they had come from; she had looked up in pain and there they were, staring at her, except for the young one, who looked away in embarrassment. She knew they were not casual hikers. She did not understand their language, only a word here and there; and when a tree branch caught her leg and she cried out, the one with the lisp looked at her and snarled, Silence, American! She was appalled. It could not be true that they thought she was American. Idiots, oafs—she was French and had always been French. One had only to look seriously at her to know that, her turned-up nose and the swell to her upper lip, the way she did her hair and—simply everything about her. It was true that she was married to an American, but they did not know that. Probably in her pain and confusion she had spoken English, thinking they might better understand her since English was supposedly the universal language. She remembered saying "Please." And for that they had misapprehended her nationality, and had she the strength she would have said to them that her name was Florette and she lived nearby in St. Michel du Valcabrère and had only gone for a walk as she did every Sunday after lunch. The others were still loud at table, some private joke. She had cleared the dishes and stepped out the back door, leaving Thomas and his guests to finish their business, though she could hear them laughing as she walked through the courtyard and the grove of olive trees beyond the courtyard, the day so sunny and fragrant. And then, much later, nearing the shelter, she had stumbled stupidly because she was tired, having walked much farther than was her custom; no doubt the wine at lunch had made her careless. But the afternoon was warm and she was distracted by the honeyed voices of the owls. The owls called and she answered back. She thought there were three owls, a loud bull-owl and his demure girl-friends. Now she listened to the men complain but she did not have the strength to set them straight. Setting them straight was not worth the effort. And if they thought she was an American they would be more careful with her, expecting a fine American reward, an automobile or a Swiss watch or a sack of gold. Munitions du jour. Perhaps a visa to the promised land. Florette smiled wanly at that, listening again for the honeyed voices of the owls, but for the moment the owls were silent and she heard only the breathing of the men and the creak of the stretcher.

When they reached a clearing they lowered the injured woman to the ground. The one with the lisp pressed a canteen to her mouth and she took two swallows, the water so cold it hurt her teeth. He stared at her with his pig eyes, then turned his back. She heard them move off the path and presently she smelled tobacco. They were talking quietly in their incomprehensible language, out of her field of vision. One voice rose above the others, then lowered to a whisper. She heard the lisp and wondered if it was part of the language, like the Zulu click. Castilian Spanish had a lisp but this was not Spanish, and he was no grandee. Thomas had taught her a few phrases of Zulu, thick with clicks. She could say the phrases but she had forgotten what they meant. They were everyday phrases: So long, see you tomorrow. Do you think it will rain? Phrases of that kind. She shifted her weight on the stretcher, trying to move her head so that she could better see where the men were located. But it was too dark now to see anything and her chest hurt when she moved. There was nothing to be done about the leg, which seemed to her an independent part of her body, an offshore island with its own government. The pain was less now than it had been, confirming a strongly held opinion of her mother's: the body contained a finite supply of pain and sooner or later it exhausted itself, a well run dry. You had to wait it out, a question of patience. The size of the well varied with the character and personality of the woman, but in most cases a woman's tolerance far exceeded a man's. Childbirth was the worst, yet all women got through it unless they were unlucky or had a butcher for a midwife. A woman's body was conditioned for pain, anticipating childbirth, whereas a man's was conditioned for pleasure. Pain always came as a surprise to men. Her mother had been very good about pain, even the pain of childbirth, an experience that had eluded Florette; and of course now she was too old. Thomas was even older. But her mother had never broken an ankle and been obliged to depend on the compassion of strange, sullen men who appeared out of nowhere, reluctant samaritans. So she waited, worrying about the leg pain that had migrated to her chest, hoping that her well was receding. She knew she looked a mess but there was nothing to be done about that, either. She remembered that Thomas had told her that Zulu women had a fantastic tolerance for pain, rarely exhibiting emotion of any kind. Stoics of the school of Marcus Aurelius, Thomas had said. But she guessed they looked a mess all the same.

Above the tops of the trees there were no stars, and then the trees themselves were lost to view. In her efforts to put her mind in another place altogether she was thinking gibberish, Zulu clicks and the like. Stoic philosophers. Bull-owls and their honey-voiced girlfriends. Her mother's theory of female pain. Florette was not at all in a good way, her thoughts confused as they were on those nights when she awakened in a cold sweat a few hours before dawn, half inside a dream and half out, uncertain where she was, filled with four o'clock dread, Thomas snoring softly beside her; and when she nudged him awake he was always easy with her, preparing to talk her through her dream, waiting with her until dawn. Often he wanted to make love but he knew he had to talk her into it, so he talked her into it and afterward listened to her describe her dream. Her mother was a frequent dream-visitor and Thomas was expert at coaxing the details from her, what her mother looked like and what she was wearing and how she figured in the narrative. What did you say to her, chérie? And Florette had replied: I said, Why do I have to make my bed when I'll only be getting back into it? Not the answer her mother wanted, and so she turned her head in disgust and flounced from the dream.

Florette's feet were cold in the morning and they were very cold now. Also, she had to take a pee. But she did not see how she could remove her trousers and her panties; and if she did, what then? She could not move with her leg hurting so. Asking the men to help was an invitation to grief. Her situation was insupportable. She shivered once again, the cold advancing until it seemed she was ice-wrapped. Surely these men could spare a pair of socks and a sweater but they paid no attention to her, as if she weren't there. Something touched her forehead, a snowflake so delicate she had to guess what it was. The forecast had said nothing about snow but mountain forecasts were often unreliable, assembled as they were in Paris or Toulouse by urban meteorologists who did not understand microclimates, as individual and erratic as human personality. Her mother had been a fine weather forecaster, unerring in her predictions. She knew everything about weather and not very much about being a mother and nothing at all about men. The three skills must be incompatible, chalk and cheese and lambswool—and then she knew she was thinking gibberish again. She tried to pull herself together, back into present time. She reckoned they had another hour or so of march before reaching St. Michel du Valcabrère, and the longer they rested the more difficult the march would be, that was obvious; and at once she had the solution. One of them could run on ahead and fetch Thomas. Thomas would return with the doctor and a proper litter with blankets and trained orderlies to make her comfortable because they were people familiar with mountains. Mountains held no terror for them. That was the efficient way to go about things, and she knew she could survive so long as she was not bounced about by strange men. No one wished to be with strangers at such a time.

She wished to God she had a cigarette. The thought came to her unexpectedly. She never took tobacco with her on her walks, not wanting it to interfere with her sense of smell. But now she craved a

Gitane. She called out in English and French but her voice was weak and she suspected they did not hear her. Certainly they were indifferent to an old woman in distress; that is how they would see her, a crone, though she was not yet fifty-five. She knew she looked a fright. They had no interest in her. In any case, they made no reply. If only she were given the opportunity, she could explain to them about Thomas and his American generosity. It would help if she had a Gitane, such a commonplace amenity given her distress, the unlucky circumstances of her present situation. The aroma of tobacco was delicious and she decided then that the gods had conspired against her. The gods of the Pyrenees were good at conspiracy. They were cruel. They rode the mountain winds and went where they pleased, very old gods grown spiteful with age. Nothing was forgiven, not the slightest misstep. They were omniscient and they were deaf to explanation. Mountain gods were especially vengeful toward women who invaded their domain, careless uninvited intruders who did not know their rightful place in the world. Such women were an affront and would be punished.

Florette dozed awhile, her thoughts blown this way and that. The thought would appear at a window in her mind, look in, and disappear. She tried to think of the future, tomorrow and the day after tomorrow, the moment she would return to her normal life, routine as that life might seem. Probably she had grown complacent. Many women did when they reached middle age and enjoyed the life they had made for themselves, even if it did not conform exactly to the life they had imagined or hoped for. When she was a girl she wanted to be a dressmaker, a great couturier with a shop on the Place Vendôme in Paris. She had seen such a place in an article in *Paris-Match*, a high-ceilinged second-floor salon with wide windows, spacious dressing rooms, and models in various states of undress, important clients arriving by appointment only. The client pressed a buzzer and a model admitted her and whomever she was with, often a man of a certain age and bearing. All the work was done on the premises, sewing machines whirring from early morning until late at night. She was the toast of Paris. Even the wife of the president of the republic owned one of her backless gowns, white satin, one of a kind. To wear a Florette was to admit to a particular attitude toward the world; the word for it was ardent. What a life that would have been! But the article did not explain how a girl from Aquitaine might get to the Place Vendôme. Characters in Balzac's novels managed it easily, arriving in the capital by fiacre, ox cart, or on foot from Angoulême or Tours and marching off directly to find their fortunes.

But she was not a character in a novel. She was Florette DuFour, and Florette DuFour had never been north of Toulouse. So her dream was deferred and upon graduation from secondary school she arranged for a job at the post office and at night knitted sweaters, which she sold at the Saturday market in the square at St. Michel du Valcabrère. She designed a label, *Florette* in cursive script, pink on a white background. She sold as many as she could knit during slow times at the post office and at night. She hoped that a couturier from Paris, perhaps on vacation, perhaps only passing through, would admire one of her sweaters and offer to take a consignment. *Florette* sweaters would become as desired as a Schiaparelli evening dress, and in due course *Paris-Match* would take notice and schedule an article, "Florette of the Saturday Market." That was how film stars were discovered; why not sweater makers? But it seemed that couturiers were not in the habit of visiting St. Michel du Valcabrère because she was never discovered, in that way or any way, except as a village artisan admired by her neighbors. Instead, she married the postmaster, an older man, most considerate, who insisted she resign from the post office so that she could stay at home to look after the many children they were sure to have. But there were no children and ten years later the postmaster developed a cancer and died, leaving her a little money, not much, enough to live on; and of course she continued to knit sweaters.

For the longest time she believed that no man would ever look at her, thirty-five years old, a widow, plump around the hips, a trace of gray hair at her temples. Men would look through her as if she were a pane of windowglass. She would live for Saturdays at the market and dinner alone or with her girlfriends (some of them widows as well), talking about their absent husbands and the life that lay ahead. St. Michel du Valcabrère was not a village that renewed itself. Handsome strangers did not arrive on horseback, as in American movies. Most families had lived in the district for generations, and it went without saying that everyone knew one another and there were the usual feuds and friendships handed down through the years. So it was hard to start afresh in the village because everyone came with a history, intimately known and impossible to revise, and the same was true of reputations. Not long after the postmaster's death, Monsieur Bardèche, father of three, husband to hatchet-faced Agnès, came by her table at the market and bought a sweater, and the next week he bought another and suggested they were so well made and nice-fitting that he might want one tailored to his own specific dimensions, a bespoke sweater, and to that end he would be happy to come by her house any time for the fittings, although Monday would be best because he closed his café early on Mondays; that would give him ample time for the fittings. So it was not true after all that men would look through her like a pane of windowglass. She had many such opportunities and was extremely choosy about which ones she accepted and which she declined but her Monday evenings were filled, mostly. All this reminiscence was in and out of Florette's memory in seconds, and she was left wishing she had taken one of the sweaters with her, the white cardigan or the blue turtleneck, when she had begun her walk that afternoon. She smiled when she thought of the article in *Paris-Match* and how she had read so carefully each word and examined the photographs, particularly the one of the handsome atelier on the second floor of the building at Place Vendôme across from the Ritz. Beautiful automobiles were parked nearby; strollers had stopped to peer into the windows of the jewelry store close to the second-floor atelier. Her eyes filled with tears. And then she heard a rustle in the woods, and someone cursing, and returned to present time.

These four were rough, not casual hikers out for a Sunday stroll.

She thought probably they were smugglers of drugs since they did not carry heavy packs. Whatever contraband they were transporting was lightweight, probably penny-ante goods, though the men themselves had an air of seriousness about them. She wondered if they were Berbers. They were dark-skinned and bearded, generally unkempt. She did not like the sound of their language, guttural and hard-edged, a sneering language, no music in it. The one with the lisp spoke so softly he could barely be heard, but his voice was coarse all the same, a sandpaper voice filled with menace. His tone reminded her of her long-absent father, a man whose anger was so deep it seemed prehistoric, the dumb anger of beasts, indiscriminate anger on eternal simmer until suddenly it boiled over. He had a head filled with golden curls and transparent blue eyes. Her father's soft voice and sly smile were always an announcement of violence, his accusation a quotation from Scripture, most often Psalm Forty-seven: For The Lord Most High Is Terrible. He Is A Great King Over All The Earth. He Shall Subdue The People Under Us, And The Nations Under Our Feet. He Shall Choose Our Inheritance For Us . . . Her father recited from the Bible as he advanced from one room to the next, her mother retreating before him, hissing like a cat; and then a clamor, a table overturned, a dish smashed, and her father's low monotone. Florette was told to remain in her room until the storm passed but she never forgot her father's words and her mother's cat-hiss, the house filled with discord. He is not one of us, her mother said. He is an alien. Who knows where he comes from or who made him. He said he was born in the Alsace, son of a missionary. His name was Franc DuFour. His father's mission was in one of the former German colonies in East Africa. He worked with the heathen who lived on the shore of Lake Tanganyika. One day the father went away to Africa and never returned. The missionary's son turned up in St. Michel du Valcabrère, a dealer in farm implements, which he sold from the back of a prewar Renault truck.

As Franc was attractive, her mother said, I married him.

I did not know he was a lunatic.

I thought he would provide for us.

Instead, he had a bad outlook on life.

I think he was badly brought up.

Soon enough, Florette and her mother went to live with Tante Christine in Toulouse. When they heard that Franc DuFour had left St. Michel du Valcabrère—a dispute with a farmer over an invoice—they returned to the house in the village. Florette never saw her father again. She was just five years old and her mother told her to forget about him. He was a lunatic with a bad attitude. He was violent and untrustworthy, mean with money. Pretend he does not exist, she said. And that was what Florette did and after a time she ceased to think about him in any specific way, except when she heard a soft voice with a lisp. Then he returned to her whole, his head full of golden curls, his ice-blue eyes, his heavy hands and wide shoulders, his broad brow, and his terrifying words from the Bible. She remembered the only phrase that he had ever said to her personally. She had no recollection of the occasion, only the words themselves: "Tidy up." Those must have been the words he lived by. Florette was distressed that the memory of her father was with her now. She did not want his memory anywhere near her but when she opened her eyes he was still there in the darkness, his bulk, his heavy brow, and his shoulders as wide as an ax handle, his lisp when he recited Psalm Forty-seven, and of course the curls and the evident necessity to tidy up. Her mother told her he was dead and Florette wanted to believe her, but didn't, quite. Well, they were both gone except for the life they maintained in Florette's imagination. This gave her an obscure satisfaction. She was lying injured on pine needles in the snow, her mind teeming with stories. They were her own stories, personal property. No one could take them from her. The conquistador's lisp had reminded her of her father and suddenly her father was alive in her mind. Risen from the dead. They were a family again, if only hallucinatory. He could not harm her, so she reconsidered and welcomed him to her dreams, a ghost from the distant past. She was certain now that she would be all right if she kept her nerve, lived inside herself, and never doubted that help would come. Florette struggled unsuccessfully to get comfortable, wrapped her arms around her chest, and closed her eyes. Light danced behind her eyelids.

When she woke, she was thinking of Thomas. The night was so dark he would never find her unless he stumbled on their bivouac, perhaps heard the men's voices or smelled their tobacco. Surely by this time he would have realized she was lost and set about organizing a proper search. He knew the trail very well. On Sunday afternoons Thomas often came walking with her, carrying a blackthorn stick and telling amusing stories as they ascended the trail, snow glittering on the slopes of the high mountains to the south, Catalonia beyond. They rarely met anyone on the trail and always returned before nightfall. Florette insisted on it. Mountains were unsafe after dark and the Pyrenees were no exception, inhabited as they were by vengeful gods without conscience. So Thomas would know her approximate location and there had always been a kind of sixth sense between them similar to the shared oneness of identical twins. They noticed when things were out of place and read each other's moods as easily as they read the weather; and they knew when not to inquire too closely on those occasions when there was silence at the other end. An explanation would come in due course. But night had fallen and there was no sign of Thomas. She thought she had never seen a blacker night, as if the gods had pulled a curtain over the heavens.

She tried to imagine him now with his American friends, the table disheveled, candles guttering, something on the stereo, Broadway show tunes or a hummable opera, *La Bohème* or *Cavalleria Rusticana*, songs by Edith Piaf or Billie Holiday. The friends did not speak good French so their conversation was in rapid English, usually politics, difficult for her to follow even when Thomas turned to her and translated. Capitalism's responsibility for the turbulence of the modern world, its heedlessness and chaos, its savagery, its utter self-absorption, capitalism the canary in the mineshaft. But it's what we have, isn't it? No turning the clocks back. Against the jihadists, we have capitalism. Will money trump faith? They all had stories of catastrophe from remote parts of the world, Thomas filling glass after glass of Corbières as they made their way through the cauldron of cassoulet. Bernhard Sindelar had stories from NATO headquarters and the various security services of Europe and elsewhere. Russ Conlon, overweight and semiretired, was content to eat and contribute anecdotes from unnamed friends at Interpol and the Paris bourse. Florette's mind wandered as she gazed out the window at the golden afternoon, the sky a washed-out blue, the trees beginning to turn. Autumn in Aquitaine was a natural masterpiece. What a mistake to remain indoors. When Bernhard lapsed into German, Florette knew the men were back in the factories of the small Wisconsin town they grew up in, red brick factories now abandoned, windows shattered, industrial locks rusting on the Cyclone fence that protected the property from vandals, though there was nothing left to vandalize and no one to care if there were. Capitalism's song: the downtown began to decay and then, overnight it seemed, the streets were full of Puerto Ricans and no one knew what there was about wintry LaBarre, Wisconsin, that would attract people from the sunny Caribbean—and here Thomas turned to her and explained that the Puerto Ricans had been there all along, the grandchildren of workers imported to do manual labor at the wire mill and the foundry during the Second World War, labor brought by rail from Miami on the very same tracks that now lay rusting beside the clapped-out factories that during the war had been running eighteen-hour shifts, good wages, good benefits, job security, war's prosperity. And now the grandchildren were grown up with children of their own who lived in a community with a dead economy. Now they called it an enterprise zone. Famous photographers came to take pictures of the factories, exquisite examples of early-twentieth-century industrial design. Form followed function and how quaint it all seemed, as quaint as a tin lunchbucket. Capitalism's epitaph: form followed function and sometime around 1955 the money evaporated, went west, went south, went back to Wall Street, Qué pasa, hombre? Qué pasa? And that was how a community founded by central European immigrants came to be mostly Hispanic, growing old together in an enterprise zone. Florette enjoyed listening to them speak of the village where they grew up, as exotic to her as Moscow, if Moscow had a dozen nationalities all crowded together in one small space. How ever did they manage it? What means "clapped-out factory"?

Florette had cleared the dishes, made a pot of coffee, and slipped out the back door for her walk, having a pretty good idea that the conversation would remain in LaBarre, Wisconsin, of which she had heard quite enough. Thomas had thoughtfully located his hometown in an atlas but she could not visualize it, a black dot in an unfamiliar region of an immense country. A river with an unpronounceable Indian name ran nearby, flowing into a great lake. Minnesota was north, Iowa west; such strange place names. St. Michel du Valcabrère had not changed since she was a girl and her mother said the same thing, yet it was also true that tourists came to take photographs of the church and the pretty square and the memorial to the fallen of the Great War, *Mort pour la France*, thinking them quaint. She had paused at the kitchen door, pleased by the afternoon light streaming into the courtyard, in use since the middle of the eighteenth century, scuffed cobblestones the size of melons underfoot. Thomas and his friends were speaking a kind of pidgin German, remembering their childhoods in once prosperous LaBarre before the Hispanic Anschluss. Russ was the one who had kept up, exchanging Christmas cards with high school classmates, privy to the news: one passed away, another in jail, a third a superior-court judge. Beautiful town to grow up in, Russ said, no town to stay in; and so we left it without a thought because there was nothing to look forward to except decline, and now we remember it as a kind of lazy American paradise where the days seemed to go on forever to the rhythm of crickets. Florette thought America had a cult of restlessness, people moving on as a matter of course. If you didn't like the hand you were dealt—the wife, the job, the color of your hair or the shape of your bosom—you dealt yourself another. She herself had shuffled the cards, bewitched by an article in *Paris-Match* that described a couturier in Place Vendôme, merchant to the haute monde. But when the chance came to go to Paris she had done nothing. She had thrown in her hand. Place Vendôme was not beyond her wildest dreams, in fact it was her wildest dream; but it was only a dream and so she had stayed behind.

In the spirit of a mariner who wished above all else to visit the caves at Altamira, Florette had tried to encourage Thomas to take her to America, New York City with a side trip to LaBarre. You haven't seen your country in ages, she said. Aren't you curious to see what's become of it? How people are getting on since the attacks? The sense they make of them? I suppose they won't like it when you tell them you live in France. Probably they'll think you're a traitor and have changed sides. But still. So much has happened in so short a time. Aren't you interested? He looked at her with a strange smile and said, There isn't anyone I want to see in America. Maybe sometime, for you. But sometime never arrived because both she and Thomas were gripped by the stubborn inertia that came with living in an out-of-the-way place, hard to get into or out of. Mountains limited the horizon. Naturally there was more to it than that but Florette did not feel she could insist. She had lived all her life in St. Michel du Valcabrère and a few more months or years would make no difference. In any case, they were content where they were. Florette had never been outside France and only recently had begun to think about travel to America. She wanted to see the empty place where the twin towers once stood and see the Statue of Liberty up close. She wanted to stay in a fine hotel and ride a Fifth Avenue bus and visit Saks. She wanted to go to the opera in a long black dress, Thomas in a tuxedo. And she wanted a long detour to Thomas's birthplace. She wondered if provincial LaBarre had a town square with a stone monument to the fallen, *Mort pour l'Amérique*, and a church that was as beautiful as the one in her square.

Florette moved stiffly on the stretcher and put her hands to her temples. She could not remember the name of the church, the one she was baptized in and attended every Sunday of her life. She closed her eyes and concentrated hard but the place in her mind where the church was, was suddenly blank. She did not understand how this could be. She thought and thought and when she finished thinking she looked up with an expression of the most poignant embarrassment.

Florette noticed pinpoints of light in the forest and knew they were smoking again. The Gitanes smell reached her, hung a moment, and disappeared. She thought she heard one of them laugh but dismissed it as her overheated imagination. These were not men who laughed casually, unlike Thomas's rowdy American friends. She closed her eyes, knowing her mind was wandering, reeling actually, stuttering from one subject to another. Her mind seemed to have a will of its own. She was so very cold, it was hard for her to concentrate. She wanted desperately to pee but did not know how to go about it. She was not all in one piece but scattered, a skein of yarn that had unraveled. She knew she must stay alert so that she could call to Thomas when he came for her with the men from the village. His sixth sense would tell him she was injured and in danger. Thomas would never allow her to be mistreated. She missed him so, his good humor and generosity, his easiness, his sincerity in most things, his superstitions (a knock on wood, his habit of placing pebbles on the gravestones of strangers) despite his professed atheism, his touch, and his excitement. She even missed his absent-mindedness, his habit of being there and not-there at the same time; she called it his equilibrium. She wished he took better care of himself and like all men he covered things up. As the women in the village said, his shoes were full of stones. Gaps in the biography, Thomas called it. Missing years, years that had dropped from sight, interregnum years when he was, as he said, absent without leave. Out of the way. In the evening after dinner he would disappear into his not-there state, a private smile appearing from nowhere, lingering awhile before it disappeared and he took up his book once again, and settled in. The smile infuriated her; you could almost hear the rustle of bedsheets. She didn't mind that he'd had a prior life, everyone did. He was past fifty when she met him and past sixty when they married, his manner suggesting a life very much spent in the world. His face looked it: laugh lines in combat with worry lines, the laugh lines winning but only barely. However, she did not like the private smile. One night she asked him about it, what he was thinking when he was smiling privately. And he told her it was a passage in the book he was reading and then he recited the passage. Of course he knew what she was asking and added that he had drawn a line between past and present, the present beginning the winter Sunday when they met in the church at St. Michel du Valcabrère and walked across the square to the café for a tisane. Remember the snowflakes in the air? The café windows were misted over. Most everyone wore their Sunday clothes, dark suits for the men, flowered dresses for the women. He had decided not to go to Mass that day but promised to meet her outside when it was over. He sometimes went to Mass because he liked the music and the carved figures of the saints behind the altar, St. Michel's foot worn smooth by the touch of thumbs, supposedly good luck, a propitious thumb-touch. They walked across the square to the café and took the table next to the pinball machine. Old Bardèche arrived with the tisane almost at once, smiling, complimenting Florette on her dress.

Thomas kept his right hand in his jacket pocket, fingering the small square box that contained an engagement ring. He had decided to ask her to marry him but did not know exactly how to go about it. He was as nervous as a teenager. Thomas reminded her of the first day they met and had gone across the square to the café and he had explained to her that he was an artist, a portraitist who had traveled all his life and was content now to settle in a farmhouse in the country. And she had said yes, she knew his house, the property next to the Englishman. Florette remembered that Thomas lit her cigarette with a gold lighter and gave her the lighter, and the next day they went for a walk on the mountain, trading personal histories; and a week after that she moved from her little house in the village to his farmhouse next to the reclusive Englishman's. They had not been apart since. That afternoon Thomas reached into his jacket pocket and said, I have something for you—

They both looked up, aware suddenly of a contretemps at the table next to the door, three men, two women, expensively turned out, tourists from the look of them, though this was not the season for tourism. One of the men was blind, talking loudly to old Bardèche, thumping his fist on the table for emphasis. The women seemed to be egging him on. The sightless man was complaining about the wine, racehorse piss, he said. He wanted another bottle, something drinkable, and did not intend to pay for the bottle in front of him because it was racehorse piss, give it to the racehorses. Old Bardèche looked from the blind man to the women and back again, understanding only that the wine was not wanted. He was short-tempered in the best of times and now Thomas watched his face color. The other two men lounged insolently in their chairs, their arms folded, as the young women—one blond, the other dark—watched avidly with the expressions you saw on spectators in the ringside seats. Whenever the blind man mentioned racehorses, the quartet laughed unpleasantly. One of the men began to pick at his fingernails while his friend yawned. They behaved as if they owned the café and everything in it. When the blond woman stuck out her tongue at old Bardèche he pointed at the door and told them in French to get out, they were no longer welcome. Take your whores with you, Madame Bardèche said from her position at the caisse. The men looked up. The blind man rose then. He was built like a stevedore, broad in the shoulders and half a head taller than the Frenchman, eyes hidden behind wraparound sunglasses, a black baseball cap with the legend *NYPD 9/11* pulled low over his forehead. He wore a tan chamois jacket, expensive from the look of it, black jeans, and leather ankle boots. He stood with his fists loosely at his sides, his head moving left and right. The racket of conversation ceased, the café grown abruptly silent, old Bardèche at a loss as to how to proceed with the American.

He said, You. Garçon.

Thomas turned to Florette and said, Excuse me. I have to see to this.

Who are they, Thomas?

My countrymen, alas.

Garçon, the American said again. Come here.

The patrons of the café were nonplused, divided by their natural sympathy for a sightless man and appalled at his behavior. Surely he had reason for grievance but old Bardèche was not the cause and he was not a garçon, either. It was well known that Bardèche had no sympathy for Mussulmen. None of the villagers did. They looked at each other and wondered what was expected of them. This blind man was spoiling for a fight, and for what? Suddenly he lunged at the Frenchman, who easily sidestepped, and the blind man crashed into the table, cursing loudly as glassware shattered. His four friends remained seated, content to let their comrade settle the matter. That seemed to be the agreement among them. Honor was at stake. Now most of the men in the café were on their feet, prepared to come to old Bardèche's aid, but in the general uproar Thomas got there first.

Thomas said, It's best if you and your friends leave before there's serious trouble.

Who the fuck are you?

Thomas saw that the blind man did not look directly at him but off to one side. He was trying to judge Thomas's position by the sound of his voice. Thomas said, I live here.

Fuck you then, the blind man said, and Thomas saw that his face was pockmarked by dozens of tiny scars and one long scar that ran from the outside corner of his right eye to his chin. He had once been a handsome man, except for the sneer. Thomas wondered if the sneer had always been there or if it was a consequence of his injuries. He must have suffered terribly.

I think you're outnumbered, Thomas said equably enough, as though this were a casual misunderstanding among friends.

It's racehorse piss.

Try the café in the next town, why don't you.

The blind man swung at him and missed and the friends at the table laughed once more. One of the women clapped her hands sarcastically.

Old Bardèche had come up behind Thomas with a heavy alpenstock but hesitated. He did not sincerely want to use it against a blind man but he was running out of patience. He only wanted the Americans out of his café.

Forget it, Jock, one of the men at the table said.

We don't care about them, his friend added.

Nobody cares about them, the blond woman said. Crummy little café in the back of beyond. She slapped a twenty-dollar bill on the table and gathered her coat. Let's get going. I'd like to be in Andorra before midnight.

Good advice, Thomas said.

He's right in front of you, Jock.

The blind man swung again but he was off balance and the blow landed on Thomas's shoulder, hard enough to turn him around but not so hard he couldn't push back, and the blind man went sprawling into the table again. Blood leaked from a tear in the chamois jacket but he was oblivious.

Get him out of here, Thomas said to the blond woman.

Don't fuck with us, one of the men said.

What's your name? Thomas said.

Harry.

Well, Harry. It's time for you to go. He looked at the blind man, who appeared disoriented; Thomas's face was reflected in the sunglasses. Look, he said finally. I'm sorry about your friend. Was he a policeman?

Cop? No, he wasn't a cop. Jock sold insurance. Except in New York City we're all cops now. You wouldn't understand that.

He was in the twin towers?

Look at him, Harry said. What do you think?

The blind man said, Go to hell. He was seated now, one elbow on the table, his hands clasped in his lap, his face soft as putty. It was impossible to know what he was thinking or if he was thinking anything. Thomas noticed that his hands were scarred. Blood continued to spill from the tear in his chamois jacket. Everyone noticed but no one said anything. Thomas felt tremendously sorry for him even as he wanted him out of the neighborhood.

Racehorse piss, the blind man muttered. But now his friends had their hands on his elbows and were moving him toward the door, awkwardly, as if he were a heavy piece of furniture. They took their time, five finely dressed American tourists, out of place in the café. They were through the door at last when the blond woman turned and looked Thomas up and down as if she were appraising a piece of meat.

You were a big help. There was a time, Americans stuck together, members of the same tribe. Cut one, the others bleed.

I don't remember that time, Thomas said. When was that? Pearl Harbor?

New York, she said. Right now. This minute. It's beautiful.

So is St. Michel du Valcabrère, he said.

What's that?

The village you're in.

Shit, she said and laughed.

He said, It was a terrible thing, nine-eleven, but—

But nothing. But *nothing*. Jock's life is ruined. And he's angry. He's going to stay angry and that's his right because his life is ruined. He might have been you, except you don't live in New York. You jerk.

The others stood in the doorway, listening. The blind man, towering above them, had his back turned so he was facing the street, though perhaps he didn't know that.

Come on, Helen. Leave them to their racehorse piss.

Old Bardèche asked Thomas to translate.

Thomas said, They're sorry for the damage.

Bardèche said, Tell them to leave at once.

They're leaving, Thomas said.

Watch your mouth, asshole, the woman said.

Close the door behind you, Thomas said.

The blind man turned. Thomas noticed that in his mirrored dark glasses, the interior of the café was caught in a frozen moment. He moved his head left and right. It seemed to Thomas that he was straining to see what was before him.

Goodbye, Thomas said.

Bardèche watched them leave, then slowly turned and walked back to his place behind the bar.

When Thomas returned to their table, Florette embraced him. Everyone in the café was talking, the noise level rising like that of an excited theater audience at the end of a powerful performance. No one knew precisely what they had just witnessed. Did the gravely injured have special rights? There was something mortifying about the blind man, lunging and missing, swinging at Thomas and missing again. He must have had a terrible ordeal, the tiny scars and the long scar and the sneer on his mouth. You sympathized with him even as you realized he was out of control. Well, they were gone now but there was no guarantee they would not return. Men crowded around their table congratulating Thomas. They had no quarrel with Americans generally but these Americans were no good. There were bad apples in every nationality, the Germans and the Belgians especially, and the Dutch. All nations had bruta figuras, even Italy. When old Bardèche sent over a bottle of the racehorse piss, everyone drank to Thomas's good health and Florette's also.

When they were alone at last, Thomas and Florette sat in a zone of silence, working the incident in their minds. There seemed nothing of it to discuss usefully except the question of forgiveness, mercy offered to a man living in darkness and hating every second, knowing all the while that those most directly responsible were dead and could not be called to account. He was an awful son of a bitch but his situation was not enviable. Grievous injury did not ennoble a man except in special circumstances. Later they would refer to the incident often, how it began and how it ended and Thomas's role in the departure of the Americans, everyone in the café crowded at the windows watching them climb into their Mitsubishi van and speed away, the blind man in the front passenger seat, the others in the two rear seats.

Will you marry me? Thomas asked.

Of course, Florette said.

Her body showed no signs of exhausting its pain ration but the memory of the Sunday afternoon in the café with the wretched

Americans and his proposal at the end of it warmed her and brightened her spirits. Thomas would not fail her but she wondered again what had detained him. They were so close. Thomas was always within earshot, working alone all day long without interruption except for lunch. He worked in the downstairs room that looked south up the couloir, the land rising until the roads ended and the snow-covered summit began, the route of smugglers for many centuries and refugees of the Napoleonic War at the beginning of the nineteenth century, Francisco Goya's war. There had been a stream of refugees from the Spanish Civil War. Thomas claimed that at the end of the day when he looked up from his easel to the panorama beyond his window he could hear the sound of marching feet, the strangled cries of the wounded, and the creak of leather and weapons. Thousands fled Catalonia in the miserable years 1937 and 1938, settling mainly in Aquitaine. A few were still alive, men and women of very great age, and their descendants were scattered all over southern France, a Spanish diaspora. Not even Franco's death could reconcile them to their homeland because so much had been lost, too much to forgive. Forgiveness was a blasphemy. Thomas thought often of the Spanish refugees when he was working because he was a species of refugee himself, a displaced person.

He told her that with no explanation.

And you still feel displaced?

Not often, he said. Almost never.

Florette heard piano music and immediately raised her head to discover its source. The notes rose and faded away and when her head fell back to the canvas she realized the music was inside her, refugees abruptly assuming the guise of a tune that she could not identify, though it stayed with her, the tempo resembling a heartbeat or the pain-throb in her ankle. She lay still, trying to imagine herself in other circumstances. She wondered what Thomas would do and what he would be thinking; at least he wouldn't have to worry about a pee. Thomas was good under pressure, as he had been that day in old Bardèche's café. She had never told him about Bardèche-on-Monday-evening—where was the need to do so? Certainly that was not the occasion, the afternoon in the café when he shyly proposed to her. You never knew how men, even worldly men, would react to such a declaration. It was always a mistake to believe you knew someone's heart, even if it was the person closest to you in all the world. Publicly, Thomas kept his thoughts to himself, using courtesy to disarm his adversaries. Now and then people came to the house to see him. Thomas said they were journalists and sometimes they were, critics from newspapers and magazines eager to know whom he was "doing." But there were others who didn't look like journalists, in their business suits and city hats, their polished shoes, always carrying briefcases, even the women; the smaller the woman, the larger the briefcase. They were often brusque. Thomas would usher them into his office where they could take account of the photographs on the walls, Thomas in a variety of locations and wearing a variety of hats, a bowler, a trilby, a beret, a kaffiyeh, a topee, before being directed to admire the view, the mountain route of refugees.

A trail of misery, he would say.

And what the refugees found was scarcely better than what they had left behind, except for the killing.

Thomas would close the door, having arranged with Florette to knock in one hour and propose tea. She would bring in the tea tray and watch while the visitor, with evident chagrin, switched off the tape recorder; and all this time Thomas was looking at her and beaming, as if tea at four P.M. were the most important moment of the day. Thomas poured the tea and made small talk before explaining that he and Florette had chores, a trip to the market or the post office, a long-delayed visit to the dentist because a molar was acting up. And the visitor would look appropriately crestfallen, how disagreeable for Mr. Railles. Then, rising reluctantly, the visitor would point to the canvas on the easel and say, Very interesting. It definitely has your signature. Who is it? And Thomas would reply, An old friend. Does the friend have a name? the visitor would inquire, offering an encouraging smile. And Thomas would reply, I have been painting him for many years, in his youth and now in his old age. As for his name, I have forgotten it. As you can surmise from our conversations, my memory isn't what it was. The years wash into one another, a watercolor memory. One fact bleeds into another. Emotions bleed. Faces bleed. I am forced to make lists, the latest list of familiar train stations, Santa Lucia in Venice, Keleti in Budapest, Atocha in Madrid. I have inventories of the natural world also, mountains and rivers, deserts, seas. It helps having a list of hard facts, don't you agree?

Facts anchor the work, whatever it is you're composing, a picture or a piece of music or a novel or poem.

But memory has to anchor the facts, alas.

And so I fall short.

Florette can vouch for that, can't you, chérie?

And the visitor would turn to her with a pained expression and she would give him chapter and verse on simple things her husband forgot, bills unpaid, letters unanswered, ordinary tasks ignored. She spoke with conviction because everything she said was true. The visitor would smile and Thomas would smile back and murmur something ambiguous. Forgetfulness is the old man's friend. Forgetfulness is a dream state, wouldn't you agree? When the visitor took one last look at the canvas, Thomas announced that the portrait was far from completion. He needed more time, perhaps a lifetime's worth. This man's personality changed with each season. Probably he would never finish it. The portrait would be an uncompleted work of great but unfulfilled promise, like Mahler's Tenth Symphony or Fitzgerald's *Last Tycoon*. The other portraits were safely locked away elsewhere, in another region of the country. Arson and theft were common in St. Michel du Valcabrère, owing to the many itinerant travelers, so often undocumented.

Then the visitor would leave and the portrait returned to the closet, where it would remain until the next inquiry. Florette thought these briefcase-wielding visitors were colorless people, with the closed and locked faces of suspicious landlords. She objected to them. She didn't like them in her house but Thomas insisted it was altogether easier talking to them for an hour than refusing to talk to them at all. They were persistent. They could make things difficult for him, and for her, too, if they chose. Trouble was, they didn't know specifically what they were looking for. There was something they wanted but they didn't know precisely what it was. Unk-unks, in government argot: unknown unknowns. Still, they had to say they tried. They had to make the journey. And they're gone now, he said, touching wood.

We can be ourselves again.

You were superb, chérie.

Would you like a tisane?

Florette listened now for his step but heard nothing except the movement of the men in the woods. She had forgotten where she was. She opened her eyes and saw that the snow had ceased. Stars burned overhead and off to the south. Through the branches of the trees she saw the horned moon. She was counting the things she had and the things she was missing, a warm coat and gloves, wool socks, a cigarette, and the company of her aunt, always a welcome presence. When she was young and ill with the usual childhood diseases, Tante Christine was always on hand to nurse her. Her own mother couldn't be bothered. Her mother was not on speaking terms with illness. When illness was in the house, her mother went away and Tante Christine arrived. Tante Christine had a saying about the horned moon but she couldn't remember what it was except it was lewd. One more lost story. She and Thomas forgot things all the time and now she knew that in her life she had forgotten much more than she remembered, fragments of herself gone forever. Soon she would be a tree stripped of leaves, bare to the winter wind. Thomas claimed that things were never forgotten, merely stored in momentarily inaccessible places, usually in l'esprit profond; so it was not unknown for the inaccessible to become accessible, such as when you were in a dream state or otherwise bewitched. She supposed that was why he made his lists of train stations and the rivers of the capital cities of central Europe. Thomas was so American. Nothing was ever lost, only misplaced; and when something unwelcome entered his mind, he knocked wood. Now she craved a cigarette. The

Gitane smell was close but wafted away. She shut her eyes and put her hands on her face, her hands like claws, her fingers so very cold against her skin. Her nails were like chips of ice and she wondered if she was feverish. Her throat was sore, constricted as if a hand had closed around it. She did not understand why Thomas did not come for her. She was waiting for him.

He was occupied with his friends. She tried to remember why the Americans were with them for lunch. Yes, of course. They had come for the funeral the day before. The funeral of the Englishman who lived in the farmhouse adjoining their own. He was over one hundred years old when he passed away in his sleep. Thomas and his two friends were pallbearers at the service, sparsely attended, only a few loyal neighbors and the mayor besides herself and Ghislaine, the village woman who cooked and kept house for the Englishman. The abbé was circumspect in his eulogy, a generic affair that took account of Monsieur Granger's long life and quiet death, his modest habits and unobtrusive character, before commending his soul to the grace of God, though the abbé's manner suggested that God might wait awhile before attending to it. The light was soft inside the church, yellow flowers banked beside the casket. Florette had picked them herself from the Englishman's greenhouse. Thomas and his American friends listened attentively, solemn expressions broken now and again by raised eyebrows. They buried the Englishman under the cherry tree by the wall in the meadow beside his house. There were no tears because the Englishman had led an agreeable life for a very long time, and if he had a complaint no one ever heard it. Ghislaine had turned to Florette and said that the Englishman had left her nothing, not a sou, after all the years she had looked after him and his wretched dogs, cairn terriers, filthy brutes, biters, six in all over the many, many decades he had lived in St. Michel du Valcabrère. Ghislaine looked after the dogs and the dogs' graves, can you imagine such a disagreeable chore? The dog remains were on the south side of the cherry trees, while he will be on the north. They were all under the shade of the tree. Wasn't it appalling and unwholesome? And that was not all. He left the farmhouse and its contents, including the wine cellar and the English silver, to a niece in America and she was selling everything sight unseen. They had never met, Monsieur Granger and the American niece. They were perfect strangers. Yet for me, there's nothing. An irregular situation, Ghislaine said. She had only come to the funeral so that she could curse him silently and in person, another foreigner who arrived unbidden to enjoy French hospitality but refused to honor his debts. Debts were for other people. Also, he was not amiable, was untidy in his manner, often curt, one of those who thought the French owed him something. Yes, that was true. He had a grudge against us. He believed all France should be grateful that he chose to come and live among us, as if it were not his choice but our choice. They think we are innkeepers to the world! That was the way with foreigners estranged from their own countries. Wasn't it true that a person deserved to die under his own flag, among his own people? He will never be at rest. And I will say this also, Madame, between us two only. He had a stone in his shoe, something concealed. He had a dark past, that one. As with so many foreigners. He should not have been here. Ghislaine heaved a great shrug, her mouth turned down at the corners. No one asked him to come. Yet here he was.

When Florette repeated the conversation to Thomas, he was unsympathetic. Ghislaine had done all right for herself while the old man was alive. She has no cause for complaint. It was true that Captain St. John Granger had a personal history that was not entirely comme il faut, but Ghislaine was in no position to judge. The Englishman was both more and less than he seemed. He had arrived in St. Michel du Valcabrère in 1919, evidently having done his service in the war. He was slender as a walking stick, with a thin mustache and a cap of fine yellow hair, dressed up in a blue blazer and flannel trousers, a regimental tie at his throat. Owing to his clothes and his bearing, people were certain he was a lord, perhaps a second son obliged to leave his homeland. Many veterans had migrated to the region, attracted by its privacy, its distance from the world, its wild beauty and extreme climate, its taciturnity. In the beginning, he was the only Englishman in the valley. When other English people arrived, he became yet more reclusive, growing vegetables, tending his flowers, rarely leaving his property. He had no visitors from the outside and gave the impression he was without family, an Englishman who had severed all ties to his native land. In any case, he seemed content living alone in a plain style, reading constantly. The Englishman had a beautiful library, books mostly of the nineteenth century, the century of invention, adventure, and capitalism. Once a month Thomas was invited to dinner, the meal cooked and served by Ghislaine. A companionable game of billiards finished the evening. Thomas always returned home tipsy and thoughtful and when Florette asked him what they had talked about, he replied that the Englishman was spare with words. He spent them as a miser spent money. He had a fine sense of humor but used it infrequently, being easy with silence. Despite his great age, the Englishman's mind had not lost its edge. He quoted Trollope and Dickens from memory and also Proust but with a Mayfair accent. He talked about books while Thomas retailed what village gossip he had—the schoolmaster's mysterious disappearance, the quarrel between the gendarme and the mayor—but the Englishman was more interested in books than he was in gossip. Gossip was interesting only if you knew the personalities involved and the Englishman had but a nodding acquaintance with the inhabitants of the village. However, he did have an intimate attachment to Ghislaine. Thomas was certain of this because one evening at table, pouring wine, she had straightened his shirt collar, in the circumstances a most private gesture. The nature of the intimate attachment could only be guessed at. But the Englishman pretended not to notice and continued the conversation as if nothing had occurred.

Florette said, But Ghislaine is nearly seventy years old.

And Granger is—over a hundred, Thomas said.

So what manner of "intimate attachment" do you suppose it is?

Billiards, Thomas said. They play billiards together.

Very funny, Florette said.

When Thomas's friends arrived on their visits he took them to the Englishman's for tea. Florette declined to go on grounds that it was a masculine occasion and she would be in the way, by which she meant that the conversation would bore her. The Americans brought news of the outside world, NATO capitals and the Middle East, the famished nations of the equator and the awakening of the East, China and the Indian subcontinent. The Englishman was always attentive, leaning forward in his chair, his hand cupped at his ear. He liked stories of international fuckups, especially if they involved Americans, but rarely volunteered any of his own. But of course he had been disengaged from the world, having lived in Aquitaine for a very long time. He had no firsthand knowledge of current events and rarely read a newspaper. His prewar radio did not receive the BBC. If asked, he could not have been able to name the American vice president or the British chancellor of the exchequer. He volunteered that he had once seen Winston Churchill from a distance, and as a child had been introduced to T. E. Lawrence. Boyish face, iron handshake. Shame he isn't around to settle the present mess, what? When Russ Conlon professed disgust at the promise of paradise for Muslim suicide bombers, the Englishman smiled and said that people who had nothing must be promised something. And they would believe the promise because God was both great and benevolent. No God would condemn a man to live as wretchedly in the next life as he lived in this one. That would make a hoax of life and of God also. Surely that would not be God's will. And so the imams promised paradise, and who is to say they are not prophets? Revenge has many forms, would you not agree? Revenge is the animating principle of our world. And in the division of the spoils is it not logical that if the faithful merit heaven, the faithless merit hell? In the puzzled silence that followed, Thomas observed that for that one moment the Englishman had abandoned his attitude of ironic detachment and spoke from the heart. And then his attention wandered and he began to doze in his chair. The Americans left shortly thereafter, promising to return again next year, when they could once again discuss the connection between faith and murder because neither would disappear in their lifetimes. Revenge would figure in the discussion as well.

Florette listened to Thomas's dry account and wondered aloud why he never invited the Englishman to dinner. She was a good cook and enjoyed having people in. Thomas replied that the old man preferred dining at home, at his own table among his own things, Ghislaine cooking according to his specific diet. Florette was not satisfied with this answer. Thomas should insist. Hospitality should always be repaid. Was he ashamed of her? Their table? Their cellar? Not at all, Thomas said equably. It was only a question of what the old man was prepared to undertake. He lived to suit himself. He did not go out of his way for other people and did not expect other people to go out of their way for him. He lived by his own rules, simple rules but immutable. Thomas added, unhelpfully, that Captain St. John Granger was a species of ghost and that was why they got on so well, because he, Thomas, was a species of ghost also, except he preferred the term "displaced person."

Florette heard a rustle in the underbrush and guessed they had finished their conversation and were ready to move once more. She listened hard for the voice of the pig-eyed conquistador, the one with the lisp, but heard nothing. She called again, louder, for a Gitane but her voice was husky, barely above a whisper. Her voice was gone and no one heard her. The pain in her chest interfered with her vocal cords and she found it difficult to breathe. She noticed that the pain in her leg had almost vanished, replaced by a heavy numbness. Snow was falling again, softly, a slow-motion fall, and a great silence had settled over the forest. The horned moon had vanished. The wind died. She felt someone touch her arm but when she looked up she saw only the snow and the white-limbed trees. The touch felt like her mother's hand but when she spoke aloud, Mama, Mama, are you there? and heard no reply, she knew the touch was imaginary, her mind wandering again. It was confusing for her, looking through the snowflakes, collecting now on the boughs of the fir trees, settling in blankets. In this country it often snowed for days, roads were closed, communications disrupted, the hills and fields motionless in white; and when that happened it was possible to believe that time had hurtled backward at great speed, centuries dissolving, Merovingian kings ruling still in Aquitaine, the community returned to the tenth century where it belonged. The trees resembled overweight women in white aprons, and she thought again of dear Tante Christine. She called again in her weak voice, speaking French so that her aunt might understand and come to her aid. She had waited such a long time. She raised her voice and promised the men reward money if they delivered her safely home. Her house was not far, barely an hour's walk. Thomas would be grateful. Thomas would reward them if only they would pick up the stretcher and carry her down the trail. Please, she said, remembering her manners. Didn't everyone deserve courtesy? But there was no sound in the forest, not even a whisper of wind. She waited, holding her breath, feeling time whirl backward, listening for the man with the lisp, the conquistador who reminded her of her absent father. His voice was unmistakable. She would know it anywhere.

Snow continued to fall, collecting on her legs and stomach, collecting on her fingers as she raised her arms to the unseen stars, time continuing to reel backward until she saw herself quite clearly as a young girl, seventeen years old and dressed in white, listening to church bells on a sunny Sunday morning, everyone gathered in the square, talking companionably as they waited for Mass. She was standing with friends, classmates, and a boy she was interested in. The boy thought she resembled Jeanne Moreau, star of that year's wonderful film *Jules et Jim*. The boy's idol was Jean-Paul Belmondo, the *Breathless* Belmondo, the Belmondo with the swagger, the leer, the truculence, and the mountainous nose. She could not take her eyes off the boy and thought of him as her personal Lord of Misrule. He wore his trousers short, his thumbs tucked behind his belt like an American cowboy, a black hat. He had plans. He intended to move to the Pigalle district of Paris and begin a career as a gangster so that he could afford fast cars and late nights in cabarets. Adieu, St. Michel du Valcabrère. He wanted to live according to his own desires. Tante Christine discouraged her interest in the boy, an unsuitable boy, louche and unstable and without prospects. What would life be with such a boy? What would become of her? Such boys existed in every village in France, perhaps in every village in every country of the world, and no good came of them. Florette could do ever so much better, she was so attractive and well disposed, warm and likable to a fault. And abruptly the bells receded and fell silent and the people filed into the church until the square was empty except for Jean-Paul Belmondo insolently astride his motorcycle.

It took Florette a few moments to realize she was alone, and a few moments more to understand what that meant. The men had abandoned her, gone back to wherever they had come from or wherever they were going. She began to shiver, turning painfully on her side, wrapping her arms around her chest. My God, it was cold. She had never been colder in her life. She waited and waited some more, she had no idea how long. She could not bear to think of dying alone, so she worked hard to keep her wits intact, banishing all thoughts of her injuries and dying in the mountain forest. She wanted to look at her wristwatch, for she had no idea of the time. She brought the dial close to her face, squinting, and saw the hands upright, forming the number 1. That would make the time six o'clock, and how surprised she was. It was only early evening and she had imagined the hour to be nine or perhaps ten, well past the dinner hour. She was suddenly filled with hope, the hour seemed to her a lifeline, time at last on her side. Thomas was certainly en route now with men from the village, so she needed to remain alert to the present moment, as elusive as that moment might be—and in that state of euphoria, as she found herself grinning like a circus clown, she began to pee. She did not understand this, why her body relaxed just then, like flopping into an armchair after strenuous exercise. She peed and peed some more, such a strange sensation lying on her back but so welcome; and at last she was done, her bladder empty, and she wondered how she had endured it as long as she had. But the men were gone. She had nothing to fear, nothing at all save for the possibility that Thomas would not find her. The mountain was as broad as the world itself.

So she clasped her frozen hands and prayed to God, first in

French, then in English, finally in Latin. Her English was not good enough for the prayer. She thought she had forgotten her Latin but she spoke as fluently as any cleric at the altar of her church, until she forgot where she was in the prayer, the sense of it, what she was saying and whom she was saying it to and why. The words had flown away. She was forgetting even as she lay alone in the darkness, unquiet, diminished, snow collecting all around her. She was dependent on the mercy of others and that made her cross. She had shied from turmoil her whole life, even as a little girl; there was turmoil enough within the four walls of her own house. Her regret was that she had no children but that was God's will, and now she was being punished again for no reason she could understand. She had never been adventurous, and now she was lying frozen on a mountainside waiting for rescue. Other people were adventurous. The boy she had been interested in had ridden away on his motorcycle one afternoon in the spring. He promised he would write her from Paris. When he was settled he would send for her. They would conquer the capital together, just like all those provincial characters in Balzac's novels. If you pushed hard enough, Paris gave way. They would work as a team, she preparing her assault on the Place Vendôme, he at Place Pigalle. And if she failed—well, a great film director would see her one day on the street and offer a screen test. She would be the new Moreau, her face on the cover of magazines and her voice on the radio. They would have a fine apartment and he would be a respected gangster with men of his own and money to burn. They would take midnight drives in the Bois du Boulogne in his yellow Alfa-Romeo convertible, she with a summer breeze in her hair, and over his left shoulder the tapering candle of the Eiffel Tower. But she never heard from him and always wondered whether he had gotten to Paris, and if he had, what he was doing there. Had her Lord of Misrule realized his dream? She hoped so. Tante Christine believed he would be driving a bus, that was what happened to boys from the country who ran off to Paris to make their fortune. Boys never understood the odds. Boys did not know how hard Paris could be when you arrived there alone, penniless, frightened, friendless, every hand turned against you. Montparnasse station was the gate to perdition. Florette had smiled at her aunt's vehemence, the natural contempt of the country woman for the city. Of course she spoke the truth as she saw it. But even so, Florette wanted to think of him as a great success in his chosen life of crime, a respected gangster with men of his own and money to burn, driving his yellow convertible through the Bois du Boulogne at midnight, the Eiffel Tower over his left shoulder.

Florette's mind continued to reel, memories tumbling from it, her spirit becoming lighter as it freed itself of its burdens. What once was thick was now loose; and all this time her thoughts were escaping and dispersing like a plume of breath on a cold day. The yellow convertible in the Bois du Boulogne disappeared. She could no longer remember the boy's name. She was further inside herself than she believed possible but this was comforting. She was no longer so cold and was content now to wait. The present moment slipped away, irretrievable. She tried now to gather her memories but they continued to elude her, dancing away into the night. They were quicker than she was. Florette was consoled and in limbo and that was all she could think about as snow continued to fall, tiny flakes as hard as gravel. She closed her eyes, concentrating, but there was nothing to concentrate on. Her memory began to drift away, shuddering, almost vacant, and weightless. She saw herself from a great height, the horned moon over her shoulder. She knew she was falling asleep because she was no longer cross and no longer remembering. She was not conscious of time except for the faint beat of her heart. Then the Gitanes smell was close by and something warm against her throat.

What is your name?

Florette, she said.

Goodbye, Florette.

Goodbye, she said.

Granger

THOMAS RAILLES, in their bedroom, sorted through the items on her dresser one by one. They were everyday familiar, but he had rarely noticed them: photographs of her mother and Tante Christine and the postmaster, husband number one, looking official in a blue hat. He had been dead some years and she seldom spoke of him except to remark on his loyalty to the post office, one of the sublime achievements of French civilization, established by Louis XI and nationalized by the immortal Bonaparte himself. There were two photographs of her and Thomas in the mountains, snow-covered peaks in the distance. Florette wore a black beret and they both carried walking sticks; same beret, same walking sticks in both pictures. He leafed through a stack of postcards, then straightened them as you would straighten a deck of cards. He paused to look left at the Matisse sketch over the bed, the head of a young woman so ardent you felt she might fly off the paper and become flesh in front of your eyes. He had bought it for Florette on their first wedding anniversary and he had never seen her so pleased. The price would have appalled her but she never asked. With difficulty Thomas turned back to the task at hand, his inventory. There was a sewing kit and a crucifix on a silver chain with strands of her hair and next to the crucifix an alligator jewel box he had bought in Rome years before. A company of elephants ranged in a semicircle around the photographs: marble elephants from Thailand, stone elephants from South Africa, ebony elephants from Kenya, and a silver elephant from India. The Indian elephant came with a howdah and a miniature maharajah wearing a pointed turban. All of them were gifts from Bernhard Sindelar and Russ Conlon. Wherever they went in the world they bought elephants for Florette. Elephants were good luck. Also, they had excellent memories and were faithful to one another. Thomas touched each elephant in turn, then reached into his pocket and put the gold cigarette lighter next to the jewel box. She had left the lighter on the dining room table the afternoon she went for her walk in the mountains. He looked again at the photographs of himself and Florette, and the one of the postmaster.

When he asked her about him, she waved the question away.

What attracted you to him?

The usual things, she said.

Really, he'd insisted. I'm serious.

He never asked questions, she said. That was what attracted me to him. Then, softening some, she laughed dryly. I can't remember, she said. It was so long ago. He wasn't a brute, I can tell you that. And, my God, he did love his post office.

From the bedroom window Thomas could see the driveway, cars parked haphazardly along it. He watched the mayor and his wife and daughter walk to their Citroën, get in, and drive away. He knew people wouldn't leave until he put in an appearance, accepted their condolences, thanked them for coming. Thomas did not move when he heard a knock on the door, and whoever it was went away. He wanted them all to go away but did not know how to go about telling them. Grief could not be shared or even communicated except in slovenly ways. Bernhard and Russ promised to take care of everyone but they hadn't succeeded. One voice rose above the others but Thomas could not identify it. Ghislaine, perhaps, or the doctor who lived in the village. Florette and Dr. Picot had been childhood friends and she was good enough to supervise the autopsy herself, and that morning at the service she offered to—explain anything he wanted explained.

I can't tell you much that you don't already know or suspect, Dr. Picot said.

Thomas was standing next to his car, the urn containing Florette's ashes in his arms. The burial was private.

She said, Florette was in good health, strong as an ox despite her filthy cigarette habit. Her ankle fracture was very serious and naturally there was hypothermia due to the cold. The cut at her throat was not deep and there was very little bleeding because her body was so cold. Her blood was beginning to congeal. Strong as she was, all this was too much for her. When she was cut her heart stopped. I am certain she was unconscious so at the end the cold would not have mattered to her. I'm bound to say that one hour would have made the difference but I'm sure you and your friends did the best you could under the circumstances. She had a bad time of it, I'm afraid. It's a blessing that at the end she was surely unconscious. The cold, her injuries. She had tremendous faith, as you know, and her faith would have helped her through her ordeal. Still, the experience would have been very lonely for her and frightening. Is it true there were four men? Whoever they were, they deserve to rot in hell.

I'm sure they will.

Poor Florette. It's not the first time something of this sort has happened, men from outside the region, poaching, smuggling, running guns or drugs or just running away.

These mountains—the doctor began but did not finish her thought. Instead, she shrugged and walked away.

He wondered what Dr. Picot wanted to tell him about the mountains. Probably she had an urge to explain the local superstitions but thought better of it. So he was left with Florette's urn in his arms, imagining her blood going cold as her heart failed. The other details he put at the back of his mind.

Thomas watched the doctor make her way to her car, head down, moving slowly. When she turned suddenly to look up at the bedroom window, he gave a little wave of his hand and knocked wood. She blew a kiss and continued on her way. The doctor was not an agreeable woman but she was a good friend to Florette; and he did not believe that one hour would have made any difference. He watched Dr. Picot's car move off, the sunlight so bright it hurt his eyes. He did not know what he would do for the remainder of the afternoon. He had thirty people in his house. They were good to come but he didn't want them there. Thomas moved the silver elephant so that it stood beside the photograph of him and Florette having their picnic in the mountains. The time was spring. She had bought cold chicken and a block of pâté and a bottle of the local rosé. She told risqué stories of village life when she was a girl, hilarious stories with the flavor of Rabelais. They were nothing like the stories of LaBarre when he was a boy. Thomas stared at the photograph and tried to remember the exact spot on the mountain where they had had their picnic but he could not; it was so long ago and all mountains looked the same when you were on them.

Thomas pressed the heels of his hands on the dresser top and leaned until his forehead touched the windowpane, warm from the autumn sun. The noise downstairs continued. He did not want to face them but knew that he must for Florette's sake. He took a sip of wine from the glass on the dresser. He had forgotten it was there but almost at once he felt better, moving into some variety of equilibrium. The person he wanted with him was St. John Granger, dead now nearly one week. Granger knew how to get rid of people. He had been successfully getting rid of people for decades. Granger, master of the silent stare, connoisseur of the oblique and puzzling remark; and all the time he was laughing inside, as he said, "where it counted." Also, he knew what to do with himself of an afternoon. A single glass of wine at lunch, a book, a nap, tea at four o'clock, a stroll before dinner. Granger swung on a tight compass, having seen as much of the world as he cared to see. He was not tempted by pyramids or South Sea islands. He believed the world was overrated. All a man needed was his health, a comfortable house, his books, and a billiards table on which the varieties of experience were near infinite. He laced his talk with billiards expressions, angle shots, balance points, bad hits, corner hooks, feather shots, force-follows, time shots, table runs. He believed restlessness was the enemy of achievement—not that he valued achievement. Granger called himself a species of ghost and that was surely true. He cast no shadow on the earth, and an evening's conversation over the billiards table, broken as it was by interminable silences, seemed to halt time itself.

Granger had had one profound experience as a young man and spent the rest of his life feeding off it, existing in a realm where experience was irrelevant. His life was a kind of force-follow, extreme overspin with a hesitation when it encountered resistance. Thomas laughed suddenly, looking at the elephants and thinking about Granger.

Do you know, Granger said one night, that no American has won the world three-cushion billiards championship since 1936?

No, I didn't know that.

Belgians have won it twelve times. Not one American. Or Englishman either. One German.

Why do you suppose that is, Granger?

Granger, sighting an angle shot over his left knuckle, waited a moment before replying. Too much war experience, Thomas. Too little patience.

Captain St. John Granger had been with Allenby's Third Army at La Boisselle, July 1, 1916, the worst day of the war, a German-expressionist horror from sunup to dusk. Along the salient that day there were 58,000 casualties including 20,000 dead, the numbers rounded off because no one had a precise count. Bodies disappeared, blown to pieces or lost in the mud. On July 2, Captain Granger crawled out of a hole and began walking. The battlefield was shrouded in early morning mist the color and density of pearls. The air smelled of fish. Granger glided over the scarred and barren terrain of no man's land, stepping carefully to avoid the corpses and pieces of corpses. He was bound for the British lines. No one noticed him and in his shock and confusion Granger believed he had become invisible. He had become one with the thick and swirling mist and so he continued unchallenged through the lines and the headquarters behind the lines. Aid stations gave way to hospitals that gave way to makeshift morgues. The fish smell grew stronger with each step he took. Granger walked across the hills until, that evening, he found himself in Albert, clad now in the blue work clothes of a French peasant. The day after that he was in Amiens, and that night in Paris, well turned out in a light-colored suit and a straw boater. He dined at Fouquet's and went home with a girl. The next week he was in Geneva, arranging a transfer of funds, a more complicated business than it might seem because by then he was reported missing in action and presumed dead. His brother, Adrian, worked for a bank in the City of London and so the transfer was made, but made most reluctantly because his banker brother did not believe in desertion in time of war, a scandalous affair, the coward's way out, letting down the side. Thank God our father and mother are gone, they could not have borne your disgrace. What will you do now? St. John said nothing, listening to his brother's voice as if it were a stranger's overheard in a railway car or on the street. He was neither insulted nor angry. He was certainly not chastened. He was indifferent to his brother's opinions because they were unearned. His brother had never seen a trench, an aid station, a morgue, or an armed enemy. He knew that in the end Adrian would comply, and in the end Adrian did. When St. John was told the details of the money transfer, the account numbers, and the verification procedures, he said a curt goodbye and hung up. They never spoke again.

Granger liked the Swiss, who kept to themselves, and liked Geneva, which was orderly and quiet. But he hated the weather so by the end of 1916 he was in Barcelona, and the following year in Málaga, fetching up finally in the pretty Andalusian village of Arcos de la Frontera, where he rented rooms to wait out the war. He was eighteen years old but had already acquired the reclusive habits that would remain with him his entire life. He discarded his memories of the war, which were elusive and fragmentary, as if they did not belong to him but to someone else. He knew that the Somme had taken something vital from him but he did not know what it was, and when someone suggested that it was his youth, he scoffed. Youth held no interest for him and he had no wish to prolong it. Later, Granger decided that the experience had not taken something from him but had given something to him—but he didn't know what that was, either. He wondered if it was anonymity. He had no specific recollection of July 2, 1916, crawling out of a hole into a pearly landscape to begin his walk from no man's land to the

British lines and beyond, the unobserved movements of a sleep-walker, and it seemed that was what he remained—unconcerned with his surroundings, one step removed, becalmed, friendless. Perhaps what he had been given was the dance, not the dancer. Ghost dance, he thought. And if he awakened suddenly? Granger knew in his heart that he would live a very long time and he had to acquire the circumspection to build a life abroad in the world. He had no desire to return to England. England was foreclosed in any case, because in England he was a dead man. His only relative was the appalling Adrian, and then, one month before the war ended, he learned that Adrian had been killed in a road accident. He saw a newspaper obituary by chance in the reading room of the British consulate at Málaga, and from it he discovered that his brother had a wife and young daughter, the wife an American from Pennsylvania. The obituary was brief but it contained this sentence: "Adrian Granger's younger brother, St. John, posthumously received the Military Cross for heroic actions on the Somme salient, July 1, 1916."

Can you believe it? Granger said. Don't you think it's droll?

The Military Cross! And I don't remember a thing. The day's a blank, except for the weather and the fish smell and the sense of inevitability. It's as if July 1 were a dream.

What do you suppose I did to deserve the MC? Or didn't do.

I suppose it's not wise to inquire too closely. But—what do you suppose happened to the medal?

He said, I imagine it's buried with Adrian. Brother Adrian was a history buff with a particular interest in the Irish question. To which, I may add, he had no answer. I fancy the Military Cross redeemed me in Adrian's eyes. Do you suppose he was just the slightest bit tempted to tell them I was alive after all and on the run in Europe and then deciding finally, no, what was the point? Raking old leaves.

Officially alone now in the world, Granger was free to chart his own course. He made his way north to San Sebastian, stayed awhile, then pressed west through the French hill towns until he found himself in St. Michel du Valcabrère. He put up at the auberge, struck at once by the lovely valley that ran into the high Pyrenees, disappearing into the Spanish summits. There was one road into the village. The inhabitants kept to themselves and were not inquisitive. There seemed to him no good reason to move on, and so in October 1920 he bought the farmhouse and settled in for what turned out to be a very long furlough.

When Thomas came downstairs at last, most of the guests were leaving or had gone. Bernhard and Russ were cleaning up in the kitchen. He said a few words to each of the friends who remained. They were ill at ease, at a loss what to say, their expressions genuinely aggrieved. Thomas's haggard appearance was not encouraging. No one stayed more than a few minutes and finally only Ghislaine, severe in a black dress and one of Florette's cardigan sweaters, was left.

I'm so sorry, Ghislaine said.

I know, Thomas said. Me too.

Monsieur Granger and now Madame. Both in one week. It's a horror.

Yes, Thomas said. It is that.

She had so many friends. All of them came to pay respects. I will come tomorrow to clean. And each week thereafter if you would like me to.

Yes, that would be fine.

I know how Madame likes things done.

I know you do.

Madame was meticulous.

Thomas suppressed a smile because Florette hated housework and meticulous would not be the word when she got around to it. Yes, of course, Thomas said.

I will charge you the usual rate.

Fine, Thomas said.

Au revoir, Monsieur.

Tomorrow, then, Thomas said and closed the door. He stood

with his hand on the knob, realizing that he had come within a heartbeat of raising his voice, calling to Florette, Do you want Ghislaine to come and clean tomorrow, chérie? And waiting patiently for her answer, which likely would have been no. She thought Ghislaine was a snoop. Probably that would be the way of things for a while, speaking aloud to empty rooms, brewing tisane for two, buying dinner for two, buying women's shampoo in the pharmacy and *Paris-Match* at the newsstand. When he realized at last that she was no longer with him and that this was for keeps, the knowledge would come as no comfort at all. That would mean she was absent from the background as well as the foreground. Of their intimate life together Thomas refused to undress himself. Aphrodite herself could not lure him. He was, for the time being, endimanché, the lovely French word that meant buttoned up in your Sunday best.

Meanwhile, there were the elephants to consider, the family photographs, the mementos, her cosmetics in the bathroom, the six varieties of shampoo, and the soap in various pastel shades. In time he would become accustomed to living alone, buying for one, and that would hurt just as much, more really, because there would be nothing to wait for except a miracle, and miracles were not in his repertoire. The mountain would always be in his vision when he was working unless he chose to turn his easel to the wall, and still he would be unable to forget, and he was a man who forgot things all the time. He was a champion forgetter. The mountain would be a predictable presence, benign, enduring, lush in the summer and barren in the winter, impassable in all seasons. The villagers called it Big Papa, a kindly massif when treated with respect. Watch the weather forecast, never trek after dark, avoid the higher elevations, beware the sullen mountain gods. Thomas was standing with his hands pressed against the door as if the mountain somehow sought admittance. It was inside his house anyhow.

How had this come to pass?

He and Bernhard and Russ hadn't seen one another for nearly a year. They were telling stories, laughing so hard they didn't hear

Florette when she called to tell them she was going for a walk. He knew she'd called. She always had before. She would never leave the house without telling him where she was going and when she would return but Russ was in the middle of one of his Washington stories, a respected senator fallen on hard times, the usual mischief and bad timing; so they had not heard Florette. I'm going for a walk, back in an hour. Stupid of him, unimaginably careless. But when Russ finished his senator story, Bernhard had one about an ambassador and an astrologer, the ambassador grown slack and torpid in the heat of Southwest Asia, losing his bearings, searching for consolation in the astrological houses, his cables to the State Department ever more obtuse and bad-tempered, and then he disappeared into the northern mountains, apparently kidnapped, held for ransom. Special Operations wanted to dispatch a team but the secretary of state counseled caution, thinking something along the lines of "The Ransom of Red Chief." Soon enough the ambassador would wear them out and the kidnappers would capitulate—

When Thomas wandered into the kitchen to look for Florette he surmised she had gone for a walk and would return soon, for the sun was low in the sky and the air smelled of snow. She had stacked the dishes and pulled another bottle of Corbières from the cave. He stepped into the yard to wait for her, noting at once the evening chill. When the sun disappeared, all warmth disappeared with it and he stood worrying in the cold with his empty wineglass, staring hard at the road and the path that led away from it, knowing—not all at once but gradually as the light failed—that something was wrong because she was not in sight. He scanned Big Papa from base to summit, left and right, looking for any movement or flash of color, but the distance was great and the mountain vast. She could be anywhere. Even so, the massif looked as empty and useless as the glass in his hand. He shivered in the cold and took a step forward, calling her name. The sound of his voice echoed in the valley, rising and repeating, expiring at last as darkness continued to gather. Then he had the idea she had gone into the village on an errand but when he looked into the garage their car was still there, so he called again and again with no result. He was furious with her, behaving so recklessly. She thought of the mountain as her private reserve, having lived in its shadow since she was a child. Then he remembered her telling him about malevolent mountain gods punishing trespassers, superstitious nonsense. He remembered looking up and seeing headlights on the road but the headlights disappeared. Night fell like a curtain and he realized he was sweating.

When Thomas turned from the door, pushing off from it, he found Bernhard Sindelar and Russ Conlon emerging from the guest room with their suitcases, Russ leading the way—Bernhard, half a head taller, much wider in the shoulders, filling the doorway behind him.

Russ smiled. You look like you just saw a ghost.

Thomas poured them each a glass of wine and said, I was thinking about Granger.

Funny, Bernhard said. From the look on your face I would have sworn it was Florette. Bet money on it.

It was Granger, Thomas said.

He was a good scout, Russ said.

He lived too long, Bernhard said.

Why do you think he lived too long?

He was worn out, Thomas.

No, he wasn't. He went to bed and didn't wake up.

Same thing, Bernhard said.

I think he was a hundred and six, Thomas said.

Yes, you told us.

Thomas poured wine for himself and they clicked glasses, saying what they always said on such occasions.

LaBarre.

LaBarre.

LaBarre, Thomas said. Granger, too.

He watched Bernhard check the time and glance out the window. Their taxi was due to arrive any time. Bernhard and Russ were eager to be on their way and Thomas was no less eager to have them gone, to reclaim his house once again, listen to the clock tick if it came to that. He wanted to get back to work and just then remembered a remark of de Kooning's, who loved his brushes and canvases so much he could sit and watch paint dry. A sudden chill came on the room, the fireplace gone cold, the long sofa and the chairs surrounding it unoccupied, the coffee table heavy-laden with empty wineglasses and the ceramic ashtrays Florette favored. The remains of a cheese board and heels of bread littered the dining room table. He loved the spaciousness of the room, its high ceiling and white-washed walls, wide windows looking up the valley. An oversized poster of Piaf in full throat hung on the wall near the dining room table, his portrait of Florette over the fireplace. The two stared at each other from opposite ends of the room. Quite suddenly Thomas had a tremendous desire to hear cabaret music, Piaf, Mabel Mercer, Billie Holiday. He wanted the room filled with music, music turned low, city music, barroom music that conjured dimly lit memories. Then he could sit like de Kooning and watch paint dry. But first he had to get his friends out of the house. Thomas said, I want to thank you both for staying on. Changing your plans. Helping out. It means a lot to me.

Bernhard drew back. You know how much we cared for Florette.

I couldn't have managed without you two.

We don't like leaving now, Russ said.

I'll be all right. I'll call in a few days.

Stay in touch, Russ said.

I will. Count on it.

Bernhard cleared his throat and said, You're going to be lonely here. Florette, of course. Florette most of all and indispensably. But Granger, too. Your dinners together, billiards, conversation with someone who'd led the sort of life you understand. Where you don't have to explain the references—

Granger didn't talk much, Thomas said.

—and winter's coming on.

But we were good friends, Thomas said.

Hard to make friends at our age, Russ said.

Impossible, Bernhard said. You can't get through the preliminaries, too much has already gone by. Where you come from. Who you know, who you don't. What you do for a living and how long you've done it.

LaBarre, Russ said, raising his glass.

Our case, Bernhard said, the government.

Yes, Russ said. That, too.

So you invent stories, Bernhard said with a smile.

Granger never did, Thomas said. Someone asked him where he came from, he said he couldn't remember. Someone asked him what he did, he said a little of this and a little of that, and if they pressed him, he said he managed his investments. And then he changed the subject.

So, Russ said after a moment. I suppose you'll go back to work.

Right away, Thomas said.

You'll need more than work, Bernhard said.

No, Thomas said. *You* need more than work. I'm content.

I don't think content is the word you mean, Thomas.

I'll think of a better one when I get around to it.

We're wondering how you'll get on day to day, Bernhard said. This place is pretty remote. You're way off the beaten track. Are you sure you belong here? Is this really your place, without Florette and without Granger? Only your work to keep you company? Sounds lonely to me.

Oh, it's my place all right.

You know you're welcome at my flat in London. Come when you want, stay as long as you like.

Thomas nodded but did not reply.

Bernhard peeked out the window. Where's the damn cab?

Russ said, Do you think we should call?

He'll be here, Thomas said.

Anyway, will you think about it?

I will, Thomas said. I surely will.

Bernhard's flat was in South Kensington, around the corner from Harrods, four small, ill-lit, badly heated rooms so situated that sunlight never touched the interior. The neighborhood was crowded with shoppers. Four young Englishmen involved in the Portuguese wine trade lived raucously in the flat above and when the noise became insupportable Bernhard went up and joined them, usually returning with one of the young women who were always about. Bernhard kept his fridge well stocked with champagne and Iranian caviar, or it had been the last time Thomas visited. The telephone rang day and night, friends, or friends of friends, or someone from he government asking for a favor. When he wasn't on the telephone, Bernhard was hunched over his computer, reading his e-mail and hacking into various private accounts, "keeping abreast of things." Bernhard's apartment was always busy with ringing telephones and messengers arriving with mysterious packages. The atmosphere combined the towel-slap of the locker room with the feral anticipation of the casino.

I've gotten used to the country, Thomas said after a moment. I like the hours, the weather, the pace of things, the silence. Florette—but he could not remember what it was he wanted to say about Florette. It was something she had said about the pleasures of living in a valley surrounded on all sides. He went on, I came for a summer, just fetched up the way Granger had in 1920. I was dead tired and depressed, too. God, it had been an awful year. The year of the Spaniard, as you'll recall—

Bernhard shuffled his feet and said, No need to mention that.

Thomas said, Why not?

It's private, Bernhard said.

You know the rules, Russ said.

Too bad the Spaniard didn't.

Really, Thomas, Bernhard said. Basta.

Think about Bernhard's offer, Russ said.

The apartment's there any time you want it, Bernhard said. I fixed the heat, by the way.

Good idea, Russ said.

The boys in the wine trade are gone, too.

Even better, Russ said. Any replacements?

Boys in the fashion trade.

Noisy boys, I'll bet.

Quiet as little mice, Bernhard said.

Thomas looked from one to the other as they did their verbal soft shoe.

I'm worried about the damn cab, Russ said. Shall we call? The train leaves in ninety minutes.

Bernhard cleared his throat. I didn't mean to be abrupt about the Spaniard, Thomas. I was startled. I wasn't prepared. So I over-reacted.

Thomas peered into his wineglass. He hadn't been listening to them. He said, Do you think an hour would have made a difference?

Russ looked at him blankly. A difference in what?

Florette, he said.

No, Russ said. Not one hour. Not two hours. Put that thought out of your head. Where did you get such an idea? It's ridiculous.

The doctor said something about it.

Oh, that's helpful of her. That's so helpful. What does she know? Was she there?

She was there at the autopsy, Russ. An hour might have made the difference. Florette alive today. Exact words.

She doesn't know what she's talking about, Russ said. It's only speculation on her part. Guesswork.

I think an hour might have made the difference, Thomas said. I think Florette would be alive today if we'd realized she'd gone for a walk, kept track of the time. We would have started earlier. Got help sooner. Raised the alarm, arranged for a search party instead of opening another bottle and telling another story. And she'd be alive right now. What do you think?

Russ was silent a long moment. Finally he said, When my Sandra was sick we went everywhere, Boston, New York, Paris. God, the treatments were painful. No success in Boston, New York, or Paris. So we thought about Mexico. They were supposed to have wonderful experiments in Mexico, things the Americans have never dreamed of and therefore discounted. But Sandy wasn't convinced. I wasn't convinced either. The doctors in Boston definitely were not convinced. So we didn't go to Mexico. We went back to our apartment in New York City and waited. Long months, as you'll remember. I've thought a hundred times about the things we might have done differently. There were plenty of them. And so what, Thomas? They weren't done. If they had been done, maybe the outcome would have been different. Maybe not. At the end, you know what made the big difference? Morphine. I'll tell you something else. She didn't die with a smile on her face. Turn the page, Thomas.

Sure it's possible, Bernhard said.

So you agree, Thomas said.

We started late. What can I say?

We started when we realized she was late. We didn't imagine she was in danger, Russ said, looking sideways at Bernhard.

Too late, Thomas said. I believe an hour would have made the difference. It was dark when we started. Because we were telling stories and having a hell of a good time.

Russ looked away and said nothing further.

Where are you going with this, Thomas? Bernhard looked at him steadily and moved a step closer.

Thomas ignored that and spoke to himself, as if he were in an empty room. And we still don't know who they were or where they came from. Or what they wanted. Why they took her to that place and abandoned her.

I've made inquiries, Bernhard said patiently. I'll know more in a few days. The people I spoke to had no good ideas, at least not yet. They were almost certainly not locals. Maybe they were small-time smugglers, drugs or whatever. Not weapons, because of the weight. Maybe they were only illegals moving from one place to another. Why did they abandon her? Attempt a coup de grâce? Because they thought she could identify them. That's one logical motive. But maybe it was for another reason altogether, something we haven't thought of or even imagined.

If only—

I'd forget the if onlys, Thomas, Bernhard said. If only this, if only that. Dead end there. Blind alley.

Fuck you, Bernhard.

That's enough, Bernhard, Russ said.

We did what we could and it wasn't enough, Bernhard said softly. We don't live in an ideal world, he added, his voice rising. He looked up when he heard a horn in the driveway. The cab had arrived.

Not an ideal world, Bernhard? And all this time I thought it was.

Then you were mistaken, Bernhard said evenly.

Thomas opened the door to a landscape flooded with yellow light from the dying sun. He had spoken more sharply than he intended but Bernhard's mordant certainties had struck a nerve. Often Bernhard lost himself among the inflections of his many languages, caustic as a Frenchman one moment, sly as a Levantine the next, while remaining the sharp-eyed baker's son from LaBarre, Wisconsin, determined to get ahead in the wider world where the odds were assuredly—the assurance coming from his immigrant father, who kept a handbook on the side—not in your favor. When something was lost you accepted the loss and set your face. Whatever responsibility you bore was only an inconvenient detail in the larger scheme of things: getting even. Bernhard was mistrustful by nature and therefore a natural investigator who always went, as he said, the last inch. LaBarre's decline had made him a firsthand witness to the obvious truth that everything collapsed eventually and that the world was inherently unstable, so you disciplined yourself or someone else would do it for you. They were all midwestern boys, no matter where they were living or what language was in the street. They had taken different lessons from LaBarre, Russ the milkman's son and Thomas the son of a doctor. His mother was the doctor's nurse, medicine the family business. The consulting room was in an annex off the front parlor and when Bernhard and Russ went home with Thomas after school the parlor was always crowded with patients, people stirring awkwardly or coughing while they turned pages of the *Saturday Evening Post* or *Reader's Digest*. Often there was one patient who did not bother with a magazine but sat stoically staring into the middle distance. Russ wanted to rush through the parlor but Bernhard always paused for a long look at the patients before climbing the stairs to Thomas's bedroom to listen to the afternoon radio programs, *Terry and the Pirates* and the others. When Thomas warned him that they weren't to bother the people in the waiting room, Bernhard replied that he wasn't bothering them, he was only looking at them. What was the harm in looking? Sometimes you could tell a lot by looking and remembering what you saw. Bernhard said you could tell which ones were in pain and not long for the world by studying their faces, where their eyes fell and what they did with their hands, and he mentioned the woman staring blankly into the middle distance as the case in point. Leave them alone, they don't want to be bothered, Thomas said. The woman's thinking about what she's going to tell her family, Bernhard said. But I'm only looking. And besides, they never see me, as if by that assertion he had made himself invisible. Bernhard was old beyond his years and had an answer for everything.

The cab's here, Thomas said.

We have to move along, Russ said.

I'll call very soon, Bernhard said. When I have news.

Thomas opened the door.

I know how painful it is, Bernhard said. But you have to get to the bottom of it. That's the first thing. And I'm going to start turning over rocks, every rock I can find. Whoever did this will not succeed. Trust me. They're dead men. We owe that to Florette.

Outside, they shook hands, promising to stay in touch. Russ proposed a weekend in Paris at the end of the month, nothing grand, a few decent meals and a stroll through the Grand Palais where an exhibit of Degas drawings was newly installed. Beautiful exhibit, Russ said, and by the end of the month the crowds will have thinned. Promise me you'll come. Thomas said he would think about it and let him know. Bernhard promised again to call when he had news of value. Thomas thanked them both and Bernhard said he adored Florette and would remember her always and meantime he would do whatever was necessary to settle the score. We won't let it rest, Russ said. "Without haste, but without rest," Bernhard added, quoting somebody, looking hard at Thomas, a private warning or perhaps a threat, one or the other. And then they were gone.

Thomas watched the cab winding down the drive to the road. The cab's were the only lights in the vicinity. Granger's farmhouse was dark and Big Papa was very dark against the sudden night sky. Thomas watched the headlights rise and dip, like a ship navigating ocean swells, until the cab vanished at last into the darkness. He said aloud, Bon voyage, but he was thinking of Bernhard's score-settling skills. His American friends lived in a world where scores were always settled because the alternative was unbearable chaos. Chaos was a world without justice. In some sense score-settling was what they did for a living. Florette would become a civic project—a wrongful death, an unnecessary and violent death in the world-that-was-not-ideal, a crime that demanded vengeance. A death in the mountains, and how many of those were there on any given Sunday in November? Deaths in the Alps, the Himalayas, the Caucasus, Atlas, Andes, Blue Ridge, Urals, Pyrenees. He had the idea that in the death-stakes, mountains resembled oceans, brutally dangerous and unpredictable weather with the possibility always of a misstep or marauders, sometimes both at once. A mystery always surrounded an unwitnessed death at sea, the circumstances unknowable; and then Thomas wondered what Bernhard would turn up and whether his findings would bring consolation, meaning facts better known than not known. And now he had a motive, the better to discount the despised randomness. Randomness was the enemy of coherence. The day before, out of Russ's hearing because Bernhard was convinced Russ had lost a step over the past year (Notice how his hearing's gone to hell and his memory's a sieve and he's simply not on top of things; he's become repetitious and he's always talking about Sandra, who's been gone at least a decade), and was therefore an unreliable collaborator, he had confided: I don't think it's likely but you have to consider the possibility that Florette's death may have to do with you, Thomas. Payback for one or another of the odd jobs you've done for us over the years, maybe a job you don't even remember, it seemed so routine at the time. Truth to tell, Russ and I often thought you were too cavalier, doubting the seriousness of your tasks. It's true you never knew the full context of things, safer for you and safer for us, and naturally there were consequences, and these, too, were inside the parameters of need-to-know. And the Spaniard would be in this category.

I know that's come between us in the past.

A job that got out of hand. A betrayal.

That's usually the way.

So we have to consider all the possibilities, disagreeable as they may be.

We have to consider this. Other people have long memories and carry them around like you'd carry cards in your wallet. So this is the possibility that cannot be overlooked, someone from your past deciding to make payback. Bottom line: what happened to Florette may not be random at all. Nothing random about it, bad luck, bad weather, Florette in the wrong place at the wrong time et cetera, assaulted by persons unknown, probably smugglers. But what's to smuggle on the trail of Big Papa in St. Michel du Valcabrère? Don't you see? It all adds up. And Thomas had replied, That idea is insane, not bothering to enumerate the reasons why because the reasons why were obvious. Bernhard, offended, had said what he always said in defense of coherence, his word for conspiracy.

Well, it's possible, isn't it?

Coherence demanded that Florette die for Thomas's sins, the message conveyed from one place to another, the document read upside down on the interior minister's desk, the surreptitious drawing of the valet attending the Saudi banker, the seascape drawn to scale at Antibes, boats in the harbor, one boat in particular. The yachtsman bought the painting and invited Thomas on board for a drink and dinner and he stayed for a week, the vagabond artist-in-residence watching the comings and goings aboard ship. His odd jobs were like that, the small change of snooping, though Bernhard preferred the word "espionage." Look, can you do us a small favor, won't take much time, no danger involved, we'd be grateful . . . And there was excitement in it, the technique similar to portraiture, slipping into an alter ego of your own making, a not-quite-authentic doppelgänger, observing closely, enjoying the performance for the most part, assured that the consequences, whatever they might be, were not momentous. Meaning: no one will get hurt. Meaning: you are not responsible. Naturally he was not fully informed but there were advantages to that, too. Meanwhile, there was nothing at all to be done about Bernhard in his search for coherence. His suggestion was monstrous but that would not keep him from full pursuit because in the world he lived in, anything and everything was possible and if you did not believe that, you were a naif who subscribed to a child's history of the world. Only chaos was inadmissible.

Thomas stood in the chill of the evening, his hands plunged deep in his pockets. This tiny domain, a smallholding in a remote province, was what was left of his world. In his lifetime he had visited all the continents and had traveled the great oceans and seas, and he knew this place better than any of them, perhaps because there was less to know, perhaps because village life was lived on a subterranean level, life at its most personal. In any case, he had lived longer in St. Michel du Valcabrère than anywhere else in his adult life. His traveling days were ended and he had difficulty remembering how he had managed it, traveling and working, now here, now there, moving from hotels to rented studios; truly a vagabond's life, entertaining as far as it went, a life without strings. Thomas strained his eyes, squinting, and made out the wan glow of the town square. He imagined the café, crowded at this hour, its windows misted over and tearing, the villagers playing cards and the pinball machine, gossiping all the while. Surely they would have words to say about Florette's funeral, her American husband and his American friends alone in the front pew. Monsieur Railles did not move during the service. He sat with his eyes fixed on the plain pine casket yet at the same time did not appear to be engaged; no doubt his mind was elsewhere. When the service ended, his American friends had to nudge him twice. It's over, Thomas, time to go to the cemetery. It was true he had been elsewhere during the formalities, remembering the patients in his father's waiting room in LaBarre and how Bernhard Sindelar seemed to enjoy watching the hands of those who were very ill, not long for the world. Years later one of his father's patients actually did die on the examining table. She had said she was not herself, feeling tired and unusually forgetful. Why, some mornings she could barely get herself out of bed, and when she did she was out of breath. The doctor was scanning an x-ray and when, alarmed at what he saw, he turned to speak to his patient, she was gone. It took him a minute to understand what he was seeing; and when he did, and rushed to his patient's side, he was too late. Three days later they went to the funeral and the woman's husband, now widower, refused to shake the doctor's hand. Thomas, then seventeen and big for his age, had to intervene to prevent a scuffle. Sitting in the front pew of the church at St. Michel du Valcabrère, staring at his wife's coffin, Thomas remembered the awful look of grief on the widower's face and noticed also his fists lifeless at his side. His wife was dead and someone would have to own up to the responsibility because she had left for the doctor's office in perfect health and returned in a hearse. But in the end the old man only shook his head and walked away to his car, where his young children waited for him.

Thomas watched a shooting star fall and disappear. The night was peaceful, no wind and the prospect of a bright morning. He had forgotten the day of the week. Was it Friday? Yes, Friday. Each day was associated with a specific event. Florette died on Sunday and her body was not found until early Monday and even that was a sort of miracle. One of the men had stepped off the trail to take a leak and, moving his flashlight, he had spied her through the trees, an unnatural shape in the woods, a spot of color, curled up like an animal.

Oh God, he said, and everyone went still.

In seconds they were all around her, staring dumbly at her body, the broken ankle and the thin line of blood frozen at her throat. Thomas forced his way through them but his arms were roughly pressed to his sides and one of the gendarmes stood in his way so that he was unable to step forward. Then Bernhard and Russ moved him away from the scene. He did not have the strength to resist, his bones turned to liquid, and so he stood passively as the men wrapped Florette in a blanket and lifted her off the slope and onto the trail. Her foot hung at a right angle off the edge of the stretcher until someone noticed and tucked it back under the blanket so that it made a tiny hill in the blue weave. Thomas did not move his eyes from the stretcher, so brilliantly illuminated by halogen flashlights as they manhandled it through the trees.

Careful, one of them said. Careful.

The senior gendarme came slowly back and put his hand on Thomas's arm and said how sorry he was, he had known Florette since school days. He opened his mouth to say something more but in the end said nothing and returned to his men, already commencing the descent. Thomas turned away when they were out of sight, and he immediately regretted that he had not gone with them, seen Florette down the mountain to the hospital or wherever they were taking her. He was not thinking straight. He somehow believed he should stay where she was found so that he would be available if they needed him. Russ remained with Thomas while Bernhard joined the two gendarmes examining the spot where Florette had died. Thomas shook free of Russ and stood on the perimeter of where Bernhard and the gendarmes were talking. One of them asked curtly if Bernhard was police and he said yes, he was a sort of policeman, a retired investigator familiar with violent crime, familiar enough to observe that the killers had spent some time on the slope. Probably they were wondering what to do with Florette. They were weighing assets and liabilities. Bernhard pointed out the cigarette butts, Gitanes, and pointed out that there were none in Florette's vicinity though Florette was a smoker. No doubt she had asked for a cigarette and they had refused. What does that tell you about them? Bernhard said, There were four of them, perhaps five, and they were careful, though not careful enough to dispose of the cigarette butts. There were remains of food also, something packaged. They were here for some time, worrying the problem of Florette . . . The gendarme with the notebook wrote down every word. Bernhard's voice and manner commanded respect and his French was serviceable, except for his American accent.

Thomas remained in the darkness, staring into the night, wondering where they were now. They could have followed the trail south into Catalonia or north toward Toulouse and beyond, into the Dordogne. Their destination was unknown. The morning thaw had melted the snow and the bivouac had been well trampled by the boots of the gendarmes and the volunteers from the village. Thomas

knew that Florette's killers would never be found, not by the authorities and most assuredly not by him. Bernhard Sindelar's "inquiries"
would come to nothing, even though he was owed favors by half the
security services of Europe, and these were people who routinely
settled their debts. They lived by favors given and favors received—
and then Thomas wondered how much he wanted to know. Was he
avid for details, where they had found her and how far they had carried her? How her ankle was broken? Had she broken it in a fall or
had they broken it for her? Had they spoken? Had they made her
plead for her life? And what of the motive behind the killing? He
supposed they were members of some despised minority, Basques or
Chechens or Tamils or any one of the numerous Muslim tribes and
brotherhoods. They would have souls full of grievance, over God
or land or Western music or imperialism or women's provocative
clothing. Nostalgia would play its insidious role—was it not true
that the ancient world's greatest library was flourishing at Alexan-
dria when the English were painting themselves blue? Perhaps none
of the above. Perhaps they were psychopaths, only that and nothing
more: American teenagers on the loose, killing Florette with less
thought than they would give to shooting up a high school gymna-
sium. No, not likely. These killers were people who had been insulted and left behind, and some combination of these grievances or
other grievances or just for the hell of it had taken Florette's life with
a clean stroke of the knife, coup de grâce. They would have known
no more of her than she of them. Probably she had asked for cigarettes and they had refused because a woman smoking tobacco was a
blasphemy. Perhaps when they looked at her they saw a bourgeoise,
an accomplice of the degraded ruling classes of the West. And when
she looked at them? God knows what she saw. Whatever it was, she
would have made a snap decision, friend or enemy with not much in
between. Snap decisions were Florette's specialty and once made
were rarely reversed. And what now? If Bernhard called to tell him
they were dead, some preposterous shootout in a village no one ever
heard of, a positive ID, he would be grateful. Fine, they're gone.
Thank you, Bernhard, you're a good friend, a reliable friend, a

friend who keeps his promises. But Florette was also gone. Their disappearance would not equal her disappearance. The two were not equivalent. The scales would not be in balance. However, his own heart would be a little less heavy—for a while. Grief was difficult to measure. Grief damages your faculties. Grief was not transferable. It had its own great weight and came and went like the ocean tides and in that way was uncontrollable.

Thomas had never put much thought into vengeance. He had enemies as everyone had enemies but they had never done him serious harm. So while he got mad, he rarely got even; it was not worth the effort and was an insult to one's own integrity. Was that the attitude of a saint or an egomaniac? Thomas knew a man who had made his divorce a life's work. He believed he had been traduced by his wife and was determined to take his revenge. He intended, as he said, to screw her six ways from Sunday. Litigation, with the inevitable appeals, continued for five years. He could think of nothing else. Screwing her six ways from Sunday was his way of taming his own restless soul and when he finally achieved what he sought, that was not the end of it. The rest of his life he spent gloating, and he died, too young, still in full gloat. His honor was at stake, he said. His honor must be satisfied; and so that was his life. But Thomas thought him absurd. Vengeance might be solace for the seeker and perhaps rough justice for the sought but the object of it would remain—he supposed the word was unconsoled. Would you be consoled, chérie, to see them dead? To watch them die, hear their cries, perhaps spit on their corpses? Would your soul rest easier? Perhaps it would. To expel them from the earth would be a blessing, a civic virtue, because if they killed once they would kill again, kill without remorse or a second thought. When she looked at them she saw—strangers. Strangers certainly, no doubt speaking a tongue she did not understand. She would have been annoyed if they were not French, if their language had been some guttural Slavic or Middle Eastern speech. *Eet waas 'orreeeble, Thomas, zee speech of animals.* He smiled at that, heard her voice so clearly she might have been at his elbow. He saw her pout, upper lip closed over lower, her head tilted like a young girl's. She was flirting with him. Thomas was weary in his bones, his eyesight blurring and his thoughts thick as molasses.

He turned to look at his house, ablaze with light. There was warmth inside and if he could pull himself together enough to light a fire, some cheer as well. He and Florette had always made a ceremony of Sunday lunch, a roast chicken or a leg of lamb or a cauldron of cassoulet either alone or with friends. They would sit together with a glass of wine after everyone had gone home, play dominoes, put something cheerful on the stereo, gossip about who said what and wasn't so-and-so clever, and always her complaint—it came as a partial non sequitur but that was the way with their after-lunch conversation—that Granger would not accept her invitations for a meal. She said, He is not comme il faut, your friend. I think perhaps he does not know how to enjoy himself with women. Women are a mystery to him. No, Thomas always replied, Granger just goes his own way. He is comme il faut in his own way. He is one who prefers the task of host to the task of guest. He likes to select his own bottle. When Thomas said that Granger lived a simple life of repetition, Florette said, Bah, he is selfish, that's the truth of it. She was innocent of the manner in which displaced persons got through life, their petty evasions and iron routine and the harmless lies that attended them every hour of every day. Now both Florette and Granger were gone in the space of one week. Neither would have to worry about the other. Granger always asked politely after Florette but he had no interest in prolonging the inquiry.

Thomas stepped around the side of the house to the woodpile and selected a few sticks of oak and carried them to the doorway. He looked inside at the heavy-laden coffee table and the cold fireplace and the lunch things on the sideboard, books crowding the low shelves on either side of the hearth, his portrait of Florette in a square wooden frame above it, the portrait a profile, her chin raised in anticipation, perhaps of an afternoon puttering in the garden, dimly seen in the background of the painting. He remembered trying to enter the portrait so that he could see through her eyes, the subject viewing the artist; and he had succeeded, mostly. He drew the garden through her eyes, as she would see it, something unfinished, cubist in nature. Overhead a twelve-bulb chandelier cast a gray light. The room seemed to him in suspended animation, as if Florette had stepped away for a moment to fix her hair or pull on a cardigan against the evening chill. They habitually cleared away the glassware and the dishes after the domino game, an Italian opera turned low on the stereo. In a perfect world he would ask her now what she had thought when she came upon them on the trail. She would be disabled by her ankle, angry and in pain, cursing her bad luck, but grateful that these strangers had come by. How did they seem to you?

And she would tell him what they looked like and what they wore, the language they spoke and whether they were comme il faut. Did they frighten her? And why did she go to the mountain alone when she and Thomas had agreed it was dangerous? But I called you, chéri, from the kitchen. I always call before I go out. I thought you heard me. Was Russ's joke really as funny as that? You were all laughing so, perhaps you didn't hear me. He watched the moon rise over Big Papa, clothing the valley in pale light, the mountain's contours brittle in the cold. In a perfect world she would now be walking up the drive, weary from her climb, though not so weary she did not have a swing to her gait, a kind of girlish lope. Her hand went up and she wiggled her fingers in greeting, giving a huge smile. All was well. She had been detained, a misunderstanding. She had tripped and if she had not caught herself in time—well, a broken ankle or worse. But the view was so lovely I could have stayed forever, and so I took my time walking down. I'm sorry to be late. Did you miss me? I hope you weren't worried.

Did the boys make their train?

Yes, he said aloud. I'm sure they did. You just missed them. They sent you their love.

Oh, dear, she said. I wanted to say goodbye.

They understand, he said. They were sad to go. But they were expected.

They are not the sort of boys who miss trains, are they?

No, they're not.

The trains run on time and so do they.

That's it.

I suppose they had instructions for you.

Of course they did, he said.

How to live your life?

Bernhard always knows best, he said.

How lonely it will be here, and winter coming on.

Yes, he said.

And Bernhard offered his apartment?

Bernhard the apartment, and Russ a weekend in Paris.

Choose Paris, she said. I know you will. But not right away. Settle in. Give yourself time to adjust. I'll be watching. She turned away, suddenly in profile, her chin rising in anticipation, and laughed and laughed, her laughter so infectious he joined in at last, mockery of his hapless state.

A breeze came up from the south. Heavy snow was predicted in the morning, road closures expected, a three- or four-day blow, locking-in time. He had nothing of a practical nature to worry about; the pantry was full and he had plenty of firewood. At least he would have no visitors and that was a relief. If he craved company he could ski into St. Michel du Valcabrère, two hours to get there, half that to get back, but he was not certain he had the energy for cross-country. He knew he had to learn to live alone, depend on his own resources after he had had time to "adjust." He knew also that the way ahead was hard, the odds stacked against, and so he must look beyond the present moment, beyond the slick surface to the deep chaotic structure of things, the vision of a man of faith, and not necessarily religious faith. Political faith would serve. Thomas had known a Spanish communist—"the Spaniard," called Francisco—who had an unshakable faith in the revolution despite its many difficulties and contradictions, among them injustice, cruelty, corruption, and a willful obscurantism. The Spaniard brushed them aside as the faults of men—he called them the iron-teeth, Stalin, Mao, Gomulka, and their many accomplices and acolytes—and had to be seen as such. The revolution itself was pure and only awaited a savior, a philosopher-mensch. You'll see, Thomas. It's only a matter of time.

We await our General Washington, he said.

Of course our Washington will not be a general. Nor a slave master. Nor an aristo. Our Washington will be a man of the people.

He will have wooden teeth, Francisco said.

And what do you believe in, Thomas?

I believe in a pure brushstroke.

Ah, but that is not justice. It will not clothe the poor or feed the hungry. Your pure brushstroke, bourgeois decadence. Bad symbolism.

No, Francisco. Sometimes a pure brushstroke is only a pure brushstroke.

The Spaniard laughed in high good humor.

Thomas turned his back to the mountain, noticing that the moonlight had vanished, clouds gathering to the south. Bad light tomorrow for painting but he had no good ideas anyhow. When you were drained of emotion, you were drained of ideas also. Your memories were less vivid because your imagination had gone AWOL. You lived in the half-light of dusk or the crack of dawn when it seemed time could go either way. On the easel was the half-finished portrait of the *patron* of the café, old Bardèche's heavy arms resting on the zinc bar, an expression of—he supposed the expression was one of suspicion. Thomas had made the sketches one afternoon in September, sitting at his usual table near the pinball machine. He was waiting for Florette and making sketches while he watched the bar action. The *patron* moved with circumspection, as if he had all the time in the world and his customers had all the time in the world also. His hands were so big the glasses seemed to disappear into them and when he placed them on the bar the effect was of a rabbit pulled from a hat. Old Bardèche habitually wore a years-old white cardigan sweater with leather patches at the elbows, a Florette. His café reminded Thomas of the Spanish communist's utopian state. However disagreeable or uncooperative his customers became, the café itself was sublime, an oasis of conformity and democratic socialism; things never got too unruly because there were laws strictly enforced. With old Bardèche behind the bar and his hatchet-faced wife, Agnès, supervising the caisse, a superior authoritarian order prevailed. In fact, the café did not serve the customers. The customers served the café. That was what made the behavior of the American tourists so shocking, the blind man seeming to instigate a counterrevolution. The Americans came from a world far distant from the café, an aggressive democratic world where rights had pride of place, including the right to spit in anyone's eye. Thomas thought often of the Americans when he worked on old Bardèche's portrait. He was certain the *patron* would be pleased with it and ecstatic when he presented it to him as a gift. He might even stand Thomas a lager on the house. Two, if he was feeling generous.

Fat snowflakes began to fall, tumbling in slow motion. The patterns of the snow in the air suggested faces and Thomas was convinced he was looking at the men who had harmed Florette; and then the apparitions vanished as the wind disturbed the snowfall. What was owed the dead? And when he discharged his debt, what was his reward? Thomas was unable to think it through, his spirit so crowded with the events of the week and his own fathomless distress. One day bled into another and here he was, alone at last on a Sunday evening discovering faces in the snow. Thomas could not see his way forward because he was empty of feeling and that was why his life would become difficult. Always in the past he had managed to submerge himself in work, slip comfortably between the paint and the canvas; that was how he got on, one day to the next. Certainly he could gain time by returning to old Bardèche's portrait, a neutral subject, and then he recalled that he had given the old man Florette's eyes, their slant and glitter and the wrinkles at the corners, a suggestion of mischief. Wasn't there every possibility that her eyes would draw him into some kind of reconciliation, meaning a way of finding his new place in the world? Thomas did not know what was required of him and if Bernhard's monstrous suggestion turned out to be true, what then? Bernhard in his zeal to find coherence where there was no coherence made life intolerable; that, and his insistence on worst-case wagers. Thomas knew in his heart that Florette had met with misfortune, a misadventure, some combination of the two, wrong time, wrong place.

He had always thought of his odd jobs as a lark, some jobs more larkish than others, but definitely the small change of espionage. His work was such a solitary business that he often felt the urge to break out, as a bank teller might take up polo or high-stakes poker, anything to escape the routine, something with the potential of danger, an experience useful in the studio—in other words, a second life hidden from the first life. Of course you were an impostor fashioning a bogus alternate destiny but there was something exhilarating about it, pulling on a false face and stepping into the unknown. And in his own case it would be a fulfillment of all those civics lessons at the grade school in LaBarre, the class that was the first of the day, the one that met after the Pledge of Allegiance. When your job was done you returned to your solitary business.

They were having drinks at a hotel bar in Paris, Bernhard and Russ having returned from unspecified business somewhere south. The times were fraught. Nixon was president.

You could help us out, Thomas. We can use your help.

There's a man we'd like you to meet.

We'd like to know more about him. What he does, who he sees, how he lives. When he's home and when he's away, dates and times. Nice fellow, harmless.

You have a way in, Thomas. He's an art collector. Fine collection, we're told.

Also, he likes portraits. Portraits of himself. Picasso did one. Braque did another.

We can arrange a commission, Thomas. He pays top dollar, by the way.

And he knows your work. Admires it.

That's all you need to know. Keep your eyes open, make his portrait.

Befriend the poor bastard. He doesn't have many friends, except a few we'd like to know more about. It's a bagatelle, Bernhard said.

A lark, Thomas said.

If you like, Bernhard said.

In the early days they had given him a revolver, a snub-nosed Smith & Wesson .32, all the while assuring him that he would never have occasion to use it, though they sent him to an instructor to learn how. The work he would be asked to do was not intended to bring him into that sort of danger but the book said to take every precaution. When Thomas tried to refuse the gun, they said, No, no, the world was never ideal or predictable. The world was untidy and one could never predict what might happen. A man had an obligation to protect himself against the unforeseen. As soon as he decently could, Thomas disposed of the gun, dropped it off the Pont Neuf late one night. And soon enough Bernhard arrived unannounced with a heavy coffee table fabricated in Grand Rapids, the table ingeniously equipped with compartments that opened at the touch of a button that operated a hidden spring. Inside one compartment were half a dozen passports in half a dozen names from half a dozen countries. A second contained currency, American dollars, British pounds, Swiss francs. A third had room for legal-sized files. A fourth had precision fittings for the Smith & Wesson, and Bernhard snapped one into place—since, he said, I understand you lost the original.

I didn't lose it. I threw it away.

I know, Thomas. I know. Don't do it again.

Why do I need all this gear?

We take care of our people. We let them know they're valued.

I'm not your people, Thomas said. I have no need for this stuff.

You never know, Thomas.

And by the way, Bernhard went on, you have a commission with our friend. He expects you tomorrow, ten sharp.

Russ said, This is important, Thomas. Our art collector has some extremely interesting friends. It's the friends we want, not him. Our art collector wants the gift of friendship but he's a naif. You'll like him.

Thomas laughed out loud at the presumption of it but Bernhard only smiled and turned his attention to the table, of which he was tremendously proud. American cabinetmakers had not lost their old-world skills. You had only to give them the specs and pay in advance. The Grand Rapids table was still in Thomas's possession, the currency long since spent, the passports returned to the embassy, the revolver to Bernhard. The Grand Rapids table was ungainly, graceless, the dimensions off-kilter, built to survive an earthquake or a firebomb. Florette wanted to get rid of it but Thomas refused. He told her the table had sentimental value and then he put it in his studio where she wouldn't have to look at it. He was often tempted to show the compartments to Granger, who had an appreciation of artifacts of dubious provenance, but he never did. He never spoke to Granger or anyone else about his odd jobs; that was part of the contract. Granger, accustomed to shadows, accustomed to living with contradiction and ambiguity—familiar with false faces, familiar with flight, familiar with altered biography, vastly disciplined—would propose, not a solution to the problem, but a way to think about the problem.

The world is too much with you, Thomas. Step back. Take stock.

Never discount the value of negligence.

Find out what they want you to do. Then do the opposite.

You want a kiss shot. Just brush the ball into the side pocket.

Something along those lines, Thomas thought.

The snow was steadier now, falling in bunches, flakes the size of marbles falling from a hidden sky. By morning the valley would be covered and he would be locked in whether he wanted to be or not. That was just as well. He had nowhere he wanted to go and if he could not get out, no one could get in; a fair trade. Bernhard and Russ would be boarding their train just about now, stowing their luggage, finding their seats, and departing at once for the bar car, checking their wristwatches en route, calculating the time of arrival in Paris. Surely there would be time for a nightcap somewhere in Montparnasse, and in the morning Bernhard could move on to London and begin his "inquiries." They disliked the countryside and provincial life generally. The pace was too slow, the days predictable, nothing to do and winter coming on. From the look of things, winter had arrived, sooner than usual. How can you stand it there? What will you do all day long? It's unhealthy to spend so much time alone, a situation that gives rise to morbid thoughts.

The wind came up again, the snow swirling, eddying like a river current. There was warmth inside the house but Thomas did not move, remaining on the threshold for many minutes, the sticks of wood in his arms, imagining the train gathering speed as it left the terminal at Toulouse.

Au revoir, gentlemen.

Mind your own business.

Thomas shivered in the cold, shivered as Florette must have shivered. Had she anything to say to her captors? At the end she would not have been capable of conversation. She would be with herself. Perhaps a prayer, not spoken but thought, a wish that someone would arrive with help. She was slowly freezing to death. Her thoughts would come to her piecemeal and in slow motion. The thought was unbearable. Thomas looked through the window into his living room, Florette's portrait over the fireplace, Granger's on the long wall, Piaf near the dining room table. A room of comfort and good cheer, the sense of one conversation just ended and another about to begin. He decided to follow Bernhard and Russ's example and walk to the bar car. He opened the front door but still did not step through it. He shivered, considering vengeance and the satisfaction it would bring dear Florette. Dr. Picot had said she was surely unconscious at the end so would not have felt the knife's blade. But Dr. Picot had also said that Florette was strong as an ox, which she was not. Thomas watched the snow tumble, wishing he were twenty years younger, when he had a young man's certainty and a young man's energy and guile and love of the game, avid for adventure. He wished he had led a different sort of life.

Lebenslüge

THE WIND BLEW every which way all night, carrying with it a foot of snow. Thomas slept fitfully, ill at ease in the howling wind. He slept, woke, and slept again. The old house creaked and time and again he thought he heard footsteps. He rose at dawn, awakened by a frightening dream, lost to him almost at once. What he remembered was a cell-like room with a low ceiling and bone-white walls. He lay quietly trying to reconstruct the dream while outside the wind howled and snow flew at the windows. Finally he pulled on his bathrobe and went downstairs to brew a pot of espresso, feeling all this time like an imprisoned sleepwalker. He stood dumbly for a while looking out the window at the blowing snow, colorless in iron-gray light. He drank one cup of sugared espresso after another, trying to bring himself into present time, wondering which chores to tackle and in what order. They had no obvious precedence and they were all disagreeable. The frightening dream was still a shadow on his spirit. He supposed the cell had to do with his snowed-in state. And then he remembered his portrait of Francisco, the Spanish communist, made in the old man's one-room adobe in the mountains west of Granada, at that time a sparsely populated region. The walls were whitewashed inside and out and the room itself was austerely furnished: a bed, a dresser, a table with two ladderback chairs, and a three-shelf bookcase. He owned a beautiful edition of Cervantes's works. Thomas drew the Spaniard seated before a narrow window that gave onto a field but the sun's glare was such that the field was obscured. The old man was a great subject, his heavy pock-marked face speaking of an outdoor life; inside, he would always be the ugliest man in the room and the one you were drawn to. Francisco was on the run from the authorities, suspected of complicity in the assassination of a captain of the Guardia Civil. His other crimes dated back many years but they were not specified, except they were known to be political. Bernhard had said, Paint his picture, talk to him, find out what's on his mind and what he sees in his future, if he sees anything. And when you have the chance, tell him he ought to change locations. He's not safe where he is.

He's a good man with a mother lode of information.

What he doesn't know about the movement isn't worth knowing.

His politics aren't worth dick. But he shouldn't have to rot in a Spanish jail before they give him the noose or a firing squad.

Some question, by the way, whether Francisco was involved in the Guardia Civil hit. We think he wasn't. Franco's people think he was.

Do your best, Bernhard said. Do him a favor, and us, too.

All afternoon as the sunlight moved across the tile floor the Spaniard talked of his admiration for the poet Baudelaire. Baudelaire of the lower depths, Baudelaire's passion, the ecstasy of creation, the ecstasy of liberation from the bourgeois corset. It was necessary for a man to live with excess. Live with it, die from it. Paris was central to Baudelaire's ambition, Paris the living heart of the revolution, where the masses took to the streets as a matter of civic responsibility. Paris was a pillar of fire. How lucky the French were to have Paris! By contrast, the Spanish had only Madrid, a gray city lacking spirit, a dull provincial city of government like Brussels, Basel, and Washington. Thomas tried to give Francisco instructions; perhaps if he could be quiet a moment, the artist might see his face in repose. But the Spaniard plunged on, heedless. Madrid had no imagination. The civil war had seen to that. The war had ended thirty years before but the wounds still bled. The defeat was complete, and so, in the fullness of time, Catalonia would secede and the capital of the Iberian Peninsula would be Barcelona. Barcelona would lead a renaissance free of Spain. The Spanish people were terrified of what they were capable of, and so they became like oxen—ponderous, looking neither to the left nor to the right, putting one thick hoof in front of another. They are a disenchanted people.

The war changed them forever.

The Spaniard went on and on in an ecstasy of his own, moving from French to Spanish to English and back again, depending on the aria. And Thomas, caught up in the old man's imagination, painted faster and faster in bold, slashing strokes, thinking of himself as an orchestra conductor, the Spaniard's face a brilliant score of nineteenth-century music. Halfway through he put away his brush and applied paint with a palette knife, the oils as heavy as the Spaniard's burdens, his suspicion, his fear, his many disappointments, his ambition, his morbid love of the idea of Spain. Thomas finished the portrait as dusk fell and the blade of sunlight ceased its slow transit across the tiles. He knew at once that the portrait was finished and stood looking back and forth at it and at the Spaniard until the man and the portrait seemed to merge. The old man did not notice, so complete was his concentration, talking compulsively of the Spanish people, the urban masses and the campesinos, so divided, so wary, a family torn to pieces, afraid to speak. The Spanish people had a split personality animated by opposing furies. They would never be reconciled in this generation or the next. The fascist army and the bastard priests would divide and conquer as they always had and the nation would remain outside the reach of the revolution. The Pyrenees were a barrier as vast as any ocean. Yet the struggle would continue underground, one corpse at a time. It is my life, the Spaniard said. Poor Spain.

Thomas was not listening. He stood in the gathering darkness with the palette knife in his right hand and the palette in his left. Finally he sat down, exhausted. God, we are an old country, Francisco said. We are the oldest country on the face of the earth. He fell silent at last, poured wine for them both, lit the table lamp, and peeked around the corner of the easel to look at the portrait. Francisco stared at it for a long minute and then he said in English, Oh, very fine. And you painted it in an afternoon! My dear Thomas, you are a prodigy. And you are sweating like a goat. As if you had been rutting in a field under the hot sun. Wearing yourself out and the she-goat, too. But it's me, all right. It's me down to the ground. I would call it of the school of Goya, and that is logical because I am a graduate of that school.

You are an admirer? But of course you are.

What a shame, Francisco said with a broad smile. It will never hang in the Prado.

Maybe when Franco goes, Thomas said.

He will never go, Francisco said. El Caudillo is eternal.

Everyone goes, Thomas said.

Not him, Francisco said. He is our Dracula.

You must leave this place, Thomas said after a moment.

But it's my home, Francisco said.

Nevertheless, Thomas said.

It's perfectly secure. I have people who watch out for me. And I have friends elsewhere.

Not secure, Thomas said. Not perfect.

Nonsense. I have confidence in my friends.

Misplaced confidence, Thomas thought but did not say. Instead, he murmured, You should listen to me.

Why should I listen to you?

Because I know what I'm talking about. And we're comrades.

That's true, Francisco said.

I hear things—

Francisco had been staring at his portrait but now he turned and asked softly, What things do you hear, Thomas?

He paused, uncertain how far he should go. He and the old man were in a zone of trust and Francisco had a sensitive ear for the false note, the thing not said or said incompletely. A false note would not be forgiven. Thomas looked at him and said, I believe this place is not secure for you. We have not been friends forever but we know each other well. I would not mislead you.

I will never abandon my house, Francisco said.

We trust each other. Trust me now.

I know you are sincere, Thomas.

Thomas was silent a moment, cleaning his brushes, distracted by the paint smell. The canvas would take days to dry. He said, Do you have plans?

No plans, Francisco said.

Please reconsider. Make plans.

New arrangements take time. Maybe I should hang a clove of garlic from my doorknob.

Francisco, be serious.

The Spaniard laughed softly and shrugged, as if he had no say in the matter. He turned away, in deep thought, and when he spoke it was with profound resignation. I have lived a very long time but I am not ready to give up. Be assured.

Thank you, Thomas said.

I wonder if I might ask you a favor, my friend. From an old man to a young one. May I have the portrait?

Yes, Thomas said. I want you to have it. Thomas lifted the canvas from the easel, signed it in the lower left-hand corner, and handed it carefully to the Spaniard. It seemed the very least he could do.

After looking at it a moment Francisco said in a voice filled with emotion, A pure brushstroke.

Thomas said, I had good material.

I wish I had a talent for art or music. But I don't. It must be a comfort.

Comfort? Sometimes it is. I can't imagine life without it.

Where will you go now, Thomas? Now that you have finished with me.

I'll be back soon, Thomas said.

Very soon, Francisco said. I'm old. I haven't much time.

More than you think, Thomas said.

We'll see, Francisco said with a ghost of a smile.

Thomas had no idea what the Spaniard knew or didn't know. He remembered that the longer he remained in the room the smaller it got, closing in on itself, as claustrophobic as a prison cell. It was true that they had not known each other a long time, barely five years since their first meeting in an artists' café in Barcelona; but he believed they knew each other well enough and trusted each other and he hoped the old man trusted him now. Thomas gathered his paints, brushes, and easel and said goodbye to Francisco, but not without a final look at the portrait he had made; one of his best, he thought. The old man had beautiful bones and a surface as weathered as a cathedral. At the doorway they embraced and as Thomas walked away Francisco gave him what he always called his Spanish salute, a clenched right fist at his temple, knuckles in, elbow out, the salute he first gave at Montblanch, near Barcelona, October 1938, a black beret on his head, a bright red scarf around his throat.

Thomas drove south to Málaga, where he spent the night, then meandered east to Almería and Cartagena and up the coast to Benidorm, with its wide vacant beach and fish restaurants open to the air. He planned to stay a week sketching fishermen and the women in the market. He met a young woman who was happy to pose so long as the sittings were kept private, owing to her strict Catholic family. The one week turned into three weeks. All the time he was with the señorita he was thinking of Francisco in his adobe in the mountains west of Grenada. One morning Señorita Carolina told him she was moving on. She had a job in one of the hotels. There were three large ones with three more to begin construction the following week. The Bavarians had arrived, she said, with satchels filled with deutschemarks. It is the first time we have been occupied since the Mussulmen in the fifteenth century. In five years you won't recognize Benidorm. Meanwhile, she said, I am training to become a receptionist. You are very sad about something, Thomas. What is it? And will you give me one of the sketches?

Thomas stayed on a few more weeks because he had nothing better to do, hoping Carolina would tire of her receptionist duties. In the morning he swam and in the afternoon he sketched and took long walks and in the evening he listened to the villagers enthuse about the hotel construction, prosperity at last. Carolina did not appear. He sent Francisco a postcard of the Benidorm beach in midwinter, empty as the Sahara. No message, only the card. At last he gave it up and drove to Barcelona, arriving at his apartment at dawn, discovering that while he was gone someone had broken in and taken his radio and phonograph and the stash of pesetas in an envelope behind the Michelin guides. He looked in the drawers and closets, cursing, finding that the thieves had also taken a pair of shoes and his good blazer. The Grand Rapids table was undisturbed and his portraits were in the closet where he had left them. The thieves had come in through the window via the fire escape and left the same way, probably weeks before. In minutes he decided to quit the apartment—Barcelona had lost its savor—and the next day was on his way to Paris, where he rented a two-room apartment in Montparnasse, good light and a decent restaurant on the ground floor. Francisco was mostly absent from his thoughts. A month later the Spaniard's portrait arrived, carefully packed and sent from an unfamiliar address in London. There was no note. He had no idea whether Francisco had taken his advice or not. He feared not. And beyond that Thomas was unwilling to go.

That night he called Bernhard, who said he could not speak just then. He would call back in one hour.

Thomas said, What happened to our Spanish friend?

Gone, Bernhard said. Disappeared.

Safe? Thomas asked.

I hope so. I don't know.

Thomas said nothing. In the street below, a musician was playing an accordion, badly.

You're not to blame, Bernhard said.

Thomas said, Why not?

You did what we asked. Something went wrong.

What? What went wrong?

Missed communications. Someone betrayed us. One of those two, perhaps both.

Bullshit, Bernhard.

The telephone was silent. In the street, the accordion music stopped abruptly; someone had probably paid the musician to stop.

I've told you what I can, Bernhard said. I don't know the details.

But you think the worst.

I think the worst, he said.

A fine old man, Thomas said.

Yes, Bernhard said. He was.

Were we actually trying to help him?

Yes, we were. Believe that.

We were on his side?

Yes. We were on his side. Bernhard's voice was as subdued as he had ever heard it. Bernhard said, We'll settle the score. It may take awhile. It may take years but we'll settle it. When Thomas didn't answer, Bernhard mumbled a word he rarely used, and never to a friend. He said, Sorry, and rang off.

That was effectively the end of Thomas's career in espionage. He undertook two more odd jobs over the next few months, both in Paris, minor business. Russ handled the assignments, apologizing, but they were in a jam; would he do it as a favor? At the end of the year Thomas handed over the currency, the passports, and the Smith & Wesson; they insisted he keep the Grand Rapids table. Thomas did not hang Francisco's portrait but propped it against the wall of his studio where he could see it while he worked. He knew that he was responsible for the old man's death and he believed that Francisco knew it, too, and knew it from the moment Thomas appeared at the door with his paints and his easel. As Bernhard said, missed communications, betrayal, something like that, but Thomas was not responsible. Like hell.

For a while Thomas carried his knowledge around like a lump in his throat. He wished to atone in some way but did not know how. The old man had no family. No one knew where he was buried, if he was buried anywhere. In due course Thomas sent the portrait back to Spain, not to the Prado but to a new museum across town, the small one that featured twentieth-century art. The portrait was not a favorite of schoolchildren but there were usually one or two old people looking at it, men and women both, always with somber expressions, remembering whatever it was they remembered. Thomas knew this because not long after he dispatched the portrait he flew to Madrid and spent a morning in the gallery watching the traffic.

Snowfall continued without letup. Discouraged, Thomas poured a cup of espresso and went upstairs to shower and dress. He shaved quickly and chose corduroys and a heavy sweater against the chill of the room. He looked into Florette's closet, six feet of clothes on hangers, dresses, slacks, blouses, and what seemed an infinity of shoes. Some of the items he associated with specific occasions, Christmas Mass, Sunday lunches, and dinners out. She had worn the black shift on their last visit to the auberge south of Toulouse, where they had eaten great blocks of foie gras followed by a veal something. Both of them were tipsy by the end of the meal. The dress still had a stain where he had clumsily dropped a spoonful of sorbet while passing it to her across the table. He made a ribald remark and she shushed him.

Be quiet, Thomas. Be good.

Stop laughing. People are watching.

That was only last month. Thomas had no idea what to do with her clothes. He knew it was not right to throw them away as if they were garbage. No doubt there was some established French custom and when he had the time he would ask Ghislaine or Monsieur Bardèche. No doubt a charity existed for the efficient distribution of the used clothes of dead Frenchwomen, all but the shoes. Shoes, like underwear, were nontransferable. Finally he turned his back on her clothes closet, at a loss.

Now he inspected Florette's dresser top, crowded with her cosmetics, her photographs, and the elephants. Thomas decided to remove an elephant a day, saving the silver elephant with the maharajah in the howdah for last. The elephants would be happy out of sight in the cedar chest in her sewing room. He looked at each of them in turn, memento mori. One of the elephants from Kenya would be the first to go, a crudely carved, utterly forgettable animal from an African country he did not care for. He remembered it had been a long-ago gift from Bernhard, who had said he loved Kenya with all his heart. Thomas put the Kenyan elephant in his pocket. Chore one.

Well done, he said aloud.

That wasn't too difficult, was it?

Thomas went to Florette's knitting room, opened the cedar chest, and dropped the elephant inside, where it fell noiselessly on her blue Brittany sweater, the one she believed was too heavy for indoor wear. He heard her voice now, complaining about the dense weave and the buttons on the shoulders. The elephant had fallen tusks-up, surely a signal of Florette's dissatisfaction. Florette thought the sweater suitable for seafarers, not inhabitants of the interior. The sweater was not comme il faut and so it was consigned to the cedar chest until she met a mariner who would appreciate it. So it was obvious that the elephant had no place in the cedar chest and a Brittany sweater was not a suitable bed. He reached into the chest and retrieved the elephant and again put it in his pocket, stepping back to survey the room. He had an idea he would commandeer it for this very place, his new studio. He took the elephant from his pocket and placed it on the windowsill.

Thomas visualized the easel and paintbox in front of the window, north light the color and vivacity of lead. Elephant gray, he thought. Unlike most painters, he did not care for north light. He thought it came from growing up in Wisconsin. The room was much smaller than he was used to. The ceiling was low. The room smelled of damp wool. The windows were small-paned and dusty, as if they were unaccustomed to being seen through. Naturally Florette's presence was palpable. When Thomas looked through the windows he could see St. John Granger's farmhouse and the modest backyard orchard where the graves were, the stone markers barely visible in the falling snow. The house looked abandoned and he hoped that Ghislaine had not let it go cold; but he knew at once that she had. There were no lights anywhere and no smoke from the chimney. The graves were as forlorn as graves anywhere.

Thomas trudged downstairs to his studio, gathered up his paintbox and easel with the half-finished portrait of Monsieur Bardèche, and set them up in the knitting room. He placed the portrait on the easel and moved back three steps until his shoulders were against the wall, knowing at once that the room was too small for artwork. Cozy would be the word for it. He tried to remember the French for "cozy" but could not. Florette liked it well enough but knitting was a cozy activity. What it shared with artwork was solitude and a scrupulous attention to detail. That, and patience. Probably patience more than the others.

This room won't do, he said aloud.

Even old Bardèche looked uncomfortable in it.

The light's wrong, not elephant gray but penitentiary gray. LaBarre gray.

He picked up Florette's sewing basket and put it beside the easy chair and sat in the chair. He looked at the book she had been reading, one of her accounts of contemporary scandal. This one was about Onassis, his houses, his yacht, his airlines and oil tankers, his strange friendships, his many enemies, his distant children, his footloose women and the financial arrangements he made with them. What would it mean to have an airline at your disposal? A private island with a cadre of servants in situ? Permanent suites in half a dozen hotels? What would it mean to have your own intelligence service reporting on your enemies and your friends, too, to ensure that they remained friends? Florette was fascinated by the means of accumulation and disposal of millions, and by the conspicuous lack of remorse. The lack of embarrassment when sordid details of your private life became public. Conscience was not included in the tycoon's repertoire of personal qualities because it would indicate a failure of nerve, and then they would be on you like a school of piranhas. Well, Florette remarked one day, perhaps tycoons were remorseful after their own fashion. Those would be private moments, never shared; and no doubt there was an element of self-pity, so much mythmaking, so misunderstood. So few could comprehend the responsibilities and hazards of great wealth.

Have you ever considered what it would mean to you to have a great deal of money, Thomas? And he had told her truthfully that no, he never had. He had never considered the consequences of being born blind, either, or being beautifully coordinated like an Olympic athlete. He had known a few very rich people and they did not seem to him to live easily, worried as they were that someone might take their money away. One of them had commissioned a portrait but seemed to want the portrait to contain certain inalienable qualities, and now that he thought of it, one of the qualities was lack of conscience, implied in the don't-fuck-with-me expression of the subject's mouth, though the tycoon preferred habit-of-command. And you? he had asked Florette. She had, she said, when she discovered her ambition of becoming a couturier with a shop in Place Vendôme. Jewels from Cartier, a car and driver, an Old Master in the living room and a Fabergé egg in her bedroom and frequent journeys to New York and London. But such an ambition was not realistic for her so she was not ruined when it failed to materialize. Hers was only a girlish dream inspired by a photo essay in *Paris-Match*. She was disappointed of course, but only a little. She had an agreeable life in St. Michel du Valcabrère even though it was out of the way, a mere vestibule in the great house of France. In St. Michel they were undisturbed and able to fashion a life according to their own lights. In that way they had been fortunate.

Yes, he said. They certainly had been.

But they were no longer young and needed an occasional tonic, such as a trip to New York City, the Statue of Liberty and Saks on Fifth Avenue. Also, she wanted to inspect the place where the twin towers were. She wanted to see it with her own eyes. She wanted most of all to attend a musical on Broadway and take a hansom cab through Central Park at midnight. Onassis had often been in New York, not that he ever seemed to enjoy it much. I want you to read the Onassis book, she said, and tell me what you think. Whether he had a life worth living. Yes, he had some good times, who wouldn't with all that money? But the end was not good, not good at all, because no one loved him. Instead, he was feared. You wouldn't wish such a fate on anyone unless you thought he had it coming.

Thomas sat in her overstuffed chair and read two hundred pages, falling asleep somewhere in the Aegean. It was dusk when he awakened with a start. At first he did not know where he was. The room was chilly and unfamiliar. He had a cramp in his thigh, the muscles twitching and needling. He waited until the cramp eased, the odor of wool in his nostrils, then rose and hobbled downstairs to pour a glass of wine, staring out the window at the blowing snow, skidding over the fields, drifting against the garage, a scene not out of place in Siberia. Thomas finished one glass of wine and poured another, thinking now about dinner and what there might be to accompany the remains of last night's roast chicken. The fridge was bare except for eggs and the leftover cheese and terrine and heels of stale bread from Florette's wake, the odds and ends of a confusing afternoon. Nothing looked appetizing and he wondered if Onassis had ever found himself alone in the early evening staring into a desiccated fridge. Not likely. Onassis would never have such a problem. Onassis would shout for a servant to fetch the caviar and toast. Fetch the champagne. Fetch the musicians. Fetch the girl. Now get lost.

That was the first full day of Thomas's new life.

Toward nightfall on the twenty-fifth of November Thomas stood at the kitchen counter reading the American newspaper, now two days old, not that it mattered in the Siberian scheme of things. He had been away from America for so long that he read the facts as if they were fiction, tall tales from the new world, blank columns of type side by side like a regiment of infantry, disciplined infantry, trained not to venture into no man's land. He always began with the facts, weather reports from distant cities—raining in Cincinnati, torrid in Riyadh—and moved from there to the Dow Jones Industrial Average, activity on the Paris bourse and the Hang Seng and the Tokyo exchange, and the fluctuations of the dollar vis-à-vis the euro and the yen. Facts anchored the world. He had never seen a basketball game in his life but always consulted the standings of the NBA, the won-lost column, the percentages, and the games-behind, and only then returned to page one and the unstable milieu of reporters' narratives where he had to guess at the life behind the news. What he saw often was the world of his youth, the vast expanse of the Midwest, proper names and place names inspiring buried memories, the strange mnemonics of interior cities: Chicago, Indianapolis, St. Louis. He thought of these reports as light from distant campfires. Thomas always looked for news of Wisconsin but rarely found any.

Instead he found column after column of government news from Washington, a vigilant capital ever alert for evidence of provocation from other, more sinister capitals in faraway regions of which little was known. These were tales of unrest. The tone of the reports suggested an America exclusive of other nations, a remote empire on a fabulous continent that worshiped a benevolent god and fortified itself in order to remain apart, a garrison state exempt from natural law and under the special protection of a watchful providence. Yet there was fear in everyday life. Fear itself was healthy, quite normal, for terrorists could strike any time, any place.

And of the other regions, news reports suggested Conrad's trackless interiors, unknown and unknowable, murderous as a matter of course. Travelers lost their wits when they ventured there, something medieval about their way of life, an urge to turn the clock back and a refusal to accept, even to contemplate, the modern world. Things happened in the torpor of the third world. Nothing worked and everything was cheap. Women, liquor, governments, life itself. Fatalism came with the heat. Whatever compass you brought with you was boxed. You knew that you didn't belong there, at least in your present capacity, whatever it was. All you could count on was a valid passport, a wallet full of greenbacks, and a return ticket home. The irrational became rational. Hard to convince an outsider of the appalling facts of daily life, the furnace-heat, blinding sun all day long, the windless afternoons, the insects, the animals, the heaviness of the night, the bad dreams, the sweat, the surveillance. The fear— no, certainty—that the true rhythm of life went on elsewhere and that you were in a fundamental sense quite irrelevant. You begin by washing three times a day in order to keep clean, a specific against disease. Then the regimen slips to twice a day, then once, and finally every few days until you notice the crud between your toes and elsewhere on your vulnerable body, and meanwhile you're trying to negotiate with the government or simply gather routine information and you hurry the groundwork because you can't wait to get out of the heat, back where you belong, and you screw it up because you forget the most basic procedures, procedures you've followed for a lifetime. You fall into a kind of swoon, deracinated, preoccupied by the past, places you've been, people you've loved, and wonder what it was that has brought you to this point.

That was what Thomas gleaned from the journalism in the American newspaper.

All things considered, he preferred the weather reports, the NBA standings, and the traders' statistics on the various bourses.

Thomas turned back to the newspaper, reading the report from Guantánamo, a detailed discussion of the methods of torture, what was justified and what wasn't under the codes of the Geneva Convention. He was brought up short by a photograph on the following page, a private ceremony marking the anniversary of the assassination of John F. Kennedy, the surviving brother and surviving daughter alone at the president's grave at Arlington, their heads bent in prayer. Thomas stared at the photograph a long time, remembering Kennedy as a young man, a golden prince of a man, a young Tannhäuser; and then the biographies and memoirs came and he was no longer golden nor much of a prince but a man pursuing Venus fully as recklessly as many other men but without the redemption promised the penitent Tannhäuser. Perhaps Kennedy would have repented, too, but there was no time. No doubt he was undone by Washington's torpor, where the irrational so quickly became rational.

Thomas was in his New York studio when the news came. He was sketching a girl who had offered to model for an afternoon. The telephone rang and rang but they did not answer, believing they were safest alone; instead, the model called her mother to make sure that she was all right and that their neighborhood in Baltimore was secure. He stayed with the model, Karen, that night and the next night and the night after, watching television with the sound off. The pictures told the story. He made a hundred sketches, and when he wasn't drawing he and Karen made love. In the sketches he tried to see her fresh each time and tried to bring something of the moment to it. He had to come to terms with November 22, to bring the wreckage of the day into her face and figure. He could not pretend it was some other day, an ordinary day in November, overcast, the weather cool. At night he decided to use the bare expanse of the south wall of the studio and began a portrait in oil, Karen lying sprawled in the tangled sheets, a troubled spirit even in sleep, her arms set at unnatural angles. She seemed to be in motion, her face resembling the sleek crest and pointed red beak of a bird, her eyes hooded. Her hands clawed the bedsheets. When she woke, Karen was abashed and not entirely pleased. She did not recognize herself, though the bed was familiar enough. She thought it was another girl. She turned her back on it and flounced into the kitchen to make coffee and when she returned she was in tears.

Such an ugly piece, she said. And you draw so nicely. Who is she? What does it mean?

He didn't know what it meant and told her so. It was what it was and would remain permanently on the south wall of the studio, next to the double windows. The next day he caught her looking at it out of the corners of her bird eyes. While they were watching the funeral she said the portrait was growing on her and it might surprise him to know that she saw something of herself in it. Ugly as it was. Somber as it was. Very well, he said, I'll call it *K Number One*. The riderless horse and the throng of mourners were shuffling down Pennsylvania Avenue when she suddenly reached to turn off the television. She said, Come to bed. They were together one year and in that time he painted six *K*'s, each of a radically different mood. The original did remain on the studio wall but all the others he sold, and with the money he decided to go to Europe. He described the grand time they would have together but she refused to go with him. I could never live abroad, she said. I could never leave my mother. My place is here. I would like to have a child, she said, but I know that's not in your future. This is your future, she said, gesturing at the sketches and the portrait on the south wall. He said tentatively, You wouldn't have to stay if you didn't like it. Don't you think we need a change of scene? Karen smiled enigmatically and remarked that he was lucky, to love a thing as much as he loved his work.

When Thomas looked up from the newspaper he noticed lights

downstairs in St. John Granger's farmhouse. A thin rope of smoke rose from the chimney. The night was cold and dead calm, the sky brilliant with stars. He was happy seeing the lights and the chimney smoke; no doubt Ghislaine had decided to clean house at last. Thomas was laying a fire when he heard a knock at the door, three sharp, official-sounding raps. Thomas had seen no one for days and he did not want company now. He was remembering the model Karen, a girl with the most beautiful shoulders since Garbo, with a smile to match; when he left for Europe she had gone west to find work in films, but the West had not worked out and she returned to New York and married a diplomat posted to the United Nations, an Argentine or a Brazilian, a successful marriage so far as he knew. *K Number Two* was now in Milwaukee, an acquisition that caused the resignation of two museum trustees and prompted a furious editorial in one of the newspapers. The headline read: "Pornographic Trash."

Another knock, louder than the others.

Thomas was not interested in talking with anyone just then, quite content to rummage about in his memory as he read bits and pieces of the newspaper. It seemed to him that he had not had a conversation in months, discounting his nocturnal discussions with Florette; that was enough, except now Karen had interfered, and someone was at the door.

She was American, fiftyish, bundled in a green parka and ski hat, a tartan scarf around her throat, sealskin boots on her feet. A fringe of gray hair peeked from under the hat. She stood in the doorway shivering, introducing herself as Victoria, no last name, from Pennsylvania, no city specified, direct descendant of St. John Granger. His heir, she added. I would like to speak with you, she went on, handing Thomas a bottle of wine, an excellent vintage that he recognized as living in Granger's cellar. He took her parka and indicated the chairs by the fireplace. She removed her gloves finger by finger, with some difficulty because she wore heavy diamond rings on her left hand and a single square-cut sapphire on her right. She handed him the gloves and said she would keep her scarf. She rubbed her hands together, rattling her bracelets. Thomas again indicated the chairs by the fireplace but she waited a moment before moving. This dreadful place, she said. Do you always keep your houses so cold? I wonder how you stand it. Did the old man freeze to death? I don't know why anyone would want to live in a climate like this. So hostile.

I arrived today, she added. To inspect the place.

It's a fine house, Thomas said. Granger and I had many good times there. I'm sorry he's gone.

I never met him, Victoria said. No one in the family had. He was a mystery man. But he left the house to me in his will. She looked here and there in the living room, a strained expression on her face. She went on, I am his only relative. And my children. Of course they are his relatives also. She moved closer to the fire, warming her hands. I would have called but I didn't have your number. I don't know how the phones work anyhow. Do you wait for a dial tone?

They're ordinary phones, Thomas said. He pulled the cork from the bottle and poured two glasses. Your health, he said, watching her sip slowly and taste with evident suspicion.

Too much tannin, she said.

Do you think so?

Definitely, she said. And it's weak. Past prime.

I agree it's lost some shape. He held his glass to the light, appraising the color of the red. He said, Granger spent eighty years putting his cellar together. Bordeaux red, mostly. Some of the bottles could be sold at auction. If you don't care for this wine, that might be a good solution.

I will, definitely. Thank you, Mr. Railles.

I might buy some of it myself. And call me Thomas.

Thank you, Tom.

Thomas, he said. Only my mother ever called me Tom.

Very well, she said. Thomas.

In the awkward silence that followed she looked around the room once again, eyes narrowing as if she were measuring for curtains. She said, I hope I'm not intruding.

Not at all, he said.

The notaire told me you were a painter.

That's right, he said.

Portraits.

Yes, he said.

So. Are any of these yours?

This one. He pointed to the likeness of Florette over the fireplace. And that one, he said, indicating St. John Granger on the far wall near the refectory table. She made no comment or any sign of recognition.

He said, Will you be here long?

As little time as possible. I wanted my husband to come with me but he refused. He had business in San Francisco. It's just as well. He does not care for France, whereas I adore it. She moved her wineglass out of reach and said, I intend to put the house on the market at once.

Good idea, Thomas said.

I have no use for it. I prefer Paris to the countryside.

Many do, Thomas said, refilling his glass.

It is a beautiful city. The French don't deserve it.

He had no answer to that.

What do you think about a price?

Price of what?

My house—what did you think I meant? The house here.

I have no idea, he said.

You must have an idea. You live here.

I would ask the notaire. The notaire knows the price of everything.

I've been told he's a scoundrel.

Thomas cocked his head thoughtfully. Her information was sound and he wondered where she got it from. Monsieur Villaret was two hundred and fifty pounds of chicanery and bad faith, one to be avoided at all costs, yet he was unavoidable if you intended to do business in St. Michel du Valcabrère. This surly American woman would be no match for him. Villaret was known in the village as

Monsieur Corpse-counter. He knew where all the bodies were buried. Thomas said, Unfortunately, he is the man to see.

I don't trust him, she said.

No one does. But that's beside the point.

He speaks no English, she said.

He speaks a little, Thomas said.

All the same, I intend to have my own lawyer from Paris.

Very wise, Thomas said. That will help a great deal.

You don't sound convinced.

I'm afraid that in his domain Monsieur Villaret is king.

Small potatoes, she said, nodding decisively. I think my lawyer will be able to handle him. Victoria went on to describe the lawyer from Paris. He and his American wife lived in a hôtel particulier in the Sixteenth Arrondissement, a very well-known address that had been visited often by the friends of Marcel Proust. The wife was a patron of the arts. The lawyer rode horses. He had outstanding connections in the government, including an extremely close friendship with the president of the republic.

He knows how things are done in the provinces, so my little problem is as good as settled, don't you see . . .

Thomas took another swallow of wine, his attention wandering. He was remembering the model, her Garbo shoulders and quick smile, her green eyes and good cheer, always ready for anything. They had had a wonderful collaboration. Karen loved to pose as much as he loved to paint. For the time they were together they were indispensable to each other. At night they haunted the downtown artists' bars, where things were always just slightly out of hand. But when the time came for him to leave she refused to go with him, insisting that her destiny was to live and die in America with a man who loved her and wanted to be father to her children. She and New York City were soul mates. That was what yoga had taught her. Thomas never understood about yoga, as he never understood the attraction to America. Last he heard, Karen and the diplomat had gone back to Rio or Buenos Aires, one or the other. The diplomat had persuaded her to change homelands, something she said she would never do, no matter what. Probably the diplomat had promised a child, in fact had insisted on it, muchos niños. Thomas hoped to God Karen was happy. She deserved a rich and uncomplicated happiness.

So there won't be any trouble with the notaire.

I certainly hope not, Thomas said.

The fat boy's history.

I'm glad to hear it, he said, imagining the sleekly coiffed and tailored Paris lawyer and Monsieur Villaret in close conversation in the notaire's office across the street from the Mairie, the walls crowded with dossiers in file folders. The meeting would take place toward the end of the day; the Parisian would have brought a bottle of something, probably calvados. They would toast each other, then discuss precisely how the pie would be cut, the size of the slices, and how much of it would remain for their American client.

Victoria nodded sharply, case closed. And then she murmured, I'm very sorry about your wife.

Thomas took a step backward, startled by the sudden change of subject. He said, Yes. Well. Thank you.

The experience must have been terrible for her.

Yes, he said. It was.

And for you, too, of course.

Yes.

The notaire said she died in a fall on the mountain.

Yes, she did.

And that there were others involved.

Yes, there were.

And she was abused.

Abused?

Yes, they abused her. That was what the notaire told me.

It took Thomas a moment to understand the word, to understand it as she apparently wished it to be understood, this contemporary American word that did not exactly fit the situation. Abused? They cut Florette's throat. He said, I suppose you could say that.

Ghastly, she said. I'm so sorry.

He nodded slowly, an acknowledgment. He said, I wish you good luck with the notaire. If I hear anything about prices, I'll let you know.

Is that her picture? She pointed at Florette's portrait, reaching to touch the frame, not two feet from where they stood.

As she was five years ago, Thomas said.

She is a lovely-looking woman. Was she French?

Born in the village.

How amazing!

We were married in the church here.

Extraordinary, she said.

Florette insisted. And I was happy to oblige.

I can hardly believe it!

We wanted a quiet ceremony but the whole village showed up. Filled the church. Rained all day long.

I can't imagine it! Victoria was silent a moment—dumbstruck, it seemed to Thomas, by these fantastic events. And then she said, I meant no harm, what I said about the French.

It's a common enough opinion, he said.

We're having a difficult time with them now.

You are?

Why, yes. Our government. It's a time of strained relations. We want one thing and the French want another.

Ah, he said. You mean Bush's war.

An American war, she said.

And getting more so every day.

It's the world's war, really. The world war on terror.

Much of the world doesn't agree.

So shortsighted, she said, sighing heavily. The French are the worst. They are afraid to look the future in the face. They're afraid of it. They're afraid history will repeat itself, so they want to stop the clocks. They're afraid of tomorrow and they've lost their spirit of adventure. They've lost confidence. Instead, they're attracted to pessimism. And when we say to them that we're working for a better tomorrow, they don't believe us because their better days are right now. This is the problem, you see. They hate and fear the twentieth century and they think that's coming around again. That's what the Americans have in store for them, a new world war. And when it's over only we'll be left standing. Perhaps the Chinese as well. They don't understand that a small war will prevent a larger war. Islamists must be punished for what they've done and plan to do, that's the simple truth of it.

Not simple, he thought. Not the truth. But she was not as dumb as he thought. Thomas said, They're afraid of the future because they're afraid of America.

You've been in France too long.

It's a different perspective than Pennsylvania that's true.

Thank God for George Bush. And—she smiled triumphantly— Maître Brun agrees with me.

Maître Brun?

My lawyer in Paris.

Thomas looked at his watch and took another swallow of wine. He put a log on the fire and stood back as sparks flew. It had been years since he talked politics with an American outside his own orbit, a stranger. The American woman—he had forgotten her name—now stood with her hands primly clasped, staring at the portrait of St. John Granger. Thomas poured wine into his glass and stood waiting for her to say her goodbye. But she was not ready.

And that is my great-uncle?

Yes, it is.

Is it a good likeness?

I think so, Thomas said.

He looks emaciated.

No doubt the fault of the artist, Thomas said.

The notaire said you were his closest friend.

I suppose I was, he said.

Other than you, he saw no one, according to the notaire. He lived alone except for that wretched servant girl. God knows what they were up to.

Her name is Ghislaine and I doubt if they were up to much.

He was a recluse, the notaire said.

He enjoyed his own company, that's true.

A selfish life, she said.

Thomas, looking at the portrait from afar, knew it was not one of his best. Granger was a concealed personality at the best of times and he was most uncomfortable sitting. He only did it as a favor. Come on, get it over with, he said in a voice as thin as paper. In the event, Thomas had made a quick sketch, took half a dozen snapshots, and worked on the piece for more than a month. He never got it right, and when at last it was finished all he could do was frame it and hang it in his own house; Granger wanted no part of it. It was the concealment, the sense of a deeply hidden history, that Thomas was attempting to catch but the quality eluded him. And quite right that it should, he concluded. Staring at the portrait, sipping his wine, Thomas almost forgot about the American woman, who had fallen silent.

He was a very good friend, Thomas said.

She said, A recluse is one who has something to hide. What do you suppose it was?

Sometimes a recluse is just a recluse.

Oh, no, she said. Not him.

He had lived a very long time. Probably he forgot what he was hiding.

She said, Nonsense. I doubt if he ever forgot anything. Not forgetting, that would be his revenge.

Strange sort of revenge, Thomas said.

Depends on what he was not forgetting. And he was always reclusive, according to the notaire. For as long as he lived here. Yes, no doubt about it. He carried a secret. A nasty one.

As you say, the notaire is a scoundrel. He can't be trusted.

At that, she smiled, her first of the evening. She said, So I'm sure you know what he was up to. The nature of the secret.

We didn't talk much, he said. We didn't tell stories. We didn't confide. We didn't share secrets. We played billiards. How easily these lies slipped from his mouth, in perfect actorly cadence. He surprised himself; he was out of practice.

Yes, she said. I guessed.

Guessed what?

That you played billiards. Nothing straightforward about billiards. It's a sly game, isn't it? Positioning, always leaving your opponent—

Uncomfortable, he said.

Yes, she said. A game of nuance.

He was deft at it.

Oh, I just bet he was. Deft as all get-out. She was still gazing intently at Granger's portrait. She said, I like it. Would you sell it to me?

It's not for sale.

Even to his heir?

Sorry, Thomas said.

Too bad, she said. I have just the place for him in Pennsylvania. I have a set of Audubon prints in my living room. They're quite valuable. He could go at the end, next to the great crested grebe. She smiled thinly and added, I imagine he enjoyed posing for you.

I had to talk him into it. Once he was settled he was all right. It passed the time.

But he didn't give much away, did he?

Thomas did not reply at once. The American woman bore no resemblance to Granger. It was hard to imagine they were members of the same family. She was solidly built to industrial specifications; he imagined her playing field hockey as a girl. Probably now she played golf at her Pennsylvania country club, long off the tee but not so good around the greens and disastrous in the rough. The rough was unacceptable and her temperament would work against her, never failing to yield to the temptation to improve her lie. Granger was built of piano wire; this American woman—he suddenly remembered her name, Victoria—of concrete, even her hair.

She said, There's a family story. I don't know whether to believe it or not. It's an unpleasant story. Most unpleasant. A scandal. She waited for Thomas to reply, and when he didn't she reached for her wine and swallowed a thimbleful, making a face. She said, It's a story that has to do with the war. That would be his war, the First World

War. He enlisted when he was very young, hardly more than a boy. He was headstrong. He didn't notify his parents or his brother. He apparently wanted to prove something, don't you see. Though it has to be said in his defense that in those days patriotism was a given. When your country was at war, you fought for it. The men went and the women waited for them to come back, or not. Pride was involved both ways, don't you think? The facts of my great-uncle's conduct in the war are scarce. But his name was never again mentioned in the family.

I don't know anything about it, Thomas said.

Too bad, she said. I thought you might be willing to help a fellow American fill in the blanks.

Thomas shook his head, neither yes nor no.

He's gone now, she said. Whatever he was protecting has gone with him, unless he shared his story. Which I am highly confident he did. It's ancient history anyway. What difference can it make to you? Or is this the unspoken male code at work?

I don't know anything about it, Thomas said again.

He was my great-uncle, after all. I don't like family mysteries. I'd like to see this one cleared up. It has caused great distress in my family.

We differ, then, Thomas said. I do like mysteries. I cherish them, as a matter of fact. Not everything in this world is destined to be known. And some things are better left unsaid. The dead have rights, same as everyone else. My God, he thought, I'm sounding like a New Age lawyer. Rights of the unborn, rights of the dead, both trumping the rights of the living. Probably a truly believing evangelical lawyer could find evidence that Jesus Christ himself had rights as the son of God, divine providence having been cited in the Declaration of Independence, no less. Suppressing a smile, Thomas said, In any case, it's really none of my business. I can't help you.

But we have rights, too, she said. The family does.

So many rights, so little time, he thought but did not say. He looked at his watch and said, Good luck.

She said, Your wife's death is a mystery. Surely you don't cherish that. Surely you don't believe her death is destined to remain unsolved and that's the way it should be. Don't you want to get to the bottom of it? Fill in the blanks? See that justice is done? Discover who's responsible and have them punished? Even if you have to do it yourself, because if you don't, no one else will. Doesn't it hurt knowing the men who abused her are still at large?

My wife is my affair.

As my great-uncle is mine. Difference is, you can help me. I can do nothing for you.

I can't help you, Thomas said.

She said, Our family has been unlucky. It's like we're cursed, some dark spot in our blood, a never-ending wrong. We have illness. We have accidents. We have had two suicides. She turned again to look at Granger's portrait. My children, she said, lovely children, sweet-natured . . . But she hesitated there and did not finish her thought. How am I supposed to account for these misfortunes? Our family is heir to misfortune and I have come to believe it begins with him, your great friend. He lived more than one hundred years. He retired from the world but that doesn't mean he was unhappy. That doesn't mean his life was not worth living, and he lived quite well. But he lived with a secret, and the secret was passed on to his descendants. I wish you would sell me the portrait. And if you did, I wouldn't hang it next to an Audubon bird. I would burn it.

I don't know where to turn, she said, openly pleading now. Where would you turn? What would you do? She moved slowly to the center of the room, still looking at Granger's portrait. Her whole body trembled when she said, The story is that he deserted in the face of the enemy. Ran like a rabbit. Deserted his comrades, ran away to the south of France and allowed the world to believe he was dead. But not before he bullied his brother into sending money, his share of the inheritance. His brother was humiliated. He quit his job, began to drink, finally killed himself by driving into a tree. His widow had no wish to live in America but that's where she went, to our little town in Pennsylvania, with their child. And soon she died also, leaving my mother an orphan. My mother was just eight years old. Victoria sighed as if it were her last breath. The story never became known outside the family. That was where it belonged. But it had an awful effect on my mother. Awful.

It was a very long time ago, Thomas murmured.

So what? The when doesn't matter. The what matters. The who matters.

Give it up, Thomas said. There's a statute of limitations on everything.

Your wife. Is there a statute of limitations on her?

I am very tired, Thomas said. And I wish you would leave.

I'm sorry. I shouldn't have said that.

No, you shouldn't've.

I'm not myself, she said.

It's late, Thomas said.

My husband was in the military, she said. He knows what people think of a deserter. And what the deserter thinks of himself.

Not Granger, Thomas said. He was shell-shocked. *He was lost.*

And what did he do then? He disappeared. And in due course, years later, he fetches up here, this place, to hell and gone. Victoria's voice rose to an accusatory soprano and Thomas thought she would break down. But she gathered herself and spoke once again. I had no idea he was still alive, she said. It's hard to conceive even now. Then I got the letter from the notaire telling me I was his heir. How did my great-uncle know my name? Where I lived? To me, the letter seemed to come from beyond the grave. The notaire knew nothing about my great-uncle's past, and believe me, I asked. He said there was only one person who might know and that was you, his great friend and confidant, his billiards partner. And then he told me about your wife and her accident and the abuse by persons unknown. So I believed that when we met I would find someone sympathetic, someone who would listen with an open heart and give me the help I need.

I have told you what I know, Thomas said. Now I have work to do.

You have a cold heart, Mr. Railles.

You aren't the first to say so, Thomas said.

He had a cold heart, too. He stepped out of his family like one of those characters who leave the house to buy a newspaper and are never heard from again. How I would have liked to be a fly on the wall at your dinners. What a treat! She walked off then, collecting her parka and her ski hat and gloves, giving one last loathsome look at Granger's portrait. The old man looked back at her with his fixed half-smile and his pale eyes that were not quite level. She turned to Thomas and said, I have never understood people who choose to live outside their own country. Why is it important to them to live among strangers, speaking a foreign tongue, eternally on the outside of things. Who do they think they're kidding? It's like trying to escape your own shadow, except every time you look over your shoulder it's there. Is it something you're afraid of? Something low and dishonest in your own past, some betrayal or misprision that makes it impossible to live among your own kind? That kind of decision always seemed disloyal to me, abandoning your family and becoming a voluntary orphan. Something scummy about it.

Goodbye, Mrs.—and he realized he did not know her surname.

Granger, she said.

So you kept his name.

My mother's name. She insisted on it.

She had paused at the door, a heavy woman, bulky in her parka, her face drawn as if she were in pain. She seemed uncertain what to do. Surely she would not relish an evening in her enemy's house, an old man's house with an old man's neglect and an old man's many memories. Thomas's sympathies were suddenly with her. She was wrong about many things but not about everything. Like Cézanne, you could admire the pugnacity without liking the man. She was very sure of herself. She was not an attractive personality and that would hold her back; things would be difficult for her here, and in a day or two she would be home in Pennsylvania with nothing resolved, except the farmhouse would be on the market. She would want to believe that when the farmhouse was gone the curse would go with it and her family would be free. But it also sounded as if the curse had done all the damage in its power.

He was a nice man, you know.

She made an abrupt, dismissive gesture with her jeweled hand and muttered something he did not hear.

Lived harmlessly, Thomas said. Kept dogs. Read all day long— the English classics, mostly. Kept to himself. Kept out of the way. Kept busy according to his own lights. Kept his own counsel, definitely. Thomas paused before continuing, then found himself with a fresh thought. He said, I think Granger would be surprised to learn that he had laid a curse on his family. What happened to him had nothing to do with his family. He rarely spoke of them. It's true that he and his brother were not close. Different temperaments, different beliefs. In any case, Granger was not a superstitious man. He was modest in his expectations. He was worldly, though not much of the world. Really, Granger was only trying to survive.

She laughed harshly. Survive what?

His past, Thomas said.

Thomas turned from her and drank some wine, considering the circumstances of the last night he saw Granger. They spoke very little, a word or two from him on the book he was reading, Strachey's *Eminent Victorians*, and a few more words from Thomas on the recent London subway bombings. Granger said he remembered the King's Cross station from his youth. After a long silence, Granger said, I never told you that I visited Thiepval once. It was sometime in the thirties, only time I ever left this valley. When Thomas asked him to explain Thiepval, Granger replied that it was the Franco-British memorial to the battles of the Somme, the missing and unaccounted-for in the period from July 1 to September 26, 1916. Seventy-two thousand names inscribed on the monument, he said. Ugly structure but affecting because of the names, row on row. I found my name high up in the center arch, needed binoculars to read it. Stayed a few hours, then left and came back to St. Michel. Shall we play billiards?

That was all Granger said of his afternoon at Thiepval. Granger threw a log on the fire and he and Thomas bent to the table. They finished billiards and Thomas was walking away down the path to the road when he realized he had forgotten his hat. He returned and looked through the front window to see if the old man was still up and about. Granger was seated in his customary chair by the billiards table, his hands covering his face. He was motionless, as if he were frozen in ice. All the world seemed excluded from his meditation. When the hands came away, Thomas saw a stricken expression, one he had never seen before—and he was certain that the events of the old man's life were marching one by one across his vision. His attitude was that of a prisoner, not shackled but detained. He sat straight up in military posture. The terms of his confinement were that he was prohibited from looking away; each episode had to be accounted for and justified. Thomas stood at the window a minute or more, Granger as still as a statue, except for his right foot, which seemed to move to some mysterious rhythm. The field of the billiards table was as brilliant as a meadow in sunlight. Thomas turned away, the moment was unbearably private. He decided to leave his hat for another day, and when he turned back he saw Granger lit as if by fire. A chimney downdraft had caused logs to flare, and subside almost at once. But for that instant it seemed that Granger himself was ablaze, a sudden inexplicable illumination. Thomas wheeled at once and walked away down the path; two days later, the old man died in his sleep.

Only trying to survive, Thomas repeated.

Really?

I believe so, Thomas said.

Victoria Granger looked him in the eye a long moment, concentrating as if she were lining up a difficult putt. She said, You think such an attitude is admirable. Manly, heroic even. "Lived harmlessly." "Kept to himself." Hide away somewhere and your past will cease to exist. You won't have to account for it. You'll feel no obligation to explain your actions or justify them because you've gone into hiding and promised to cause no more harm. You've gone away and you expect your victims to go away, too. It's like leaving the scene of an accident, wouldn't you say, Mr. Railles? Or a marriage. Even a field of battle.

Head high, she marched to the door. Then she looked back at

him. One last instruction. She said, Only one month ago my great-uncle made a codicil to his will. He left you the billiards table, the cues, the ivory balls, the rack, the chalk. The lot. Wasn't that thoughtful of him? Make arrangements with the notaire to have it delivered.

And then she was through the door, closing it hard behind her. Thomas stepped to the front window to watch her advance through the snow down the driveway to the road. He wondered what it was she wanted to say about her children before she caught herself; they would be troubles too intimate to be disclosed to a stranger. Bad blood, she said, and all of it the fault of Captain St. John Granger, scapegrace. She did not want to hear that the old man was innocent. Innocent, he lost responsibility. Innocent, he had no value. Thomas believed that with Granger there was nothing to forgive—or nothing Thomas could swear to with confidence. He had no way of knowing if Granger had embellished his résumé, contrived his own narrative, a story he could live with. You either believed him or you didn't. Amnesia was the curse of the modern world, or its redemption, depending on whether you held to the Old Testament or the New. Forgiveness was the consequence of amnesia. This American woman, this Granger descendant, was a hanging judge and Thomas wondered now if this was something fresh in the American character or if it was yet another arid legacy of the joyless Puritan horde, Cotton Mather and his ilk. No doubt the attacks of September 11, 2001, played a part, revenge sweeping the nation. Kill the Islamists and two objectives were accomplished. Vengeance was sweet. They would kill no more, once they felt the full fury of righteous American anger. The Spanish communist had a German word that covered it: Lebenslüge, the lie that makes life bearable. Citizens of the former German Democratic Republic knew it well. Russian troops were not marauders and rapists, they were liberators. East Germans were at last free of the fascist Hitler, owing to the Russian occupation; he was in any case a Western capitalist phenomenon, for whom the Eastern proletariat bore no responsibility. Thomas had the idea that most everyone had a Lebenslüge and Victoria Granger's was her own great-uncle, deserter, coward, scourge of the family, a kind of terrorist. She was a determined woman and he guessed he had not seen the last of her. She certainly walked with purpose. He watched her turn right, in the direction of Granger's house, her head bent against the wind, her scarf flying. But the night was dark and soon he lost her among the drifts and shadows.

Thomas poured the last of Granger's Bordeaux and switched on the television set, the drizzle of the eight o'clock news. A strike had crippled Charles de Gaulle and Orly, one of every three flights canceled, all delayed. Farmers were outraged at new EC rules concerning livestock and they, too, threatened action in Paris. A car bomb had killed a dozen Iraqis and one American soldier in Baghdad, the bomb concealed in a police car. More Americans were among the injured. The words flew by too fast for Thomas to grasp the details. The news anchor habitually bit his lip for emphasis and this was another distraction. Then the scene shifted to a cemetery in one of the Baghdad suburbs, the funeral of a child killed the day before. The wailing of the women and the howling of the men seemed without limit, anguish beyond words. The women clung to each other and the men to themselves, tugging at arms and shoulders, clothes stained with sweat and tears. Their cries reached to the very heavens, unconsoled, raw, unbridled, final. Thomas moved closer to the television screen, remembering the funeral of a few days before, at Arlington, a Marine captain laid to rest, the American flag carefully folded and handed to his widow, her face partly hidden by a black veil, two very young children at her side, a pantomime in perfect silence until somewhere beyond the gravestones the first baritone notes of taps, limpid in the cold. Thomas found himself near tears, watching the disorder in Baghdad and remembering the restraint at Arlington. Identical grief, dissimilar expression. Not less deeply felt at Arlington—no one watching the widow's trembling fingers could doubt she was near collapse. But she uttered not one word and did not appear to weep. Perhaps she felt her anguish was no one's business but her own and that of her children. Thomas had an idea that

Muslims were as a rule restrained in their laughter; more restrained, in any event, than Americans or Europeans. Perhaps the formality of their religion discouraged laughter. Did laughter mock God?

He turned from the screen to look at Florette's portrait.

What do you think of that as an idea, chérie?

Not much, Florette said. American laughter is the worst.

Have you ever listened to the English? Or the Germans?

I prefer French laughter, Florette said. Although I do not prefer French television.

Thomas and Florette had made a ritual of the evening news, Florette translating when he missed a phrase or nuance, when there was any. She made her own commentary on the events of the day, ribald for the most part. She believed the evening news a Paris fantasy designed to lull the good people of the countryside into a bovine sense of well-being, confident that their affairs were being scrupulously handled by skilled civil servants at the many important ministries located in the capital, and if they only knew what the civil servants knew of the complexities of managing a modern industrial state they would sink to their knees in gratitude. And here Florette's ribaldry reached its eight o'clock summit as she gathered the dominoes and commenced to shuffle the bones on the table between them. Then she said in her cool announcer's voice,

Alors, chéri!

Fetch the wine.

The evening news continued, a fast segue into a promo for that night's showcase program, an inquiry into the sources of the civic genius of Bonaparte, the film followed by a panel discussion of leading authorities, including the adorable and provocative communist academic so often in the news. The final item caught Thomas's interest—the anchor chewing on his lower lip with more compassion than usual—for it had to do with the restoration of brown bears to the Pyrenees. The few remaining native bears had died out at last, and eighteen had been imported from the Julian Alps in Slovenia, the Slovenian bears identical in every respect to their lost cousins in the Pyrenees. Schoolchildren had been enlisted to support the importation, which they were delighted to do since all children loved bears. Six-year-olds took to the streets in noisy approval, with the happy result that the bears were now occasionally seen as well as heard, though only at high elevations. A survey showed that bears were the most popular animal in France, a curiosity, since only a few shepherds had ever seen one. And even the shepherds were delighted, since each time a bear fell upon a sheep and dismembered it, the shepherd was compensated to a formula that worked out to twice the sheep's value. Thus was ecological, monetary, and sentimental balance achieved in the great mountains to the south. The segment ended with a grinning child displaying a bear's tooth that had been taken from the skull of one of the unfortunate sheep, as the announcer's compassion spilled over.

Alors, Thomas said, in a fair imitation of Florette's voice.

All those walks. We never saw a bear.

Probably we didn't go high enough.

Thomas was looking at her portrait over the fireplace. He confessed he was touched by the footage of the bears. Bears were relics of prehistory, drawn on the walls of caves and prominent in European legends, creatures of mythic stature, especially in Russia and Germany. They belonged on mountains or in forests, the more remote the better. When Thomas was a boy, brown bears were common in the northern Wisconsin woods, feeding on lake fish and berries, fiercely protective of their young. Thomas had never seen a bear in the wild but he was confident they were wonderful animals. Slovenian bears were welcome in the Pyrenees no less than the mighty birds, the royal eagle and the Egyptian vulture. If it took enthusiastic schoolchildren and cost-conscious shepherds to make it happen, so much the better. Of course there remained the question of whether the bears minded being extirpated from the Julian Alps to the Pyrenees, unfamiliar territory, not that they had any choice in the matter—unlike, say, a human expatriate. That was almost always a matter of choice, and then the choice became a habit, and you learned the language and discovered a fresh persona outside the norms of your own country yet not entirely inside the norms of your new country, and so there were no civic responsibilities. Elections came and went. Prominent citizens died. Your own country changed in unfathomable ways, the ways gathered by the American newspaper and foreign television. The context of things vanished. Still, you were working well, and if you were lucky you found a French woman and settled down with her, and up to a point her context became your context. There were tax advantages also. Bears and expats were brothers. Bears had no tax worries either. There were no secrets for them to hide and nothing for them to be afraid of except trophy hunters and other bears. They wouldn't worry about being condescended to by neurotic Pennsylvania women with chips on their shoulders. They weren't kidding anybody and certainly betrayals were not involved. They were beloved by schoolchildren and even the shepherds became their friends and protectors, and in the winter they retreated to their dens and slept.

They wouldn't worry about expressions of grief and laughter.

Thomas opened another bottle of wine, one from his own cellar. He rummaged in the domino box until he found the double-six. He stacked the bones one by one until he had a domino tower a foot high, the blank bone at the summit. It was a beautiful structure, tall, slender, and symmetrical; he could see it standing in downtown Milwaukee, ten, twelve stories high, an ornament of the city. Thomas Railles, architect.

He removed the stories one by one and returned the bones to the domino box. That left the matter of the billiards table. He poured a glass of wine and tipped it in the direction of the portrait of St. John Granger. The only room in his house large enough for the table was the living room where he sat, so that would be its place. He did not know how you went about playing billiards solo. Billiards, dominoes, gin rummy, all companionable games. Probably you would play it for practice only so that you could know the feel of the cushions and the stick as well as you knew your own body or your lover's body, and no doubt if you thought about it seriously you could invent rules for a game with imaginary opponents. Granger, for example, or Francisco, a kind of round robin of dead men. Billiards was an amiable way of passing the time and Granger's equipment was superb, the sticks as finely balanced as a violin bow; they had been made in Austria at the turn of the previous century. If the table was in the living room it would be as much a part of things as the bookcase or the television set and no two setups would ever be the same. Billiards was a game of infinite variety. He could play billiards while listening to opera or jazz music.

Thomas needed an evening activity.

Something that involved repetitive motion.

Something other than the evening news.

He reached into the domino box and rebuilt the ivory tower with the blank bone at the summit. He contemplated it a moment, and when he touched it with his finger the tower collapsed and one of the bones splashed into his wineglass. When Thomas glanced at the portrait on the wall above the fireplace, Florette seemed to be staring at him with reproach, her off-center eyes and her mournful mouth, one eyebrow raised. He apologized for comparing her to felt cushions but her expression did not change; then he knew she disapproved of a billiards table in the living room. That was the meaning of her severe expression. Thomas had painted her in a plain white shift in a white room—white walls, white floors, white sunlight. Her skin was pale. He had worked on the portrait for weeks and finished one afternoon in a characteristic burst of speed. At first she had been impatient with the long hours of sitting still and then came to enjoy it, putting herself into a trancelike state, remembering things. She said that sometimes she forgot he was in the room, so complete was her abstraction. When he asked her what she was remembering, she said it was none of his business what she remembered. The last week he worked alone. The oils seemed to him to explode off the canvas. He sat looking at the portrait for an hour before he called her in to see for herself and when she did tears filled her eyes. This was not at all the reaction he had hoped for or expected so for a time he said nothing, allowing her to look at her portrait in her own way before she spoke. But she remained silent for many minutes, motionless as if she were holding her breath.

Well, he said finally, what do you think?

Oh, she said. It's beautiful.

I'm pleased, then, he said.

Do you mean that?

Oh, yes, he said. Of course.

Naturally I wonder, she said.

Why would you wonder?

You've made me look so sad, she said, and burst into tears, her hands over her eyes. She made gasping sounds as though she were short of breath.

He was astonished. That was not his intention at all, and that was not how he saw her. He reached for her and took her in his arms. She was trembling, peeking through her fingers at the portrait.

She said, White on white on white. You did that with Francisco. And that's the saddest picture you ever painted.

Look for yourself, she said. Look at the eyes you've given me.

He explained what he saw in her eyes, which was not sadness or disappointment but understanding. Sympathy, he said, and wit. At some level sympathy implied knowledge and knowledge had a melancholy aspect. He believed that was universally true, no exceptions. When you knew too much you felt a natural distress but that was something quite different from fundamental personal sadness, sadness as a trait, like blue eyes. Her distress was not temperamental but intellectual. They argued the matter all that night and the next night, and in the end there was no resolution. God, she was stubborn. So the portrait had not been a success, at least with Florette, and he never forgot the sound of her weeping, a moan that seemed to reach to the heavens.

Freehand

JUST BEFORE CHRISTMAS Thomas received a long handwritten letter from Bernhard Sindelar, postmarked Washington. Bernhard had been called back to headquarters for a conference, a general review of current operations with special attention to methods and sources, connecting dots while they walked back the cat, a dispirited and dispiriting exercise. Morale was terrible, the fudge factory's bureaucracy nervously broken down without energy enough for rebellion. Congress was asniff, the Pentagon frightened, and the White House in deep prayer. So many of the old boys had retired that Bernhard was now the senior field man, sitting around the long table with people young enough to be his children and, in two cases, his grandchildren. "The problem here is Gulliver's problem, if you get my meaning." Still, he was able to bring the youngsters one or two items of interest, pristine material from impeccable sources, produce from Tiffany's window. They were childlike in their appreciation, Bernhard said, going so far as to offer a polite round of applause. And so there'll be no fuss about the renewal of my contract. As to the urgent matter at hand, he had nothing new to report. Several promising leads had fizzled, but one was very much alive. Not Tiffany-window produce but not dross, either. Stay tuned, Thomas. More anon. I know you're anxious but these things always take time, as you know. The goods were almost certainly still in France. No one had given up, and in time they would find what they were looking for. No doubt of that, none whatever. And when the time came they would set about doing what they did best, breaking faces, an honorable revenge for a terrible wrong. And the score would be settled. The letter ended with a long paragraph of instructions, one old friend to another. Sixty years of friendship, Thomas, so trust what I say.

It's evident to me that you're not cut out for the country. You're an urban man, a rootless cosmopolitan, as a matter of fact, wholly unsuited to the rustic life. You should sell the Schloss and head at once to the Sixth Arrondissement. It's time you kissed the dreary weather in dreary Aquitaine bye-bye. You need a time-out, Thomas. Come to London, take a cruise, go skiing, find a girlfriend, see a bullfight, attend the opera, *get out of the house.* By the way, Russ is in Tripoli but should return to Paris very soon. He wants to see you, and sends this reminder: Degas is at the Grand Palais until the end of January.

Thomas read the letter in front of the fire and when he was finished pitched it into the flames, Bernhard's standing orders. He wondered if Russ was truly in Tripoli or if Tripoli was code for Tbilisi, Timbuktu, or Trenton. Thomas never knew which parts of Bernhard's letters to believe. His friend was at heart a fabulist, living always for a glimpse of Tiffany's window, contemplating honorable revenge by breaking faces, quick to issue instructions in the certainty that he knew best what was good for you, anticipating applause. Bernhard Sindelar was a stranger to solitude and unacquainted with doubt and that was what made him a capable intelligence agent. Also, people were afraid of him, his glare and his huge hands. Thomas would have been afraid of him too, except they had been friends for so long. Even so, Bernhard's bite was much worse than his bark.

For the hundredth time that day Thomas wondered if he should buy a Christmas tree and a wreath for the front door, decorations they had always had when Florette was alive. He poured a glass of wine and went to the billiards table, selected a cue, and began to practice three-cushion shots, drastic angles. Dead men's round robin. After a while, studying the drastic angles, he was able to put Bernhard's letter and the last-paragraph instructions out of his mind. The prediction that Florette's killers were still in France was alarming. He didn't want them in France or anywhere. He had nearly succeeded in forgetting about them altogether, as one does with unwelcome strangers who arrive unannounced, invading one's domain, troubling one's sleep. In that sense they were dream-visitors. He concentrated hard while he chalked his cue. Maybe a wreath, he thought. No tree.

After New Year's a false spring arrived in St. Michel du Valcabrère, the temperature rising to nearly 10°C. under a watery Mediterra-nean sky. The snow remained but here and there brown patches were visible in the fields, along with the persistent sound of running water. Each afternoon Thomas drove to a different village and sketched churches inside and out. Many of the churches dated from the Middle Ages. He had an idea he could discover the medieval rhythm of life from the altars and choirs—bare ruined choirs, ac-cording to the Bard—and the worn wood of the pews, heavy stones underfoot. The fathers had ruled things to suit themselves, in those days and later, and now the churches were relics, sparsely attended, mostly by old people. The priests were old. There was great beauty in the architecture, in the silence and the overhead space—a beauty, he concluded, of a sentimental kind, the beauty of a very old woman praying fiercely. He was unable to judge the inner beauty of men, since there were so few in church of an afternoon. Surely men had as many troubles as women but did not visit church to solve them. Thomas looked at the old women and tried to imagine them when they were young, as young as Florette when he first met her, or the model he'd lived with when he was twenty-one and struggling to discover if he had talent or merely a flair for illustration.

He thought Karen could help in the discovery and to that end listened to her comments with the attention New York collectors had given Bernard Berenson. Then it turned out that Berenson was not all he seemed to be. He knew everything there was to know about Venetian masters including the devious ways of the doges, sharp practice as second nature, and then he met Duveen. Karen knew nothing of sharp practice. She was rarely devious, and when she was, it was inadvertent. She said that she often wished she could care about something as much as Thomas cared about his art. She said, You'll have it as long as you live, no matter what else happens to you, because you'll never use it up or wear it out. Whether that will make for a happy life, I'm not sure. Maybe not. Maybe that one thing is so large it crowds people out. And then again it's possible you can get along without them. The other people, including me. Maybe you can tell me what inspires such devotion. Believe me, I'll listen. I'm all ears. He told her that a true picture came from loving the work itself—the paint, the brushes, the canvas, the look and feel and smell of it, the space itself, negative space until you made the first stroke—confident that at a certain moment the oils would explode off the canvas, the picture revealing itself as dawn revealed the day to come, not its weather or its events but its presence. He had forgotten all that in the weeks since Florette's death and searched now to get it back, something he believed was second nature to him, his own version of sharp practice. But apparently not, and so in the afternoons of the false spring he went from church to church in search of—he supposed he would call it enlightenment. In any case, some way of beginning again.

The churches were empty but if he stayed awhile he would hear the creak of the portal and someone would enter and take a seat and begin to pray silently. Often the penitent would light a candle and then Thomas would wait for the decisive clink of a coin slipped into the metal box behind the vase full of white tapers. Of course it was cold inside the churches and noisy, too, with wind and the creaks and groans of centuries-old stone and wood. He never believed he was alone, owing to the unsettling noises. When he was far enough inside his work he believed he could apprehend souls gathering around him, scrutinizing his sketch and deciding it wasn't worth their attention; it was only a sketch, after all, something provisional. After a while his eyesight began to fail in the dim churchly light. When his fingers seized up, the cold locking his knuckles, Thomas gathered up his paper and charcoal pencils and stood, his knees stiff as wood. Lightheaded, he had to grasp the back of the pew to steady himself. He walked to the alms box and deposited ten euros and walked out of the church and into the square, feeling every bit as old as the women he watched at prayer. The time was always dusk or near dusk and he would walk at once to the café across the street— there was always a café in the church square—and order an espresso and a pony of the local marc, firewater to chase the chill from his bones. He sat at one of the round tables and listened to the conversation that often involved local gossip and horseracing, with the usual gibes at the government. No one ever paid much attention to him, an elderly foreigner who evidently desired solitude.

When Thomas finished his espresso and marc he paid up and drove home. Often he forgot the name of the village he was in and how he got there and had to ask someone to give him directions home. Then he heard Florette's baritone laugh, rich as chocolate and as seductive. She was with him every hour of every day and he wondered how long he could live with a ghost. He began to think of her as a kind of benign god, present everywhere and visible nowhere. She was with him in the church and the café afterward and when he drove home in the darkness and later in the evening when he played solo billiards, the only sounds in the room the click of the balls and the soft thump when one of them struck a cushion. Billiards was now an essential part of his evening repertoire, along with the nightcap when he finally gave it up, racked the cue, and sat heavily in the high-backed chair that oversaw the billiards table. He used the remote to put an end to *La Bohème* and listen instead to the piano music of Art Hodes, blues in the old style. With the billiards table and the portraits, his living room had the look and feel of a men's club in London or a bar in the tropics, British India or Malaya, except it lacked ceiling fans and a white-coated barman. But as Thomas poured a glass of cognac he was remembering not the Garrick or the wide-verandahed resort hotel in Mysore but the lobby bar of the Hotel Pfister in Milwaukee, all dark wood and cocktails in large glasses. He remembered portraits of women on the walls but may have been mistaken; this was more than forty years ago. He drank beer, his father a bourbon and soda. They were in Milwaukee on some errand, had dined together at Mader's and stopped by the Pfister for a nightcap before driving home to LaBarre. His father was upset about something. What are you going to do with your life, Tommy? What are your *plans*, boy? Yes, it was the semester he was on probation at the university. The dean had written a sharp letter and the doctor was embarrassed and irritated at the imperious tone. Thomas remembered that it was Christmas vacation and they had been shopping, a grim business because his father was so upset about the dean's letter.

Thomas said, My plans are to go to New York and learn how to draw.

My God, his father said.

I'm leaving school at the end of January. Madison doesn't have anything I want.

God, Tommy.

He said, Sorry. There's no other way. Madison's just an awful waste of my time and your money.

What are you going to live on?

I'll get a job, he said.

His father sat for a long moment looking into his glass. Jesus, he said finally. New York. Why New York?

New York has jobs, Thomas said. Restaurant jobs, driving a cab. The important thing is that New York is where the artists are. New York is where things are happening. Then Art Hodes began his set and they listened quietly for a while, neither of them speaking. His father finished his drink and ordered another and a beer for Thomas. Hodes, slender and hawk-faced, beautifully turned out in a tuxedo, was playing stride. The room filled up and they moved to the far end of the bar.

It'll kill your mother, his father said.

I don't think it will, Pop.

Well, he said, and offered a hint of a smile. Maybe not right away.

Thomas remembered laughing and touching his father on the arm. The old man could be droll.

He said, What about Bernhard and Russ?

They'll finish up, get their degree. A degree's important to them.

But not to you, his father said.

No, he said. Not to me.

And what will they do when they graduate?

Work for the government, Thomas said.

His father looked at him blankly. The government?

Yes, he said. The government. Our government. The Kennedy administration.

What do they intend to do for the Kennedy administration?

It's all arranged, Thomas said.

Government work, his father said, still trying to put things together. He had never known anyone who worked for the government except the LaBarre postmaster and the local Social Security administrator, both of whom were patients of his and good Republicans. Do you mean they'll work for the government in Washington?

The Department of the Army, Thomas said, dropping his voice. Russ had told him that the Department of the Army was their official cover until they finished training at the place everyone called "the farm" and then sent abroad to work in a friendly advertising agency with offices in all the European capitals. They were NOCs, Russ confided, meaning they would be living under non-official cover, pronounced *knock*. But this information was strictly hush-hush. NTK, Russ explained, available only to those with a need to know.

His father pulled a face. He said, That's just the damnedest thing I ever heard of. Why don't they simply enlist?

It's a different kind of army work, Thomas said lamely.

Are you putting me on, Tommy?

No, he said. It's all arranged.

I suppose this was Bernhard's idea.

Russ, too, he said.

Strange boy, Bernhard, his father said. He's a snooper. He pokes his nose into places it doesn't belong. I always thought you and Russ were at a disadvantage with Bernhard. He grew up awfully fast, too fast. And his father was no help. Hardheaded German, wasn't good with his wife or with Bernhard, either. But I think Bernhard gave as good as he got. He was a forbidding presence, even as a kid. That hair, like an animal's pelt. Thickest hair I ever saw, like a Labrador's, tight against his scalp. That strange golden color.

Bernhard's all right, Thomas said loyally, turning from his father to listen to an especially silky Hodes riff. But he had a point about Bernhard's hair, woven as tight as a rug. Women liked it, according to Bernhard, when they weren't frightened.

I hope those boys know what they're doing, his father said.

It was impossible for Thomas to explain to his father how Bernhard had found his new purpose in life. The gears were set in motion by his German professor, who suggested that Bernhard meet an old friend, a historian who did special work for the government. I've told Mr. Green about you, the professor said, and he wants to get together for a chat. Bernhard agreed and when he asked what time, the professor said that very afternoon. He's eager to watch your match. Bernhard was a wrestler, heavyweight division, and the captain of the Wisconsin team. Hard to miss Mr. Green, Bernhard told Thomas later, he wore a Borsalino hat and a bomber jacket that looked as if it had seen thirty missions over Tokyo. He was big as a horse with hands the size of pie plates, bigger even than mine, Bernhard said. So I made short work of my opponent and went to meet Mr. Green. He wanted to speak German, so we spoke German while he asked me about myself, my family, my friends, my interests, and finally he asked me what I intended to do with my life. He said he could offer interesting work—second time that day I'd heard the expression—if I was willing to go to Washington for an interview and a psychological test, nothing very demanding but a necessity. Expenses paid. All this was in German, Bernhard said. Naturally I mentioned Russ and you, too, Thomas, but when I said you were an artist at heart he seemed to lose interest. Hell, I thought they could use an artist. But I guess not. Funny thing was, Mr. Green really was a historian, except his histories are all classified. But he liked the cut of Russ's jib—his phrase—so we're going off together to work for the government. Wish you could be with us, Thomas. They want us for overseas work and in the meantime we have a little apartment in Georgetown, around the corner from Kennedy's old house, arranged by Mr. Green.

That aroused Thomas's envy because he was so taken by the romance of the Kennedys, the thrilling rhetoric, the campaign that promised a new kind of government and a new generation to run it. Kennedy's people were idealistic but they were tough, too, animated by a kind of European fatalism. The other important thing was that they weren't from Wisconsin. They were eastern men from Boston and New York, widely traveled, cosmopolitan even, an altogether different milieu from provincial Madison with its earnest protest marches and student manifestoes. Kennedy's people were coastal as opposed to inland-bred, familiar with boats and oceans. They knew how the world worked but in their dissatisfaction were determined to change the rules. And there was one final important thing. Thomas had seen a magazine photograph of the president and his beautiful wife at a dinner party in New York. On the living room wall of the apartment was a portrait of a woman, a nude unmistakably drawn by the hand of Henri Matisse. Kennedy seemed to be looking at it out of the corner of his eye, a rapt sidelong look of admiration and deep respect. So the president-elect was an art lover as well, Matisse no less, the century's greatest artist.

You're being evasive, Tommy. It's not like you.

Thomas looked up from his reverie. Evasive about what?

The boys, his father said.

What about them?

It's intelligence work, isn't it?

I don't know what it is, Pop.

Intelligence work, his father said again, and barked a laugh. God save the republic. Then he signaled for the check and after a moment of thought said, All right, goddammit. I'll stake you a thousand dollars. But that's *it*, not another dime.

Good luck, Tommy. You'll need it.

Thomas smiled at the memory of his father's slapping a twenty-dollar bill on the bar, dismounting from the barstool, reaching for his coat, and hurrying into the frigid Wisconsin night.

He poured a thimble of cognac into his glass. Thomas knew he was drinking too much but could see no good reason to quit or slow down. Alcohol was an old and valued friend, most reliable, always ready to jog your elbow, recollecting hidden memories, specifically the pitch and swing of actual language, language as it was spoken: *But that's it, not another dime. Good luck, Tommy. You'll need it,* the old man's voice in his ear, a raspy voice from his three-pack-a-day cigarette habit, the vowels as uninflected as the surface of Lake Michigan on a still summer's day. His father's voice brought him out of his Camelot reverie. Probably the old man was reading his mind and that would account for his sardonic smile under the raised eyebrows. You always had the face but the trick was to put a voice to the face, and when you did you had a portrait and a story inside the portrait. Thomas had to know what the subject was thinking and the voice he was thinking in. Was that not the crux of Rembrandt's late self-portraits, the voice inside the rutted and disheveled head? Thomas thought that Matisse's portraits were not really portraits, they were expressions of Matisse himself, his own voice and whatever he was thinking at the time of composition. In the case of the portrait of the nude in the New York apartment, Henri Matisse was thinking what John F. Kennedy was thinking, and rapt would not be the word for it.

Thomas's father had not lived to see his first show at the two-room gallery in Greenwich Village, sparsely attended, no sales, until an unexpected review appeared in one of the afternoon papers, so well written and provocative that people were drawn in. They wanted to discover an artist at the beginning of his career, things not fully worked out but the destination not in doubt. Portraiture was at the bottom of the food chain then, overwhelmed by abstraction and expressionism and finally abstract expressionism. Jackson Pollock was a kind of unruly god, no doubt as unhappy in Valhalla as he had been on Long Island, but still with vast supervisory powers, arbitrarily applied. In the end Thomas sold most everything and his prices were not low. He would have given anything to have been able to write a check for a thousand dollars and present it to his father right then, so he wrote one to his mother instead and discovered later that it had been endorsed over to her church. She had come from LaBarre for the opening and had been offended by the many nudes and embarrassed when he introduced her to Karen, braless and alluring, already tipsy on Almaden and weed. Isn't it great? Karen said. Don't you just l-l-l-love it to death? Isn't Thomas divine? she added, pointing proudly to the portrait of her own sweet self nude in bed. She had found the most wanton pose, enjoying herself in the voluptuous folds of a chalk-white sheet. My shroud, she said, and laughed and laughed.

Thomas had tried many times to make a portrait of his mother but had never succeeded. He finished the pictures but they were no good because he was never able to see beneath the skin. They were stillborn. He was never able to settle on the expression, although he was attracted to the disappointment on his mother's face when she looked upon Karen's portrait and had pulled back from it as though she had been physically struck, her abrupt motion dramatic enough to have drawn attention from those around her—who leaned in to look at nude Karen to see what there was about her that had caused such a reaction. Thomas had seen the same expression many times, most often when his father had taken one bourbon too many and had said something coarse or unfeeling. Her son was unable to locate his mother in relation to himself or his father. She seemed to be a star in a distant orbit, now bright, now far away. Her orbit had nothing in common with his orbit or her husband's orbit, yet was studied meticulously by both, studied with the care of astronomers—amateur astronomers, it had to be said. Astronomers who reckoned her orbit in relation to their orbits, not as something unique in itself, and no doubt she did the same. Your mother is fragile, his father said to him once, yet to Thomas she did not seem fragile at all. From her distant location she seemed to rule things, though he reached that conclusion years later, when she was gone. The half-dozen times he had tried to paint her portrait he felt as if he were painting a stranger, but that was no explanation because he had successfully painted many strangers. Strangers were his métier, fifteen minutes' acquaintance and a series of snapshots all he required. But she refused to come to life on his canvas, still a distant star.

He had resolved not to paint his father until he himself was sixty-seven, the old man's age when he died. He wanted to see his father through mature eyes, remembering his voice and his manner when speaking to his patients, his voice so soft it could barely be heard. His voice was his manner. No one delivered more bad news than a doctor, bad news a part of the day's portfolio. At the end of the day his father's voice was wan, used up and wrung out, the wrinkles in his face so deeply etched they might have been carved in stone. At the end of a very long day at the easel Thomas's own face had a similar look, not quite a thousand-yard stare but close to it, the day's events pressing in, the details clear but soon to fade. The day's bad news always lingered but it was his own bad news, not another's, and he was under no obligation to share it, still less an obligation to cure it. Of course a portrait never captured a single moment but an accumulation of moments, and the older the subject, the greater the accumulation. Thomas could begin his father's portrait any time now but he knew he would wait until his own life was more settled, equilibrium achieved, so that he could recollect with confidence. If he attempted his father's portrait now he would end up with a self-portrait disguised as his father's portrait. To some degree all portraits were self-portraits, as all novels were to some degree autobiographical. Trouble was, the artist could never calculate the precise step on the ladder, the exact degree of separation; and the viewer knew even less. That which appeared true was false, and vice versa. A visage was sometimes true and false at the same time, the natural effect of a hundred brushstrokes or a dozen rewrites. Autobiography resided in the style of composition and from that the viewer could conclude whatever he wished or nothing at all. The possibilities were nearly infinite. Thomas thought he would wait before attempting his father's portrait. The old man was entitled to a picture that was his very own. His mother deserved her own, too, but that would have to wait a little longer.

Thomas covered the billiards table and extinguished the bright, green-shaded overhead light. He put his empty glass in the sink, then thought again and fetched the cognac bottle and poured a generous measure, all the while sensing a shudder of disapproval in the room. He took a swallow, allowing the disapproval to gather. That was Florette, glaring at him from her space above the fireplace, irritated that he had drunk something before dinner and one bottle of wine during dinner and was finishing now with cognac, one, two glasses, and, still not satisfied, a third. This was insupportable. Drinking after dinner was dangerous unless you were entertaining guests. After-dinner drinking was unwholesome also, an unfortunate indulgence, in no way comme il faut. Florette was sympathetic toward the bored or the lonely or the melancholic, but not toward drinking as a solution. He tried to explain to her that drinking usually increased loneliness or melancholy but was a specific against boredom because alcohol cast a cockeyed light on your surroundings. That which was dull became vivid. That which was static became a whirlwind. Grief became hilarity because the world was skewed. Thomas turned his back on Florette's portrait and sipped his cognac. The time was midnight. He finished that glass and poured one more, turning now to give a sideways look at Florette, glaring back at her with what he hoped and believed was a rapt expression of admiration and respect.

The room was in near darkness and he was happier now, filled up with cognac, living inside himself, his ghosts gathering around. Florette was there and Granger and the Slovenian bears and the appalling Victoria Granger, a repertory company obliged to follow an unfamiliar script. Thomas was writing it now as he sipped his cognac in an enviable zone of well-being, snug in a well-made house, at that moment without a worry in the world. Something came into his mind and went out again, a fugitive thought that made him smile and then laugh out loud in the empty room. The world was elsewhere and might not exist at all, an incoherent VSOP-cognac milieu majestic in its carelessness. He tasted cognac and blew an imaginary smoke ring from an imaginary cigarette. The wind had come up, whistling loudly in the eaves, perhaps the signal of another storm, most likely not. No storms tonight. The wind produced a strange sharp sound and that was what came from living alone in an old farmhouse, ominous sounds that could put your nerves on edge if you listened carefully enough and paid attention, something he had no intention of doing, conjuring trespassers in the shadows—and then Thomas understood that the telephone was ringing, one bleat after another, six, seven, eight bleats, and sudden silence as the answering machine connected and he heard his own voice and after a pause the voice of another, not at all welcome at this hour. He had not received a telephone call in days.

Thomas? Are you there? I know you're there. Pick up, it's Bern—

Bernhard, Thomas said, his hand on the telephone at last.

—calling from London.

Yes, Bernhard.

Thomas? It's late, I know, Bernhard said. But I'm glad you're still up and about. What are you doing?

Playing billiards, Thomas said.

Who with? Get rid of him.

Nobody. I'm alone.

Playing billiards alone? That makes no sense to me. Billiards is a two-man game.

Not my version, Thomas said.

Bernhard's laugh rumbled down the line and died out.

But I've finished now. I'm going to bed.

I need a minute of your time, Thomas.

Later. In the morning.

This won't take long. And it can't wait.

Morning, Thomas said.

Are you sure you're alone?

Your voice is not clear, Bernhard.

I'm calling on my mobile.

Where are you? And as he asked the question, Thomas knew he had made a mistake, prolonging the conversation. He did not care where Bernhard was. He wanted Bernhard off the phone and now he had to listen to an explanation.

I'm not at home. I'm away for a few days, here and there, the usual. Thomas heard voices and a discreet round of laughter, as if Bernhard were in someone's living room or an after-hours bar. The background language did not seem to be English but it was hard to be certain. Bernhard said, You're sure you're alone?

Thomas said, Victoria's here.

Who's Victoria?

Granger's great-niece. He left her his house. And now she's come to sell it, and she wants my advice as to an asking price. Also, she wants to destroy my portrait of Granger but I won't let her have it. So that's the situation with Victoria Granger. She's from Pennsylvania. Have you ever been to Pennsylvania?

Yes.

So have I. Years ago. I didn't like it. You know what they say about Pennsylvania? No great picture has ever been painted in Pennsylvania. It has to do with the damned light. Eakins is the exception. Goddamned artistic wasteland like the Rocky Mountains. Unless you count Bierstadt, which I would never do.

Thomas?

She's got the house on the market for eight hundred thousand euros, which is a joke. She'll never get it.

Thomas?

She's appalling.

Pauling's in New York.

Well, she's in Pennsylvania.

She's not there, is she?

She was here but she left early. Last month.

So you're alone.

I was happy sitting alone in the dark but now there are trespassers.

Focus for a minute, please.

I'm tired, Thomas said.

I'm going to talk LaBarre. Do you understand?

Thomas sighed. More cloak and dagger.

Jesus, Bernhard. It's late. I don't know what time it is, but it's late and I'm a little drunk. I'm ready to go to bed. No codes at this hour.

It's necessary.

I'm sure it is.

There's a man I want you to meet.

Thomas did not reply. The wind came up once more, whistling in the eaves. He felt a soft breeze, a reminder that the house was not as snug as he thought. Nothing was. He looked at his watch, past midnight; tomorrow had arrived and he had not even noticed. His future was filled with dread, score-settling on Florette's behalf. Just then he thought he heard her voice inside the wind-whistle but the words were swiftly carried away. Bernhard said something but Thomas did not hear what it was, owing to the background noise and the wind in the eaves. Whenever in the past Bernhard had a man he wanted Thomas to meet, trouble always followed. He had been a fool to answer the telephone. What he should be doing was listening to Billie Holiday or Art Hodes but the stereo was at the other end of the room so he had Bernhard Sindelar instead. Thomas tucked the phone between his neck and his shoulder, opened the fridge, fetched the bottle of white wine inside, and poured the last of it into his glass, spilling some, neglecting to notice that it was the two-ounce pony. He threw it back as if it were whiskey and put the glass in the sink.

I want you to make his portrait, Bernhard said. Will you do that?

No, Thomas said.

You wouldn't recognize him, Bernhard said, but he has an un-usual head. Bernhard went on to describe the head but in terms Thomas found difficult to grasp. Late at night, Bernhard's descrip-tive powers often failed. He said, Because of the shape of the head I think you'd like to meet him. Talk with him, get to know him, do his portrait. He's interesting, this man. Not your usual subject. And he has friends, and the friends are also interesting.

I'm not accepting commissions.

Thomas? Pay attention.

It was true his concentration had wandered, Florette's phantom voice, the puddle of wine on the kitchen counter, and his obligation toward Billie Holiday. Swing, brother, swing. Thomas was watching a car wind up the road to St. Michel du Valcabrère and wondering what it was doing at this late hour. People went to bed early in the village, rising at dawn to commence the day's chores. No doubt this was Monsieur Bardèche returning from an assignation.

Did I tell you Granger's niece was here? Grandniece.

Yes. Now listen to me.

A Pennsylvania matron.

Can you get up to Paris tomorrow?

Most unpleasant.

Noon train?

I'm working, Bernhard. I'm working damn hard, day and night. I don't want to go to Paris because Paris will interfere with my work.

You're being selfish, Thomas.

Not now. Maybe later.

—paint his portrait. And the portraits of his friends.

No commissions.

I'm afraid this can't wait, Thomas.

Have to wait, he said. He thought an eternity was about right. He was much happier alone with his ghosts than he was talking to Bernhard Sindelar. He said, Florette was here a second ago but she had to leave. It's late. I'm tired.

What was that about Florette?

Nothing. Forget it.

I'm worried about you, Thomas.

Don't be.

All right. But guess what? Russ is here with me.

Well, tell him hello.

Thomas, Bernhard said. Focus just for a moment.

He watched the car dip over a hill, its headlights lost to view. Country rhythms, Thomas thought, a single car on a lonely road late at night, destination surmised; and still the hubbub in Bernhard's phone, voices and soft laughter. He said the thing that came to mind and knew at once that he had made a mistake, the conversation prolonged once again. He said, I haven't heard from Russ for a while. How is he?

Not so good, Thomas.

What's wrong?

They're not renewing his contract. They've said bye-bye to Russ. Thanks very much. They're giving him a medal. But on the whole, he'd rather be working. So that's another reason to come to Paris, help out old Russ. He's pretty broken up about it.

I'll be there, Thomas said. But not tomorrow and not next week. He paused, searching for the car that had passed over the hill, surely Monsieur Bardèche's green Peugeot. I'm tired, Bernhard. It's late. I couldn't walk across the street. Give me a number, I'll call you tomorrow. We can make plans tomorrow, meet whoever it is you want me to meet. What did you say his name was?

I didn't.

That's right, you didn't.

His name isn't important.

I don't care who he is anyway. I'm not accepting commissions.

Yes, you said that.

Thanks for the call. Give Russ my best. Tell him I'm sorry about his retirement.

Don't hang up, Thomas.

Goodbye, Thomas said and hung up.

He knew he had been abrupt, but Bernhard's conversation made no sense to him, except the part about Russ. Russ should have retired long ago. The idea of Paris filled him with dread, the raw urban chill of January, washed-out Monet skies and bare plane trees, Giacometti women in the Tuileries, a leaden atmosphere of everyone wishing to be somewhere else, a ski resort in the Alps or a beach in Morocco or the Costa del Sol. And he was not accepting commissions. People called you late at night and assumed you were eager for a jolly chat when all you wanted was to go to bed, shove tomorrow a little farther into the distance. Christ, he was drunk, already forgetting what Bernhard had said to him, something to do with a man in Paris, a mysterious man-with-no-name. Thomas lifted the pony glass from the sink and turned out the lights, startled when something brushed against the window and melted into the shadows, a shape darker even than the night. He rapped on the window and looked into the darkness but saw nothing. Through the crack in the window he could smell an alien odor, feral, musky, slightly sweet. He did not think he was imagining it or the dark shape either. Thomas stepped unsteadily to the front door and locked it, something he never did at night. Thomas stood quietly listening but heard nothing. He reached instinctively for the telephone when it rang again, most shrilly.

Russ Conlon said, You shouldn't hang up on Bernhard. He doesn't like it.

Is that right?

Yes.

Well, fuck him.

Thomas, Russ said, a voice of profound disappointment.

What does he want? It's something about Paris, isn't it? He wants me to paint someone, is that it?

No, he doesn't.

That's good. I'm not taking commissions.

Not to paint, Thomas.

That's what he said.

It isn't what he meant.

I'm tired, Thomas said. Also, I'm just the slightest bit drunk. And someone's been prowling around my house. Big bastard. Stinks.

What?

A prowler outside my window.

Russ was silent, his hand evidently over the phone's mouthpiece, for the background noise vanished. When he came back on the line he said, There isn't any prowler, Thomas.

You don't think so?

Trust me.

What do you know about it?

Thomas, you've had a long night. And Bernhard wants to talk to you again. It'll only take a minute.

Not now, Thomas said loudly.

All right, then. Go to bed.

How can I when the phone's always ringing?

Russ laughed at that. He said, We'll call tomorrow.

Thomas said, I understand you're under the weather.

I'm not under the weather.

Bernhard said you weren't so good. Not so good, he said.

I'll tell you about it tomorrow, Russ said, his voice subdued.

Not too early, Thomas said. He was staring into the darkness where the shape had been. The odor of it was still in his nostrils.

Noon, Russ said. Please be home.

Thomas tried to recollect the day of the week. He thought today was Wednesday. No, Thursday, because midnight had come and gone. Tomorrow was at hand. He had no plans for Thursday so he said, Fine.

Noon then, Russ said.

I don't like prowlers.

A nuisance, Russ agreed.

God knows who they are.

Sleep well, Thomas. Tomorrow noon.

I'm not taking commissions, Thomas said and hung up for good.

By eleven Thomas was drinking coffee in his kitchen, sorting through the mail, putting the American newspaper to one side; it was the paper that had gotten him into such trouble yesterday. He carefully stacked the bills in one pile and the gallery invitations in another. There were three invitations to openings in Paris, none of them very interesting judging from the reproductions on the invitations. It was a terrible thing being a young French artist, Matisse always at your elbow; it was like a tyrant routinely judged to the standards of Genghis Khan. That left a letter from his New York dealer, Arthur Malan, announcing that a museum in Holland was interested in one of his Karen portraits. Negotiations would commence at once and it was reasonable to expect a satisfactory outcome. Arthur inquired after his health and hoped he was getting along all right and working well. Thomas read the letter twice, pleased at the news. It had been some time since a museum had come to call. Milwaukee was the first, twenty years before. Then the Art Institute of Chicago bought one. One to MOMA, Francisco to Madrid, another to Centre Pompidou, but that had been five years ago and there had been nothing since.

The stirrings of a renaissance, perhaps.

Holland was a strange place to begin, but why not?

Maybe it was time for another show.

What do you think about that, Florette?

But Florette was silent.

He remained in the kitchen, idly making line drawings of St. John Granger's farmhouse across the way. The day was fine, warmish with brilliant sunshine. He had opened the kitchen window an inch and everywhere he heard the tick-tock of melting water, the drip of icicles from the roof, the slushy sound of shifting snowdrifts in the fields. Also melting were the deer tracks outside the kitchen window, something that had significance for him but he could not remember what the significance was. It was a good day for a drive, perhaps a visit to one of the churches in the west. The roads were clear and at the end of the day he could walk into a café and stand the regulars to a marc, courtesy of the museum in Holland. He looked up to see a pair of blackbirds wheeling in the bright sky, a good omen.

Thomas told himself he was under no obligation to wait for Bernhard's telephone call. Bernhard with his bluster, his certainties, and his insistence on score-settling, and not only his scores but your scores, too. Someone once called Bernhard Sindelar a godless son of a bitch, a judgment that Thomas thought a bit harsh but now he wasn't so sure. Still, they had been friends for sixty years and would go on being friends because they knew so much about each other and Thomas was in his debt, not that Bernhard knew or cared. That was the rub of it, Bernhard's fascination with the patients in the doctor's waiting room, and his inquisitive eye for the patient in most distress. Bernhard had seen something that Thomas had not seen, and thereafter that which had been most familiar became strange yet fraught with meaning. His father's waiting room became a stage set. The low ceiling, the dark walls, the narrow windows that admitted little light, the functional chairs, the tables with their burden of thumbed magazines, the settee by the window that his father designated the smokers' corner, a standup metal ashtray on either side of the settee, the sort of ashtray found in men's clubs. A few years later *The Waiting Room* became Thomas's first attempt at ensemble portraiture, realism in the manner of Georges de La Tour, though his art instructor at the time thought the piece owed more to Norman Rockwell—admitting reluctantly that Rockwell would not have used such somber colors, nor given the room such a shabby appearance, and surely a Rockwell would have had the doctor's kindly face appear at the door of the examining room, summoning the next patient. The doctor was not present in Thomas's waiting room, only the patients, in attitudes of anticipation or dread. He gave his father's likeness to the middle-aged man on the settee, a cigarette in his fingers, nonchalantly turning the pages of *Time* magazine. Bernhard Sindelar was the boy in the wing chair, a bandage on his forehead, a sullen expression on his mouth. The woman next to Bernhard was Thomas's mother, her face turned so that her features could not be seen. Her body was a blur of dark wool, her purse in her lap. Her purse caught the eye of the viewer, perhaps because her fingers were tight on its handle, as if it contained not only her worldly goods but her soul as well. And all the time Thomas was painting the picture he was imagining his father behind the closed door; the force of the picture was the closed door. So he owed Bernhard Sindelar his attention, and when the call came he would answer it. Of course the message would have to do with Florette, some "break" in "the case" that would bring "closure." But no break in this or any other case could bring her back to him, so what was the point?

He did not have the energy for it, or the desire. Desire in all forms had left him and what he wanted now was to live quietly in a simple fashion, keep his own counsel, and find a means to begin painting again. The churches were a beginning, and in their authority and stillness as good a beginning as he was likely to get. He lacked anger of the sort that swept all before it and became a cause in itself, a way of life, the anger of the American in old Bardèche's café not long after September 11. His friends had called him Jock, a boy-man whose anger defined him. His anger was directed at the world as a whole, meaning anyone who got in his way. The lawless world had robbed him of his sight and the lawless world would pay, and if he found a simple café in the French countryside wearing a hostile face, then the café would pay, too. Thomas also recalled the confusion of those in the café, grown silent, divided between sympathy for the blind man and outrage at his behavior and that of his friends, who so enjoyed an atmosphere of menace, establishing a would-be tyranny. They looked at the blind man and saw some aspect of themselves, had the cards fallen differently. When the blind man lunged at old Bardèche and crashed into the table the room went dead still, and then came a heavy sigh of regret and dismay. The episode was so unsettling that he and Florette spoke of little else for days. She said it was as if September 11 were present in the village—at least the aftershocks were. And he had said yes, that was one of the objectives. A month later they were married in the church.

She said to him that night, I don't want us to be a part of the American war on terror.

He said, We won't be.

I can't get the blind American out of my mind.

Me either, he said.

But we're safe here, aren't we?

Of course, Thomas said.

Not one death or a hundred deaths, silent or noisy deaths, public or private deaths, could bring him consolation. What nonsense to speak of consolation. The dead had consolation for eternity, but the living went on living with the consequences of the lives they had made for themselves, and consolation didn't come into it. Thomas became aware of sudden desolation, as if a knife's blade had pierced his heart. The feeling was physical, a sharp pain that reached to his marrow, and for a moment he wondered if he was having a cardiac event of the sort that had killed his father so many years ago, his father looking up from his dinner plate with an expression of the utmost bafflement, carefully putting down his knife and fork, and falling from his chair in slow motion, dead when he struck the floor. He had uttered no sound. Remembering his father's untenable expression, Thomas now sat very still, his charcoal pencil in his hand, raised as though he were aiming a dart at a distant target. His vision blurred, the fields of snow weaving before his eyes. He swallowed once and held his breath, then exhaled slowly, searching for neutral respiration. He felt very tired.

Thomas let the pencil fall and watched as it rolled across the uneven surface of the kitchen counter. The pain stayed with him a minute or more before it eased, slipping away. His sense of desolation remained. The landscape was unfamiliar. The blackbirds had vanished, the field was in motion before his eyes, the land rising to burst forth in snow-capped mountains, Spain beyond. The sun seemed to him less bright though there were no clouds, and for a second he thought he heard Florette's step. Far in the distance he saw the spire of the church at St. Michel du Valcabrère. He listened hard for any sound but he heard nothing. Thomas's breathing was now near normal and he took a sip of coffee, his hand trembling. The landscape appeared to him in shadows until he heard the bells tolling the noon hour and he knew at once where he was, as if he had turned a page in a picture book and found himself looking at the Arc de Triomphe or the wood-paneled bar of the Pfister Hotel. He wondered what his father saw in his last seconds. Probably he saw nothing at all. A religious would assert he had glimpsed the void beyond the stunned expressions of his wife and son, some intimation of the presence of the afterlife; then Thomas realized he had no idea of his father's religious convictions. Father and son talked about politics, medicine, sports, and sex. They often discussed the delivery of bad news, the terms a doctor used and the tone of voice he employed using them. He and his father were not churchgoers, not even on the holy days, and "holy days" was not an expression the doctor would ever use. Thomas's mother took care of the family church business most conscientiously and so presumably did not die bereft. Thomas looked again at the sketches he had made that morning, discouraged at the very facility of the work, five-finger exercises. He picked up the sketches and turned them over so that he wouldn't have to look at them.

Instead, he looked at the telephone with something like dread.

Come on, he said aloud. Get it over with.

Then he gathered up his sketchpad and charcoal pencil and stepped outside into a splash of sunlight. The air was cold and he stood looking at Big Papa, its ridges and summit blending into the mountains behind it. Sunlight blinded him so he began to sketch freehand, not looking at the pad, his fingers guiding the unseen pencil. Almost at once his spirits rose, work a kind of catechism. Thinking was optional. Thomas believed in work the way a pious soul believed in God and the hereafter; that was the way his father approached medicine. In his life Dr. Railles took nothing else seriously. Medicine was life and death, and his family was pleasure, a respite at the end of the day. He was fond of saying that his family made his medicine possible, not realizing that he was telling his wife and son, You are in second position. His wife understood this well enough, as did his son, but much later, when Thomas himself was in thrall to his own work. There was no room for anything else. And then came Bernhard and Russ of the outfit-with-the-unseen-hand, proposing odd jobs, nothing arduous, nothing dangerous, nothing that would interfere with his real work, and indeed he would be able to continue his portrait-making and be amply rewarded. The faces he drew were never less than interesting and a few were exceptional. Thomas liked to remember that Caravaggio began life as a thief.

The sun slipped behind a cloud.

He liked the idea of Karen in Holland.

Thomas, drawing freehand, was looking at the church spire in the distance but not seeing it. Much later he knew he had made a mistake undertaking the off-book odd jobs, his larks. After the encounter with Francisco in the adobe west of Granada, he gave them up altogether. He was in over his head. Florette thought so, too, though she did not know what the jobs were about and by the time she came into his life Thomas had definitively retired. All that remained were the occasional visits by the men and women with briefcases and tape recorders, investigators from Senate committees and historians from the Pentagon, think-tank specialists, and once a harassed assistant from the National Security Council. None of them knew what they wanted, only that, whatever it was, Thomas Railles was the man to provide it. He explained about them to Florette the afternoon in the café when the Americans had made such a scene; he couldn't think what made him tell her except that it seemed the right thing to do.

She had a right to know. They were to be married, after all.

Florette had listened to him in silence, her expression telling him that she did not understand everything he was saying. Later, when she met Thomas's friends, she confided that she liked Russ more than she liked Bernhard. She recognized the particular intimacy of friendships that began in the schoolyard and ended in the mortuary so she did not insist on her point of view. Bernhard she thought not thoroughly aboveboard, not the sort of man you'd trust with an important secret. He had so many secrets of his own, why would he care about yours? She thought his hair was a symbol of his unruly nature, a refusal to domesticate himself. Also, she believed he was ambiguous sexually. She asked, Does he like boys? Thomas's answer to that was yes, and girls, too, and Bernhard saw no reason to keep that side of his life to himself.

Florette believed Thomas was at a disadvantage with Bernhard and Russ; they were altogether more experienced and worldly than Thomas, not to say sinister. Not to say reckless. Not to say rough in their judgments.

You should be careful with them, Thomas.

I think you are sometimes naive.

They take advantage of your good nature. So be careful, please.

I've heard that before, Florette. I knew what I was doing.

Not entirely, she said.

Yes, entirely.

She said, What was a lark to you was not a lark to them.

I knew that, too, Thomas said. Basta.

She said, Thomas, you are an optimist.

He held his tongue. The French liked to equate optimism with innocence, an endemic American condition, and who was to say they were wrong? Yet one evening he was obliged to mention that the French, too, had their moments of sublime naiveté. How else to explain the rapture of the avant-garde with the Soviet system—Jean-Paul Sartre came to mind—an expression of innocence and optimism so wild you could imagine the French intelligentsia en bloc succumbing to a collective case of the vapors.

That's different, she said.

The field seemed to move before his eyes, a deer struggling through the snow, high-stepping and pausing every few yards to move her snout, sniffing, getting her bearings, watching for enemies. She looked exhausted, the soft snow a foot deep, and deeper on the slopes of the hillocks that ran away to St. John Granger's empty farmhouse. The deer had no obvious destination and no companions. In a moment she turned to climb the rise of a hillock, the snow only a few inches deep at the top. She stood quiet as a sentry, turning her head and then freezing to a statue, having heard or sensed something, her snout quivering. She moved her haunches and looked directly at him, an accusing look, the pitiless glare of an executioner. And then she flew off down the slope and disappeared, the field quiet again in the noonday sun. Thomas's fingers danced across the sketchpad, his concentration complete, happy that the strokes were still there, that they had not vanished during the night. Artwork demanded an optimistic temperament, a belief that what was there yesterday would be there tomorrow and the day after tomorrow. Now he was aware of a ringing telephone.

Thomas walked back into the house and picked up, listening to Bernhard's brusque greeting and returning it in kind. He began to sketch as soon as he heard the voice, drawing his friend as he imagined him speaking, voice low and close to the receiver, his confidential take-no-prisoners voice, glowering, thin-lipped, and remorseless. Stripped of its weird code, this was what he said:

Gendarmes in Le Havre had arrested a middle-aged Moroccan on a drug charge, nothing too severe, but his manner was so evasive they decided to investigate further. They found a reason to declare his papers not quite in order and were able then to hold him without formal charge and without—supervision. The gendarmes transferred control to agents of a special branch of the security services, who put him through the mill, one interrogation after another. They found a notebook in his hotel room that yielded no names but did have an address in Marseilles, and the address did lead to names that were known to the agents, though these names were in no way drug-related. The names were political, different nationalities, similar politics. So they ran their middle-aged Moroccan through the names one by one and after a week of round-the-clock interrogation he made one small slip—chemically induced, but no one was watching—in a high unnatural voice, as if he were reciting a classroom lesson.

The Moroccan said, Goodbye, Florette.

They checked the name on their databases without much hope of success. They had no date, they had no place. Florette was a common name in France, perhaps not so common as Françoise or Florence, but common enough. But they were smart about it. One thing led to another and at last they had Florette DuFour, deceased under violent circumstances—"wrongful death"—and next to her name was the name of an official at the American embassy, Paris. Before the day was out Bernhard had been notified. The Moroccan was being held incommunicado in Le Havre, well looked after, receiving medical attention as needed. Would you like to talk to him, Monsieur Sindelar? And what precisely is your interest in this case?

And there we are, Bernhard said.

Thomas sketched in Bernhard's eyes and the comma lines around them, busy eyebrows above.

Damn good police work, Bernhard said.

Yes, Thomas said.

They have him at a safe house in Le Havre, Bernhard went on. He's a tough nut. Self-possessed, I would say. And drugs are the least of his offenses, and as a matter of fact the drug charge was bogus. He's scum. He and his friends have caused trouble wherever they've been, and they've been all over the world. Bernhard sighed, cursing under his breath. They have all the toys of the modern businessman. This one even has a Swiss bank account.

Thomas said, Friends?

Three friends, Bernhard said.

What are his politics?

We think he's a freelancer. They all are. Basque, Al Qaeda, Tamil, Chechen, Polisario. Hell, I don't know. Whoever pays.

Mercenaries, Thomas said.

That's what we think. When Thomas didn't reply, Bernhard went on, Question is, do you want to see him? Watch the interrogation, and when the time comes have a word or two with him yourself. Our French friends are convinced that he and his three chums were with Florette when she died. And that gives you a specific, personal interest.

See him?

I can arrange it. The French are being damn good about it, very cooperative. They owe me a favor.

Has he talked about Florette?

Not yet. He has to rest up. He's been through the mill, you bet. He has to get his strength back. His brains unscrambled. Bernhard paused to laugh. He's hurting a little. He doesn't know what we know. He doesn't know what he's given away or if he's given anything away. The French are superb, really good. You watch through a two-way mirror.

The interrogation?

Yes, the interrogation.

Thomas thought a moment and then he asked, What does he look like?

Look like?

Yes, his face. Thin, fat, clean-shaven, bearded. What?

What do you care?

Small eyes? Large? Thomas penciled in Bernhard's eyes as he spoke, making them large and dead.

Shit, Thomas. Fat-faced, I suppose. Swarthy. What you might expect. He looks like a Moroccan, for Chrissakes. Hard to read, though. It's fair to say his face is not an open book. Do you see what I'm saying here?

Thomas did not reply.

So do you want to see him or not?

I don't know, Thomas said.

What do you mean you don't know?

I don't know whether I want to see him. Why would I? Thomas tried to imagine the encounter. Would the object be to introduce remorse, make Mr. Morocco feel badly? Shout at him? He didn't care what Mr. Morocco felt or didn't feel. In any case, he did not think remorse would be in his repertoire of feelings. Thomas said again, Why would I?

I think he killed Florette, Bernhard said.

I have nothing to say to him.

Is that what you want me to tell the French?

Thomas poured a cup of coffee from the carafe on the sideboard. Without realizing he was doing it, Thomas had given Bernhard a kaffiyeh and a thick, close-cut beard and wire-rimmed eyeglasses in front of his marble eyes. If the Moroccan had, as Bernhard alleged, a Swiss bank account, then wouldn't a homburg be suitable? Somehow Thomas doubted the Swiss bank account, a Bernhard fiction. Would it give him satisfaction to slap the Moroccan? Hit him very hard, make him cry out, perhaps weep because of the pain?

Thomas?

I don't know, Bernhard.

You can look the son of a bitch in the eye—

Why would I want to do that?

I think you ought to. It'll bring closure.

You think so?

Yes, Bernhard said. One of the things that will.

I don't think so, Thomas said.

If it were me—

It's not, Thomas said.

Well, it's up to you. But a lot of people have gone to a hell of a lot of trouble.

Thomas turned to look back at the fireplace, Florette's portrait in deep shadow over the mantle. He wanted a signal from her, some sign as to how to proceed. They had always shared a sixth sense. Thomas listened for her voice but heard nothing. He looked at the sketch he had drawn, a generic Arab such as you might find in a comic or newspaper supplement or on a film set, Bernhard the pentimento. This man was not flesh and blood. He was a cliché, "a Moroccan, for Chrissakes," hard to read, self-possessed, a tough nut. Thomas wondered about his voice, thin or thick, and his eyes.

I'll let you know, Thomas said and hung up.

PART TWO

Bastinado

WATCHED CAREFULLY by the men behind the two-way mirror, the prisoners came in single file up the wide plank staircase, gathering uncertainly at the top of the stairs. The time was noon. Their wrists were manacled so they hung at the belt buckle. One of the guards pointed wordlessly at the chairs placed around the long table and obediently they stepped forward and sat, their hands in their laps so the manacles could not be seen. The four wore the blue work clothes of laborers, the clothes ill-fitting but freshly pressed and starched. The belts were new and would be removed at the end of the interview. To a casual observer they were four workingmen waiting for assignment and ill at ease as to what that assignment might entail, though a closer examination would cast doubt. Three of them were middle-aged, somewhere in the vicinity of forty years old, and did not have workingmen's hands. Middle-class men, one might think, merchants or traders. The fourth was young and thin-faced, obviously nervous, perhaps a university student out of his milieu. The older men were expressionless but alert. Without being told, they had arranged themselves in a row on one side of the table according to age. The casual observer would notice also that the loft was without windows and that the overhead lights were harsh and their metal shades grilled with heavy wire. At a signal the guards stood back, giving the four men breathing room. The guards were unarmed except for leather bastinados. They were dressed casually but carried an air of authority that the prisoners did not, obviously so, since manacles reduced any standing a man might have in such circumstances. Also, the guards were conspicuous by their size and stillness of bearing. They moved sluggishly as if they were half asleep, though naturally their eyes were wide open. The guards were clean-shaven and the four at the long table were bearded except for the boy, who wore a few days' stubble.

As yet, no one had spoken.

One of the guards glanced at the wide mirror on the wall across from the four men, smiled mirthlessly, and placed a pack of Gitanes dead-center on the table, leaving it to the men to work out how they would open the pack with their hands shackled; and then they would be obliged to ask for a light. The four at the table sat staring at the pack, then the oldest rose and reached for it, sliding it toward himself where he could wrestle with the cellophane. He sat down and fumbled with it for two, three minutes, and when he opened it at last he took one for himself and politely skidded the pack laterally to the man next to him. Finally all four were sitting comically with cigarettes in their mouths, waiting for one of the guards to offer a light. But the guards did not move and in fact did not look at them, having found something in the middle distance that required their attention. There matters rested for some minutes until the oldest prisoner—his age and something in his peremptory manner suggested that he was the principal, although he was unprepossessing physically, having a soft body and large liquid eyes—took the cigarette out of his mouth and placed it on the table. The others followed suit and this was comical also, the cigarettes put down just so before each man as if they were party favors. The scene had the look of a vaudeville sketch or a magic act, in any event something worked out according to a script, the payoff or punch line to come. But there was no anticipation of laughter. With studied insolence the guards pushed off from the far wall and stood behind the prisoners and all that could be heard in the room was the slap of leather against skin as the guards began to tap each prisoner lightly on the shoulder with their bastinados.

No one had spoken.

The four at the table began to sweat, even though the room was of normal temperature, perhaps even a bit chilly. The guards were rapping to some prearranged rhythm, the blows growing sharper with each beat. The guard standing behind the chief had reached into his pocket and withdrawn a second bastinado and was using them both like a traps player in a jazz band. The chief showed no particular emotion but continued to sweat as his jaw worked; he seemed not to be thinking of the present but of the immediate future. At a sound on the stairs the guards put their bastinados away and stepped back against the wall. The footsteps grew louder and a middle-aged Frenchman appeared at the top of the stairs. He was dressed in blue jeans and a faded corduroy jacket over a black turtleneck sweater, his eyeglasses perched on the crown of his head. He was reading from a file and did not appear to notice either the guards or the prisoners. He took a chair on the empty side of the table and sat heavily, still reading, wetting his thumb as he turned the pages. Still reading, he reached across the table and took a Gitane from the open pack, lit it with a Bic, and settled back, not without an amused glance at the cigarettes before each man. The Frenchman blew one smoke ring and another, grunting now and then, rubbing his eyes as if he could hardly believe the words on the page. He turned to one of the guards and raised his cigarette hand. The guard immediately produced an ashtray and was rewarded with a nod. At last he put down the file and looked across the table at each of the prisoners, beginning with the youngest and ending with the chief.

Then he turned back to the file.

The four were watching him carefully and did not notice a movement behind them until they heard the boy yelp and nearly fall off his chair. The guard had whacked him on the back of his head with the bastinado. And still the Frenchman did not move or give any sign that something violent had occurred. The boy's face sunk to the tabletop and stayed there.

Did you see that? Bernhard said.

I saw it. He almost took the kid's head off.

No, not that. The older one, the one at the end of the table. When the kid cried out he looked over at him and I thought he was going to start bawling. That set him back, all right.

I didn't see that, Thomas said.

You watch enough of these, you learn.

Learn what?

Learn to look at reactions. Learn to watch the second man. Or the third. I knew what was coming so I didn't have to look at that. I looked somewhere else. I looked at Yussef. That's his name, by the way. The chief of this tribe.

How do you know?

They defer to him. Little things. A shift of body weight. A sideways glance. Look and you'll see a slightly greater distance separating him from the others. And while they almost never look at him, he does look at them. Seeing how they're doing. How they're getting on. This is the first time they've been together. Always before they've been interrogated separately. Yussef had no idea the others were in custody. None of them knew. So today we have the advantage of surprise. None of them know what the others have said or if they've said anything.

Frenchman doesn't talk much, does he?

Relax. My guess is, he won't speak for an hour. God knows what's in that file. Maybe something important. Maybe his laundry list.

Thomas backed away from the two-way mirror and stretched. It was crowded in the small room, he and Bernhard and three French investigators. They had been introduced as Pierre, Paul, and some other name he didn't catch, also beginning with P. Noms de guerre, Bernhard had said. Thomas had been introduced as Mr. Railles, having no need of a nom de guerre.

The Frenchman's damn good, Bernhard said. Best I've seen.

So what does it mean?

What does what mean?

The older one who almost started to cry, according to you.

The kid's his lover. That's what it means.

How do you know that?

Bernhard smiled unpleasantly. Trust me.

I do, Thomas said. I surely do. And what's to be done with this tremendously valuable information?

As a matter of fact, Thomas, it is valuable. It helps to know that

Yussef's just another lovesick oscar. The kid means something to him. So the way to Yussef is through the kid, compris? Antoine picked it up, too. He saw what I saw. Wait a minute, you'll see the kid get whacked again.

The boy was sitting face-down, his forehead almost touching the tabletop. He was gripping the rim of the table, the manacles clicking from the effort.

I'm afraid I don't have great enthusiasm for watching the kid get beaten again.

You can turn your back, Thomas. Cover your ears.

I'll go out for some coffee.

Not recommended, Thomas. Our hosts wouldn't like it, you wandering around in unfamiliar surroundings.

Le Havre is only a port city like any other.

Not this neighborhood.

Thomas saw the Frenchman rise from his seat and begin to pace the floor, still reading from the file. The guard came up noiselessly behind the boy and hit him again but this time Thomas was watching Yussef, whose face was stricken, eyes filled with tears. Yussef's composure vanished, his lips moved as if he were praying, and then he spoke.

He said, Please stop.

The Frenchman looked at him, alarmed. He put his finger to his lips as if he were warning an unruly child. Then he shook his head and went back to his reading. The boy was face-down on the table, a tiny spot of blood on his shirt collar. When he looked up his eyes did not seem to be focused, but it was hard to tell because they, too, were filled with tears.

That was a mistake, Bernhard said.

Hitting the boy?

Speaking, Bernhard said. Speak only when you are spoken to. Those are the rules and they are inviolate. Did you see the look Antoine gave him? I tell you, the man's a great natural actor.

There's a protocol, Thomas said.

Yes, always. Different services have different protocols.

The Frenchman had paused near the stairs, continuing to read, continuing to wet his thumb when he turned a page. And then he was gone, his footsteps echoing on the stairs.

What now?

We wait, Bernhard said.

The boy had not moved, his forehead resting now on the table-top. Thomas knew by his breathing that he was still alive. At the end of the table Yussef stared straight ahead, dry-eyed now, but he had developed a tic in his cheek. The guards were studying the ceiling again. Thomas thought the proceedings as stylized as a Noh play and as hypnotizing: he, too, was perspiring from the effort. His shirt was soaked through. In the room beyond the two-way mirror, no one moved or spoke. The two men in the middle seemed to be forgotten altogether, attention having shifted to Yussef and the boy.

Jesus, Thomas said.

It's interesting, isn't it?

That would be one word, Thomas said.

We'll wait a minute now. We can relax. Antoine won't be back for a while. I expect he'll want to look at the film, to see what he's missed, if he's missed anything. Bernhard pointed to the video camera on the ceiling. Thomas had not noticed it before. He's in no rush, Bernhard said. Our terrorist friends are. But he isn't.

He has all day, Thomas said.

He has as much time as he needs, Bernhard said.

Jesus, Thomas said again.

Bernhard said, You had a pleasant trip from St. Michel?

Yes, Thomas said. Uneventful. Except for the four A.M. departure.

Aren't French trains miraculous? Arrive on time, leave on time, always comfortable. At least the Grandes Lignes and the TGV are comfortable. That's what happens when a society decides to spend money on practical amenities, getting its citizens from here to there comfortably and at modest cost. Of course it takes subsidies, subsidies that never end, but the results are fantastic.

Thomas nodded and did not reply. He was watching the boy, who was still, eyes closed.

The food isn't what it was, Bernhard said.

Thomas looked at him. What food?

Train food. Remember the old TEE? Trans Europe Express. Wonderful food in the dining car, linen tablecloth, nice flatware. Short wine list but very high quality, particularly the wines of Alsace. Once I went up to Brussels and back just to have lunch one way and dinner on the return. I had nothing better to do so I spent the day on the train. Very pleasant time, I remember it to this day. You go through Picardy, so many cemeteries visible from the train. I had dinner with a NATO colonel. Bernhard shook his head sadly.

Distant footsteps announced the Frenchman's return and presently he appeared at the loft stairs, still reading from his file. Thomas noticed that the folder was now an inch thick, so he must have added papers. He stood in front of the long table and removed his corduroy jacket and pulled up the sleeves of his turtleneck. His forearms were the size of hams and covered with black hair. Also, he sported a small tattoo just above his right wrist.

Now we'll see some action, Bernhard said.

Is there no way I can get out of here for some air?

There's a chair in the corner if you prefer not to watch.

I prefer, Thomas said. But he did not move.

So, the Frenchman said. And that was all he said as he wet his thumb and turned another page. He sighed once as he read, a sigh designed to signal disbelief, though the nature of the disbelief was mysterious. Now he nodded at the guards, who noisily took up places behind the prisoners, one guard back of each prisoner. The guards struck one bastinado-tap on the leg of each chair.

So so so, the Frenchman said.

The prisoners seemed to take care to stare into the middle distance.

So, the Frenchman repeated, his voice light, almost cheerful. He turned his head to look at the clock behind him and Thomas noticed that it read five. The Frenchman looked at it for a minute or more, giving the impression that time was infinite. It was eternal. The clock could read five, or ten, or two, or four; the numbers had no meaning. In the Frenchman's domain time meant what he wanted it to mean, neither more nor less. He was his own time zone. Now he lowered his eyes to the file and began to read once again, except his posture was confidential, an attitude approaching intimacy. He had put his foot on the chair, leaning forward with the file in his thick hands, wetting his thumb again and again as he turned the mysterious pages.

Thomas felt the bottom go out of his stomach. His vision blurred and he was afraid he was going to be sick—the wretched breakfast aboard the train. He turned from the two-way mirror and stepped to the rear of the room. He removed his jacket and slung it over his shoulder, aware that he was being watched by the three French investigators. But Bernhard did not turn from the mirror and seemed unaware that Thomas was no longer beside him. A heavy drape covered the narrow window at the rear. Thomas pulled it back a half inch and looked into a nondescript street of warehouses and garages, an industrial street, paper in the gutters and a rundown café on the corner. The street was deserted and then he saw a figure hurrying alone, looking neither left nor right but down at the pavement. The pavement was his destination. Thomas remembered a description of one of the Stasi detention centers in East Berlin. People didn't walk on that street unless they had to, and then they rushed past without stopping and surely not looking because what went on in the building did not concern them. This reminded him of that. Then Thomas felt a hand on his shoulder and slowly the curtain eased back into place. The investigator pointed to the wooden chair in the corner and Thomas sat, waiting for the action that Bernhard promised.

He heard the slap of the bastinado, leather on flesh, and a howl. He heard it again and again. He stopped counting at eight, when the howling ceased. In the sudden silence he forced himself to recall who they were, the events that had brought them to this place, a room in a loft on a nondescript street in Le Havre. They were the men who sat by while Florette lay dying and then with the swift stroke of a knife had finished the job. He was unable to put the ordinary faces of these men to their actions. Did a man truly have the face he deserved? He did not recognize anything about them. Yet one of them, surely the chief of the tribe, had put a knife to Florette's throat and cut—finding that he drew but a thin line of blood. They had been with her for hours while she froze to death, and then they walked away to complete whatever violent mission they had been assigned. Blood was on their hands. That was who they were.

Thomas, Bernhard said.

He looked up.

You should watch this.

Thomas rose and walked slowly to the mirror. The boy's face and shoulders were spotted with blood and he was crying, a soft choking cry of deep pain and something else, humiliation for showing weakness in front of his friends. No doubt he thought himself a coward for not standing up to the blows of the bastinado. But he had said nothing audible. Whatever secrets he had, he kept.

This is the dossier, the Frenchman said.

Here we go, Bernhard whispered.

I have what I need here. You are expendable. The Frenchman drew another Gitane from the pack on the table and lit it, exhaling a great plume of tobacco smoke that hung in the air longer than seemed possible. He said, I have details of four of your actions that have resulted in loss of life. And I have the set of plans for your proposed action, the one in Holland. The one that will never happen.

The chief is about to crack, Bernhard said. His laddie isn't so pretty anymore, is he? Face is pulp. Broken down psychologically. Yussef can't look at him. Yussef can't stand it.

Shut up, Bernhard.

Bernhard smiled thinly and fell silent.

Yussef said, In the name of God. Please stop.

Ah! the Frenchman said. The sphinx speaks!

Please stop, Yussef said again.

But I have no interest in what the sphinx says, the Frenchman said. I have no interest in the sphinx's thoughts except the thoughts that might relate to the events of—he looked closely at the dossier—

November the fifteenth. The events on the mountain near the village of St. Michel du Valcabrère. And the days immediately before and the days immediately after. I have no interest in other things this afternoon. Later on we will explore the other things. For now I am interested in the fate of Florette DuFour.

Thomas looked again at Yussef, his doughy skin and his thick lips, his heavy nose and delicate hands. The fingernails were clean. He would not have been out of place in any souk in the world. His eyes were unnaturally bright now, and still Thomas could not connect him to Florette and the fifteenth of November or anything else. He was a man in a chair, his hands shackled.

With a turn of his head Yussef indicated the boy. He said, His name is—and the name, spoken in Arabic, eluded Thomas.

Yes, the Frenchman said. I'm sure it is.

He is from Rabat, as I am.

I see, the Frenchman said, looking again at the file in his hands.

He is nineteen years old.

An adult, the Frenchman murmured, not looking up.

He is my son, Yussef said.

I'll be damned, Bernhard said. How do you like that?

I ask you not to harm him.

We have no interest in your requests. You are not here to request. You are here to answer. The Frenchman turned a page of the file, neglecting to wet his thumb, and then he made a sudden motion with his right hand and the cigarette fell to the floor. It had burned his fingers.

Sir, Yussef began, but stopped when the guard slapped his shoulder. But Thomas thought he saw a ghost of a smile.

Silence! Be quiet! You are not to speak! The Frenchman resumed his circuit of the room, walking with the slow tread of a priest, and in a moment he had disappeared down the stairs. The prisoners could not see him and for all they knew he was still present. The guards remained at attention behind each prisoner and the room was quiet except for the on-again, off-again whimpering of the boy. He stole a quick glance at his father but Yussef did not acknowledge it, instead raising his eyes to the ceiling and seeming to settle into a meditative state, staring into the heavens or the interior of the Great Mosque, some refuge from the world. Thomas watched him for a minute or more, trying without success to divine his thoughts and to place him in the everyday world. It was easy to see him now in a suit and tie, perhaps the owner of a jewelry store or a salesman of fine carpets, the owner of a small hotel or an arms merchant, the latest gadgetry from Czechoslovakia or the broken-down warehouses of the former Soviet Union. But his face gave nothing away and his thoughts were unreadable. Odd that he should have been trekking Big Papa. Yussef didn't look as though he could walk fifty feet without pausing for rest. Thomas watched him a while longer but learned nothing. The boy was silent also, and the other two were invisible men.

That will be it for now, Bernhard said. Antoine will want to think things over. I'd guess he'll be back in an hour or two. He turned to say something to one of the investigators, who looked at his watch and said, Yes, probably three o'clock. Not before. If it's earlier I can call you if you have a mobile. Bernhard gave him the number and the investigator wrote it down.

Would Antoine like company for lunch?

Antoine likes to dine alone, the investigator said.

Very well then, Paul—

Pierre, the investigator said.

Yes, sorry. Thomas? Shall we have lunch? Oysters at the port?

All right, Thomas said.

What did you think of this? Pierre and Paul and the other one were listening but Bernhard ignored them.

I didn't like it, Thomas said.

Of course not, Bernhard said. You're not trained. You have no experience in these matters. The technique is confusing at first, what's being done and why. The pauses and the silences, the pacing, the entrances and exits. The protocol. Did you know that Chaplin said the essence of performance was the entrance and the exit?

That's what he said. And he ought to know. It's a specialized skill and you should consider yourself lucky that you haven't had to learn it. So we've had a successful beginning. Antoine should receive a medal. You've just watched one of the best, Thomas.

Thomas supposed that was true, performance art in the afternoon, an ensemble, each actor with a role, and Antoine the star. Every society needed people to do their dirty work, taking care to keep the worst of it out of sight, unacknowledged, and deniable. Certainly there was a talent to it, interrogation and torture. Patience, of course, and something else. Thomas smiled to himself. Lebenslüge would be involved. Lebenslüge, he thought, was probably in first position.

Bernhard leaned close to him and whispered, Antoine's worked with the Comédie Française. A valued colleague, I'm told. Gifted at farce. He enjoys playing *Le Misanthrope.* Thrives on it. Can you believe it?

Is that the one where they use bastinados?

Sarcasm does not become you, Thomas. The bastinados cause no permanent damage.

They don't? It looked like they did.

They hurt like hell and there's some blood. Bruising, some scarring, but nothing truly serious. Bernhard turned suddenly to Pierre and inquired, Where do you get them from?

Corsica, I believe. It's the noise that unsettles. The slap.

But there's no permanent damage, Bernhard said.

No, that is correct, Pierre said. Of course you have to know how to use them properly. In the hands of an oaf anything is dangerous.

Bernhard said, They are most often used on the soles of the feet—

But we don't do that here, Pierre said.

It is outside the protocol, Bernhard said.

Those are our instructions, Pierre said.

You can ruin a man's feet. He'll never walk again.

So it's said, Pierre agreed.

Bernhard threw his arm around Pierre's shoulders and moved off a little ways, a private discussion concerning the best restaurant in the port for oysters. When Bernhard mentioned one restaurant, Pierre shook his head and said it had a bad reputation. The freshness of the oysters was in question. There was another place, down the street, called Café Marine. Everyone goes there. Try the belons. While they discussed the merits of belons and papillons, Thomas looked again into the prisoners' room. Yussef continued his meditation, eyes closed. The boy stared glumly at the cigarette that remained at his place. The other two appeared to be dozing, unlikely as that seemed; in any event, their shoulders were slumped and their breathing was regular, their faces slack. In one corner a guard yawned and looked at his watch. Thomas tried to think of it as a picture but the composition was all wrong. A fly had entered the room and was careering here and there around the boy's head. When it lit, it lit in a path of blood and could not free itself. The boy never noticed.

We have our marching orders, Bernhard said, rubbing his hands together. The Café Marine it is.

Let's go now, Thomas said.

Monsieur Railles? Pierre approached him, hand out.

I'm very sorry, Monsieur Railles.

Thomas shook hands, having no idea what Pierre was talking about. He said, Yes—

Your wife, Monsieur Railles. I am sorry for what they did to her.

Thank you, Thomas said.

They are animals.

Yes, Thomas said.

Scum. And your wife was French?

Yes, she was.

We will find the truth.

I hope so, Thomas said.

We are very close now. Just this far. Pierre held his thumb and forefinger an inch apart. The old one, we break his balls. The old one and his so-called son.

Thomas said, The boy is not his son?

Of course not, Bernhard said.

I'm not asking you. I'm asking Pierre.

No, Pierre said. Of that we are quite certain.

Bernhard smirked. See? Quite certain.

Outside, the wind was raw and carried with it the acrid smell of the sea. Thomas shivered and set his shoulders against the wind. The air was filled with soot and woodsmoke from the shops and apartment buildings and boarding houses of the district. The neighborhood had the blank, horizontal look of a Hopper cityscape. They walked for a while, the only people on the street until they arrived at the Rue Georges Braque at Square St. Roch, where they encountered office workers and women pulling shopping baskets. And then Bernhard knew they had taken a wrong turn. They walked along the Rue Georges Braque until they arrived at the Place de l'Hôtel de Ville, a great vacant public space, the buildings dating only from the end of World War II. British bombing had destroyed most of the city in 1943. Le Havre had a strangely provisional look to it, a first rough draft of municipal life. Thomas paused to consider what the quarter might have looked like before the war but Bernhard was eager to find the restaurant and irritated that precious minutes had been lost.

Who cares? Thomas said.

You should care. I want to get back to our French friends in good time. I don't want to miss the payoff, Bernhard said, striding off.

Go on ahead, I'll meet you there, Thomas said.

The day had left Thomas dispirited. He had risen very early. Too many hours on the trains, too many minutes in the loft room watching men being beaten. Antoine's slow-motion pantomime, and nothing to show for it except a low-grade depression in an unlovely port city. Thomas walked slowly in the direction of the harbor. The breeze stiffened and he no longer smelled woodsmoke but the inviting aroma of fish sautéed in butter. The cafés and restaurants were beginning to empty but in most of them a few old parties remained at the zinc bar, nursing calvados or marc, fortifying themselves for the rigors of the afternoon. Thomas stopped at one café and sat at an outdoor table next to an electric heater and ordered a double espresso and a glass of beer. The waiter returned almost at once with the order, slipped the tab under the saucer, and went back inside. At the bar, three of the old parties were laughing about something, an escapade from the sound of it; also, they were flirting with the waitress, a very pretty sweatergirl, a redhead. They called her Grand-mère. Their laughter and flirting made Thomas smile and his mood began to improve. He sat drinking beer and watching traffic in the Rue Victor Hugo, wondering if Hugo as a young man had anticipated that after his death half—no, ninety percent—of the cities and villages in France would have a Rue Victor Hugo. Boule- vard Victor Hugo. Avenue Victor Hugo. Of course he would, the great writer was not shy. Victor Hugo always expected great things of himself. Of France itself he was a little less certain. Thomas remembered that his father had had a street named for him in LaBarre. Railles Crescent, a curvy street in a subdivision west of town, the subdivision called, alarmingly, Sunset Acres.

Thomas paid the bill and resumed his stroll toward the harbor. He was in no hurry to get there and, once there, would be in no hurry to leave. He realized that he was ravenously hungry. The precipice drew near: he was on a perfect knife's edge of indecision, believing one moment that he never should have left St. Michel du Valcabrère, believing the next that his witness was important. Ev- erything that can be known must be known, or that was the theory. But he was unable to identify the line between witness and voyeur. What he had now was an unfinished portrait, far from a work of art. He had tried to see under their skin but could not; the prisoners were as concealed as if they had sacks over their heads and Florette kept getting in the way. He hated what they had done to the boy but found it impossible not to watch, as if he were a spectator in the am- phitheater of an anatomy lesson, the corpse naked on the table. To turn away would have been false but he believed he should have done so. Not for them, not for Florette, but for himself. He had not solved the problem of who was owed what or if anyone was owed anything. Yet here he was in Le Havre.

The streets were crowded now.

In the distance he saw Café Marine, Bernhard waiting impatiently at the door. Thomas slowed down, remembering the look of the redheaded sweatergirl. He thought that pedestrians in this port city walked with a different gait than the inhabitants of St. Michel du Valcabrère, a rolling light-footed walk in keeping with the motion of the sea. Everyone in St. Michel walked with a slight stoop, feet flat on the ground. They moved slowly, in part because of the hills; at times you felt you were climbing the Matterhorn simply walking from the church to the café. The redheaded girl had a rolling gait and a skirt as tight as any ship's hull. Thomas decided he needed a vacation, somewhere warm, somewhere remote, Sardinia or Madeira. Perhaps Ireland, where redheaded girls were native. He would rent a place by the sea and paint from dawn to sundown.

Where have you been?

I stopped for an espresso and a beer, Thomas said.

Took your time about it, Bernhard said.

I was tired. The morning wore me out.

You're not as tired as they are. And you're not hurting.

I saw a redheaded girl. Beautiful girl flirting with some fishermen who were even older than I am. They flirted back so a great time was had by all. I wish to hell I'd had my sketchpad.

They paused at the entrance to Café Marine to look at the écailler's bin, four kinds of oysters and a flock of langoustines on a bed of shaved ice surrounded by a picket line of uncut lemons. On the margins were moules, étrilles, tourteaux, bigorneaux. Inside, they took the nearest table and ordered three dozen oysters and a bottle of Sancerre. The café was brightly lit and not crowded. Through the window they watched the écailler go to work. It took him under five seconds to shuck an oyster. The wine arrived in a heavy plastic bucket, sweat beading its exterior. By the time the wine was opened and poured the oysters arrived on a great pewter tray, arrayed according to type. For a while they ate and drank without speaking. Halfway through, Thomas ordered a second bottle, a demi. Bernhard added half a dozen oysters, three belons, three papillons. Thomas did not care for belons and told him so. Bernhard said the belons were for him, the papillons for Thomas. Finally the tray was empty except for crushed ice. Oyster shells were stacked on three white plates. They ordered coffee and when the waiter asked if they wanted a digestif, Thomas requested a calvados and Bernhard a cognac. The waiter smiled his approval, muttering something about their being serious men. In a zone of enviable well-being, they relaxed and drank coffee. When Thomas looked at his watch, he discovered they had been in Café Marine for exactly forty-five minutes, about one minute per oyster. He was hungrier than he realized.

He said, Do you know what I remembered? There's a street named for my father in LaBarre.

What reminded you of that?

Rue Victor Hugo. Rue Georges Braque.

My old man, Bernhard said. Bookies' Hall of Fame.

How long since you've been back?

I was back last year, Bernhard said. Drove up from Chicago just for the hell of it.

Twenty-five years for me, Thomas said. I haven't even been in the country for ten years.

You wouldn't like it, Bernhard said.

Why not?

It's a spoiled, peevish country. Whines a lot. Mad at everybody. National politics is broken and no one knows how to fix it. Economy's broken, too, because America doesn't believe it has to pay for what it buys. Someone else can pay because America's owed a free ride because it's the beacon of democracy et cetera. But what the hell. Doesn't matter to me. I only work for the government. And I don't want to talk about it anymore.

Thomas nodded, understood. Are we going to see Russ this afternoon?

Problem there, I'm afraid. He's back in the States. His daughter's laid up again.

Caitlin?

No, the other one. Grace. Russ got a call yesterday morning and was on the afternoon flight to New York. He felt he had to be with her and he probably did. He promised to call this afternoon with details.

That poor girl, Thomas said.

She's been through a lot. And she was such a great kid when she was young.

That's true, she was.

That's what everyone called her, a Great Kid. That Grace, isn't she something? From about age thirteen, most poised kid you ever saw. Polite without making a big deal of it. Filled with good cheer, smart as a whip, president of her class at whatever prep school she went to. And a knockout to look at. Then one morning she presents herself at the emergency room at Bellevue Hospital dressed in a bathrobe and nothing else. Wouldn't talk. Had no ID on her. The doctors suspected rape or some other trauma but an examination revealed nothing. No rape, no trauma. She had not been beaten. And still she wouldn't talk. It took three days for Russ and her mother to find her, and when they did, she didn't recognize them. She was away for a year and when she got out she didn't return to college. But at least she was speaking a few words. They never discovered the cause, and believe me, they tried. The best headshrinkers money could buy. But you know what I think? I think it was the burden of being a Great Kid. Maybe she didn't feel so great all the time but that was her identity. She'd walk into a room and everyone would light up. What's Grace been up to lately? Did she have a boyfriend? She's such a Great Kid she deserves the best. That look, that smile. I think it became an intolerable burden for her, a burden as heavy as the world itself. And so she bent under its weight, as she had every right to do.

I knew some of that, Thomas said. Not all.

She broke Russ's heart.

And her own, I would imagine.

That, too, Bernhard said. And her mother's. Broken hearts all around.

That's a sad, sad story.

It's what they used to call you, you know.

What did they used to call me?

A Great Kid. Tommy Railles, the doctor's boy. Just a great kid. Smart at school, a decent athlete, great with the girls, wonderful with older people. And so talented. He'll make a name for himself, that Tommy.

Bullshit, Thomas said.

Bernhard laughed. True, every word. Meanwhile, I was that little prick Bernhard, the bookmaker's son. Come to no good end. Stay out of his way, don't let your boys grow up to be like Bernhard Sindelar. He's a strange one. No one could figure out what I was doing hanging out with you, a certified Great Kid.

That's not the way I remember it, Thomas said.

Maybe that's the reason you didn't end up in Bellevue in your bathrobe, mute, no ID, no explanation. You didn't listen to the things people said because at some level you didn't believe them. Maybe you didn't care. Maybe you didn't think you were so great. And that saved you.

More bullshit, Thomas said.

So we were brothers in that one way. Not caring.

Thomas raised his glass and said, LaBarre.

LaBarre, Bernhard said.

And good luck to Russ, Thomas said and they clinked glasses.

We won't be seeing him for a while. But I have a number. We can call him this afternoon, see how things are going for him and for Grace. The poor bastard. Bernhard threw some euros on the table and stood up.

He said, Let's go.

I haven't finished my calva.

Finish. Antoine's due back any time now. You don't want to miss the afternoon show. It'll be worth your while, I promise.

I'll wait a minute. Meet you there.

You know the way?

I know the way. Bernhard? One question. Did you ever regret not having children?

He said, Are you kidding? What about you?

Yes, Thomas said. I do.

Well, Bernhard said, that's out of the way. Au revoir, he said, and then he was through the door and walking back the way they had come.

Thomas finished his calvados and ordered another espresso, a double. He watched the écailler pull a canvas over his bin, secure it, and walk across the street to a café on the corner. Lunch was over. The streets filled up in midafternoon with shoppers, the light now an oystery gray, the sun trying to pierce the cloud cover but failing. The air seemed to him to smell of oysters. Thomas imagined his children with him, everyone giddy from the oysters and wine. There would be a son and a daughter, or two daughters and a son, or two sons and a daughter, surely no more than three. They would be playful with each other and with him. Their mother was away someplace. They had all come over from London on the car ferry, everyone having agreed to a fine lunch in Le Havre before driving to Honfleur for the evening. They would meander a few days in Normandy before going on to Paris, where he had a show at the end of the week. They would stay at the Ritz, adjoining rooms on the second floor. Across the square was Florette's atelier and at dusk with all the lights on they would gather at one of the bedroom windows and watch the models go about their business, Florette in constant attendance. The children were in their twenties, unmarried and footloose. He hoped to God none of them thought of themselves as a Great Kid. One of them wanted to be a doctor like her grandfather and the others were uncommitted. When they asked his advice as to a suitable career he told them, half seriously, follow your heart—and they roared with laughter and said, Oh, that's very helpful, Papa. Can we take that to the bank? His daughter, the doctor daughter, put her hand on his wrist and pretended to take his pulse, causing a fresh round of giggles.

Thomas smiled and finished off his calva, put a banknote on the table, and shrugged himself into his coat. When he stood he was lightheaded and had to grip the tabletop to steady himself. But the episode came and went in an instant and then he was outside in the cold and wind.

Of course there could have been three sons or three daughters.

But that would be unlikely.

He bought a newspaper at the kiosk on the corner and headed for the port. He had no idea what the French shipped from Le Havre, probably grain, manufactured goods, wine and cheese. Camembert was not far away. At the quay were two Korean freighters and one from China. There were no American vessels and he wondered if the nation's maritime industry had gone belly-up like so much else. Bernhard would have the answer; you had only to ask. Thomas was trying to work something out in his head but the thought was elusive, sidetracked as he had been by his fictitious children. He didn't want to spend any more time than absolutely necessary in Le Havre, a noisy, unlovely city. Was it not possible after all to conclude his business today? Wasn't the point to get it over with and return at once to St. Michel du Valcabrère?

He watched a slender black cat slither along the water's edge of the quay and disappear under a pallet, a grace note to the bustle of the docks, a clamorous environment of arrival and departure. The Chinese vessel loosed its hawsers and was under way, sliding from the quay dead slow. Seamen on the other ships halted work to watch it go. Thomas saw the captain looking out from the bridge rail, his face as impassive as a sack of wheat. He was a Chinese of middle age, balding, heavy pouches under his eyes; it seemed that he had seen every port in the Orient and elsewhere. He turned to say something to the helmsman and then looked directly at Thomas, conspicuous in his city clothes; and no doubt that was what caused the captain to offer a halfhearted smile and a gesture that was either a wave or a signal of dismissal. Thomas returned the gesture but the captain was already concentrating on the business at hand. A French tug nosed up to the freighter's bow, took a line, and the two vessels crept forward. The freighter towered over the tug. Thomas saw the captain gazing out to sea, heavy clouds gathering in the west, the wind stiff. If he was alarmed at the weather he did not show it.

The Chinese vessel gathered speed as it approached the outer harbor, oily smoke spilling from its twin stacks. Then the freighter seemed to shudder and stall, the captain sounding the horn, two sharp blasts—and a sloop appeared suddenly, swinging around the freighter's bow, heeling dangerously to starboard, a collision narrowly avoided. The yachtsman, in oilskins and watchcap, shook his fist at the freighter, gathering speed once again. The sloop was beautiful, as sleek and composed as a fish, whereas the freighter was a crustacean, a formidable, slovenly, and unruly crustacean, careless in its habits. The yacht made for a mooring and the freighter lumbered on, and it was the freighter that enlisted sympathy, a hard-luck vessel, rusting where the deck met the hull, her paint peeling. The name on her stern was unreadable but her home port was Shanghai. The captain looked as though he had been born with the boat, a mariner who had been at his trade for many years; neither he nor his ship felt any need to keep up appearances. The captain emerged again at the door of the wheelhouse, smoking a cigarette. There was something stalwart about him, an old man on an old boat sailing an ancient route, and when the boat went into drydock or was taken apart for scrap, that would be the end of him, too. There would surely be other ports of call as he made his way south and then east—Aden, Mumbai, Singapore, Haiphong. Thomas continued to watch the Chinese freighter as she made her way beyond the lighthouse breakwater into the foul channel weather, waves crashing over her bow. The tug was long gone, the freighter abandoned to her fate. Thomas continued to watch but he did not register what he saw. He was thinking of his own business and how it might be satisfactorily concluded. He did not have all the time in the world. His questions were few in number but subtle in their own way and essential. He was formulating them as he turned his back on the quay and walked in the direction of Rue Georges Braque, wondering now what there was about the port city that inspired Braque. Tramp steamers and sailing ships would be part of it, and the low sky and the channel's gray water. He walked quickly because he had an errand to run before he arrived at the safe house.

In the loft the prisoners remained as they were, seated, still shackled. The guards had disappeared. In the room behind the two-way mirror the three investigators played cards in the corner. Bernhard stood at the mirror watching the four at the long table. They appeared to be dozing. Now and then one of them would move his head or his arm or shift uncomfortably in his chair. The clock now read eleven, Antoine Mean Time. Thomas noticed that the men continued to sweat.

Bernhard looked up when he entered the room.

He said, Antoine wants them to wait some more, do some private thinking. Antoine believes in the persuasive power of boredom combined with anticipation. I think when he says anticipation he means dread. Fear of the known, Bernhard said and chuckled. Fear of the bastinado or worse. So we wait.

Thomas said, Where is he?

Somewhere in the building. He has an office. And in the office there's a cot. I imagine he's catching forty winks so's to be alert when things recommence.

Will he show up soon?

No telling. Antoine sets his own timetable.

I'll wait, then, Thomas said.

I'm glad to hear it. I had the feeling you were copping out.

No, Thomas said.

I thought you were on your way to Aquitaine.

I'm not, Thomas said.

So where have you been?

The quay. Watching the boats, specifically a Chinese freighter. Old boat, rusted, paint peeling, a veteran in every way. Her skipper is a veteran, too, but he damned near smashed up a sloop. Looked that way anyhow, a heavyweight beating up on a girl. By the way, what do the French export from Le Havre?

Wine and cheese. A few automobiles. How the hell would I know?

I thought you might.

I don't, Bernhard said.

From the corner of the room Thomas heard the slap of cards and desultory conversation. Boredom was general in the safe house.

Thomas said, How well do you know him?

Antoine? Not very well. I don't imagine anyone knows him very well. Maybe his wife does, if he has a wife.

What's he like?

Keeps to himself. He's an interrogator, for Chrissakes. He has his own outlook on things. He's focused on his work, his calculated entrances and exits, his questions. When he has any. He's not the sort of man you have a beer with at the end of the day. Why do you want to know?

I want to talk to him.

I don't know about that, Thomas. We're here at his invitation, on his sufferance. He's repaying a favor, settling a debt, if you like. We're lucky just to be here to watch how he goes about things. He's an artist. Antoine's like you except his métier's more specialized.

Thomas grunted and thought to hand Bernhard the newspaper he'd bought at the kiosk near Café Marine.

He said, Here's the newspaper.

Bernhard said, Thank you, Thomas, and immediately began to read an account of the latest car bombing in Baghdad.

Thomas stepped to the back of the room and watched the card players. He did not recognize the game. The room was filled with tobacco smoke. When Pierre threw in his hand, Thomas touched him on the shoulder. Pierre excused himself and they retreated to the curtained window.

Thomas said, I'd like to see Antoine.

Antoine? Pierre frowned, a look of grave doubt.

Yes, Antoine.

He's resting now.

I know he is. Perhaps when he wakes up—

Pierre took a step back, worried that he had been misunderstood. He is not sleeping, Monsieur Railles. He is preparing.

It's important to me, Pierre.

To speak to Antoine.

Yes. I have a question for him. Perhaps two questions. And then, soon after, I'll be on my way.

I don't know, Monsieur Railles. It's irregular.

I am greatly indebted to your service, and the French government. The apprehension of these four . . . Thomas let the sentence hang and continued, Of course I have my own interest in this crime. My wife was very dear to me. I cannot think that my interest would conflict in any way with your interest. And therefore I would like to speak to Antoine. It's possible I could be of help.

Pierre stared at him, judging his sincerity. After a pause he went back to the card table and picked up the mobile phone at his place. He looked at it skeptically, then dialed a number and spoke softly into the receiver. Thomas could not hear what he said but after a moment Pierre closed the phone and with a nod of his head walked to the door. After a glance at Bernhard, absorbed in the newspaper, Thomas followed and they descended the stairs and went through a corridor that led to the rear of the house. Pierre knocked on a door, opened it, and stepped aside to admit Thomas.

Antoine was sitting in an easy chair, smoking and reading his file. There was something on the CD player at his elbow but the sound was turned low. He put the file aside and went to his desk and perched on its edge. There was no cot in the room. Antoine gestured for Thomas to take the easy chair. In the sudden silence he recognized the music at once.

Thomas said, That's Billie Holiday.

Yes, it is.

I have the same recording.

Yes, it's very popular. What can I do for you, Monsieur Railles?

Thomas said, Thank you for seeing me. I know it's irregular.

Antoine said, What do you want from me?

I want to see him alone. Without the others.

You want to see Yussef?

Yes, without the boy or the other two.

You want to interrogate him?

I want to explain one or two things to him and then ask a few questions. It would not be an interrogation.

This is not in the protocol.

I know that, Thomas said.

We stick strictly to the protocol. One interrogator.

I appreciate that.

Antoine leaned back, stretching, his hands on his hips, yawning. He stubbed out his cigarette in an overflowing ashtray and stared thoughtfully at the ceiling. He was silent a minute or more and then he lit another cigarette, offering the pack to Thomas, who shook his head.

What is it you wish to do to Yussef?

Not violence, Thomas said.

Truly? No violence?

I won't touch him.

You have every right—

I know. I know I do.

I talked to people in your village. Florette was very well liked. Everyone spoke highly of her, the kind of woman she was. They spoke well of you, too. And they are suspicious people, as you know.

Thomas smiled. He said, Country people.

I, too, am from the country.

I am also, Thomas said. From the state of Wisconsin.

Two country boys, Antoine said with a dry smile. What are we doing here?

They listened to Billie Holiday, "Twenty-four Hours a Day" ending and "Let's Dream in the Moonlight" beginning, the singer in fine voice. Thomas knew the band at once, Teddy Wilson's. Wilson's piano was unmistakable.

Thomas said, I heard Wilson once in Milwaukee.

Antoine said, You are a fortunate man.

I never saw Billie Holiday in person.

Nor I, Antoine said.

How much do you know about them?

Not as much as I pretend. But you know that.

I guessed, Thomas said.

My file is a prop, like Yorick's skull or the iguana that lives under the porch. I can tell you this. They are Moroccan-born and they are surely the ones who were with your wife in her last hours.

What were they doing on the mountain?

I do not know, Monsieur Railles.

Are they affiliated with any group?

They are angry men. I believe they are freelancers but Islam is their cause. The old one, Yussef, is an intelligent man. Probably university-educated. In the early stages of the interrogation they gave away some information, not very much. And I am not convinced all of it was genuine. Now this news is between the two of us, because I have sympathy for your position. It is not to be shared with my colleagues or yours—

Bernhard.

Yes, Bernhard.

He is not a colleague.

You are not attached to the embassy in Paris?

I am a painter in St. Michel du Valcabrère. Portraits.

That does not disqualify you.

Nevertheless. I am not in the spy business. I did odd jobs for Bernhard but that was many years ago. I am telling you this as earnest of my bona fides. My interest here is strictly personal.

Bernhard deceived me.

He meant no harm, Thomas said.

Deception among friends is ugly business.

He is grateful to you. I am, too.

Antoine lit another cigarette, staring thoughtfully at his hands. His fingers were yellow with nicotine.

Thomas said, Does Yussef speak English?

No, of course not.

French only? Of the civilized languages, he added with a smile.

Yes.

Thomas said nothing more, waiting for him to make a decision. Antoine was a man very easy with silence, so he would not be hurried or provoked in any way. He finished one cigarette and immediately lit another. His office was devoid of personal items, photographs or mementos of any kind. Thomas wondered what he did in his off-hours and then he remembered Bernhard's remark that Antoine spent vacations with the Comédie Française, his specialty being Molière.

Antoine said, What do you intend to do exactly?

Thomas said, First, a portrait.

And then?

Talk to him.

All right, Antoine said. You have two hours.

More than enough, Thomas said. Thank you.

You are welcome. Good luck.

You are most kind, Monsieur—

Antoine, the Frenchman said.

Then I am Thomas, he said.

Goodbye, Monsieur Railles, Antoine said.

Antoine

SHACKLED HAND AND FOOT, Yussef sat alone at the long table. The guards had been told to wait on the ground floor. Thomas mounted the stairs slowly, a step at a time, lugging the easel and the Conté crayon box and Canson paper and cardboard tube that he had bought on Rue Victor Hugo. When he entered the loft the echo of his footsteps seemed much louder than the echo heard through the loudspeaker in the room behind the two-way mirror. When Thomas assembled the easel and opened the crayon box, Yussef looked at him without expression, and then he closed his eyes. Thomas busied himself with the Conté crayons, not the type he was used to but serviceable. He backed up to the mirror and looked hard at Yussef, the shape of his head and his shoulders, the way his hair grew, his ears, the droop of his mouth, and the almond shape of his eyes. After a moment Thomas came around the table and lifted Yussef's shackled hands from his lap and placed them on the table-top. The prisoner did not resist, nor did he open his eyes, expressive even when closed. Yussef had adopted the weary, passive look of any man whose fate was in the hands of others. Thomas thought that Yussef was willing himself to disappear, vanish in a puff of smoke like a djinni. Thomas wondered about his ancestry, parents and grandparents, what they did for a living and where they lived and the relations each to each. What had brought him to this place, a safe house in an industrial district of Le Havre. Yussef smelled thickly of disinfectant and cheap hair tonic. The disinfectant, hair tonic, and sandy smell of the artist's paper gave the room the air of a hospital laboratory. Thomas moved left and right to inspect Yussef's face in profile, the noble nose, the sagging chin, the smooth brow, and the relation of the parts to the whole. All this time Thomas displayed a sly smile, one his friends would not have recognized. Finally he moved behind the prisoner and lifted his chin with two fingers and held it a long moment.

Good, he said in French.

Keep it like that.

Then Thomas went to work, drawing at speed. He barely looked at his subject but concentrated instead on line, beginning from the center of the sheet of paper and working out. The face was all in his memory anyway. He intended a credible likeness, some impression-ism around the edges but essentially a realistic portrait of the sort sought by actors or impersonators. He spent time on the mouth and more time on the eyes, which now seemed to him expressive of infinite serenity. They were old eyes, the lids wrinkled, deep pouches beneath them. He did not know enough of Yussef's milieu to judge whether his was a face attractive to women; probably it was. There were no obvious defects except a small scar on the chin, and a scar was often an interesting abnormality. When Thomas looked back at Yussef he saw that his eyes were closed once again and that his chin had sagged. It didn't matter. He was almost finished and he knew the chin by heart; not such a difficult chin in any case. Quite an ordinary face until you got to know it well, know it in its range of emotions, and then it became as familiar as your own, more familiar unless you spent your life looking into mirrors.

Thomas spent a few extra minutes tidying up and then he stepped back and looked at what he had wrought. He had always been proud of his draftsmanship and was proud again. He had set out to make a portrait of a certain kind and had succeeded, and now he was empty of energy and very doubtful that he had succeeded in Yussef's terms; what he could say with confidence was that the draw-ing was without sentimentality. He had no idea of the shape or aspi-ration of Yussef's terms. Yussef's terms would be his own. Come to think of it, he did not know Yussef's surname. The man before him was a species of ghost. As quietly as he was able, Thomas turned the paper around so that Yussef could see it. Then he walked silently around the table and stood behind the Moroccan and with a fierce motion pulled his hair. Yussef's eyes popped open and stayed open.

Florette, Thomas said softly into Yussef's ear.

I was her husband.

Thomas took a chair on the other side of the long table, moving it so as to give Yussef an unobstructed view of Florette DuFour. Florette's gaze was open and surprised—as if she had just heard something that interested her—and she was dressed as she was the Sunday afternoon she took her walk on the mountain. Thomas had drawn her head and her torso, careful to preserve the true color of her pink shirt, but the glare from the grilled lights overhead gave her skin a waxy sheen. It broke his heart to look at what he had done but he looked and kept looking nonetheless. Hers was the face he knew better than his own. As the silence gathered, Thomas glanced at Yussef, who was staring intently at the portrait, leaning forward in his chair. His manacled hands were back in his lap. Thomas thought he saw a minute shake of the head but he couldn't be sure.

I will tell you a little about her, he said in French.

So that you will have a personality to go with the name.

Florette was not an ordinary woman, though I suppose that could be said of almost any woman. No one you knew well was ordinary—and if you loved her, then she was not only not ordinary but unique. And you can see some of that in the portrait if you look carefully. Of course what you are seeing is my version. Some of the other men in her life would have a different version. But none of them were artists.

Thomas described Florette's childhood—her mother, her violent father, her Tante Christine—and her first marriage, to the postmaster, and the postmaster's early death. He described her dream of becoming a couturier in the Place Vendôme. And he described the Place Vendôme, its location in the First Arrondissement, the Ritz Hotel across the way. Thomas told Yussef about the boy in the village, the one with the motorcycle, the one who reminded her of

Jean-Paul Belmondo, the actor. Surely you know his work on the screen.

Yussef seemed to shrug, neither yes nor no.

Yes, of course you do. Half the women in France were in love with Jean-Paul Belmondo. Moroccan women also, I believe. He was tall and muscular, an athlete, a dangerous presence. Women are often attracted to dangerous men.

In the end Florette settled for him, Thomas, instead of the Jean-Paul Belmondo look-alike, as she settled for knitting sweaters instead of designing evening gowns fit to be worn by the wife of the president of the republic. She was a woman of great good cheer who nevertheless kept much to herself, as he did. But he had decided after long thought that what she kept to herself was not as important as what she disclosed to him. So that part of her life that she kept to herself was a trifle, not worth worrying about. I was bothered by it for a while and then I wasn't bothered because, as I said, I had my own secrets.

You, too, have a wife.

The boy's mother.

Perhaps your story is not so different from my own. You meet a woman and spend hours talking to her, telling stories, making a narrative of your life. Two narratives merge until they are the same narrative; one story, two characters, and when you are together long enough other characters find their way in, family, friends, children if you are lucky enough to have children . . . Thomas paused, unsettled again by the echo in the room and the knowledge that behind the two-way mirror were Antoine, his three investigators, and Bernhard Sindelar. He wished it were only himself and Yussef but there was nothing Thomas could do about the eavesdroppers. That was part of the bargain he had made, and eavesdropping was what they did for a living. Thomas allowed the silence to lengthen; Yussef had not taken his eyes from the portrait.

I am certain that you, too, have made false starts, participating in actions that had an unfortunate aftermath and which you are not proud of; you are filled with dismay and reproach yourself later.

These would include false starts with women, perhaps involving a lack of patience, or of sympathy, or a failure of nerve or intelligence. But you may also be the sort of man who blames people for getting in your way. They should know better. They got what they deserved. There are many such men, from all cultures. And women also. Women are not excluded.

How old are you?

I would say forty-five.

Younger than I am by twenty years.

So you may look forward to many more false starts, though it's possible you have another outlook on things. You do not make false starts or admit to them when you do. Or you make a point of avoiding compromising situations altogether. In any case, your false starts—your crimes, to make my meaning plain—would differ from mine owing to your nationality, your religion, your politics, and your sense of honor. Or, to be exact about it, your attitude toward them. The crimes remain the same. But you will be judged as I will be judged. Our common fate. No exceptions.

Thomas stood and walked again around the table so that he was standing behind the prisoner. He watched Yussef's muscles stiffen, his back bowing, his hands palms-down on the tabletop. Yussef expected another hair pull or similar indignity, though more painful because he expected it. Thomas gripped the back of Yussef's chair and spoke softly as they both stared at Florette's portrait. Thomas described his work, how he began in grade school and continued through high school and college, dropping out in his last year, moving to New York, and the four days following John F. Kennedy's death. The assassination was a world event, all the world mourned. But you cannot imagine how it affected us in America. The unthought-of was suddenly thought, in front of our eyes, bright as day. So for those four days and for some days thereafter we thought of nothing else. This one thing crowded out all the other things. Of course there were places in America where he was not mourned but those places were foreign to us, an exception. What a hold John F. Kennedy had on our imagination!

I expect you were a toddler about that time, perhaps not yet born.

I believe I became an artist that day, though I'm ashamed to say it. Still, when you are rocked to the soles of your feet by an event you tend to remember it, work it over in your mind, attempt to assimilate it. I mean, when the unthought-of becomes thought.

Thomas furnished a few details of how he went about finding his subjects—or how they found him—and how he went about looking at heads. Looking for the unspoken thought and searching also for inherited physical traits. He drew Yussef's attention to Florette's full lips, a legacy of her mother. When you are trying to create life on canvas—that is, when you are trying to see life in a new way—these are the qualities you pay attention to.

I have had an exceedingly fortunate life, he added.

I was dealt a fine hand and I played it well.

For the most part.

The false starts are an exception.

I was responsible for a man's death. I think he had a great soul. He was a communist, a Spanish communist, most passionate. Spaniards are passionate and Spanish communists are notably, willfully passionate. He was not a saint. Do not mistake him for a saint. He was not a holy man. He was a good man in a bad time, a man of belief. That belief sounds tarnished now, a bit foolish even. Most of us believe that train left the station many years ago, the cattle cars filled with corpses. He argued that he believed in the system, not the men who made the system, and that is surely a distinction of a kind. He lived an adventurous life and it seems likely that blood was on his hands. I did not pull the trigger that caused his death but I was in the vicinity. A friend wanted a message delivered and I obeyed; it is possible my friend was deceived also. And Francisco died, not that day but days later. I made his portrait. It is one of my best and it hangs now in a Madrid museum, "a gift from the artist."

We all have blood on our hands, from deeds large and small.

The idea is to atone and go on.

No regrets is a fine sentiment if you are a cabaret singer.

So I have had an exceedingly fortunate life.

Dealt a fine hand, played it well.

Except for crimes here and there.

I do regret that I have no children.

So you have the advantage there. I envy you. He's a fine-looking boy. You resemble one another. You must be proud of him. It's hard for me to believe—and here Thomas walked around the long table and stared into the mirror, his back now to Yussef—that the boy was part of this, the business on the mountain near St. Michel du Valcabrère. Allowing a woman to die. Hastening her death. A woman your boy had never met, a harmless woman on her Sunday walk. I cannot believe he would willingly participate in such a— Thomas sought the word in French and came up with "scandale."

He would be following your instructions.

Papa, who is this woman? What does she mean to us?

How does it help us if she freezes to death?

Tell me what to do.

Thomas watched Yussef in the mirror. He had betrayed no emotion at any point in the narrative and betrayed none now. His eyes remained fixed on the portrait, staring at it as if willing it to life; or to disappear, vanish from his sight. Then Thomas heard a noise, a kind of whir. A bumblebee had flown up from the first floor. After a few passes in front of the mirror it landed on the long table and began to circle Yussef's shackled hands. It moved drunkenly, its yellow patch of pelt twitching. Its wings were huge, moving slowly as it reeled here and there on the tabletop. Not air-worthy, Thomas thought; the bee was aerodynamically unsound. Yussef drew in his hands, the first decisive movement he had made since Thomas had pulled his hair, forcing him to look at the portrait. The bee continued its reconnaissance, laboring forward, resting, moving again, always in circles, closing on Yussef's shackled hands. Its hairy body concealed its stinger but Yussef knew it was there. The bee had stopped an inch from Yussef's wrist. Thomas watched Yussef's fingers begin to tremble, and the bee crept forward. Yussef's hands were steady now. He had evidently concluded that fear of the known trumped fear of the unknown, and that to move his hands would be a provocation. The bee rested and seemed about to tumble on its side—and then it rose, hovering a moment, rising and circling until it beelined to the stairwell and disappeared back the way it had come. Thomas had been watching it in the mirror and realized now that the bee was a trick up Antoine's sleeve, an airborne version of Yorick's skull or the iguana under the porch. Full of surprises was Antoine, and pure dumb luck that the bee had landed on the long table.

Thomas allowed the moment to settle and then, still not turning from the mirror, he said, So the boy went along with your plans. Whatever the plans were.

But when he said, What does this woman mean to us? what was your answer? How did you identify my wife as your enemy? Was it something she said? She didn't know you. You had never seen her before. She meant nothing to you. She meant nothing to your son. And she meant everything to me.

But I've said too much.

We did care for each other. As your wife cares for you, I imagine.

Did she complain when you took the boy with you? Where are you going with him? He is too young to be involved in such business. Let him grow up before he joins you in your work. Perhaps she said nothing. Perhaps she held her tongue, kept her thoughts to herself, including the prayer that he would return safely.

Did she know where you were going? And what you intended to do when you got there? That would have been Florette's question. Western women are inquisitive. They are often at their best when in an inquisitorial frame of mind. As they almost always are. They don't give up. Often it's necessary to confess to them in order to keep a good face on things. But perhaps your wife has a different outlook. Perhaps she does not feel entitled to press her questions. And in that case she would be a most unusual personality. I would say a most unusual mother. I'd like to meet her. But, alas, that is an impossibility. We will never meet.

What exactly is your work? What brings you to this place?

And with that, Thomas seated himself and lit a Gitane, his first cigarette in fifteen years. His throat caught but the spasm passed and he blew a fat smoke ring into the middle distance, where it hung, well defined, for a surprisingly long time.

One hour later they were still at the long table, Yussef having said nothing, Thomas deep in thought. He had said what he could say. There was more but he did not choose to give voice to it. This was the last act, and when he glanced at Florette's portrait she seemed to him as mute and lifeless as the Moroccan. He suspected she was as disgusted with the loft as he was. Thomas let his thoughts meander until they settled on the late St. John Granger, his supposed experience in the war and the life he had made because of it. What had brought him to the farmhouse at St. Michel du Valcabrère? What brings us anywhere? You take one turn instead of another, you meet one woman instead of another, you have good health or you don't, luck vies with misfortune, you break down and arrive at Bellevue in your bathrobe on a Saturday morning or—what was his father's antique phrase?—you pulled up your socks and got on with things. Your heart adapted to changing times. Your body did. Or it did not and you passed your days in a muffler of regret. And that was what they called intelligent design.

Thomas was drowsy in the heat of the room. It seemed to him that he had talked for hours, though in fact it had been little more than thirty minutes. The time was just about up, though he assumed Antoine would not be exact about the time. Thomas believed he had made no particular impression on the Moroccan, who had remained expressionless as he scrutinized the portrait of Florette. Thomas had heard somewhere that Moroccans were an especially handsome people, tall and fine-boned, lithe in their movements, often with vivid blue eyes. They were said to have a subtle sense of humor. Of course that was according to Western norms, Nordic in origin. Yussef was not handsome, not even very interesting; there was something ponderous about him. Thomas wondered if his people were from the city or the desert, if somewhere in his ancestry there were renowned hunters with falcons on their forearms, austere men at home in the sand. Thomas had no idea how he would go about making Yussef's portrait if called upon to do so. But that was a commission he would refuse in any case. Then he was back in the billiards room with St. John Granger, the old man laughing in his dusty way at some gossip he had learned from Ghislaine, mischief in the village. He missed Granger. Granger was, in his problematic way, an anchor to windward, a ghostly anchor to be sure, but one that held.

Thomas wondered if it was wise for him to remain in St. Michel. His wife was gone, his closest friend was gone, and if he remained the face before his eyes would be the Moroccan's. Dead or alive, he would be unforgettable. He decided then to finish the portrait of old Bardèche and after Bardèche there would be other villagers to paint and before long he would have canvases enough for a show. Arthur Malan had been pestering him for a year. Make yourself visible, Thomas. Get out and about. Collectors must be reminded that you are still alive and at work. Thomas lit a Gitane and thought about working again, not in St. Michel but somewhere unknown to him, another country altogether, perhaps someplace near the sea. He could take up fishing. One thing was certain. He wanted no more to do with Le Havre, the loft room, the two-way mirror, or the man seated across the table.

Yussef made a guttural sound as he tested the strength of the shackles, *click-click* as he forced his wrists apart just so far and no farther. His forearm muscles stiffened with the effort. He held the pose a moment, then brought his wrists together and let them fall to the table.

The Moroccan said, My name is not Yussef. I don't know where they got that name. It is a pretend-name. They found it in a telephone book.

As to why I am here, you must ask your friends on the other side of the looking glass.

And my work is my own affair.

I am here against my will.

The voice was soft, the French grammatically correct but badly spoken with a coarse accent. Thomas did not look at him. He gave no sign he had even heard him. This was not an act performed for the Moroccan's benefit. Thomas was beyond artifice. He was listening but he was indifferent to what he heard because the truth was not present, not the exact truth of Florette's last hours. The loft room had its own special aura and truth was not part of it. A useless exercise, he thought. Better he should have remained in St. Michel du Valcabrère. Nothing he could hear would ease his heart. Lies wouldn't and the truth wouldn't.

You're afraid, I can see, the Moroccan went on after a moment. Yes, it's evident. Are you certain you want to hear what I have to tell you? It is not pleasant. You will not like to hear it. Give some sign so that I will know what to do.

The Moroccan had a slight lisp, more pronounced in the echo of the loft than it had been in the few words he had spoken hours before. Thomas remembered Florette telling him her father had a lisp, and so in her last hours she would have been reminded of him. Thomas shook his head, thinking of this. There was no end to it.

I did not kill your wife, the Moroccan said. She was a foolish woman who stumbled and broke her ankle. She was careless. She was not dressed properly. I had nothing to do with her ankle. Her ankle did not interest me. We carried her some distance on a litter. I do not know how far. She was heavy and complaining every minute and the load was difficult. The trail was steep. Surely you know it well, the turns and switchbacks, the steep dips and rises. A pig of a trail. The task was not simple. The boy tires easily and the others were unhappy at the delay and our compromised position. So when we found a clearing among the trees we set her down and considered what to do next. We needed a solution. We had business of our own. She interfered with our business. We were on a timetable. Then the snow began and it became impossible for us to go on with her. She was unconscious.

We did not ask for her to be there.

She was not our responsibility.

She was on her own. She was dying.

And I saw to her. We continued on our way.

You killed her, Thomas said.

An act of mercy. When I drew the knife, she was already dead.

Thomas looked into the eyes of the Moroccan. He believed he was listening to a rhapsody, a kind of romance, Scheherezade's thousand and one nights of epic verses and in every one a kernel of truth. Find it if you dare.

The responsibility is yours. Why would you allow your only wife to put herself in such danger? You are a restless people, you Americans. You expect others to clean up for you. We did what we could and then we went away and the result is that I am here where I do not belong—

Florette was French, Thomas said.

American or French, it makes no difference.

Why did you think she was American?

She spoke English.

Florette spoke English?

Yes, the Moroccan said with a smile. Once she said "Please."

She said "Please." And so you left her to die.

We had business. And what of our situation now? We are insulted. We are shackled. We are beaten.

And Florette is dead, Thomas said.

You must hope that God has welcomed her. The Moroccan paused a long moment, looking at his hands. He said softly, Inshallah.

As he listened to Yussef, Thomas felt dissociated, as if he were in a dream state, some place from which it would be difficult to return. He watched the clock on the wall. At the moment the prisoner began to speak of the difficulty of the trail, the hands began to move counterclockwise, and when they stopped the time was two. The hands moved in spasms, indicating that they were being turned manually. Thomas wondered why Antoine chose two. Why not twelve or ten? But Antoine had his own way of going about things, his protocol, so probably there was a logic to it. You could always find a logic to things if you searched intelligently and looked for patterns, connections of things one to another. You could explain the way of the world by cause and effect or blind luck or misadventure or a random god in the universe; but explanation did not always lead to comprehension, a ready grasp of the matter. Frequently it didn't. Thomas waited to see if the Moroccan had anything he wanted to add, some fresh detail of how they did their duty and the part played by the foolish, careless American woman. He had spoken only a few sentences. But evidently there was nothing more because he remained silent. Thomas considered moving close to him, whispering something dramatic in his ear: You will rot in hell. But perhaps he wouldn't rot in hell. God might welcome a Moroccan. Who knew what God intended? God-in-all-his-mysterious-ways, God whose shadow never diminishes, the Moroccan an inscrutable instrument of God's will. Probably the prisoner would be amused to hear his words, the infidel American rattled at last. The solution was to kill him or leave him alone. There was nothing in between.

Thomas stood and stretched, lightheaded from sitting for so long. And then he remembered the wine and the calvados he had drunk at lunch; that would account for the drowsiness. It would not entirely account for the bad taste in his mouth, nor the knot in the pit of his stomach. Nothing more to hear, he thought. This is the end of it. Thomas stepped to the easel and dismantled it. He rolled up the Canson paper, wrapped it in glassine, and inserted it in the tube. He collected his Conté crayons and returned them to their box. From habit, he spilled a little turpentine on his hands and patted them dry with his handkerchief. The smell of turpentine had always been a mnemonic for him, vivid recollections of portraits made and anticipation of those to come. But it did nothing for him now. He intended to leave everything at the safe house—no telling when they might need artists' supplies. The portrait he would burn when he returned to St. Michel du Valcabrère. Thomas looked around to see if he had forgotten anything and noticed the pack of Gitanes and the lighter on the table and put them in his coat pocket, and when he did, his hand brushed the hard leather of the bastinado. Antoine had insisted he take it, in case the Moroccan got ugly. Thomas picked it up, weighed it in his hand, and looked in the mirror at

Yussef seated at the long table, his eyes cast down. Thomas thought about using it, a smart slap across the eyes. Easy to break his jaw, dislodging teeth in the process. Such a blow would be extremely painful, pain that would be hard to forget. With a broken face and ruined eyes, the Moroccan would never look the same. And at the same time he would be recognizable wherever he went, an object lesson. Look! That was what the American did because his wife died, an eye for an eye—except his wife lost more than an eye. But the American was satisfied, even though the scales were not in balance. The American would remember the blow forever; he would hear the bones crack, hear the Moroccan's scream. He could carry that memory for the rest of his life, perhaps recall it on his deathbed, when it would bring a smile to his face. Perhaps the blow was hard enough to kill him, score evened. And that memory would be more satisfying still. It would never be forgotten. His memory of Florette and the Moroccan would coexist, in perfect balance. It would be with him every time he painted a portrait; the sound of leather against bone, bones breaking, broken skin slick with blood, the scream as the Moroccan fell and lay still, slowly dying. That would take awhile. Thomas turned away. He turned with a heavy heart, bile in his mouth. He weighed the bastinado in his hand, then slipped it into the tube that held Florette's portrait. He looked around one last time. That seemed to be everything.

Thomas stood quietly a moment, irresolute, uncertain how to proceed. He sensed the faces at the mirror, Bernhard and Antoine and the investigators. Probably they expected him to do something or make some comment to the prisoner. He had earned the right to do so. But what was there to say? Words seemed to him beside the point, unequal to the burden he carried. With difficulty he gathered up the easel, the tube, and the crayon box and stepped to the stairwell. All this time he had not looked directly at the Moroccan or given any indication of what he thought or what he intended to do with the information he had been given. It was dark at the foot of the stairwell. Thomas paused at the top, then lumbered on down the stairs and deposited the supplies in the hallway. The guard looked at him with a sympathetic expression but did not speak. Thomas slung his overnight duffel over his shoulder and stepped out the door into the gray dusk of early evening, coal dust in the air, a light snow falling.

Thomas retraced his steps to the port, easily finding Café Marine. The écailler nodded at him and said he had plenty of oysters left. Thomas gave him a thumbs-up and went on through the door. He sat at a table and ordered an espresso and a calvados. The room filled up with seamen, their voices loud and jolly. The *patron* presided with the formality of a bishop, a bishop with fast and competent hands, easily holding three beer glasses in one hand while with the other he pulled the porcelain handle. All the time he was pouring he was conversing, now with one customer, now with another, a man happy at his work. Thomas ordered another espresso and lit a Gitane; the air was heavy with tobacco smoke and beer smell. He drank the espresso but saved the calvados for the third cup. For the first time that day he felt at ease—the first time in months, he amended. Thomas took off his jacket and placed it over the back of his chair and listened to the confused conversation around him. The language was so filled with argot and punctuated with laughter that it was hard for him to parse—mariners' talk mostly, ships in the harbor and ships due to arrive, the weather forecast. Mariners paid attention to the weather. Then a shadow fell across the table and a hand rested heavily on his shoulder.

May I join you?

Thomas looked up and indicated the empty chair.

Thank you, Antoine said. A waiter appeared at once and he ordered a Dortmunder, the big glass.

I like a glass of beer at the end of the day, Antoine said.

We all need something, Thomas said.

This is a favorite café of mine, Antoine said. The *patron* is an old friend. Surprising the things you hear in a seamen's café in a busy port. But I never come here for business. This is my off-duty place. I come here to relax with friends, have a glass and a plate of something.

How did you know where I was?

In a strange town, people always return to that which is familiar. Unless they are fugitives. And sometimes even fugitives, the ones who are less than clever. Bernhard told me where you had lunch.

And where is he?

Wondering where you are, Antoine said with a smile.

The waiter arrived with Antoine's Dortmunder and a platter of langoustines. The beer looked so appetizing that Thomas ordered a glass. They ate for a while without speaking, Antoine shelling the langoustines with the speed and skill of a surgeon. When they were finished, Antoine signaled for another plate and two more glasses of Dortmunder. He talked about seafood in Le Havre—homard, turbot, coquilles, all superb. The restaurants were not grand but they were not expensive, either. The food was honest and the prices likewise. Unfortunately, he himself was obliged to live in Paris, a filthy place where cheating was an art form. There was no trouble in France that the elimination of Paris could not cure. But alas, all the world loved Paris, so Paris will be with us a while longer. It is said that America would not be America without Paris for Americans to go to. Also Germans, the brutes. But I will tell you this. The Parisians are not comme il faut.

Thomas smiled at that.

You live in the Pyrenees. Do you like it there?

I do. It's quiet.

Landlocked, Antoine said.

Yes, landlocked.

Mountains bother me. You never feel caged?

Not caged. Sometimes it's lonely.

The winters are a tragedy, Antoine said.

Very cold, Thomas agreed. Snow to the eaves.

But the food. Bah!

No, Thomas said. The lamb from the Pyrenees is the best in France. Duck is a specialty, the confit. Cassoulet is a specific against the cold. You know cassoulet.

Of course, Antoine said. But it's heavy. It's anvil food. It's not like this—he held up a langoustine shell and let it drop—light and succulent, food for an angel. And it's a dangerous place, the Pyrenees.

Yes, it is.

Antoine looked at him with an apologetic smile. I meant the bears.

Oh, yes.

The imported Slovenian bears. Vicious creatures.

Thomas nodded and took a swallow of beer. He was trying to work out an idea that had just come to him. The idea depended on a rental car. But surely in a port city there would be rental agencies.

Antoine held his beer glass to the light, watching the bubbles. And how did it work out for you?

You heard it. What did you think?

We didn't learn much. He's an awful little shit. He's like a reptile. He responds only to provocation. By the way, contrary to what he said, his name is Yussef. I was surprised that he talked to you at all. Something you said must have angered him. I imagine it was your own confession.

Could be.

You were most candid with him.

I said what I wanted to say.

So you were involved with Francisco.

Yes, Thomas said.

I knew him. I had occasion to interview him once. An interview, not an interrogation. We had no charges against him. Even so, he was a difficult interview. I liked him immediately. I knew at once who you were talking about. Poor Francisco, he carried a whole world inside his head. A walking archive. It was an ugly business for him at the end. A betrayal, I imagine. Someone sold him out.

Thomas looked sharply at the Frenchman.

Not you. This one can be traced back to Bernhard.

Thomas said nothing to that.

Americans are so quick to act. So slow to repent.

Thomas looked at his watch. Too late to engage a rental car.

Well, Antoine said and raised his glass. To Francisco.

Francisco, Thomas said.

Antoine turned in his chair and held up two fingers. The waiter nodded and said something to the *patron*.

I watched you with the bastinado, Antoine said. You had ideas. But you dismissed them. Put them out of your mind.

I did. What was the point of another beating?

To watch him suffer. Listen to his jaw crack. Watch him weep. Beg for mercy. Lick your shoes. They're not good with pain, these four. Yussef is better than the others but not by much. They don't mind watching violence but don't like it when it's them. And of course Yussef is protective of the boy, who may or may not be his son. We think he is. Your Bernhard disagrees. Bernhard says he has a hunch, and he always follows his hunches. A DNA test will settle the question.

I've known Bernhard for many years, Thomas said. We grew up together in a small town in the American Midwest. His hunches are usually sound. Thomas stopped talking while the waiter put down the Dortmunders on fresh coasters. From behind his back the waiter produced another plate of langoustines. Thomas said, Bernhard was a wrestler in college.

Sweaty sport, Antoine said.

Isn't it, Thomas said.

So you didn't use the bastinado.

No, Thomas said.

You decided to spare him. Yussef.

Thomas shook his head. Sparing didn't come into it. I don't care if he's spared or not spared. My wife is gone. What do I care what happens to him?

Antoine moved his beer glass in circles on the table. Surely you believe in justice, he said. A society cannot function without it. I am forced to conclude you are without conscience.

Civic conscience, Thomas said.

Yes, civic conscience. The other kind, too.

Perhaps, Thomas said.

I watched you. I watched you very closely. You wanted to do it. I wasn't sure you wouldn't beat him to death, one blow after another. I know that look. It's the look of anticipation of high satisfaction, justice done and seen to be done. No question of the Moroccan's guilt.

My satisfaction doesn't come into it, Thomas said. He took a long swallow of beer and looked again at his watch.

And if we release him tomorrow?

You won't.

No, we won't. You're correct about that. He'll be with us for some time. Yussef and the other three are working for someone, we don't know who. But we'll know everything before we're through. This business takes a strong stomach, you know. Patience. Attention to detail.

Good luck with it, Thomas said.

Perhaps it also requires a certain ideology.

And what would that be?

Antoine smiled and gave an exaggerated shrug. Anger, he said. The common denominator of all ideology. A belief in the righteousness of your cause and the squalor of all other causes. It comes easily to me because I am fundamentally a policeman. It's not for everyone, however. You need an excellent memory. You must never, ever forget. Forgetfulness leads to—

Forgiveness? Thomas said.

No, not that. Do you think so?

No, I don't. What were you about to say?

Antoine smiled again. He said, A lack of focus. A lack, I should say, of zeal. He raised his finger, struck by a new thought. Do you know Brahms's German Requiem? Of course you do. I should not have asked. He composed it after the death of his mother. I have always wondered whether his requiem counseled remembrance or forgetting. Not the death, surely. The circumstances of the death. The Requiem Mass, after all, is a call for the repose of the souls of the dead. It is to comfort those who mourn. Well. The Germans have much to remember. But they had not so much in 1867, when the piece was first performed. They had no more to remember than any other people, perhaps less because they were disorganized. The mountain of bones came later. So we must be careful what we forget, wouldn't you say?

We must not be thoughtless, Thomas said.

I think you mean careless, Antoine said.

They are the same thing, Thomas said.

I am sorry about my German lesson. Sometimes I talk too much.

Tell me. Do you like the Brahms?

Yes. It is not Verdi or Mozart. But it is very powerful.

It is sublime, Thomas said.

Antoine smiled and did not reply. Instead, he made a gesture that indicated the subject was not worth pursuing.

I'm glad we met, Thomas said.

Yes, I am too. I am glad we had a chance to talk. I can tell you this, for your ears only. Your wife was not a target in this business. The encounter was as Yussef described it. A chance meeting.

Thank you, Thomas said. I never doubted it.

Bernhard had another idea.

I know he did.

He is more conspiratorial even than the French.

His family background is German.

That explains it, Antoine said.

I worried about Bernhard's idea for a while and then I didn't worry.

If it had been someone else, the someone else would have met the same fate. Or if there had been two or more walking in the mountains, same thing. All four were armed, even the boy. Nothing was going to keep them from their business.

And that was?

Antoine shook his head. He said, We have classified your wife's death as a terrorist act.

Of course, Thomas said.

Antoine swallowed the last of his beer, leaned back in his chair, and looked around, raising his eyebrows at the café hubbub, every-one talking at once. He said, Do you plan to spend the night in Le Havre?

If you can give me the name of a hotel —

Antoine called for the check while he took a business card from his wallet and scribbled a name and address. He said, Show them this at the reception.

Thank you again, Thomas said.

It's a small hotel but very clean, of moderate price.

Antoine stood and they shook hands warmly.

I wish you luck, Thomas said.

Godspeed, Antoine said.

Will you let me know what you discover?

Assuredly, Antoine said. What I can. What is allowed.

Your information will stay between us.

The waiter delivered the check and Thomas put his hand over it. He said, Please allow me.

The Frenchman hesitated, then nodded politely and walked away, stepping delicately as if his feet hurt. At the door he turned and gave a wave that was half a salute, and then continued on out the door without a backward glance.

Thomas was relieved to be alone at last in a place where he was unknown. The same could not be said of Antoine, the focus of covert glances from the men gathered at the zinc bar. Thomas had noted that two of them put on their hats and left when Antoine appeared. Thomas ordered a glass of wine and a dozen oysters and sat back to collect his thoughts. But he was unable to gather them coherently so he contented himself watching the show, the bar arguments and laughter and the young lovers at the corner table who were making plans for the evening. His attention was noticed because the young woman caught Thomas's eye and winked; he tipped a glass in her direction. The *patron* continued to pull the porcelain handles, glass after glass. There were fewer now because the café was beginning to empty, and seemed emptier still in the bright glow of the overhead lamps. Thomas could not remember the last time he sat in a café alone, doing nothing, without even a newspaper, merely watching the action, such as it was. His oysters and wine arrived and he began to eat slowly, taking a tiny sip of wine with each oyster. The lovers left arm in arm and he wished he had a pretty friend to share an oyster with, someone he knew well but not too well. God, he was tired. He could sleep where he sat, put his chin on his chest and say night-night. If the girl he knew well but not too well was sitting beside him he would have to talk. He was tired of talking. And if he had this girl, what would he do with her? When the moment came, if it did, he would be forced to plead headache, sciatica, osteoporosis, or something alarming like shingles; perhaps a dangerous heart condition. Thomas glanced at the door and saw that the snow had ended; there had only been a dusting, no difficulty for the morning's drive. He hoped the hotel had a map. The next time he looked up the café was almost empty, the *patron* whistling to himself, cleaning the glassware at the bar sink. A second glass of wine arrived, and when he looked curiously at the waiter, the *patron* nodded from the bar; on the house.

Tell the boss thanks, he said.

I will do that. Are you and Monsieur Antoine friends?

Yes, we are friends.

He is a famous policeman, you know.

So I've heard.

He is from here, Le Havre. But he is often in Paris on his official duties. He and the *patron* play cards . . . The waiter described the games they played and what they ate and drank during the hands. Dortmunder for Antoine, Heineken for the *patron*. The policeman was a cautious bettor, the *patron* reckless. Thomas listened and nodded, murmuring something now and then, when the waiter looked over his shoulder and backed away, pulling out the empty chair at the table.

You forgot this, Bernhard said, setting the cardboard tube on the floor next to Thomas's duffel. He sat in the chair the waiter held for him and said, Scotch, neat.

Thank you, Thomas said. Now go away.

You didn't say goodbye. I had no idea where you were.

You found me. I'm tired. Go away.

Bernhard drummed his fingers on the tabletop, waiting for the Scotch neat. When it arrived he took a swallow and said, Prosit. Thomas called for the check.

That was quite a performance back there, Thomas. Jesus, I thought you were going to give him your life story. You damn near did. And you didn't get much for it, did you? Francisco was a mistake on your part. Clever stunt with the portrait, I have to admit that. Only time I saw the little prick shaken. Maybe not shaken. Maybe only stirred, but at least you got a reaction. That was something. Antoine was impressed. But you walked away. Just walked away from him.

The waiter arrived with the check and Thomas paid it, and the first one, and laid on a heavy tip. He looked at the card Antoine had given him and hoped that the hotel was close by. Fatigue had overtaken him. His eyelids weighed a thousand pounds. He did not believe he was thinking straight and wanted out of Café Marine before he said something better left unsaid.

But we'll have time to talk about that and Francisco, too. You cut a little close to the bone there, Thomas. Francisco's a verboten subject. He's way back in the cupboard, out of sight. We don't talk about Francisco even when you don't use his name. You know that, for Chrissakes. I can't imagine what you were thinking of.

I'm going to bed, Bernhard.

So long as you understand the seriousness of it—

Thomas reached down for the cardboard tube but had to steady himself on the chair—a shudder of dizziness. Finally he gathered both the tube and the duffel in his arms and stood blinking in the bright glow of the café.

I had a call from Russ, Thomas. His little girl died last night. She ate something she shouldn't've.

Thomas looked at him but didn't say anything.

Funeral and burial are private. New York City. I sent some flowers in both our names but you'll probably want to call him, so here's his mobile number. Bernhard passed a piece of paper across the table and Thomas took it.

He's holding up all right, Bernhard said. Probably it's a relief.

I doubt if it's a relief, Thomas said.

Whatever it is, he's holding up all right.

Thomas said, An overdose?

Russ didn't say. And I didn't ask.

Such a pretty girl, Thomas said.

A great kid, Bernhard said.

Goodbye, Bernhard. I'm going home.

You can stay if you want. Antoine likes you. On principle he doesn't like Americans. He doesn't like me. But fuck him, my future plans don't include Antoine. This is my last gig with Antoine, although you can bet I'll have a chit to call in. Antoine owes me.

Why?

I delivered you, Bernhard said.

I'll be in touch, Thomas said.

Don't forget about Russ.

I'm not likely to, Bernhard.

You're awfully damn flaky these days. Hard to talk to. Hard to get close to.

That's what they say, Thomas said.

But listen, Bernhard said. I have a new venture. Want to hear about it?

He leaned close and began to talk but Thomas was no longer listening. He tried to imagine the grief that would come from losing a child. The pain would be never-ending. Every time you saw a child of that age on the street or in a schoolyard you would have to turn away. You would turn away generally, from your family or whatever you believed in. Because it was a child you would hold yourself responsible. You would eventually recover but never completely. You would be like someone who had lost a limb: the memory of it would never cease. An image came to him suddenly, Russ Conlon sitting slumped on a bed in a hotel room eating a room-service meal, his elbows on the table. The table was covered with a bone-white cloth. In the middle of it was a slender vase with a single pink rose. But why was Russ in a hotel room? He kept a pied-à-terre in one of the downtown neighborhoods. And why was he alone? The television set was tuned to a news program and Russ watched it while he ate methodically, his arms moving like semaphore. Between bites he sipped ice water. His face showed no expression as he ate, one forkful after another while the newscaster droned on, another car bomb in Baghdad, an unknown number of casualties but as yet no group had taken responsibility. On the screen was a burning vehicle and two women weeping. Russ pushed the plate aside and sat, still slumped, his hands in his lap. He did not look up when a waiter arrived and wheeled the table from the room. The image was so powerful that Thomas put his hands over his eyes. He did not want to see more, if there was more to be seen. He suspected that someone else was in the room, out of sight. Russ was not alone.

But by this time Thomas was on the street, nodding to the écailler. Snow had ceased but the wind was busy. The streets were empty. Thomas had no recollection of leaving the café but he had his duffel and the cardboard tube. He showed Antoine's card to the écailler, who looked at it and said that the hotel was only a few blocks away. A very nice hotel, very clean. The service was good. Thomas thanked him and walked off, but when he saw a taxi he hailed it and rode the three blocks in warmth and silence.

Early the next morning Thomas was in a black Citroën driving east from Le Havre. The day was chilly and overcast, iron-gray clouds hanging so low they seemed close enough to touch. He drove slowly through Bolbec to Yvetot and Rouen. He thought of stopping to see Notre-Dame cathedral in Rouen, the one that Monet liked so much he painted it twenty times in one year. But Thomas decided not to; he preferred Maître Monet's versions. Between Rouen and Amiens he passed from Normandy into the Department of the Somme. Beyond Amiens the land flattened some and the clouds lowered some more. The wind died. The roads narrowed and traffic thinned. The terrain seemed featureless, the villages uniform and lacking charm. They were working villages, and certainly to the inhabitants they would not seem charmless. But they were anonymous. Lahoussoye was followed by Franvillers. This was farmland although here and there were small copses, tufts of trees growing from the bald earth. Everywhere in this part of France were the cemeteries, carefully maintained and watched-after, more carefully than the villages. There were French, British, German, Canadian, and South African cemeteries, the result of the slaughter along the Somme salient in 1916 and later. Some of the cemeteries were very large and others quite small, only a few hundred graves, some with names and others blank. *Mort pour la France. Died for King and Country.* Thomas wondered about American graves, but they were farther south, near Soissons and Belleau Wood. He easily identified the German cemeteries because of the Gothic crosses that marked each grave in stone so dark it was almost black. *Gott mit Uns.* There were few billboards along the route. In January the cemeteries were deserted. Tourists and relatives of the dead tended to arrive in the more temperate seasons, combining a remembrance-duty with a holiday. At Albert, Thomas turned north along the sluggish River Ancre, passing through Aveluy and Authuille on the way to Thiepval. He spied the memorial beyond a slowly rising hill. The surrounding countryside seemed to him as desolate and barren as a desert but it stood to reason that the inhabitants would object to such a description. It was not their fault that a million men died in the vicinity; to them the Department of the Somme was home.

With the help of one of the gardiens, Thomas found the name of St. John Granger. It was engraved high up on one of the inner vaults, so he could not read it no matter how hard he squinted. He thought he would give up. The name was there according to the register; there was no need for him to verify it. Still, he had come all this way. Thomas stood on the stone floor of the vault and looked upward into the shadows, name after name and all of them too far away to read. The wind picked up again and it was cold standing in the central arch of the memorial.

Would this help?

An elderly Englishman in a beret and a Barbour coat, trimmed military mustache and a very red face, was at his elbow. He handed Thomas binoculars.

Thank you, Thomas said. He focused the binoculars and commenced to scan the vault's ceiling at the place he understood Granger's name to be. But he had no luck, moving the glasses back and forth through the rows of names.

Can't find him, Thomas said.

A relative? the Englishman said.

Friend, Thomas replied.

Mine's a school chum of my father's. He died some years ago and I promised him that if I ever got near Thiepval I'd find the name and say a few words. So I found him and said a few words.

You kept the promise, Thomas said.

I did, the Englishman said. What's your name?

Thomas put out his hand and said, Thomas.

No, I mean the feller you're looking for. I've good eyes. I'll find him.

Granger, Thomas said. First name St. John.

The Englishman pressed the binoculars to his eyes and stared up into the shadows. Thomas moved off a little and lit a Gitane, first of the day. Standing under the vault, he was surrounded by names, so many names that if they were raindrops they would be a deluge. He and the Englishman were the only visitors except for a young couple sitting on one of the stone benches, talking earnestly, their heads close together. Thomas thought they were on a tryst, working out a difficult romantic problem. Suddenly they kissed passionately. Their arms flew around each other's necks and Thomas turned away, grinning. Problem solved.

Got him, the Englishman called.

Thomas walked back to where the Englishman stood and took the glasses from him, aiming where he was pointing. It took a minute to find the name and the rank. So that much of the old man's story was true. But staring at the name, Thomas was unable to connect it to his friend, whose bones lay under a tree in St. Michel du Valcabrère. The disconnection was perverse. It seemed to him a monstrous joke.

Thomas handed the binoculars to the Englishman and thanked him.

The Englishman said, An old friend?

Thomas said, Very old.

I was puzzled when you said he was a friend. I still am. These men died almost ninety years ago, their bodies never recovered. The bones are scattered all over these fields. Thousands upon thousands of troops. The Englishman looked at him blandly but his blue eyes were ice cold.

Family friend, of course, Thomas said. Our two families have been friends for generations. Thomas smiled, feeling seven kinds of fool; but he had made a recovery, and it was plausible.

You're not supposed to smoke here, you know. Respect for the fallen.

I was just leaving, Thomas said.

The regulations are quite clear, the Englishman said.

Goodbye, Thomas said and strolled off past the young lovers and down the gravel path to the parking lot. Along the way he pitched the Gitane onto the grass and then thought better of it and retrieved it, holding the stub until he reached the Citroën. He started the car and waited for the heater to warm up, all the while looking at the monument, seventy-two thousand names. He wondered how many Grangers there had been, men who wandered away from the battlefield and made another life for themselves. Not very many, surely, but more than a few. Granger would have been the last. When the car was warm, Thomas reached into his coat pocket for his mobile phone. He tapped in the numbers Bernhard had given him and waited. On the sixth ring Russ picked up.

He said, Hullo.

Russ? Thomas.

Oh, Tommy. It's so good of you to call. Where are you?

Flanders. I'm calling from a parking lot in Flanders. I'm so sorry about Grace.

Thank you, Tommy. It's a terrible business.

Is anyone with you?

No, I'm alone. Caitlin's flying in from Los Angeles. Russ's throat caught then and he was silent a moment. In the background Thomas could hear music. Brahms, he thought. Russ said, I'm expecting her later on today.

Do you want to talk about what happened?

No, he said. We can talk later, face to face. I'm just trying to get through the damned day. Funeral's tomorrow. Family only. She had so many troubles in her life, Grace. Too many for her spirit to bear.

Yes, Thomas said.

And so much of the time I was abroad.

Don't start that, Russ.

Fact, he said. The simple truth.

Thomas watched the Englishman stride down the gravel path and into the parking lot, bound for an old green Land Rover. He unlocked the door and got in and in a moment was gone. The young lovers were behind him, walking slowly, their arms linked. They got into a Deux Chevaux but did not start the engine. Thomas watched them embrace and soon the windows began to mist over. He wished them great good luck in their adventures, whatever they were.

So she was alone when she died, Russ said.

She was a sweet girl, Thomas said.

Yes, she was.

I can be there tomorrow, you know.

Thank you, Tommy. I know. But we're going to do this alone.

I understand, Thomas said.

I had a crazy idea that we should take her back to LaBarre. But Caitlin didn't want that so we'll bury her in a cemetery in Queens. I don't remember the name. Old cemetery. Her mother had some connection to it. So that's where she'll be. Queens, he concluded and grunted a half-laugh.

Thomas said, When this is over you're welcome at St. Michel. Any time. Or I'll meet you in Paris. We can see the Degas.

Yes, the Degas.

We'll be able to talk.

I'll be staying on here awhile, Russ said.

I understand.

What are you doing in Flanders, Thomas?

Looking for St. John Granger. I found him, too. I'm looking at the monument right now. Granger and seventy-two thousand others. It's cold, the wind is blowing, and I'm about to return to Amiens and get a train for Paris and another train to Toulouse and with luck I'll be home by midnight.

How did things go in Le Havre? Did it help, seeing them?

The question was sudden and Thomas paused before answering. No, I don't think it did. I didn't expect it to. I don't know what I expected. Nothing good, that's for sure. I had a conversation with the head man. Nothing conclusive there, either, except they thought Florette was American, not that it made much difference. Did you ever watch torture up close?

Once, Russ said. A prime suspect who had valuable information et cetera. He talked, they always do. But what he said could not be verified. Also, his language was garbled. In the end the valuable information et cetera was lost because the subject died.

A disappointment all around, Thomas said.

A mighty disappointment, Russ agreed.

All that work wasted.

Well, Russ said, they got him off the streets.

That's something, I suppose.

He was an awful son of a bitch.

Funny thing, once or twice I thought I felt Florette in the room.

Yes, Russ said, I know what you mean.

Listening quietly, Thomas said.

Bernhard was doing the interrogating?

No, Thomas said. A Frenchman named Antoine.

I met Antoine once, Russ said. He went on to describe Antoine as a younger man, new to the security trade but already a natural. Thomas watched a bus lumber into the parking lot, stop, and discharge its cargo, schoolchildren from Lille. The children looked to be ten or twelve years old, milling around the bus until two teachers alighted and they all moved off up the gravel path to the monument. The children were subdued, no doubt the result of the lecture en route from Lille. This is hallowed ground. Many thousands died here. Be respectful. No skylarking. The children and their teachers strolled up the path, the colors of their winter clothing bright against the monotone of the field.

And what do you think of Bernhard's move?

What move is that? Thomas asked.

He said he told you last night. But he also said you looked a little out of it and may not have understood. He's resigned from the government. He's been asked to become managing director of Edwards. Edwards et Cie., Edwards Ltd., Edwards Inc., depending on the country. It's the security firm, the one that's filled with ex–Special Forces, ex-SAS, ex–Foreign Legion, ex-Wehrmacht, ex-cops, ex–Chicago goons, Los Angeles shamuses. You name it. They've got the firepower of an army but none of them know how to run a business. They can overthrow a government but they can't read a balance sheet. They have to have someone who understands the ins and outs of the peculiar business they're in and the even more peculiar people they employ. So they found Bernhard.

Bernhard doesn't know anything about running a business.

He says he does.

Thomas began to laugh. Bernhard Sindelar, CEO. Is that it?

That's it. Bernhard says everyone needs a fresh challenge after the age of sixty-five. This is his fresh challenge. They're paying him a ton of money plus stock and stock options and a fat expense account and a car and driver. And he doesn't have to move to the Cayman Islands, where the company is chartered. And he wants me to come aboard as vice president in charge of expenses because he needs a man he can trust, someone who wasn't born yesterday. All those warriors seem to think that money grows on trees. I'll be there to tell them it doesn't.

Are you going to do it?

I was, until all this.

Don't make a decision. Wait a little.

I suppose I will. Probably I ought to retire.

Let things settle, Thomas said.

You're awfully good to call, Tommy.

Will you let me know if there's anything I can do?

I'll see you when I get back.

We'll go somewhere, Thomas said. We'll go to Baghdad. Give Bernhard a hand.

Wouldn't that be something. There was a pause and Thomas

heard shuffling sounds over the telephone, as if something were rubbing against the receiver. For a moment Thomas thought the connection was broken and then he knew that Russ was sobbing and gasping for air at the same time.

Thomas said, It's going to be all right, Russ.

He said, No, it isn't.

Not right away, Thomas said.

I don't know why they wouldn't let me bury her in LaBarre, Russ said. I don't understand why. There was another long pause and then Russ sighed, murmured goodbye, and rang off.

Thomas got out of the car and stretched. He lit a Gitane and stood quietly smoking. The schoolchildren and their teachers were coming back down the path. He could hear high-pitched voices and laughter. They had not spent much time at the memorial. But probably they had an itinerary, La Boisselle, the Lochnagar Crater, the marshes at Frise, and the graveyards in between, all of Somme 1916 that could be crowded into one afternoon. Probably they would also be reading the books of Blaise Cendrars and Georges Duhamel, veterans both. The memorial at Thiepval was but one detour among many and at the end of the day the schoolchildren would be exhausted; their teachers, too. Not all of what they saw would stay with them. Surely the graveyards would, row upon row of stones, and so many nationalities. If they were considerate, the teachers would spare their students specific knowledge of the many ways the millions had died: gunshot, grenade, bomb, bayonet, poison gas, hand-to-hand combat. In the spring rains infantrymen sank into the mud and disappeared. Dysentery, pneumonia, gangrene, heart attack, and stroke, all were present. Nervous breakdown was epidemic. The Great War was a titanic struggle, a soul struggle, a struggle of civilizations, except it was the same civilization divided only by language and national custom. No one who lived through it returned from it entirely sane. No revenge was too harsh for the victors, no bitterness too deep for the defeated. The war glorified the values of the slaughterhouse. Nothing could justify it. Nothing would even the score, though a generation later the Germans would try. Hard to say what the schoolchildren would remember of their tour of Somme 1916.

Thomas pitched the Gitane onto the concrete and watched sparks fly. The school bus pulled slowly out of the parking lot; the children gave him a wave and he waved back. He had never heard a voice as broken as Russ's voice, a voice as toneless as modern music. It was without color. All he wanted for his daughter was that she be buried at LaBarre, an inland place where she knew no one. Probably he thought she would be safe there from the forces that had taken her life. Russ would be remembering his own benign childhood and somewhere that childhood existed still. Whatever LaBarre had become, something of what it had been remained. No doubt that was the point. His own birthplace, his daughter's grave. Soon enough he would join her, and that was the meaning of LaBarre. So he would plead with his older daughter and the other family members and be turned down. They would look at him as though he were crazy, a man maddened by grief. Whatever was he thinking of? Russ had lived too long abroad, outside the family orbit. LaBarre meant nothing to his older daughter or to Grace's friends or Grace herself. LaBarre was personal to Russ.

Billie Holiday

IN EARLY FEBRUARY another false spring came to St. Michel du Valcabrère. Monsieur Bardèche arranged metal tables and chairs on the sidewalk and everyone came in the afternoon to enjoy the sun and temperatures that reached almost 15°C, knowing that in a few days the thermometer would fall and freezing rain or snow would follow. But the false spring lasted for a week, the entire village giddy with the excitement of it. The days were longer, too, and soon the café was filled from lunchtime on with people in shirtsleeves, their faces upturned toward the sun. Thomas had walked into the village to collect his mail, then walked to the café in the square for a glass of something while he opened letters. That day there were three from Russ, long letters painfully composed on a vintage typewriter with a faded ribbon and an *a* that jumped right. He confided that he was not in a good way, sleeping poorly and drinking too much, at loose ends and quarreling with his surviving daughter. Here he was in the strange position of blaming himself for Grace's death and having his Caitlin enthusiastically concur. She wrote that the time had come for him to take stock, examine the damage he had done. He was a bastard and had always been a bastard, fundamentally unfaithful, unstable, erratic, and selfish, more concerned with his disgusting work than with his family. He had never been there for them. What does that mean, Thomas? "Never been there for them." I was always there for them, except when I wasn't. When I was on the job earning the money that kept them afloat. His blame of himself was easier to take than his daughter's blame of him, which must mean that his feelings of self-blame were false or at least not thoroughly thought through.

If Sandra were still alive she'd set things straight.

The girls always listened to their mother.

Russ wanted absolution but Caitlin wasn't giving any. Caitlin refused to communicate except by e-mail, her messages written in a tumbling stream of consciousness that became ever more strident until she was nearly incoherent with anger. E-mail encouraged that sort of thing, picking thoughts off the top of your head like popcorn from a box and flinging them into the ether of the universe without benefit of mature reflection, meaning the anguish they might cause the recipient, and all the time calling it candor-for-your-own-good.

For all that, Russ said he was enjoying himself in New York. Most days he went to the Met, the Morgan Library, or the Frick and lunched at his club. There was always someone he knew in the bar, retired men or men at loose ends like himself. Every Saturday morning he went to visit Grace's grave in Queens and that gave him some solace. He was upset that she was not resting in LaBarre but he had come to terms with that. Maybe it was for the best. Something forlorn about the grave, though, the earth still bare and the gravestone yet to arrive. She had been dead such a short time and it felt like forever. Thomas looked up from the letter, realizing he had not visited Florette's grave since he had been back, not once. Until lately the weather had been wretched, but that was no excuse and not even much of an explanation. The truth was, he had visited Florette only three or four times—no, three—since her death in November. On his way home, he thought, he would stop by. And do what? Pay his respects? He did not want to think of Florette in the ground but somewhere in the air, one of the spirits that hovered about, enjoying the sunshine of the false spring. Thomas turned back to Russ's letter.

In any case, Russ wrote, New York day to day had much to recommend it. The people were brusque but that was because there were so many of them on one small island. Sharp elbows were obligatory, and so the city was off-putting if you were used to the more relaxed European environment. And the noise! But you got used to that, too, and when you wanted entertainment every movie you ever heard of was playing somewhere in the city or on cable—music, too.

His apartment downtown was comfortable, though the neighborhood was somber. He was living only a few blocks from the former World Trade Center. Russ did not think he would be returning to Paris. Maybe he had run out his string in Paris. That happened with cities; suddenly you were no longer comfortable in them and had to go elsewhere. Russ offered his apartment to Thomas any time he wanted to use it. He disclosed that his contract with the Agency had expired. They had proposed a one-year renewal, part-time work, but he figured that his string had run out there, too. Isn't it hard at our age to get the hang of new systems and the personalities that went with them? Bernhard said he saw you in Le Havre but provided no details. I did not mention that we had spoken. I told him nothing of your thoughts on the matter. Wasn't it true that Bernhard was sometimes careless with personal information? Russ closed—Thomas could sense his shyness in the roundabout way he put it—with the news that he had begun to write again, a very long story that had possibilities. He was working in the early morning as he had done in the old days, when he was much younger and had energy and ideas to burn. At five A.M. the city that never slept was asleep, and if you were awake you were comfortably alone and could go about your business unimpeded.'

That was letter number one. Letter number two was the same letter in different words, somewhat more cheerful. A new deli had opened in the neighborhood, his long story was going well, he had one more or less successful conversation with Caitlin, and he had met a merry widow who had a place up in Washington, Connecticut, so his weekends were occupied. The third letter was a reprise of the other two, with a final paragraph on the activities of Bernhard Sindelar. Bernhard had found Edwards in terrible financial shape and was putting the books in order and establishing a budget. Bernhard wanted Russ to join up as comptroller of the company, essentially the wallah in charge of expenses. But Russ thought not. He liked working on his story. He enjoyed his Connecticut weekends with the merry widow. Bernhard sounded as though he were having a fine time inspecting the books and visiting the company's many foreign outposts, Iraq and Afghanistan and West Africa and unnamed East Asian nations, all of them beleaguered and in need of professional threat-assessment. Each week new clients showed up, Russian industrialists and Latin American supremos and, just the other day, a worried American board chairman. The chairman wanted competent bodyguards but he didn't want gorillas, so Bernhard said he could find two out of the pages of *Gentlemen's Quarterly* but the chairman would have to ante up for the Armani suits, Bruno Magli shoes, and Blancpain wristwatches, along with fresh haircuts.

Thomas put the letters aside and ordered an espresso and a glass of beer. He glanced at the front page of the American newspaper but there was nothing new or interesting. Nothing that wouldn't keep until dinner. The air was balmy, the sun warm on his face. Around him the townspeople were sunning themselves, sleepy in the afternoon, as if there were no other place to go and nothing in particular to do. The moment was sufficient unto itself.

Old Bardèche brought his order and said someone had been asking for him.

Who was that?

American woman, Bardèche said. Unpleasant woman, middle-aged, expensively dressed. She said she saw no lights in your house and wanted to know if you'd gone away. I told her I didn't know that you'd gone and didn't know when you'd be back. I don't think she believed me. Were you gone?

I was in Le Havre last week.

Bardèche said, She looked at me wrongly, as if I knew where you were and wouldn't say.

If she comes back, tell her I'm still away.

I will be happy to. I didn't like her.

Thanks for telling me.

I thought you should know, Bardèche said.

Thomas said, I'll have your portrait before long.

The Frenchman broke into a wide grin. I am eager to see it.

Next week, Thomas said.

You have worked on it a long time.

It's always the way with interesting subjects, Thomas said. He looked around and saw that most everyone had left the café, leaving the sun unattended.

Did you walk from your house?

Thomas nodded.

I thought so. You should leave at once. A storm is coming from the west. Bardèche pointed over the roof of the church where the first black clouds were visible. And then Thomas felt a cool breeze.

I can get someone to drive you.

No, I'll walk.

You should leave now.

It's not far, Thomas said.

He paid and they shook hands. He stuffed the letters and the newspaper into his jacket pocket, picked up his walking stick, and began the two-mile trek to his house. The air had an electrical odor but underneath it was the unsettling smell of spring lilacs. He was thinking about Russ and wondering whether to write him about his vision in Le Havre: Russ alone in a hotel room eating a room-service meal and watching television news and the strange intimation that he was not alone but accompanied, someone out of the frame of Thomas's vision; and then Thomas knew he had composed a portrait, the other party felt but not seen. But there was no need to trouble Russ with visions. It was good that he was writing again. He had not published anything for thirty years. He said that his secret life kept intruding. He loved the camaraderie of the secret world, really a tremendous esprit in the clandestine service, more esprit than there ever was at home. Esprit was not one of the things Sandra was good at. They drifted apart and came together again after her illness. She had tremendous courage. He abandoned the field and took a liaison job in New York so he could look after her, and he wondered later if their tenderness toward each other then distanced them from their daughters. He wondered if in the last months they lived in a locked room.

When Sandra died he went abroad again because secret work

was the only work he knew how to do. Other jobs came along but he always turned them down. Mostly they were offers from private companies that wished to capitalize on his special knowledge, which he believed belonged to the government. In that sense he was not entirely his own man and so his thoughts often returned to his early efforts at fiction. They were stories set in LaBarre, tales of small-town life always narrated by the same character, a middle-aged doctor who knew too many secrets for his own good. The secrets weighed on him but exhilarated him also. They gave him a kind of power in the community and so he was feared. The stories usually opened in the doctor's waiting room, an ambiance that reminded Thomas of his father's, the shabby furniture and out-of-date magazines. When Thomas asked Russ once if he thought he could make a living writing fiction, he said instantly, No. It's an avocation, that's all. But I loved doing it. I didn't need an audience.

The sun was gone now and the wind had come up, no longer cool but cold, a wintry gust from the mountains. The clouds were boiling up out of the west and Thomas stepped up his pace, taking long strides, the clock-tick of his walking stick a comfort. If a car came along he decided he would try to hitch a ride. He heard thunder somewhere back of him and he knew from the look of the sky that the region was in for a drenching and possibly something worse. He remembered that the windows of his house were open, the car windows, too. One car and then another flew by, too fast for him to wave or put his thumb out. The cars were traveling much too fast for the narrow road but everyone was hurrying home. Then the rain began, fat drops that hit the pavement like pistol shots. The wind increased and the rain became a deluge, first a *thumpa-thumpa* and next a minutes-long pause. Thomas thought of a prizefighter circling the ring before closing, playing rope-a-dope, knowing his opponent was defenseless and giving him time to consider what was about to happen, a terrible beating. Thomas put his head down, determined not to yield.

The deluge came, rain so heavy he could not see the road beyond twenty yards. When he looked backward the village had vanished behind a curtain of water. He was a mile or more from his house when he wondered if the distance was not too great and if he would be better off in a crouch, hunkering down for as long as it took. A gust so fierce it nearly knocked him off his feet caused Thomas to wheel around and face the advancing tempest. He raised his walking stick, brandishing it like a medieval warrior in combat with a dragon or other supernatural phenomenon. Drenched now, he stood his ground and fenced with the wind as if it had a human face and the face was known to him, a face from the past or a face to be seen in the near future. Thomas talked to it in a kind of growl, egging it on, all the while thrusting with his walking stick. The sky was black as the ocean depths except when brilliantly illuminated by lightning. This was the known world. The face was all around him, overhead and underfoot, in front and behind. He was forced backward by the strength of the wind, and yet he believed he must close with it, not yield one inch. He remembered Florette's intimate descriptions of the gods of the Pyrenees, cold, remorseless, reckless, indifferent, heedless of consequence. They could not be grappled with. They were permanent and implacable, like the force of gravity or of inertia. Thomas bellowed a great roar and turned his back on the wind, which seemed to him to slacken slightly. No doubt it was his imagination, a vainglorious belief that he had prevailed. From somewhere overhead or underfoot he heard what he thought was a ghostly cackle but it was only the drumming of the rain on the pavement. As if to emphasize the peril of the moment, a gigantic thunderclap and a string of lightning arrived simultaneously. But now the lightning illuminated nothing but itself.

Thomas knew he had no choice but to soldier on, one footstep after another, the wind and rain at his back, no slack. His trousers were plastered to his legs, his shoes soaked also but holding the ground. He counted as he walked, trying to calculate feet per step and wondering all the while if his house would be there when he arrived or was floating downslope like the biblical ark. Close by in the field to the north the firs were bending in the wind with bits of branches and unidentifiable debris flying here and there. He had been a fool not to accept old Bardèche's offer, and he wondered again if he would be wiser to quit the road and find shelter until the storm passed. But there was no shelter nearby. He knew the storm would blow itself out, nothing could maintain this level of rage forever, and then he thought of Granger's war, four years of carnage and the end was as bloodthirsty as the beginning. He had been walking uphill and now he sensed he was walking downhill, a feeling only, because the wind had thrown off his balance. He believed he was no more than half a mile from his house. That hopeful thought vanished when he saw a blaze of light not far to the south followed by a furious roar of thunder. The rain backed off, seemed almost to give up, then recommenced in a flood of water.

He thought they were in competition, the lightning, the thunder, the rain, and the wind. There were two more flashes, close together in sound and in location, and he believed that the storm had him bracketed like coordinated artillery fire. No point to try to dodge it; the storm was living in its own context. So Thomas continued on, one foot in front of the other, his eyes on the pavement, which now resembled a river in flood. And then he was down, carried in the cold current, ship's wreckage bound for some appalling void. His elbows and backside scraped concrete and for a moment he lost consciousness, a sense of where he was and why, his mouth full of water, his shoes gone. He had fetched up in the ditch, and not fifty yards away was Granger's house, and beyond it his own. The treacherous wind paused and he made off across the field, sloshing through water a foot deep, mud beneath the water. He saw the silhouette of his house and the thick plane tree in the front yard but his strength was waning and he did not believe he would make it. Thomas leaned against the tree, embracing it, holding on, his arms slipping on the wet trunk, his knees collapsing, the tree itself seeming to give way. His brain was stuck fast in neutral, an ox-brain without agility, animation even. Thomas struggled to his feet. His house was twenty yards distant but in his confusion and ox-mindedness he did not recognize it. Oxen had no memory. Still, everyone had an emergency reserve, something extra when the limits of endurance were reached. The idea was to concentrate. Forget the hopelessness of the situation. Forget exhaustion and forget pain. Pain was ephemeral, although it, too, had something in reserve, a little extra in the event you tried to forget it was there. And so Thomas stood on his rubber legs and focused on the front door of his house and the warmth beyond. The wind and rain gathered force once again but Thomas's attention was elsewhere and he did not notice, any more than he noticed the serial claps of thunder and lightning now far distant in the east. Thomas leaned on the front fender of his Renault and peered through the windshield. Seeing what appeared to be a foot of water in the car, he rolled up the windows. Then he stumbled forward and stepped inside the house.

An inch of water covered the floor. He bumped the front door shut and stood shivering, listening to the rain and the hollow rolls of thunder echoing in the mountains far away. Everything here was familiar to him and he knew he was home at last. When he reached to turn on the overhead light his hands were shaking so badly he could not grasp the switch; finally he moved it with the palm of his hand and the room filled with light. His body was shaking, the cold deep into his bones. So this was how it felt to be a castaway, or the first reptile slithering from the ooze onto dry land. Some part of him was back on the road and later in the ditch; he had no recollection of the trek from the ditch to his house. His face was frozen and he had no feeling in his feet. He knew he should change into dry clothes but did not have the will to do it. He had left everything in the storm. He thought to grab the bottle of calvados and a glass from the sideboard and with them in hand he sloshed his way to the armchair in front of the fireplace, wood and kindling already expertly laid in the grate. After a dozen or more tries he managed to get paper to burn and then sat back, watching the flames, his ruined feet as close to the fire as he could get them. The fire assumed fantastic shapes as he watched, a man hypnotized. Thomas had forgotten the calvados although the bottle and the glass were still in his hands. He watched the fire and in minutes was lost in a dreamless sleep.

Dr. Picot arrived at noon the next day to check him over. She bandaged his feet and the scrapes on his arms. He had a deep cut on his forehead and she bandaged that after sewing five stitches. All the time she complained about the storm and his behavior, stupidly walking from the village in a downpour, and worse than a downpour because of the wind, which according to the radio was eighty kilometers an hour and gusting to one hundred. You could have been killed walking alone on that road. You are a reckless old man without the sense of a baboon. You are fortunate to be alive, and as it is you may have a fine case of pneumonia in your future. Stop smoking at once, she said and gingerly picked up his pack of Gitanes and threw it into the wastebasket. She checked his blood pressure and his heart, commenting that he had a murmur. Have you always had it? she asked, not waiting for an answer. She listened to the rattle in his chest and shook her head in disgust. She jabbed him twice with three-inch-long needles—antibiotics, she said, and vitamins. Then, putting her instruments away in her black bag, she began to talk about Florette, how much she was missed in the village. He, Thomas, had the sympathy of everyone; even old Bardèche was running a pool for anyone who wanted to predict how soon he would marry again. Men your age are a menace, she said, chortling fractionally to indicate the humor of the situation. How could such a thing happen to Florette? People still can't believe it. Do you know if anything's been done? When Thomas shook his head, either yes or no, it was hard to tell which, the doctor said inaction was typical of the authorities at Toulouse and Paris. Tragic occurrences in the countryside did not interest them. They were not concerned with the countryside. We might as well be living in Timbuktu. In France every community lived in its own orbit and Paris was the worst. It has always been so, she said. She stood up and snapped shut her black bag.

Goodbye, Thomas.

Come to my office in one week.

Meanwhile, remain in bed. Do not smoke.

You are a very foolish man.

But you have very good luck.

Thank you for coming, he said, but by then the doctor had already left his bedroom and was clomping down the stairs. He heard the front door open and close and immediately turned on his side, shut his eyes, and waited for sleep. He thought he could sleep for a week. In his mind he retraced his route from the village, remembering now when he had wheeled around to do combat with the storm, the storm that he believed had a human face. He attempted to slay it as if it were a dragon, raising his walking stick—and what had become of that? In a ditch somewhere, probably miles away. He wanted to retrieve it, the physical evidence of his moment of blindness. Lunacy was the better word. He remembered thrusting and thrusting again as if the storm could be skewered, run through and bled to death. The moment had come and gone in an instant but it was vivid still. He could not remember what he had been thinking but he was sure it had given him no pleasure in the sense that Florette had given him pleasure, or his work did, or even the sense of well-being on a clear autumn day when it was sufficient merely to be alive. Merely. Well, he had survived the tempest but had lost something, too. He could never do it again. He could not summon the required rage, hot-blooded and hot-minded. You needed a certain lunacy for artwork, a lunatic's confidence that you could finish what you started, that you had a God-given right to make portraits. But the life should never be confused with the work. His actions were vainglorious, but there was a possibility that they had saved his life.

He rose late that afternoon and pulled on slippers and a bathrobe and shuffled downstairs to survey the damage. He could tell that Ghislaine had cleaned up. The floors were dry. The cloth skirts of the furniture were damp. The kitchen was immaculate, the counter polished and the plates and glasses neatly put away, a shipboard ambiance; the bottle of calvados sat in a bath of bright sunlight. He stood at the foot of the stairs, then stepped painfully to the billiards table. Thomas was shocked to see a damp spot dead center, and when he looked at the ceiling he observed drops of water clinging to the timbers. The green baize was black where the water had dripped and spread. He bent to look under the table but could not bend far enough. His feet and back hurt so much that he was unable to see if the leak had soaked through. He stood looking at the table, worried that it would warp or the baize soften and separate, making the table useless for play. He had grown used to it in the living room of his house. Removing it would be like removing one of his portraits, Florette's or the unsatisfactory Granger. He moved slowly to the front door, opened it, and stepped outside.

When he looked at the roof he saw the damage at once. A ten-foot-long branch from the plane tree lay athwart the roof. His house looked like a dismasted schooner, topside in bad repair but most everything secure below decks, except of course the billiards table. The billiards table was the ship's rudder and without it no navigation was certain. He pulled the cloth robe closely around himself and inspected the plane tree. Two large branches were missing and the lawn was scattered with debris. Here and there were deep puddles of rainwater. His Renault was plastered with leaves but otherwise intact, and then he noticed the windshield cracked from side to side, one of the wipers askew. The other downed branch of the plane tree was at the end of the drive; it would take two men to remove it. He saw the scars of tire tracks across the lawn, the doctor's Peugeot. Thomas's feet were cold now and when he looked at the mountains to the south he saw new-fallen snow glittering like ice. On the low slopes houses were buried in snow. What caused people to live in such inhospitable conditions? Probably they were born to it and couldn't imagine anything different. He had had a friend in Madison who went on and on about the beauty of the Great Plains, the horizon as flat as an infinite ruler. His name was Ballard, a farm boy from Nebraska, training to become a chemist. What ever happened to him? Thomas stood shivering, surveying the wreckage of his lawn, the car windshield, and the roof of his house. He plucked a Gitane from the pocket of his robe, lit it, and immediately began to cough; he remembered that Ballard was a chain smoker. They all were then. He peeked around the corner of the house to look at the olive grove and saw to his surprise that it was mostly intact. Florette would not have been surprised. She loved her olive trees and knew they were tough. After a last look around, he turned his back and went inside to brew a pot of coffee. From the kitchen window he could see Granger's low-slung farmhouse, apparently undamaged. However, one of the fruit trees in the back yard was gone, its branches tangled like razor wire. It looked to have fallen on the dogs' graves.

Thomas poured a dram of calvados while he waited for coffee, mentally making a list of things to be done. Repair the roof, repair the car windshield, fetch wood for the fireplace, lay in some wine, get someone to inspect the billiards table. The lawn could wait until spring. He had never been good with repairs. His instinct was to ignore them, move along, another city, another country. But this was the only place he had ever actually owned, held title to, paid taxes on, insured; and in its particulars the house was Florette's. Florette had handled the insurance and he wondered now if automobile windshields and the roofs of houses were included in the coverage. Likely not, nor billiards tables either. He had never in his life collected on an insurance claim. Thomas poured coffee and drank, making a face; much too strong. He ran his hand over his chin, feeling two days' stubble. Nearly dusk now, shadows lengthening, a bite to the air, unshaven, unshowered, wearing his bathrobe at four in the afternoon, sipping coffee corrected with calvados, he thought he had a glimpse of the future. His domestic arrangements were breaking down, his house damaged, his lawn in ruins, a tree branch dug into his roof, Granger's beautiful billiards table damp with mountain rainwater, and in the adjoining field the orchard was dying. Ghosts were in every corner of his house. Thomas felt as if he had wandered from the pages of one of Chekhov's stories, a character surrounded by decay.

A week later, late on a Tuesday afternoon, he finished the portrait of old Bardèche. He cleaned his brushes while he looked at it; there was nothing more to be done. The piece was finished. He lit a Gitane, inhaling especially deeply as he remembered the lecture that morning from the officious Dr. Picot, how fortunate he was to have escaped pneumonia but he would learn soon enough that he was on parole only. If he continued to use tobacco, pneumonia would be the least of his worries. Emphysema and heart disease would surely follow, at which time he could look forward to an early and unpleasant death. Gitanes were the worst. Meanwhile, she poked and prodded, looked into his nostrils and ears, his mouth and eyes. She announced she would leave the rectal exam for another occasion, nor would he be required to cough. The cut on his head was not infected. His feet were almost healed. All in all, a fortunate outcome which smoking would negate. All this time he had said barely a dozen words, half of them "yes" or "no" in answer to her impertinent questions. He was thinking about old Bardèche's portrait, finishing it in his mind. And when she was done at last he thanked her, paid her, and departed, but not before she reminded him of his heart murmur. She advised him to consult a cardiologist. Cardiology was not one of her specialties.

How are you getting on otherwise?

Fine, he said.

You don't look fine. Your color's not good. You should lose weight. Fifteen pounds at least.

Nevertheless, he said as he closed the door to her office.

Thomas cleaned the last brush and put it in the oversized coffee tin. He looked up when he heard two sharp raps on the front door. Through the window he saw a black Mercedes in the driveway, a man in a Bailey hat at the wheel. He could not see who was at the front door but he knew who it was.

Victoria Granger was snugly turned out in a red beret and a loden coat, eskimo boots on her feet. She smiled nicely and said she was back for the closing on her house, the buyer an engineer for Airbus in Toulouse—a German, as it turned out. She didn't have to come back but she wanted to, for a last look around. Also, she wanted to meet the German. This time she brought her husband with her—she gestured at the man in the car—so that he could see the place.

We'd like to invite you for a drink, she said.

A last get-together before the German takes over.

Well, thank you, Thomas said.

She looked at him, wrinkling her nose. Have you been painting?

Finishing up, he said.

I didn't realize oil paint smelled so.

It's the turpentine, he said.

She wrinkled her nose again and looked at her watch. Come at seven.

He said, All right. I'd like that.

We sold the wine cellar with the house. But I held back a few bottles. We might as well drink them.

Even with all that tannin? he asked with a smile.

Victoria laughed merrily and returned to her car, waving as it backed up and sped away down the driveway to the road.

Thomas showered to rid himself of the paint smell and pulled on a fresh pair of khakis and a work shirt. As he was leaving the phone rang but he decided not to answer it. He thought, One thing at a time. He marched across his frozen yard and into the field that separated his property from Granger's. The night was clear, the sky filled with silver stars, Orion directly overhead. He noticed that the fruit tree in Granger's back yard was still down but the debris was gone. Ghislaine must have cleaned it up. The cold air felt good after his long day in the studio. He thought he needed to get out more, clear out his lungs, take advantage of the beauty of the landscape, the snow-blanketed mountains, the spire of the church in town. He paused to take it in while he lit a Gitane. The Americans were certain to have no-smoking rules in place. The night was windless so the wire of tobacco smoke rose straight up. He remembered Ballard saying something about seeing all the way to heaven when you were alone on the Great Plains at night. What Thomas saw was the mass of Big Papa crowding the valley. He threw away the Gitane and continued his march in the direction of the Granger house, lit from within. When Thomas rang the doorbell he heard rustling sounds and then a man's voice.

Come in, Tom.

They were seated in the easy chairs on either side of the fireplace. Victoria was in Granger's old chair, her husband in Thomas's usual place. The husband rose and greeted Thomas at the door, asked him what he wanted to drink, offered to take his coat, waved him amiably to the sofa.

I'm Ed, he said.

Thomas gave Ed his coat and said he'd like a glass of red wine.

He took in the living room, unchanged since Granger occupied it except for the bare space where the billiards table had been. That made it a different room. Thomas said to Victoria, Did the German buy it furnished?

Every stick, she said. And everything else, flatware, dishes, garden tools. The books in the bookcases. The rugs on the floor. He loved the furniture. Ed says that's because all of it is brown, the color of fascism. Isn't that right, Ed?

You got it, Vic.

How old is he? Thomas asked.

Younger than you, she said. So he wouldn't know the Nazis firsthand.

Historical memory, Ed said, handing Thomas a glass and returning to the chair by the fire. Ed was as big as a football lineman, his face ruddy, his blond hair close-cropped, military style.

So you've met him, Thomas said.

Oh, yes. He seems nice enough. He designs airplane fuselages. Speaks perfect English.

We're rid of it, Ed said. That's the main thing.

And I got what I asked for, Victoria said.

Good for you, Thomas said.

Yes, she said.

So the notaire worked out after all, Thomas said.

Her face clouded and she admitted not quite as well as she'd hoped. Her Paris lawyer seemed unable to find the time to devote to the sale so the notaire had a free hand. It took a very long time, she said. His fees were appalling, just appalling. How do they get away with it?

Same reason that American lawyers charge a thousand dollars an hour, Thomas said. Because they can.

Well, she said. It's disgusting.

We're rid of it, Vic, Ed said. Look on the bright side.

I'm trying to, she said.

The goddamned house is haunted anyhow, Ed said. Let the Kraut deal with it.

Ed thinks Granger's ghost lives here, she said to Thomas.

I wouldn't be surprised, Thomas said.

I think he's gay, she said.

The ghost?

The German, she said. He keeps talking about his partner. That's the word he uses, in English, "partner." My partner this, my partner that. He's worried that the partner won't like the drapes.

The doors slam all the time, Ed said.

That's the wind, Thomas said. The house has always been drafty.

The damn drapes are brown, Vic.

Maybe the partner's anti-Nazi, Victoria said.

Strange noises, Ed said. In the night and the daytime, too.

It's an old house, Thomas said. It creaks.

Ed did not reply to that. Instead, he refilled his glass, Victoria's, and Thomas's, draining the bottle. Thomas observed that one of his portraits was still on the far wall. It was a sketch he had made of Ghislaine. Granger liked it so he gave it to him. Thomas supposed that the German bought the portrait along with the dishes, the flatware, and the Berchtesgaden furniture. Suddenly the house seemed not to be Granger's domain but another place altogether.

That's one of yours, isn't it? Victoria said, following his eyes.

It's Ghislaine, Thomas said.

Well, it's his now.

I have to make a call, Ed said abruptly and left the room.

Tokyo, Victoria said.

Thomas looked at his watch, four A.M. in Tokyo. Thomas said, I hope they keep late hours.

All hours, Victoria said. They follow the various exchanges, Seoul, Tokyo, Singapore. Currency speculators. Ed always calls at about this time. What's that bandage on your head?

We had quite a storm a week or so ago and I got caught in it. Trees down, branches everywhere. Seventy-mile-an-hour winds.

She nodded absently. She had no interest in the storm. She sipped her wine and said, Have you been getting on all right, Thomas?

I've been worried about you, she added.

You have?

Yes, she said. I have.

I'm fine, he said.

I'm afraid I wasn't very cordial the last time we met. In fact, I was pretty much of a bitch.

It was a difficult time, he said. For you, too.

I was so angry at him, Granger. Glad he was dead, angry he had taken his secrets with him. I'm sorry I took it out on you. I had no right to do that. She looked up, saw his glass was empty, and said he should open the bottle on the sideboard. Ed's conversations go on forever, she said. Ed likes to stay in touch. He loves his BlackBerry. That way he's always in touch.

Thomas was carefully working the cork from a bottle of 1983 Margaux, wondering what a BlackBerry was.

Tell me something, Victoria said. Isn't it strange for you, being back in this house, Granger gone, strangers here, a German soon to be.

Don't forget the partner, he said from the sideboard.

Yes, the partner.

New faces, he said. Maybe they play billiards.

I went into town today, walked around the church for the first time. It's a beautiful structure. I walked into the café for a coffee and asked about you. No one would tell me anything.

My instructions, he said.

They protect you, she said.

That they do, Thomas said. Common village practice.

Still, she said. Don't you find it lonely here?

Thomas paused a moment and said, Yes.

Always, or just now?

Not when Florette was alive.

You could get married again, find a girlfriend—

Thomas smiled and did not reply.

Of course you have your work. That's fortunate.

Thomas returned with the bottle and poured wine into their glasses. From somewhere upstairs he heard the rumble of Ed's voice.

You can have the portrait of Ghislaine if you want it. The German will never miss it.

No, it should stay with the house.

As you wish, Victoria said.

But thank you. I appreciate the offer.

Does it look like her?

Pretty much, he said.

I've only seen her from a distance. She wasn't friendly.

Thomas shrugged and sipped his wine. Thin, he thought.

So you'll stay on here, she said.

Looks like it, he said.

I couldn't bear it.

No wonder. You don't like the French.

I never said I did. I like France and that's a different thing. And even so, this valley is not of the modern world.

As opposed to Pennsylvania, he said.

Pennsylvania's beautiful, she said. You can make a life in Pennsylvania. She went on to describe the hill towns of the Poconos and the mountains farther west, the border towns south of Pittsburgh. The suburbs were superb. The Susquehanna and the Allegheny north of Pittsburgh, beautiful rivers. Her mother's family had lived in Pennsylvania for generations, William Penn himself a shirttail relative. Surely he knew the work of the Wyeths, she herself could never keep them straight. Thomas listened with attention and after a while her Pennsylvania sounded as exotic as the Czech Republic or Bhutan, inland nations with rich histories. She said, Wouldn't you agree that St. Michel du Valcabrère is a closed book? But I'm intruding again. I promised I'd stop that. Victoria stared into the fire a moment, then began to laugh quietly. She said, I'm a tennis fanatic. I play every day when I'm home. Tennis is a game of repetition. You place your feet just so back of the baseline when you're serving. You toss the ball at a specific angle to a specific height, and if the angle is off or the height too high or too low you retrieve the ball and do it again. One small mistake with your feet or with the toss can throw your serve way off—the ball goes long or wide left or wide right or into the net and you lose the point. That's my chaos theory of tennis; the butterfly's wings flutter in Mexico and a year later a typhoon hits Japan. One of the things I don't like about St. Michel is that there are no tennis courts. No chaos theory either. So yes, I prefer Pennsylvania. Aren't you the least bit curious about the United States?

Not personally, he said.

People are friendlier in Pennsylvania.

I'll keep that in mind, he said.

We're leaving tomorrow, she said. I expect we won't see each other again.

Likely not, he said.

Perhaps sometime when you get to Pennsylvania.

He glanced at his watch and drained off his wine. I must go now.

Thank you for coming, she said.

I have one bit of news for you, Thomas said. A while ago I visited Thiepval, the graveyard and the monument. Your great-uncle's name is there along with the thousands of others who died at the Somme. In case you or your children are ever in the neighborhood you could visit. He paused at a blast of Ed's laughter from upstairs, something hilarious from Tokyo. He said, It's not cheerful. But it's interesting. And there he is, high up in the central vault.

I'll take your word for it.

No interest at all?

Not personally, she said with a smile.

It's worth a visit, he said.

Not anymore, she said. There's a statute of limitations on everything. That's what Ed told me. Ed's good at putting things behind him. I can't fix what Granger did any more than I can change the course of the stars in their heavens. So I decided to let go. Does that make sense to you?

Yes, it does, he said.

I thought it would.

Say goodbye to Ed for me.

It's a good feeling, letting go.

Let me know if there's anything I can do for the Germans. Or if you need help with the notaire.

The notaire is out of my life, she said with a grimace. And good riddance.

We're off to Holland tomorrow, she added.

He said, Holland?

The Hague. Ed has business in The Hague.

Thomas shook his head. Holland seemed to enter his life at the strangest times.

Goodbye then, Thomas said. He opened the door to a frigid night. He pulled his coat shut and buttoned up. The mountain wind was like a knife. It seemed to him that the stars were not fixed in the heavens but in motion, wheeling this way and that, rising and falling on the gentle swell of a fathomless ocean. Orion had disappeared. The starlight was wan, the southern sky invisible. He thought of saying something to her about the stars but decided not to and closed the door firmly. Thomas stood for a moment on the front steps of Granger's house, wondering why it was that people felt themselves small when they looked at the stars in their orbits. People were not small. Stars were small.

Home, Thomas put a potato in the oven and stood for a long time in the kitchen looking across the field at Granger's house. He had the feeling he would never enter it again; the Germans would keep to themselves. They were lucky to have Ghislaine's portrait, and if they ever discovered its value it would be gone the next day. Thomas turned away to inspect the billiards table, the discolored surface where water had settled. It was damp to the touch but there was no depression that he could see. He rolled the cue ball from different angles and decided the line was true. Then he racked balls and played quickly, imagining Granger as his opponent. He realized with some satisfaction that he had become a decent player, good with finesse. If he ever moved from St. Michel he would take the billiards table with him, along with his portraits and the Matisse sketch that lived in the bedroom. He would not take the furniture, which seemed to him to belong to the house; it would not translate elsewhere. The furniture would always have Florette's signature, her scent, and its arrangement was as fixed as the marks on a ruler. He did not like to think about moving, a chore at any age.

Six ball in the side pocket.

Ten ball in the corner.

Twelve in the corner.

Thomas kissed the eight ball into the side pocket and put the cue stick away. He covered the table and went into the kitchen to check the potato, wondering if it was worthwhile to cook the steak outside, cold as it was. Thomas debated the matter, deciding finally that charcoal was definitely required. He stepped out the door with some newspaper and a basket of briquets. Thomas set a match to the paper, shivering all the while. Wine was cold in the glass. The night was eerily still, as if the universe had paused to catch its breath, a moment that could never be caught on canvas, although Vermeer tried. At last the fire caught and he hurried back inside where he noticed the blinking red light on his answering machine.

The voice was Russ Conlon's, cracking here and there with laughter. Had Thomas seen the *Washington Post*? Well, no, of course he hadn't seen the *Washington Post*. On page one was a photograph of the secretary of defense, his assistants, and his generals gathered around a table in the Pentagon, battle maps in the background, a top-secret briefing from field commanders in Iraq. The war was going extremely well and improving every day and the question was whether there was time enough for the improvements to become definitive—that is to say, a time frame elastic enough to extirpate the insurgency in order to move the ball down the field. So it was a question of metrics. Russ said, Our secretary has invented a whole new war-language, the vernacular of mathematicians though it bore the stamp of the social sciences and the locker room also. Arranged along the wall behind the grandees was a row of about a dozen seated civilians, identified only as aides. One of them had ducked his head at the moment the photographer shot, so all that could be seen of him was Labrador hair, big ears, a thick neck, and broad shoulders made broader by the padding of a bespoke blazer. Bernhard Sindelar, Thomas. And the word is that he's received a marvelous cost-plus-guaranteed contract from the Department of Defense, his warriors now among the well-paid outsourced armed militia providing security, so necessary for success in Baghdad and elsewhere in that tragic war-torn land. Bernhard, it seems, has a place at the table.

He's moving to Geneva, Russ said, to a fine villa outside of town with a splendid view of the lake and a little dock in case he wants to provide himself a yacht. Switzerland's anonymous, Bernhard says. And he wants to be close to his money.

He asked me to tell you he's on top of things.

I hate to wonder what that means.

Call me, Thomas.

What are your plans?

Russ's voice trailed away and the recording stopped. Thomas stood watching the machine, deep in thought. Then he remembered about the steak on the grill and hurried outside. He turned the steak and watched the flames leap, thinking about Bernhard living large in anonymous Switzerland. He wished he had seen the newspaper photograph, the battle maps, and Bernhard's big head and ax-handle shoulders, recognizable anywhere if you knew him well. It was hard imagining him in a Genevese villa with a boat dock; and then it was not only imaginable but logical. Bernhard Sindelar could find a place for himself in any city in the world with the exception of little LaBarre, Wisconsin. Thomas speared the steak and went back inside, forgetting Bernhard. He was thinking now about his evening music.

Thomas laid out flatware and a cloth napkin, lit two candles, placed the salt and pepper within reach, poured a glass of wine. He sat at his usual place while he ate his steak and potato. Billie Holiday's ruined voice filled the room so he could not hear the rafters creak. She was singing about a sailboat in the moonlight, though there didn't seem to be anything nautical about the song. It was an ordinary love song except for the way she sang it, the sailboat standing in for a hundred dreary hotel rooms in a score of cities. Thomas wondered if Billie Holiday had ever been on a sailboat in the moonlight, on Long Island Sound perhaps, or the Hudson River. Probably she had. She'd done everything else. A sailboat in the moonlight would be the normal thing for Lady Day, her many friendships and her fierce imagination. At the helm would be Prez Young, trying to figure out the compass and how the sails worked and what the tide was doing, struggling to keep his mind focused on navigation because all the while Billie Holiday was singing blues. At a certain point, weary of maritime chores, he'd drop anchor and heft his sax and soon be off on a signature riff and there they'd be, making music on the deep. Teddy Wilson was below decks playing a bone-white cabaret piano. Tide in, tide out, no difference because they were lost in music of their own making, moonlight dancing on the surface of the water. Now Billie Holiday was singing about getting some fun out of life, definitely not a normal thing for her or for Prez Young either, except when they were playing blues or recreating in other ways. Fun was always at the top of the agenda but the agenda was often mislaid, forgotten in the general turbulence of living. How could you keep an agenda in your head with so many competing desires, and always fear and unspeakable grief. She was putting her heart into the song, though. She was giving it everything she had and then some, her voice so worn out at the top of the register that it was more whisper than voice, yet a whisper with the force of a tornado, hushed at the eye of the melody, violent on the margins. Billie Holiday always gave full value, nothing less than everything she had and if what she had diminished day by day what remained was as hard-earned as any labor anywhere. Thomas had stopped eating and was listening to the music only. You could never know what transpired beneath another's skin. He knew the singer from the songs and that seemed evidence enough of what she chose to disclose of herself. He supposed what kept her alive was her knowledge of the world and her place inside the world, hoping for a reconciliation, an equilibrium, meaning a way to get from today to tomorrow. What she remembered was in balance with what she had forgotten, either deliberately or inadvertently; if she remembered everything, she could not possibly survive. She would be unable to sing. She died at forty-four and it seemed a miracle that she had lived that long. Probably it was a miracle even to her. Thomas was listening now to the sax, playing to the rhythm of a heartbeat. When Prez Young backed her up he often had tears in his eyes, especially the jam sessions toward the end of her life and his, too; they died but four months apart. He was at his most tender when she was singing. He was not normally tender, either as a musician or as a man. Tender would not be the word for Lester Young except when Billie Holiday was nearby.

The CD ended with "I'll Get By" and Thomas heard the rafters creak once again—in protest, he believed.

He pushed his plate away, the steak uneaten. Thomas thought of putting something else on the player, then decided not to. He was content at the table in the silence of evening, candles guttering. He absently rubbed his foot, still sore from the misadventure in the storm. His good fortune could not be said to be hard-earned, more a winning lottery ticket, a stroke of luck similar to Bernhard Sindelar's discovery of outsourced mercenaries. Bernhard always had good luck. Russ didn't. Florette had had good luck until the very end of her life. Thomas thought he had always been very lucky until recently. Billie Holiday had terrible luck, though sometimes you had to suspend the rules when appraising artists' luck. The jazz business did not encourage fair weather. Self-consciousness was part of the routine and luck was not the residue of design or anything else. The job took a terrible physical toll with the usual consequences. Jazz musicians were night creatures, natural prey.

Thomas regretted never hearing Billie Holiday in person. He had heard Sarah Vaughan and Carmen McRae many times and Mabel Mercer once. Mabel Mercer sang at a club on Third Avenue and one night, flush from the sale of a portrait, he had taken Karen to see her. The club was dark, each table with its own candle and vase with a single rose. They decided to have dinner because the club was nearly empty and it would seem as if they were being granted a private performance. When she finished her set, Miss Mercer made one bow to the house and one bow to her pianist and stepped off the platform. She passed their table, her bearing as composed as a queen's. She strolled on to the rear of the club, where a much older man was waiting in a banquette. He was very tall and slender, immaculate in black tie. When she approached he rose to kiss her on both cheeks. They held each other's elbows a moment, so happy to be together again. When they were seated he lifted a bottle of champagne from its bucket and slowly poured two glasses. They saluted each other and fell into an animated conversation punctuated by soft laughter. They were telling private stories, narratives that would be meaningless to strangers. Thomas tried to pay attention to Karen but his eyes kept straying to the banquette tête-à-tête. Their poise and good humor suggested to him that age would have superb rewards, though when he proposed that thought to Karen she rolled her eyes. While he and Karen talked, Thomas made a pencil sketch of Mabel Mercer and her black-tied gentleman, both of them looking—he supposed the word was continental, in any case an atmosphere of the fading old world, characters from a novel by Schnitzler or Fontane, people imprisoned by history and glad of it. They were their own jailers and their own judge and jury. When he retailed that thought to Karen she did not roll her eyes but laughed and laughed and at last leaned across the table and kissed him.

Thomas remembered now that it was not too long after that night that he began to think about Europe as a destination, and he wondered even then if he was in pursuit of something that had been lost or something he had never known. Was the attraction the old or the new? Alone in the stillness of his house, surrounded by memories, he recalled Mabel Mercer and her gentleman friend with absolute clarity. He remembered Karen, too, moving her chair close to his and looking over his shoulder, watching him sketch on a cocktail napkin.

She said, Can I have it?

He said, Of course.

A souvenir, she said. I want to remember this evening, she added with a wisp of a smile, tucking the napkin into her purse.

Why is that?

I don't think we'll have many more like it, she said.

We'll come again, he said.

But it won't be the same, she said.

Why not?

She laughed and said, History doesn't repeat itself.

He ordered a bottle of champagne, both of them silent while the waiter popped the cork, poured, and with great deliberation settled the bottle in an ice-filled bucket. And a few minutes after that, Mabel Mercer mounted the stage again, nodded at her accompanist, and waited for the lights to dim. Then she closed her eyes and flew into "Mountain Greenery."

Karen's instincts were sound. They never again went to the jazz club on Third Avenue, and not long after that Thomas was on the boat to France. He recalled with a start that he had disembarked at Le Havre. He had no memory of the city then and no memory of whether he had stayed the night or pressed on to Paris. Nothing about his most recent visit had reminded him of his earlier journey. It was as if he were seeing it for the first time. Antoine had asked him if he knew Le Havre, and he had said no without hesitation. How strange was that? How encouraging.

Thomas pushed a button on the stereo and Billie Holiday was back on her sailboat in the moonlight, a voice filled with regret and desire; revenge would be the furthest thing from her mind. Successful revenge required the cramped discipline of an accountant and she preferred the unruly emotions of the spendthrift. She needed protection but there was none and so she sang. He threw a log on the fire and stood staring into the flames and then he threw another on for good measure. For what he was about to do Thomas needed fortification and so he poured a glass of calvados and listened to the song, true American blues, imitated everywhere in the world, never equaled. He wondered if there was anywhere in America now where you could hear the real thing. The Mississippi Delta of course, probably New Orleans, perhaps South Side Chicago. It would be a good thing if presidents were obligated to listen to the blues in the vast formality of the White House and a good thing also if they were to drink while listening. The blues would give them an idea of the limits of human ambition and the consequences of righteous action, an appreciation of grief and ecstasy and inscrutable providence and the certainty of betrayal, along with the imprecision of memory and often its loss altogether. Truth and falsehood were next of kin. That was what Lincoln knew.

Billie Holiday was singing parlando, one of the late songs when she had lost her voice and had only her nerve in reserve. Thomas threw the last of the calvados into the fire, where it flared orange. Next, delaying matters still further, he backed away and racked the billiard balls with the triangle. He stood with the long stick in his hand surveying the field. When with one violent thrust he broke, the eight ball fell into the side pocket and the cue ball in the corner. He took this as an omen; he had hoped for a coup and now he was twice scratched and the game not fairly begun. He laughed out loud, concluding that he had committed the billiards equivalent of original sin.

Thomas put away the long stick and poked the fire. Then he stepped slowly to the coat closet and reached inside for the cardboard tube he had taken with him from Le Havre, the drawing of Florette inside. But when he gently shook the tube the bastinado fell out first, and he remembered slipping it inside as an afterthought, an appalling souvenir of the afternoon in Antoine's loft. He put the bastinado in his pocket, removed the Canson paper with its glassine wrap, and brought it to fireside. Looking at it critically, he decided he had drawn too quickly but even so it was an accomplished piece. He did not know what Florette was thinking but he thought he could hear her voice, a whisper of encouragement. The orange firelight cast strange shadows and distorted things. He barely recognized the portrait as his own work. But he was not himself when he drew it. He weighed the Canson paper in his hands and with a sudden motion placed it on the flames and watched it smolder, then flare, burning from the inside out. In ninety seconds it was ashes. Thomas adjusted the fire screen and waited one minute more to assure himself that everything was secure. Then he drew the bastinado from his pocket and dropped it on the fire, where it disappeared into the ashes. The rubber gave off an unpleasant smell. The smell followed him across the room and up the stairs into his bedroom. He checked the elephants one by one and got into bed and the smell still lingered.

He could hear, but faintly, Billie Holiday's parlando downstairs. The melody was unfamiliar to him but above the singer's voice he could hear Prez Young's soaring saxophone and Teddy Wilson's evenhanded piano, so surely the piece was from the standard repertoire. Thomas was wide awake, his thoughts tumbling, trying and failing to identify the song. Thinking hard about the future, he had an idea it was time to visit America.

Mr. Parlando

His FIRST MONTHS in America were marked by irresolution, a fate as familiar to him now as the drawn face in the mirror. He had found equilibrium, a fine balance that allowed him to live but allowed nothing more. His past life seemed to vanish bit by bit and the future was a blank slate, leaving the precipice of the moment. He did not know where he belonged or if he belonged anywhere. Thomas contrived a nickname for himself, Mr. Parlando, because he was talking his way through the song. In New York he stayed for a time with Russ Conlon, lunching with Russ at his midtown club, visiting galleries in the afternoon and going to the theater at night. More often than not he fell asleep during the third act, and when he awoke suddenly he was unable to remember acts one and two. Russ introduced him to attractive widows but the attractive widows seemed to have more troubles than he did. Every time they opened their mouths he expected a dead husband to pop out like a jumping jack; and his mouth was full also. When they asked him about Florette he avoided answering or answered falsely and that annoyed them because Russ had told them the score. Does he think we don't understand death, for heaven's sake? Thomas seemed to them one of those men who trusted no one, a man in hiding. One night at dinner the conversation turned to the uses of torture and peremptory detention of persons suspected of terrorism, and one of the widows had said, Whatever it takes. Thomas said, Where does it end? The widow said, It doesn't matter where it ends. What matters is that it stop. And if you have a better solution, please tell me what it is. Her eyes filled with tears and for a moment Thomas suspected that her husband had had offices in the twin towers. That was not true. But she had been nearby on the morning of September 11 and had seen the bodies tumbling from the heights of the buildings and she still had nightmares, terrible nightmares, and for that reason demanded action, the more severe the better. She said, There were many victims of nine-eleven and not only those who died. We deserve satisfaction, too.

You of all people should understand that, Thomas.

Thomas said he understood, but he didn't, quite.

You've seen them face to face, haven't you?

Thomas said he had.

They don't deserve to live, she said.

He did not reply to that.

What did they look like?

Most ordinary, Thomas said.

The conversation moved along to something less contentious, dessert, coffee, the settling of the bill. The widows were sympathetic but frustrated and concluded Thomas was damaged beyond their repair; and they were not eager for nurse work in any case.

Thomas was scarcely more communicative with Russ. Mr. Parlando didn't know how he felt. He didn't feel. He had lost the rhyme and melody of feelings and meantime he existed on his precipice, mindful always that there were many people in the world much worse off than he. To the extent there was a bright side, that was it. Thomas believed he had made a mistake in Le Havre but he didn't know what it was. He imagined the mistake was some form of Lebenslüge. But what was the lie that allowed him to live? He wondered if the lie was his refusal to have blood on his hands. So the interrogation at Le Havre, too, was unresolved and marked by doubt.

After a fortnight in Russ's flat he took a suite in a downtown apartment hotel and began to sketch again but without conviction. He attempted a series of self-portraits but they were not successful, owing to his minimalist approach, five or six long looping strokes; he was not Matisse. His material was somewhere else. He had no idea where. Thomas thought that going to America was a mistake, as whims almost always were. Because you were born in a country didn't mean you had a connection to it. It was only a birthplace. The country was so foreign to him that it might as well have been on another planet. But here he was, and he decided at last that he should make an attempt at reconciliation. Thomas rented a car and drove west to Wisconsin, his apprehension growing with each mile. LaBarre was confounding, like visiting the abandoned set of a familiar film and finding that the characters you knew and loved had vanished. Mr. Rick and Miss Ilsa were long gone long with Ferrari and the piano player Dooley Wilson and the crazy Russian and all the others. The house he had grown up in had been demolished to make room for a two-story apartment house called Covington Court. The lawn at Covington Court was unmowed, the garbage cans upended in the street. Cats were round and about but the sidewalk was empty. Thomas stayed at a Best Western near the LaBarre Mall, wandering the streets for a day, arriving in late afternoon at the police station. Russ had told him that a high school classmate had become chief of police. Thomas wanted to buy the chief a drink and catch up on the news of the town but the desk sergeant told him that was impossible, Chief Phillips had taken his retirement five years before and moved to Florida for the tarpon. After a few minutes of aimless conversation the desk sergeant became suspicious. What did you say your name was? What are you doing here? The sergeant sat in a swivel chair behind heavy glass and spoke through a microphone. I don't remember any Dr. Railles. That name is not familiar to me at all. You better be on your way, the desk sergeant said.

And put that out.

No smoking in this facility.

Jesus, the sergeant said. Everyone knows that. Secondhand smoke. Biohazard.

Where are you from, anyway?

France, Thomas said.

Well, the sergeant said, you better get back there, then.

Thomas left for Chicago the following morning, stopping in Milwaukee for lunch at the Pfister. He thought the bar looked the same but couldn't be sure. He had no trouble recalling the conversation with his father forty-five years before and the promise of a thousand dollars to ease his passage to New York. He ate a club sandwich and read the Milwaukee paper, filled with news of the war, two local boys killed in Fallujah, assailants unknown. He read every word of the account, then put the paper aside, wondering if he should visit his two portraits at the Milwaukee Art Museum. No, he thought, wait for Chicago. Thomas knew no one in Chicago but put up at the Drake in a room with a view of the gray lake. At dusk he stood at the window and looked at the water, flat as a billiards table. Not a painterly lake, he thought, because it lacked depth. The weather was fine and in the morning he strolled down Michigan Avenue to the Art Institute. When he inquired after his portrait, *Young Woman in a Fur Hat*, he was told it was not on display. At once Thomas expected the worst.

Deaccessioned?

No, the clerk said. In storage.

That's a shame, he said. I wanted to see it. I've come a long way. I've come all the way from Wisconsin.

Are you a friend of the artist?

I am the artist, Thomas said.

Oh dear, the clerk said.

Thomas imagined the fur-hatted woman, a friend from Barcelona days, in a dark closet somewhere in the basement weeping bitter tears over her exile, the Spanish diaspora reaching even to an air-conditioned basement in Chicago. She was a high-spirited señorita who adored the Catalonian sunlight and often sunbathed on the balcony of her apartment overlooking the Ramblas. He had drawn her in a fur hat on the balcony on a chilly sunlit morning in January. Thomas took his time in the uncrowded rooms of the Art Institute, avoiding the room where *Young Woman in a Fur Hat* had hung. But when he came upon the room he could not resist a peek and was unhappy when he saw a de Kooning in its place. Thomas enjoyed himself in the soft light of the museum, revisiting many of the rooms and standing for minutes at a time before his old favorites. He was looking at the edges of canvases, defining the limits of the idea. There were many scenes from the south of France and from Aquitaine, too. He recognized many of the villages and rivers and mountains and the people who inhabited them, and inhabited them still. French visuals, human and topographical, had not changed in centuries. He paid serious attention to American artists but was always drawn back to the Europeans. It turned out that dead European impressionists were most companionable and the plump girl in the haystack reminded him of Florette.

Thomas returned to New York but after a month decided that equilibrium did not come easily in the city that never slept; even at five A.M. it did not have repose. He bought a car and took trips out of the city, trying to find a suitable venue which, if asked, he would have been unable to define. In due course he settled in the state of Maine, attracted by the raw light and habitual fog. He rented a house on an island north of Portland, the house situated two miles from the village on a low, rocky bluff with a view of the sea. Ferry service to the mainland was infrequent but dependable. He rarely traveled to the mainland in any event. The house was small, two bedrooms up, one big room down, including the kitchen. Half the big room was given over to his easel and canvases. The ensemble reminded him of the studios he had rented in New York more than forty years before, except there was no carnival outside the windows. At night there were no sounds at all except the harbor foghorn and the occasional stutter of a fishing boat entering port or leaving it. At night the old house creaked, seemed to strain at its moorings, but these sounds were companionable, compatible with silence. In this uncomplicated zone of well-being Thomas had the idea that anything could occur, including the miraculous.

He lived a spare life, occupied mostly by his work. During the cold weather he worked in the big downstairs room making portraits. He thought that before he was through he would draw everyone he had ever known or heard of. These included many self-portraits, himself as a young man and later on, at fifty and sixty. In a number of these, remarkably, Thomas saw the pentimento of his father. Arthur Malan thought enough of the work that he proposed a show in New York.

You've turned some kind of corner, Arthur said.

I'm damned if I know what it is, but whatever it is, you've turned it.

It would be good if you'd come to the city, do some interviews, make nice.

It wouldn't kill you, Arthur said.

We'll see, Thomas said.

When the weather was tolerable Thomas spent adventurous afternoons drawing his pier. The sign at the end of it read DANGER DANGER UNSAFE PIER KEEP OFF THIS MEANS YOU but everyone knew to stay clear. The pier listed drunkenly as it fought the breeze and the tides but it was unsafe in any weather. An August storm had wrenched the mooring yet again. The wood was rotten underfoot, causing alarming gaps in the planking. Still, if it gave way the fall wasn't much, five feet into a fathom of cold water, and it served you right for ignoring the sign.

One bright afternoon in early September Thomas picked his way the twenty yards from the shore to the end of the pier, where he set down a camp stool and a canvas beach bag. The pier shuddered in the wind, a pleasant sensation, as if the pier and the ocean surge were one. Thomas stood glowering in the weightless afternoon sunlight listening to the waves and the screech of gulls diving for bait fish. His ears were ringing and he moved his jaws to clear them. This was not successful but he didn't expect it to be. He had hay fever or some other allergy. Perhaps it was only the wind. Either way, the ringing continued, a nagging companion that wouldn't leave him alone. He flexed his fingers, a pianist preparing a recital. Down the beach a man and a woman—the Duffields from the look of them—gathered their belongings and began the slow march to the parking lot behind the rocks and the shallow dune. Thomas's eyesight had worsened over the past year and the sun's glare made him squint but he gave a friendly wave. If they weren't the Duffields they were the Maxwells or the Lunds, neighbors all. Then he saw the man was speaking into a cell phone. Lund.

The beach was empty now. Thomas maneuvered his camp chair

to a solid section of the planking where he could sit comfortably with his back against a piling. He rested quietly a moment looking at the meandering line of the old pier, almost as old as he was. On the island all structures came with a history, sometimes more than one. Duffield and his father had built the pier during the Second World War. In those years, theirs was the only house on that stretch of the north shore, a modest cape heated by woodstoves and lit by kerosene lamps. They built the pier as a mooring for their two dinghies and as a place to fish from and also for the aesthetics, a hand-built pier in Maine being the equivalent of an olive grove in Jerusalem. Duffield was a retired banker from Boston who kept the house as he had known it as a boy, except for the addition of indoor plumbing and electricity. Those were his concessions to the modern world. Now there were half a dozen houses hereabouts, including the Lund monster, visible at the summit of Hall's Hill, with stables, a swimming pool, and a Le Corbusier–inspired main house, seven thousand square feet of bad taste and megalomania. At dusk the sun's rays collided with the picture window, transforming it into a blinding wall of fire. What redeemed the Lunds was their daughter Tina, a sprite aged fourteen, lovely to look at, nonstop talker. Tina usually arrived unannounced, scampering across the shaky planks like a circus acrobat, settling at the edge of the pier, her legs dangling, commencing a rapid-fire monologue. She was on the outs with her parents. Her mother disapproved of her boyfriend. The dope, her parents called him. All he wanted to do was run away to New York and start up his rock band and become a star and what was so dopey about that? Will you teach me to draw, Tom? I need something personal in my life.

Would you say something to them? They'd listen to you.

They say you're a man of the world. What does that mean, by the way?

Thomas took a thermos from his beach bag and put that beside him. Next he withdrew a worn square of plywood, then his sketchpad and pens and charcoal stick. He sat with his back to the sea and began to draw the pier, stressing its insecurity as it ran into the stony beach, the dunes and ragged sea grass beyond. A narrow rutted road disappeared into the underbrush and scrub oak of Hall's Hill, a gnarled thicket that in its complexity and antiquity suggested the land mass of Asia, including Lund's preposterous wat. This made a stark and inviting drawing, one of a hundred Thomas had made in the past year. He believed his pier had the personality of a human being, as many faces and as many contradictions, presenting one face in the birth light of early morning, quite another in the afternoon or at dusk. No drawing was identical to any other. When he thought he understood the essence of its character, the pier turned once again and he saw something utterly unexpected, a sudden shift of gravity or of shadow, desire ignited or extinguished. He thought of these shifts as mood swings. The pier aged the way a human being ages, stooped here and there, fragile in the usual places, forgetful, complaining of the cold weather, complaining of neglect or betrayal, pleading that it was being asked to bear too much weight, and all this time remembering its robust and buoyant youth, indomitable under the assault of Atlantic hurricanes. As the afternoon breeze freshened, the arthritic planks trembled and creaked, the coughs of distress sounding like hollow laughter.

Thomas worked for an hour, oblivious of his surroundings except for the ragged line of the pier, and then his eyes moved to the stony beach, the dune with its eyebrow of grass and the rising rutted road. The wind had shifted to the northwest, bringing with it a damp chill, and behind the chill a low rumble, something close to a feline purr. The unfamiliar sound made Thomas cock his head and listen, and then on the edges of his vision he saw the car easing down Hall's Hill Road. It seemed to come on forever, a stretch Mercedes limousine as long as a boat and as sleek, heeling this way and that as it tipped sideways in the ruts, emerging at last from the trees to level ground.

The intruder slid silently to a halt in the parking lot. The driver, dressed in black jeans, a Hawaiian shirt, and a baseball cap, alighted and opened the rear door. After a moment a passenger emerged, shaking the creases of his trousers with thumb and forefinger. He looked around and shook his head, apparently making some droll comment because the driver laughed loudly, the sound carrying to the end of the pier where it mingled with the cries of the gulls. Thomas had returned to his sketching, working swiftly because he knew the weather was turning. The passenger removed his blazer and handed it to the driver, who put it inside the car and stood importantly to one side, his rear against the front bumper, arms folded, the baseball cap low over his eyes. He appeared to be scanning the horizon. Then the other rear door opened and a second passenger alighted, this one shorter and stockier than the first, but judging from his demeanor no less bemused by his surroundings.

Thomas continued to sketch and the visitors made their way slowly over the dune. He could not see them clearly but he knew that neither of them were local—that was obvious from the Mercedes. Islanders favored pickup trucks and clapped-out Dodge Darts except for Lund's Hummer. Thomas guessed that the tall one was yet another urban predator in fitted slacks and a cobalt-blue shirt, a little stooped, painfully thin, moving sluggishly in the soft sand. The other one lagged behind, anonymous. Thomas bent to his sketchpad, concentrating on the gaps in the planking. No doubt his visitors were investment bankers or land speculators privy to the new wisdom, advising clients that island real estate was undervalued so why not take profits from the portfolio and buy something that's here today and here tomorrow, unspoiled real estate with a water view on an island with dependable ferry service, a nine-hole golf course, and a fine state-of-the-art helipad to get you the hell to Portland in case you were infarcted. Two mil, two-five buys you the house with the swimming pool and the water view. And what fun your young wife will have furnishing the layout. Every week Duffield received letters from real estate brokers begging him to put his house on the market. One of them even showed up at his front door. You won't be sorry, Mr. Duffield, and our splendid seller's environment won't last forever.

This one, in his Palm Beach duds, his insolent chauffeur, and his Mercedes the size of the Ritz—how did he manage to find the beach, at the terminus of such a difficult and confusing road? The visitor arrived at last at the end of the pier, leaning on the railing, gasping from the exertion. Thomas was squinting in the glare of the sun. He lowered his sketchpad and sat watching the stranger. The rings on his fingers winked in the sunlight. All in all, a stranger to avoid. Thomas picked up his pad, and then it occurred to him that Mr. Palm Beach was in distress.

He called, Can I help you with anything? The other shook his head but did not look up. He bent to remove his shoes and shake them free of sand.

What do you want? Private property here, Thomas said in his proprietor's voice. No trespassing, as the signs say.

The stranger nodded wearily. Evidently this was a story he had heard before.

And none of it's for sale, Thomas said.

That so?

That's so.

Damn, he said, his voice raised but thin.

I wish you luck getting that boat up the hill. Then Thomas saw the chauffeur on the crest of the dune, carrying three beach chairs and a wicker basket. The stranger indicated where he should place the chairs, then turned to look directly down the pier where Thomas sat. He stood back and cocked his head, no longer out of breath. The stranger mustered a toothy smile—no one who had seen it once would ever forget it—and gave a jaunty wave of his pale hand.

Hi, Thomas. Long time no see.

Bernhard?

And look who's here with me. Antoine, all the way from Le Havre.

Bonjour, Thomas, Antoine said.

The chauffeur had set up the chairs side by side and was busy opening a bottle of wine. Three glasses rested on the lid of the wicker basket.

Thomas did not move. Everything about Bernhard was diminished—his height, the breadth of his shoulders, the size of his hands, the thinning hair on his head. They had not seen each other for a year and a half, since parting company at the Café Marine. The shirt that Thomas had thought was cobalt blue was now seen to be navy and not a shirt at all but a tight-fitting sweater. In the glare of the sun he had missed everything; and he had known Bernhard his entire lifetime.

Thomas picked his way back from the end of the dock, his camp stool in one hand and the beach bag in the other. The wind was up, the dock swaying, his footing uncertain. But in a moment he was stepping over sand, embracing Antoine and putting his hand on Bernhard's shoulder. He could feel slack muscle under Bernhard's skin and bones beneath the muscle. His friend's face was gray. Thomas sat in the chair between Antoine and Bernhard and watched the chauffeur pour wine, then move off down the beach. The breeze caught his shirt, revealing a pistol in a hip holster.

He said, How are you, Bernhard?

Bernhard shrugged and gave an approximate smile. What you see is what you get.

You don't look well, Thomas said.

I got hit by an express train, Thomas. One minute I was shooting skeet with some friends at the lake, the next minute I was flat on my back. And the minute after that I was in the hospital. A heart attack, can you imagine? You didn't recognize me at first, did you? And I don't wonder. I've lost twenty-five pounds. I can't walk across the room without stopping for breath, though each day it's a little better. I'll be fine. It'll just take a while.

Ah, Bernhard. I'm sorry.

A hell of a shock, Bernhard said.

I can imagine. Does Russ know?

He does not know. Russ is not good with illness in case you haven't noticed.

I can tell him, Thomas said.

No, Bernhard said. Russ is in good nick these days. I think he's going to marry the merry widow from Connecticut. Let him be. Bernhard laughed suddenly, a flash of his old style. He said, Remember how I used to spy on your father's waiting room? I always knew which patients were at the end of the line. A day or two after the express train I looked into the mirror to see what the future would bring, and after a long hard look I knew my time had not come. Now let's talk about something else.

Thomas shivered and when he looked up he saw fog gathering to the north. He said, Why don't we go up to my place? I'll build a fire. We can talk there, out of the cold.

In a minute, Bernhard said. I like it here.

A beautiful place, Antoine said. It reminds me of Bretagne.

I'm surprised to see you again, Antoine.

Antoine's working for me now, Bernhard said. Between the two of us we know just about everybody worth knowing in the security industry.

Thomas said to Antoine, Congratulations, and Antoine smiled bleakly.

It's quite a business now, Bernhard said. You wouldn't believe the money.

More work than we can handle, Antoine said.

We're in twelve countries, Bernhard said.

On three continents, Antoine said.

Antoine's damn good, Bernhard said. Brought in some French troopers. Beautiful soldiers, good with languages, good with rough-house. We got one or two from the Foreign Legion who didn't work out, but on the whole, beautiful soldiers.

The legionnaires were undisciplined, Antoine said.

Gorillas, Bernhard said. Knuckle-draggers. He paused then, his eyes drooping. He looked up and signaled the chauffeur, who returned in a hurry, rooting around in the hamper and coming up with a black bag from which he extracted two vials. He shook a pill from each vial and handed them to Bernhard, then poured a glass of water. Bernhard said, So we let them go reluctantly because they were good men. But they didn't have a sense of proportion. They ignored protocol. They didn't play well with others. Bernhard threw the pills into his mouth and drank the water.

Thank you, Leon.

The chauffeur grunted, closed the bag, and resumed his post, watching the fog crawl in from the north. The harbor foghorn began to sound.

A fine lad, Bernhard said. Strong as an ox.

I can see, Thomas said.

Excellent with automobiles and firearms, Antoine said.

He's Welsh, Bernhard said. SAS-trained.

Thomas said, Last I heard you were living in Geneva.

Bernhard looked at him a long moment, his eyes unfocused. What was that?

Are you still living in Geneva?

I've been out of touch, I know. I'm sorry. Press of business, constant travel. My firm moves at warp speed, threats everywhere, multiplying daily. A man has to be on his toes. You have to speak the language of Mr. Chairman and Ms. CEO. You have to convince them that they're at risk every day, same's a Marine in Fallujah. Same thing exactly. It's no time to go slack, turn a blind eye. Bodyguards are part of the cost of doing business, like keeping your cholesterol down. They're fully deductible as well. With difficulty Bernhard reached for the wine bottle and refilled their glasses. He listened a moment to the foghorn, smiling blankly. And how have you been keeping, Thomas? Have you been working? I hope so.

A little of this and a little of that.

Let me guess. Self-portraits.

Those, too, Thomas said.

You should take care on that pier. It's dangerous.

I do, Thomas said.

And you like Maine?

It's quiet. I have few visitors here.

And you intend to stay on?

For the time being, Thomas said.

Well, Antoine said. It's certainly out of the way.

But you found it.

Yes, Antoine said. We found it. He cleared his throat and leaned forward. We have some news for you, Thomas.

Oh, that can wait, Bernhard said. It's so pleasant in the fog. Look at it. The color of belon oysters, wouldn't you say?

Thomas looked from one to the other but did not speak.

Antoine said softly, It's getting late, Bernhard.

Bernhard said, Look at it. That fog is my tomorrow. That's why I like watching it, so messy and opaque, any damn thing could be on its far side. The lost city of Atlantis, a ship in distress, Scylla and Charybdis, the Garden of Eden, your worst enemy or your closest friend. I may close my eyes for just a sec, if you don't mind. His eyelids closed, then popped open. You're my oldest friend, Thomas. You and Russ, but I think you predate Russ by a month or so. I heard you were in LaBarre. You must tell me sometime if you found what you were looking for.

His eyes closed again, this time for good. Leon was at his side at once, taking his pulse. He counted a moment, dropped Bernhard's wrist, nodded casually at Antoine, and walked off to the pier. They watched Leon step cautiously to the end and wait there in the swirling fog as the horn sounded again and again.

He's all right, Antoine said. He'll sleep now for a while.

I didn't recognize him, you know.

Or me, either, Antoine said.

You said you had news.

Yes, Antoine said. Some developments at Le Havre, just last week. Yussef's out. In fact, all four are out.

Out? Thomas said, louder than he intended.

An exchange, I believe. That's what I understand.

An exchange of what?

The four of them for one of ours, Antoine said.

They were just—let go?

Put on a plane for—I don't know where. My friends wouldn't tell me.

So they're loose.

Never to return to Europe. That's the arrangement.

Thomas slumped in his chair, his thoughts disordered. He was quiet a minute or more, listening to Bernhard's shallow breathing. He said, You don't know where they are?

Antoine said, No.

Beirut? Damascus? Tripoli?

I don't know, Thomas.

Thomas was quiet again. What do you propose I do with this news?

You're in no danger, if that's what you're thinking.

It had not occurred to Thomas that he was in any danger. But he was not encouraged by Antoine's assurance.

I wish I had more details for you. I was lucky to get as much as I did. My people were not happy when I left the service. I am bound to say that while they admire Bernhard they do not always approve of his methods. Bernhard is not respectful of protocols, as you know. He's the bull in the tearoom. My people did not like it when I went to work for him.

Dusk was coming on. Thomas rose from his chair and went to the edge of the water. Leon, standing at the end of the pier, was nearly obscured by the fog coming in waves. Thomas skipped one stone after another, thinking of Yussef and the boy and the other two, now at large. It didn't matter to him where they were actually, only that they had taken up residence in his mind once again. He saw them clearly at the long table shackled hand and foot, the guards behind them slapping their bastinados against the chair backs. The boy had been terrified, the other two resigned, Yussef still as death itself. That was where they were in his mind and they remained there still, until, at a mysterious signal, they rose from their chairs and glided across the room to the stairs and disappeared while Thomas skipped stone after stone across the ruffled surface of the water.

He took his seat again and said to Antoine, What did you learn about them?

The other two were common criminals, not stupid, Saudis. The boy was a courier. Yussef was a different breed, devout in his own way. He could recite verses of the Koran from memory in a beautiful haunting voice. He did that even when filled up with chemicals. He was unreachable in that state of intoxication. Ecstatic, I would say, and in that state harmless. He reminded me of a feral cat my wife took in. She was nice to the cat and after a while he lost his hostility and became a house cat like any other, except now and then, entirely unpredictably, his eyes would flash and he would bare his teeth and you saw at once where he came from and what he was and might become again if conditions changed. In other words, if he felt like it. That was Yussef when he was intoxicated. We learned that among other activities he organized public executions. He organized them the way we French organize a parade. Yussef chose the time, the place, the means of execution, and the executioners. The event had a ritual formality to it. Someone had misbehaved, betrayed a comrade, refused an order, disobeyed the Koran, mocked God. Other times Yussef arranged for the car bomb or the assassin's bullet. That was what he told us he did. His descriptions were quite poetic. Yussef had the storyteller's gift and if I had not known better I would have sworn that these stories came from deep in his subconscious and arose from his dreams of the man he wanted to be instead of the man he was. But I cannot swear to that. Much of what he told us could not be verified. Really, the only crime we could prove was the killing of Florette.

And you let him go, Thomas said.

The man we got back was a valuable man.

French?

I don't know. I imagine he was. Or, who knows? Maybe a she.

Thomas wasn't sure how much more he wanted to know. He had the idea he was lying in an open grave and the grave was being filled with sand, one grain at a time. The Moroccan would be with him for the rest of his days, arriving at unexpected times, one scrap of information after another, and he'd better get used to it. This information would come to him whether he wanted it or not. He had no say in the matter. Thomas listened to the foghorn a moment and said, Is it true they were on their way to Holland?

We think so, Antoine said. A disciplinary action. One of their people had talked to the police and Yussef was on his way to prepare the execution. He was a fanatic about security and that was why they were traveling the mountain trail. We believe they entered the country at Perpignan. Probably by boat from Algiers.

This information came from him?

Some of it, Antoine said.

After torture?

Some of it, Antoine said again.

What kind of torture?

What you saw in Le Havre and other kinds. Don't ask me to be specific. I have already said more than I should, but we felt you were entitled to know what we know. Bernhard was most insistent. I have to say that after one year with us Yussef was not right in the head. I suppose verses from the Koran can carry a man only so far. They are only songs, after all. He may have been deceiving us but I don't think so. He was unbalanced, Thomas. I don't think he'll be much use to anyone from now on but I can't give a guarantee. Much remains unexplained. Not all problems have solutions. I am unable to say more than that.

They were silent. Somewhere back of the breeze, the foghorn, and the gulls, Thomas heard piano music, no doubt a late-season cocktail party at one of the trophy houses, probably the Lunds' on Hall's Hill. Thomas explained to Antoine that in the summer a musician who did Bobby Short imitations charged five hundred dollars an hour for a three-hour gig. That included the dinner jacket and the smart repartee. The three-hundred-watt smile came with the tip. But the musician migrated to the Caribbean after Labor Day, so he would not be available. The music they heard was recorded. Thomas craned his neck to locate the Lunds' house but fog had closed in. Thomas lit a Gitane while they listened to "Ain't Misbehavin'" very faintly in the distance. He said, In the old days Bernhard would have insisted we crash the party. He'd make a pass at the hostess or maybe the host, depending on his mood, and stay till dawn. Flirting, telling stories, drinking everything in sight, letting everyone know he was a basket full of secrets.

Does your wife know what you do, Antoine?

No, Antoine said.

If she knew, would she mind?

I think she would. My wife is religious.

Florette liked the rituals of the church but she was not religious.

I think my wife would mind terribly, Antoine said. She liked the idea of the police, a stable business, guardians of the public order, an early retirement and a good pension. She thought I was a superintendent, which I was, but not the sort she imagined. She thought more along the lines of Inspector Maigret. She would not like to know what I did actually and what I do now. She would definitely not like the idea of running mercenaries for an American. It would not be—

Comme il faut, Thomas said and they both laughed.

The fog continued to gather. The foghorn's moan diminished, the piano music vanished. The pier was lost to view and Leon with it. Somewhere back of the dune an owl cried. Thomas reached into his beach bag and pulled on a sweater against the chill. Dusk was coming on fast.

He said, You can't kill them all, can you?

Antoine said he didn't think so.

There are so many, Thomas said.

Very many, Antoine agreed. On every continent.

In time—

It will be worse, Antoine said.

—they may lose heart.

Like my feral cat? Antoine snorted. I didn't tell you the end of the story. My wife's cat was an Abyssinian, quite handsome, ring-tailed with a narrow black stripe down its back. One day the brute clawed my wife from her elbow to her wrist, broke the skin to the bone. She was terrified. She loved the cat and could not understand what made him turn on her. So I had it destroyed. Or to be precise: I took it outside to our back yard and shot it dead.

And did she approve?

I didn't ask her, Antoine said.

Thomas was suddenly very tired. This was his favorite time of day, the sun shuddering in the west, the sea settling, the fog arriving to close things out. It was a perfect day for a sketchpad and a pencil. He collected a handful of sand and let it leak through his fingers. There were scores of tiny tooth-shells and other remains of sea creatures. This part of the Atlantic had long been empty of fish except for fugitives. But it was very beautiful at the end of the day.

Thomas said, Do you miss Le Havre?

Antoine thought a moment and said, Yes.

You were awfully good at what you did.

Yes, I was. I was the best they had.

An unusual skill, Thomas said.

Very unusual, Antoine agreed.

And then you didn't want to do it anymore.

It's not personal, my friend. All mechanics retire. Antoine was silent a minute or more, listening to the owl's cry. He said, I was fifty-five. My wife wanted to return to Bretagne, the village where she was born. Our children and grandchildren live nearby. And when Bernhard came along and offered me enough money to buy the house she always wanted, I said the time had come. Two years with Bernhard and then a proper retirement. A common police story: Inspector Maigret goes home to tend his garden, play boules with his friends, visit his grandchildren, grow old. And in a year or two that is exactly what I will do.

For a split second, as Antoine turned his head, Thomas sensed the ambiance of the stage, and an audience, and a skilled actor alone in the spotlight. Thomas knew that something more was coming and he waited for it, watching sand slip through his fingers. Above them gulls drifted in light wind and the nearby sound of waves curling onto the beach resembled applause.

When you are very good at something, Antoine began and then sighed, declining to finish his sentence. He said instead, I miss hearing confessions. Not the sordid details of their lives—I have no interest in their lives. The details of the crime. A successful interrogation is a beautiful thing. The truth builds so slowly you can believe the room is under a spell, time advancing by heartbeats. You would say: one small brushstroke after another. It's exhausting. It wears you out, hour after hour, and at last all defenses are broken down and the truth makes itself known. We did this and then we did that. X gave the order. Y was the target. Z was the escape route. God is great. And in thirty minutes you have everything you need and more than you need because the man in the chair cannot stop, a torrent of words. And then you must be very careful that the imagination is not in play. You must beware that the subject has not become bewitched with his story and concluded that as good as it is in fact, he can make it better by exaggerating. As with Yussef.

Antoine was silent again, staring at his hands. Thomas watched him work his callused fingers, a magician preparing to pull smoke from his thumbs.

Do you remember all of them?

Every one, Antoine said. I have an excellent memory.

And you're not troubled?

Of course I'm troubled. Not to be troubled is not to be human. But I was a policeman. I acted on behalf of the state. I came to know my subjects very well. I came to know them perhaps better than they knew themselves. Not that any of us can know more than a finite amount, and even that's prone to error. In the end we are doing a job, an assignment. There's a residue we cannot explain. Too bad. Tough luck, as you would say. But Yussef chose the arrangements of his life, not I.

You felt you knew Yussef?

Yussef most of all. Not that it mattered in the end.

That's what happens when you do your job.

You should go back to yours, Antoine said.

I intend to, Thomas said.

So that you will not be troubled.

That depends on the subject, Thomas said.

Antoine poured the last of the wine into their glasses. Thomas shook a Gitane from his pack, offered one to Antoine, took one himself, and lit both with Florette's lighter. Bernhard stirred, murmuring something unintelligible.

I was troubled in St. Michel du Valcabrère, Thomas said, so I thought it was time to return to America. I don't know why; I hadn't been here in years. My acquaintance with it is limited to what I'd read in the newspaper and now that I'm here I find that the newspapers were not wrong. America is not the place for anyone who is troubled. Still, I was not ready to return to St. Michel. I drove from New York to Boston and up the coast from Boston. I saw a car ferry and I took it. I liked the look of the village, a half-dozen shops, lobster boats in the harbor, a snug anchorage. I spent an hour on the harbor drawing boats. I liked it. And so I stayed.

And has it met your expectations?

Thomas said, Entirely.

So you're settled down.

Probably not. This afternoon's news changes things. I have to think about them again, Yussef and the boy and the other two who murdered my wife. They were locked up. But now they're back in the world. One of the things that appealed to me about Maine was the quiet, and now it's not quiet.

It will be again, Antoine said.

Don't think for one minute that the dead don't have voice, Thomas replied.

They heard an unfamiliar sound and looked up. Antoine was on his feet at once, pitching his cigarette away, crouching, peering into the fog. They heard a rattle of shingle, then silence, and once again a heavy step close by, alarming in its force. Two men, Thomas thought, perhaps three, incautious in their approach. So they had arrived at last, a final rendezvous, and as acceptable now as later. Thomas rose from his chair. From the fog a fantastic shape materialized, very tall and broad, two-headed, now at the water's edge and moving in their direction. Antoine crept away and was lost in the fog. Thomas remained standing, waiting for the fog to part. The horse and its rider arrived from the fog, Lund's young daughter astride her creamy palomino. The body of the horse, its color identical to the fog surrounding it, seemed to disappear, leaving only its head and the girl's visible. When Tina Lund saw Thomas she gave a little cry and reined up, frightened. Her horse raised its great head, quartering, its hooves slipping on the shingle. When the animal was under control, Tina grinned and waved at Thomas, and in a moment she was gone, lost again in the fog. Only then did Thomas notice Leon lumbering toward him over the stones and soft sand. Leon paused to listen to the retreating hoofbeats, then holstered the pistol he held in his hand.

He said, Who was that?

Thomas said, The neighbor's daughter.

She should be careful, Leon said.

She likes to ride her horse on the beach. She's just a kid.

She was unexpected, Leon said. She could've gotten hurt.

No harm done, Thomas said.

She was lucky, Leon said with a cold smile. Is Mr. Sindelar all right?

Thomas had forgotten about Bernhard, who continued to sleep. He was motionless except for a tic in his cheek.

Antoine stood off to one side, a disgusted expression on his face.

Leon said to Antoine, We must leave now. The ferry.

Antoine looked at his watch. We have a minute.

It will take time getting the car up the hill.

Thomas put his hand on Bernhard's shoulder and shook him. Bernhard opened one eye and looked at him blankly.

Your boat, Bernhard.

Leon reached down for Bernhard's hand and slowly hauled him to his feet. The big man stood, swaying a little, looking like a drunk trying to get his bearings. His face was still full of sleep. He said, Where are we going?

To the mainland, Antoine said.

Thomas said, You're welcome to spend the night. I have room.

Bernhard looked left and right, angry at the unfamiliar surroundings. He said, Where are we again?

Maine, Thomas said.

Christ, I don't know where I am.

You're in Maine, Thomas said.

What am I doing here?

You missed the horse and rider, Thomas said.

What horse and rider?

A girl on a horse, Antoine said. Surprised us. Looked at first like a desert mirage when they came out of the fog.

I don't know anything about it, Bernhard said.

Leon collected the beach chairs and the hamper and began to move across the beach to the dune and the parking lot beyond. Antoine offered his arm to Bernhard, who waved it aside.

Really, Thomas said. There's room here.

We have to go sometime, Antoine said.

We have important interviews in Bangor, Bernhard put in. Good lads for the team in Baghdad.

Antoine looked at Thomas and shook his head: no interviews in Bangor, no lads for the team in Baghdad.

All right then, Thomas said.

Did you find out all you needed to know? Bernhard asked.

Thanks for coming all this way, Thomas said.

I knew Antoine would deliver.

Let's go, Bernhard, Antoine said.

This is important, Bernhard said. Listen closely. If we can help, let us know. We have resources. We have the damnedest resources you can imagine. We're full-service. You have only to ask.

I know, Thomas said.

You bet, Bernhard replied.

Then Leon was back with a flashlight and a car blanket for Bernhard. He draped the blanket over Bernhard's shoulders and the three began the slow march across the rocks and sand. It was almost dark. Fog was all around them now and there were no lights visible on Hall's Hill or anywhere else. Thomas worried about Tina Lund navigating her horse in the darkness but she was a resourceful girl and the horse knew the way. Thomas gathered up his camp stool and beach bag and followed behind them, Bernhard now holding on to Antoine's arm. When Leon reached the parking lot he switched on the car's headlights and opened the rear door. When Thomas looked inside he saw a bed with a reading light fixed to the headboard. The windows were smoked for privacy. Leon helped Bernhard onto the bed, where he gave a jaunty wave to Thomas and closed his eyes. His body went slack at once, a collapsed balloon. Antoine covered his legs with the blanket. Then Leon climbed in behind the wheel and impatiently gunned the engine.

Let me know how he's doing, Thomas said to Antoine.

He'll be all right. You should have seen him a week ago. He tires easily, that's all. Antoine got into the front seat of the car beside Leon, who was busy unstrapping his hip holster and stowing it in the glove compartment.

The horse scared you, Thomas said.

I have always been frightened of horses, Antoine said.

That one's tame enough.

Antoine grunted. Leon gunned the engine once more.

I wish you very good luck, Thomas said.

And you, Antoine said.

Perhaps we can meet sometime in Brittany.

Antoine smiled broadly. Inshallah, he said, and closed the car door.

Thomas rapped the roof of the car, bruising his knuckles on the armor plate. The Mercedes eased forward and back again and stalled. The parking lot was too small for a stretch limousine. Leon restarted the engine and cranked the steering wheel but ran the car into the dune. Thomas walked around the front of the car and stood in the headlights to give hand signals, forward, left, back, left again, forward. At last the car was free and moving slowly to the road. Presently it began to climb, heeling now to starboard, now to port as it slipped in the ruts. The taillights winked on and off as the car dipped in the shallows of the road. Thomas watched it rise up the hill, the headlights aglow in the underbrush until it reached the top, turned the corner, and was lost to view, leaving Thomas alone in the parking lot. He stood quietly listening to the owl and the faint splash of waves breaking on the beach. There were no other sounds. The wind had died. Then somewhere in the distance he heard faint hoofbeats, a horse in a slow trot, and Tina Lund whistling softly.

Thomas collected his things and left the parking lot in the direction of the path over the rocks to his house. The night was very dark but he had made this passage many times before and knew it from the contours of the rocks and the bluff beyond. The path wound through sea grass and bramble thickets, spiny fingers that tore at his sweater. His house, somewhere ahead, not far, was dark. He had expected to be home well before nightfall. He had certainly not expected Bernhard and Antoine, though the Bernhard he saw was not the Bernhard he knew. Thomas thought he saw the roof's silhouette on the near horizon and stopped to take stock. He was winded, the way up was very difficult, the path slippery, the light a memory. The beach bag was heavy in his hand. It seemed to him that the fog was lifting but he could not be sure. His face was damp with it. Then he heard the engine of a boat close in to shore where the rocks were, evidence that the fog was dispersing; but it was also true that Maine skippers could navigate with their eyes closed, a useful skill at end of day. Thomas listened for the owl but the owl was silent. The boat's engine receded. He wondered if there were sea gods as well as mountain gods and if the sea gods were similarly capricious, spiteful, and cunning. Sure they were. Why wouldn't they be? He thought that tonight was a good night for a fire. Autumn was in the air.

He began to hum, then parlando one of Holiday's standards. When he hesitated, smiling at the droll notion of Billie Holiday's getting some fun out of life, it was as if the world had fallen silent, everything forgotten. It was with that thought that he struggled up the path and mounted the steps to his house, dropped the beach bag and the camp stool on the porch, and stepped inside into the familiar smell of oil paint, turpentine, and weathered wood. The chill was inside, too. He made out the silhouette of the easel and his work in progress, he and Florette seated at their table in old Bardèche's café, Florette's face turned toward the light. The day was fine. They were in shirtsleeves. She was laughing at something he had said. Thomas had proposed an alternate destiny for the boyfriend who wanted to become a gangster: instead, he had gone into politics and was now minister of the interior. Thomas had been working on the portrait for a month and would continue to work until he had what he wanted. When he knew precisely what that was, the portrait would be finished. He shivered in the chill. The single light came from the radio dial, the evening news reporting casualties from Iraq. He listened to the details, unchanging from one evening to the next, a monotonous weather report from a region where the temperature was constant. The dead were never named because their families had not been notified; and each evening he imagined the knock on the door that would precede such notification. And how many families refused to come to the door when an army major was on the other side of it, a briefcase under his arm, his face grave, the worst possible news brought to you by a stranger. Go away, this is the wrong house. No one is at home here. In that way the distant became intimate and the chaotic quite routine. Meanwhile, you waited for the stranger's knock on the door. Thomas switched off the radio, the room in sudden darkness, its silence unsettling. Then he heard the creak of the rafters and, far away, the splash of waves. He set a match to the kindling in the fireplace and watched as the wood caught, smoldering at first, then a flame, low but steady.

Thomas stepped to the window and stood there listening, allowing his eyes to become accustomed to the night. He thought that might take some time, the island was dark by nature, the green of the firs, the deep blue of the sea, the autumn days short and getting shorter. In any case there was more in front of him than he could possibly discern or even imagine. Outside, the fog was lifting, assuming fantastic shapes, swirling, aimless, unstable, suggestive. Far off he heard the bleat of the ferry's horn. It was the last boat, and a calm night for a sail. He touched the windowpane, thinking— Wasn't it something, that child riding out of the fog on her white horse, reining up, and vanishing as quickly as she had come, a moment that approached the miraculous, a moment worth remembering. They were always unexpected.

Patience, he thought. Wait it out. Wait for the light that arrives ages later, light even from a dead star. Thomas looked back at the silhouette of the canvas on the easel, then resumed his watch of the night.